"YOU ARE HOLDING A WORK OF
ART WHEN YOU PICK UP A BOOK BY
PATRICIA POTTER."
—*Rendezvous*

"Potter's recent foray into the contemporary
romantic suspense arena has been a dazzling
success." —*Library Journal*

outstanding

Praise for
PATRICIA POTTER
and her bestselling novels

Twisted Shadows

"With three fully developed characters, a number of likable minor ones, and a slew of villains, not to mention an edge-of-the-seat plot, it is nearly impossible to put *Twisted Shadows* down, once started. There is nothing better than a novel that is equally character-driven and plot-driven, and Patricia Potter excels in them . . . She knows how to entertain readers . . . For a story of love that grows amidst lies and betrayals, be sure to block out sufficient time to thoroughly enjoy this riveting, highly recommended novel." —*Romance Reviews Today*

"Ms. Potter delivers with this thrilling drama. The characters are great and the tension is kept at a high level through the whole book." —*Rendezvous*

"Potter's recent foray into the contemporary arena has been a dazzling success. With romantic flair and emotional intensity that is classic Potter, *Twisted Shadows* ensures that her success is likely to continue."
—*Library Journal*

"Fraught with danger at every turn, this read grips you with its suspense and holds your attention with the sizzling romance." —*The Best Reviews*

continued . . .

PATRICIA POTTER . . .

". . . will thrill lovers of the suspense genre as well as
those who enjoy a good romance."
—*Booklist*

". . . proves herself a gifted writer as artisan,
creating a rich fabric of strong characters
whose wit and intellect will enthrall
even as their adventures entertain."
—*BookPage*

". . . has a special gift for giving an audience
a first-class romantic story line."
—*Affaire de Coeur*

"The Potter treatment . . . is pure action and
excitement, and the characters are wonderful."
—*Midwest Book Review*

"One of the best."
—*BookBrowser*

Cold Target

Patricia Potter

BERKLEY SENSATION, NEW YORK

This is a work of fiction. Names, characters, places, and incidents either are the product of the author's imagination or are used fictitiously, and any resemblance to actual persons, living or dead, business establishments, events, or locales is entirely coincidental.

COLD TARGET

A Berkley Sensation Book / published by arrangement with the author

PRINTING HISTORY
Berkley Sensation edition / January 2004

ISBN: 0-425-19386-1

BERKLEY SENSATION™
Berkley Sensation Books are published by The Berkley Publishing Group,
a division of Penguin Group (USA) Inc.,
375 Hudson Street, New York, New York 10014.
BERKLEY SENSATION and the "B" design
are trademarks belonging to Penguin Group (USA) Inc.

PRINTED IN THE UNITED STATES OF AMERICA

10 9 8 7 6 5 4

prologue

A creak. Then another.

Creaks she shouldn't hear.

Holly Matthews Ames froze in her bed and glanced at the illuminated clock on her night table. Three in the morning. She listened intently.

Silence. Yet she *had* heard those creaks.

Fear twisted inside her. Someone had mounted the stairs and tried to be stealthy about it. She knew those creaks. She'd heard them many times when her husband returned home after a late meeting.

Maybe you're hearing things. Imagining sounds that weren't there. This two-hundred-year-old house was full of strange noises.

But this was not her husband. The creaks would have been closer together. He would have turned on the lights. He would not have closed the front door softly, and he probably would have headed for the bar first. Not to mention that tonight he had been scheduled to make a speech in another city and had planned to stay there overnight.

She would not have heard the noises had she not been awake most of the night, a conversation she'd heard hours earlier repeating in her mind like a song stuck on automatic replay. She'd tried to turn it off but she couldn't. The implications had been too horrible.

Perhaps that's why her hearing was so acute, why all her senses were tingling. She sat up in bed. A thought flashed that was so fast, so terrifying, it almost paralyzed her. Fear exploded into panic. *Mikey!* Icy fingers of pure terror ran down her spine. Mikey. Dear God, Mikey was alone in his bedroom.

He was her life.

She scurried over to Randolph's side of the bed, and the nightstand. Her husband was paranoid. Despite her many protestations, he kept a pistol in the drawer. He'd even insisted she learn how to use it years ago when they first married.

When he loved her.

If he ever had.

But those were thoughts for a different time.

She reached for the key to the drawer. It was taped underneath the table.

For the first time, she was glad he had not paid any attention to her pleas to keep the gun in a place where Mikey could never find it. She unlocked the drawer, picked up the automatic and clicked off the safety.

Her hand shook.

She had never been brave. The only way she could force herself to touch the weapon was to think of her son alone in his room.

She saw a pinpoint of light outside the door. When she was alone, she never closed the door. She wanted to hear Mikey if he had one of his nightmares.

Whoever was approaching was doing so cautiously. Definitely not Randolph. He always made his presence known. She moved away from the bed and hid behind the door, just as she had seen in films and on television.

She thought the intruder could probably hear her heart beat.

She tried not to breathe. She smelled the intruder, the heavy cloying odor of a man's cologne, before she saw him.

The wood floor creaked again, and movement stopped.

She huddled behind the door, wishing that she had bundled something in the bed and covered it. Instead the bed looked as if someone had just left it.

She heard an oath as he moved into the bedroom and apparently saw the empty bed. She saw the gun in his hand just as he seemed to sense her presence behind the door. He started to turn toward her. Her finger squeezed against the trigger in involuntary reaction.

The gun bucked in her hand. The intruder jerked back with a cry. His gun went off but the bullet missed her. She watched in shock as his body twisted and fell to the floor. He didn't move.

Barely holding herself together, she turned on the light. The intruder wore a mask and black clothes. A red stain darkened the pale carpet. She wanted to lean down and check the pulse in his throat, but she could not force herself to do that. She saw his eyes through the holes in the mask. They now stared sightlessly at her. The bullet must have struck his heart.

Paralyzed, she couldn't move for several seconds. She had killed someone. Taken a life. Nausea assailed her and she had to choke back vomit. She could not go to pieces.

Think!

The police. She should call the police. But a small voice kept her from running to the phone. The intruder had entered the house without the alarm going off, and she *had* set the alarm. He had entered her bedroom with a gun in his hand, so obviously he wasn't a burglar more concerned with theft than murder.

She forced herself to pull off the mask.

She gasped as she recognized him. She did not know his name, but she had seen him several times with her husband. She'd always thought he was a hanger-on, someone who did errands for small sums of money. Errands like taking a car to be detailed.

Blood was visible on his dark shirt.

Mikey. Check on him. But the intruder had appeared at

her bedroom door immediately after his footfalls on the stairs. He had come directly to her room. As if he had known . . .

Police. You should call the police.

Instead she leaned down and went through the man's pockets. She found a key in one. Her house key. And a slip of paper with the alarm system's code written on it. Nothing else.

He had been given a key and the code to their alarm system. No one should have either, unless her husband . . .

Her legs almost buckled under her. For a moment, she'd believed the intruder might have expected to find jewels and money in the house. But now it was clear that his objective wasn't to steal material things.

It was to kill her.

one

Meredith Rawson paused at the doorway to her mother's room and looked at her ravaged body.

She was dying. The change in just a day was shocking. She had been diagnosed with advanced lung cancer only weeks earlier, but already the disease had spread throughout her body.

Until now, Meredith had clung to hope. But a call to her mother's doctor had revealed that she had only days to live. An aggressive treatment of chemo and radiation had failed to halt the progress of the disease.

Meredith had hoped against hope. She'd known deep inside that the rapid deterioration was its own prophecy. She'd known, and yet she had not accepted it.

Grief and regret tore at her heart. Grief for her mother, for the loss of a life that was ending far too early. Regret that she had never completely made peace with her, that the remnants of old wounds had kept them apart.

She pasted a smile on her face, balanced the large bouquet of flowers in her hands, and went inside.

Her mother lay quietly, unmoving, in the bed. She hadn't been moved to critical care from the room she'd occupied for the past two weeks. Instead Meredith's father had hired private duty nurses to care for her twenty-four hours a day. He'd been convinced she would be more comfortable. Her mother always had been a very private person.

The nurse sat beside her mother's bed now. Her father, she knew, was in court. There was an important case.

There is always an important case.

That excuse had been only too familiar. A distant mother. An absentee father, except during those times he planned her life.

Her mother's eyes were closed. Her face looked skeletal, her once lustrous blond hair nearly gone. The nurse stood and took the vase and flowers from Meredith. The room was already filled with gaily colored flowers. They made her mother look even more pale. Faded.

"How is she?" Meredith whispered to the nurse.

The nurse indicated the door, and Meredith followed her outside into the hall.

"You'll have to talk to the doctor about that," the nurse said.

"I know he'll give me the medical information. I already have that. I want to know how she's feeling." Her worry overrode her usual courtesy.

The nurse—Betty Akers, Meredith remembered—did not seem to take offense. "Not well," she said softly. "She's taken a turn for the worse. I think she's . . . given up. But she's been asking for you."

"I can stay a few hours. I have a court hearing at two."

"She's drifting in and out of consciousness. I don't know how long before she wakes again."

"If she doesn't wake before I have to leave, I'll be back as soon as possible." She'd planned to visit her mother this evening, but that was before the doctor told her that her mother was failing rapidly, far faster than anyone had thought. It had been telling, but not surprising, that it had been the physician who called, not her father.

She went back into the room and sat on the chair next to her mother. She looked at the face that had been so beautiful. Beautiful and distant. Marguerite Rawson had been the perfect hostess. The perfect wife. Sometimes Meredith thought she was also the perfect mannequin. Emotion seldom showed in her face. Affection was a brief smile.

As a child, Meredith had eaten in the kitchen. Her father didn't think young children should be allowed in the dining room with adults. A housekeeper—a long succession of housekeepers—always put her to bed. Play was ballet classes, which, being taller than the other girls and more awkward, she detested.

Once Meredith finished her homework, her father always gave her another task. It wasn't good enough that she passed her courses. She had to be the best in her class. If she received less than an A, she received a bitter tongue-lashing about being lazy and worthless.

Her mother had never protected her from the attacks. She'd never dried her tears.

Meredith had learned not to cry, not to reveal any sign of vulnerability.

But she was crying now. Perhaps the tears weren't falling down her cheeks, but she felt them trapped at the back of her eyes. Tears for all that was, and all that had never been.

She picked up her mother's hand. It was purple now from multiple needle pricks. And impossibly fragile.

The touch apparently woke her mother. Eyes flickered open. Once a vivid sapphire blue, they now looked dull and sunken.

"Meredith," she said in a thin voice.

"I'm here," Meredith said, wanting to tighten her hold on her mother's hand yet afraid she might hurt her.

Her mother's gaze flicked over to the nurse, who had been reading a book. "Please . . . leave us," she said with labored breath.

The nurse rose and looked at Meredith. "I'll be right outside."

Meredith waited as the nurse retreated.

"I want you to do . . . something for me." Her mother stopped as if even that sentence exhausted her.

"Anything," Meredith said.

Marguerite Rawson said nothing for several moments. Emotions crossed her face. Meredith wondered whether she was having some kind of internal argument.

Then, haltingly, "You . . . have a . . . sister."

Meredith just sat there. The news was like a thunderbolt striking her. "I don't understand."

"I was . . . seventeen. Pregnant. My parents were . . . furious. Mortified. Daddy thought it would destroy his career." Her mother swallowed hard and pain etched her sunken face.

"Squeeze the ball," Meredith urged her. The pain medication was self-controlled now.

"Later," her mother said. "I . . . please find her. My . . . trust fund. I am leaving it to you. And to her." She searched Meredith's face, as if seeking approval.

Meredith knew about the trust fund. It had been established for her mother, who had never used it. Meredith knew it was meant to go to her. But that had been the least of her thoughts. She made an adequate income with her practice.

"How . . . ?"

"Memphis. I was . . . sent to Memphis. She was born in . . . February."

Her mother suddenly jerked. She squeezed the small rubber ball that released the narcotic into her veins. She turned back to Meredith. "Promise me."

"When, Mother? What year? I need more."

"Seven . . . seventy."

"Father? Does he know?"

A tear worked its way down her mother's face. She seemed to nod, but she didn't answer directly. Instead she looked away as if she were staring into another place. Another time. "I'm . . . sorry. Not a good mother. I . . . didn't have anything . . . left after . . ."

"You were a fine mother," Meredith lied.

"No . . ." The voice trailed off. Her mother's eyes closed. Meredith sat there for several more moments, waiting to see whether her mother would wake. She had been so determined to exact a promise.

And Meredith needed time to digest the news. A sister. A half sister. Why was it that children never believed their parents had a youth? Never had been madly in love? Never had done anything outside the norms they had set for their own children?

She had a thousand questions. Who was the father? What had happened? Was the baby taken from her?

She looked at her mother and realized she'd never known her.

She finally rose, and went to the door. The nurse stood just outside, ready to resume her place at her patient's bedside.

"She's asleep. Will you call me on my cell phone the moment she wakes again?" Meredith searched in her purse and pulled out her business card. "My cell phone number is there as well as my home and office numbers," she said. "I'll be back tonight in any case."

"Sandra Winston will be here then."

"Please give her the numbers," Meredith said.

"Of course."

Meredith was mouthing words as if everything was normal. But nothing was normal. She looked at her mother and wondered how many more secrets she had.

But she had to get to the courthouse. She had a hearing on a protection order this afternoon, and Judge Evans did not tolerate tardiness nor was he sympathetic toward postponements, regardless of the reason. And this matter couldn't wait. She was seeking a restraining order against a New Orleans policeman. The complainant was his wife. She was terrified of him. It had taken every ounce of courage she had to file.

If the hearing was delayed in any way, Meredith wasn't sure that Nan Fuller would keep her courage. She had already returned to Rick Fuller twice after receiving at his hands injuries severe enough to send her to the hospital.

As Meredith drove to the courthouse, she mentally reviewed the case. Rick Fuller was a popular man in the police department. Like many abusers, he was a charmer. His captain refused to believe Nan despite her two documented hospital visits, partially because Nan had contradicted herself several times out of fear.

Meredith checked her watch as she drove into a public parking lot. She was due in court in thirty minutes. She was ten minutes late in meeting her client at a restaurant across the street from the courthouse. Meredith had not wanted Nan to confront her husband in the hallways without her.

She hurriedly gathered her suit jacket, briefcase and purse and stepped out of the air-conditioned vehicle. The heat hit her like a furnace blast when she opened the door, even though she had grown up in this climate. She hurried toward the restaurant, knowing she must look as wilted as she felt. Of course, the light was red. It was always red when she was in a hurry.

Meredith broke the law and crossed without waiting for it to change, dodging several cars in doing so.

She hadn't expected her mother to drop a bomb on her. She felt like a piece of rope in a tugging contest, pulled on one end by a client's future and on the other by her mother's past.

Praying that Nan was still there, she reached the restaurant and rushed inside. Her client was sitting toward the back with Janet, a counselor from the women's shelter. As always, Nan looked ready to run away, and her hands were tightly clasped in front of her.

A blonde with wide cornflower blue eyes, Nan was a pretty woman, or would have been without the look of constant apprehension on her face. She was also thin, too thin. She was one of Meredith's pro bono cases, a referral from the women's shelter where she volunteered on a regular basis.

Despite the shortness of time, Meredith slid into the bench across from Nan and reached out to clasp her shaking hands. They were freezing.

"This shouldn't take long," Meredith said.

"I'll have to see him?"

"Yes. He's contesting it. I hoped he wouldn't because of his job, but . . ."

Nan stared at her. "I don't know if I can testify against him when he's looking at me."

"You won't be testifying against him. Not in the sense that he has been charged with a crime. You are merely asking for protection. Remember that."

"I'll try," she said.

Meredith looked at her watch. "We had better go."

Nan rose, as did Janet. Janet, Meredith knew, had also been a victim of domestic violence. She had been the one who had urged Nan to come to Meredith.

They reached the courtroom ten minutes before two. No one was loitering in the corridor. Rick Fuller must have gone inside.

She didn't see him in the courtroom. Only his attorney, who nodded to her. The rest of the room was empty except for a man sitting in the back.

A lump settled in her stomach. Gage Gaynor. He had been a witness in several cases when she was an assistant district attorney, including one involving NOPD members. He had testified against fellow police officers, and the rumor was he'd been dirty as well. She didn't know whether that was true. He had denied it when she'd prepped him for testimony, and the defense counsel had been unable to shake him.

But in her few sessions with him, she'd had disquieting reactions to him. A physical attraction had flared between them, a response she most definitely hadn't wanted and that had probably led her to be more distrustful and more hostile than required.

Her suspicion had been met with his obvious lack of confidence in her abilities. He'd been defensive and curt. Still, he'd fascinated her in some elemental way.

That had been years ago. Since then, she had encountered

him in courtroom hallways, and she'd always felt an odd tug deep inside at the mere sight of him.

It had never made sense to her. He was not a particularly good-looking man, at least not in the classical sense. His hair was a sandy color, straight and a little long, as if he missed haircuts on a regular basis. He had a crooked nose, obviously broken at some time, and a mouth that seldom smiled. But the rare times it did, the crooked left end of his lips moved upward in an intriguing way, and a small dimple transformed his face.

Most striking, though, were his eyes. They were a cool green that could frost an opponent in the warmest of New Orleans days. She had been on the receiving end of that gaze and shivered now just at the memory.

Still, she'd been drawn to him. He radiated a raw masculinity that he didn't try to present as anything else. Perhaps it was his self-confidence, or the athletic grace in his every movement, or the world-weary skepticism in his eyes. Whatever it was made her wary of him even as his presence created an uncomfortable warmth inside.

That kind of physical attraction was perilous to her well-being, and she had run the other way as fast as she could after the case ended.

Nan caught a glimpse of him, too, and Meredith saw her flinch.

"What is it?" she asked.

"He's one of Rick's friends," Nan whispered. "He was over at the house for a cookout."

Meredith glanced back at him, hesitated, then left her client's side to approach him. "Are you here for a reason?"

He looked amused. "No hello?"

She realized how rude she had sounded. But he had put her on the defensive before.

She decided to be direct. "My client says you're a friend of Rick Fuller. Are you here to testify for him?"

"No, and no," he said.

"I beg your pardon?"

"No, I'm not a friend. And no, I am not here to testify for him."

"Nan Fuller says you *are* a friend. That you attended a cookout."

He shrugged. "I attended with a friend who was invited."

"Then why—?"

"Do you ask everyone in courtrooms why they're there?"

"Somehow I doubt that you're a courtroom voyeur."

He stood with that loose-limbed grace she remembered to her deep discomfort. "I'm here on official business," he said.

She knew better than to ask what. He would merely counter with a nonanswer of his own. At least he did not plan to testify.

She started to turn away before she allowed her temper to get the better of her.

"Gone over to the dark side, Counselor?" he asked, causing her to turn back to him.

"What do you mean?" She knew her cheeks were coloring with anger.

"Defense attorney. I understand that you got a couple of lowlifes sprung a few days ago."

"Who?"

"L. L. Jenkins for one. He needed more than a lecture."

"The judge didn't think so. But I'm flattered that you're following my career."

His mouth turned up on one side. "Hardly. It's common knowledge. L.L. is well known in the police community. How does it feel to let criminals loose on the city? Of course the DA's office does that on a regular basis as well, so I guess it's not much of a change."

It was a well-aimed arrow. Though she believed in second chances, she'd seen far too much plea bargaining.

"Prison wouldn't help them."

"No? Neither will a slap on the wrist. It just tells them they can get away with it."

She suddenly recalled one of the facts she'd discovered about him when she was researching his background as a government witness. He had a younger brother in prison.

Drugs. It had been something she'd honed in on because she knew the defense would try to embarrass him or destroy his credibility.

"Is that what happened—?"

Judge Evans's bailiff entered the room, and she didn't have a chance to finish the question before turning around and returning to her client at the table.

In minutes, she had the protective order. It was not contested.

Bewildered, Nan looked at her.

Meredith turned around. Gaynor was gone.

She went over to Rick's attorney. "What happened to your client?"

"He decided not to contest," the attorney said.

"Why?"

"You'll have to ask him."

"Maybe I will," she said.

The bailiff said she could obtain a copy of the order in the clerk's office in the morning. Rick Fuller could not go within five hundred feet of his soon-to-be ex-wife and was not to contact her except through their respective attorneys. If he wanted to see the children, it would have to be under court supervision.

Meredith followed Nan and Janet through the door. They paused outside. "I will bring the order over later," Meredith said. "Call me if he tries to contact you, then call the police."

"They won't do anything," Nan whispered. "He's one of them."

"They will now. They have to."

"Thank you." Nan managed a slight smile.

"You're welcome."

She watched as Nan and her friend walked down the corridor. She still looked defeated and frightened. Meredith only hoped she was right, that Rick would obey the order.

She looked at the clock. Only two-thirty. She had a great deal of work at the office, but nothing was more important now than her mother and the promise she'd just made to find her half sister. If, by some miracle, she could accomplish it quickly, her mother might have some peace before she died.

It was a gift Meredith wanted to give her. Perhaps it could bring closure to her as well.

She would go to the office, cancel as many appointments as possible for the next week, and get her legal assistant started on what little information she had on her half sister. Then she would return to the hospital.

Half sister. The revelation was still sinking in. She'd always wanted a sibling. She'd even made up an imaginary sister as a child. But the imaginary friend had never quite salved her loneliness, her sense of being the ugly duckling daughter of a beautiful woman.

She walked down the halls of the courthouse, finding herself looking for Detective Gaynor. That he occupied her thoughts at all was disturbing.

Why had he appeared in the courtroom? What was his interest in the case? He hadn't answered any of her questions, and he'd disappeared much too quickly.

He'd been an enigma to her when they'd first met years ago. Every impression she'd had of him was later contradicted. Because he was a witness in an important case, she'd investigated him thoroughly. He was regarded as a lone wolf. He was not well-liked by other officers. And he had a brother in prison. None of that had instilled confidence. But he had been one of the best witnesses she'd ever had, sure and confident.

And now he showed up here. She didn't like puzzles. And she didn't like people who didn't answer questions.

Gage had forced himself to leave the courtroom once the order was granted.

It would be his last—if unofficial—act as a member of the department's Public Integrity Division. He would be back on homicide in the morning. It had taken the threat of resigning to get a transfer.

He hated Public Integrity. He didn't like being a cop investigating other cops. He already was one of the most despised cops in the department for testifying against fellow officers. He thought being assigned to the PID had been still another form of punishment, though his superiors denied it.

He had served his time, though, as he'd said he would. Now he would do what he did best.

Rick Fuller was his final case with PID. Gage had learned a petition for a protection order had been filed in civil court. A division investigator said the wife had refused to file a complaint, but had agreed to file for protection. There were photos and a statement from an emergency room doctor, enough to take the man's badge even without a complaint from the wife.

But Fuller had a superlative record in the department, and his captain wanted to keep him if possible. There had never been a citizen complaint filed against him. Apparently, he saved his violence for his wife.

Gage had talked to Fuller at length. If he did not fight the protection order, stayed away from his wife and followed the court's child custody orders, he would not lose his badge. But one call—one simple complaint—would end his career, and Gage would personally make sure he went to prison.

Gage hadn't liked the deal he'd made. He didn't like men who hit women, especially those they had vowed to protect and cherish. But he knew domestic violence. If Fuller was fired, he would go after the wife. This solution might just save her life.

He'd had no intention of telling Meredith Rawson that. He knew she thought he was dirty and for some odd reason, that bothered him. The defendants she had prosecuted had blackened his name to destroy his testimony. Rumors had been everywhere.

Perhaps he had some guilt and that had made him defensive. Not that he was on the take. But he had looked the other way too many times. From the moment he'd joined, he'd recognized that minor corruption was department culture, and the department was all he had.

Gage had accepted that culture until he discovered two fellow officers had committed a murder to cover up their sins. He'd overheard a drunken conversation about an unsolved murder. After talking with his superior, he'd found the evidence that convicted two fellow officers. He could ignore a lot, but not murder.

Meredith Rawson had assisted in trying the case. She'd been new to the office, having received the appointment—according to courthouse gossip—because of her father, a prominent attorney and an influential political donor.

She had been charged with doing preliminary investigation of all the witnesses, including the police officers involved in the case. She'd obviously thought the whole department was dirty, and her questions implied such. He certainly hadn't intended on taking guff from a socialite who played at being an assistant district attorney.

To his surprise, she had done a reasonably competent job on the case, but their reaction to each other had been immediate friction. The air had crackled with it. He had thought her too inexperienced to be involved in what had become "his" case. He'd placed his career, even his life, in jeopardy to pursue it.

To be honest with himself, maybe it hadn't been her inexperience that had made him edgy. Perhaps it had been the physical attraction he'd felt even though she was exactly the kind of woman he avoided. He did not trust debutante types who played at real life. Their depth of commitment was usually as thin as parchment.

Still, he couldn't stop thinking about her now as he cleaned out his desk. She'd looked particularly harried today. Distracted. Her short auburn hair had been disheveled and her eyes had had dark circles under them. Still, she'd looked great in the expensive dark blue suit she'd worn. Hell, he might as well admit it. With her tall, lithe body, she was the kind of woman who would look good in a potato sack.

Damn, he was mooning over a woman who was pure poison for someone like him.

He took one last look through the drawers, not wanting to miss anything. Then he lifted the scantily filled box. No photographs. Just some notebooks filled with sources he'd cultivated during the fifteen years he'd served in the department. Some personal stuff, like insurance papers, old pay stubs and his various certificates for law enforcement courses. An address book that was almost empty. A letter from Clint, his only surviving brother. The return address was the state prison. It reminded him that he needed to visit him this weekend.

A familiar pang jolted through him. He hadn't been able to save his brothers. Terry had died in a gang fight. Clint had gotten involved with drugs and gone to prison. In trying to make their lives better, he'd somehow lost them. The pain and guilt never entirely left him.

He added to the box the numerous pencils and pens he'd collected in the past year and a couple of old candy bars.

The lack of heft didn't bother him. He had little doubt that his new desk would soon be bulging with files.

Homicides were never scarce in New Orleans.

two

A new private duty nurse greeted Meredith in her mother's hospital room.

"She didn't wake up?" Meredith asked.

"No. She's slipped into a coma."

Meredith swallowed hard. She closed her eyes as a lump grew in her throat. Grief was a part of it. Need, another. She had thought she would have more time. Perhaps not much. But enough to get the information she needed, perhaps even find her sister before her mother . . .

"Has my father been here?"

"He came for a few moments." The woman's voice was chilly.

Meredith wondered whether it was because her father had been curt with her, even rude, as he could be when in a hurry, or because her father had spent so little time with his dying wife.

"He has an important case," she said.

The woman gave her a look that tore apart that defense.

"You can take a break," Meredith said. "I'll stay with her."

The nurse rose. She left without a word and closed the door behind her as if she knew Meredith wished to be alone with her mother.

Meredith sat down in the chair next to the bed and reached for her mother's fragile hand. "Please wake up."

There was no response. She looked at her mother's face, remembering the wedding photo of her mother and father. Marguerite Thibadeau had been truly beautiful, far prettier than Meredith had ever been. She'd always envied the cool elegance of her mother's flawless bone structure, the symmetry of her features. Meredith had inherited her father's firm jaw and wide mouth.

She rested her head on her mother's chest, something she couldn't ever remember doing as a child. She heard the soft beat of her mother's heart even as she felt her soul drawing away.

"Don't give me a task I can't fulfill," she whispered. But she knew she would try. She had never known her mother. Never known the agony she'd obviously carried so long. Never known she'd possessed the kind of reckless passion that produced a child out of wedlock.

How she wanted to talk to her now.

"I made you a promise. I'll try to keep it," she said, then continued in a conversational tone, "I won a small victory today. I've finally found something where I can make a real difference."

She sat there for another thirty minutes, talking about her life, reaching out when it was too late to reach out. She held her mother's hand and wished she could turn the clock back.

She thought about her father, about the coolness, even hostility, that in some strange way bound her mother and father together.

Should she talk to her father about her half sister?

Her mother had nodded when she'd asked if he knew. Or had she? Had it simply been a reaction to pain? Should Meredith bring it up now? Or should she wait? Regardless, he would have to know. If he didn't know already.

She decided she had to talk to him about it. It would be difficult. They had never spoken of important things.

She couldn't quell the resentment she felt for his lack of support now, for his few visits to the hospital.

She knew his current case was important. She also knew any other attorney would have requested—and been granted—a postponement. Any other husband would come to the hospital after court rather than interview witnesses himself. She wondered whether he was secretly glad to have an excuse to stay away from the hospital.

She would remain here tonight and face him tomorrow at breakfast. She would have Sarah cancel all her appointments for the next ten days except for one court case, and if worse came to worst she would try to postpone it. She would stay here at night with her mother. During the day she would try to find her sister.

That might be the one thing that could give her mother comfort. *If* she regained consciousness.

She turned to the nurse, who had just returned. "Will she come out of the coma?"

"You'll have—"

"I know. Talk to the doctor. I have. He wouldn't commit himself. But you must have worked with comatose patients. Have you ever seen one wake?"

"I've known it to happen," the nurse said. "Nothing is impossible."

"I'll stay with her tonight," Meredith said.

"But—"

"I'll take the responsibility. I would just like to spend some time with her."

The nurse nodded.

After she was gone, Meredith leaned back and closed her eyes. Images went through her mind. The cool politeness between her mother and father. The causes her mother espoused. She'd been on every civic and charitable board in the city, including the symphony, opera and theater guilds.

Meredith always thought it was to avoid her husband and daughter. As a child she'd thought it was because she was not pretty enough. So she'd decided to be smart and please her father. But she could never quite do that, either.

What had happened so many years ago? Why had her

mother given up the child if she cared so much? What had happened to Meredith's sister?

Meredith couldn't imagine what it must cost a mother to give up a child. She loved children, though she'd resigned herself to never having any. Growing up as she had in a loveless atmosphere, she had never seen marriage as a desirable state. Most of her friends' parents were divorced. Love, if it existed, seemed to be a fleeting thing, a condition more of pain than joy.

She didn't let herself think of loneliness. She had friends, interests, a career now veering off in an entirely new direction that gave her life purpose. She loved good music. She enjoyed art. It was all she needed.

It was what her mother had had.

Obviously it had not been enough. The despair in her eyes had not come from the knowledge of impending death, but of regret for things not done. Meredith had recognized that.

She continued to hold her mother's hand, planning out her next moves.

She could not stop thinking of the woman who was her half sister. What kind of life had she had? And would she even want to be found?

Gage went over the files dropped on his new desk. Mostly cold cases, the rest reaching that stage.

He was surprised. There was a special office for cold cases.

But this might well be an effort to keep him away from the other homicide detectives. His immediate superior had been curt when Gage reported in, and it was obvious—at least to Gage—that he had been foisted upon the lieutenant. Gage wasn't surprised. He knew he was a pariah in the police department. He'd broken the blue wall of silence.

He remembered Lieutenant Bennett. The officer had been

in robbery when Gage had testified against two of his men.
It had been a black eye for him.

Gage wondered exactly how he had been forced on Bennett. But he *was* an experienced homicide detective and had
a good record in solving cases. That was probably why he
was getting cold cases that were almost impossible to solve.

Still, he was so damned glad to be back on the streets.
And it wouldn't be long before Bennett was forced to send
him out on new cases. Budget cuts had sliced the homicide
unit in half.

He sifted through the ten old files. New scientific techniques often turned up something that hadn't been obvious
before. The FBI now maintained a nationwide bank of fingerprints. And DNA technology allowed the police to explore avenues that had been closed years ago.

Only one case really interested him: the murder of a socially prominent man fifteen years earlier.

He remembered the case. He had been a rookie then, and
he had followed the investigation. The victim—Oliver
Prescott—had been an officer in his father's bank.

The death had apparently devastated the father, who died
two years later. The father's brother had assumed the position of chairman of the board, a position the son unquestionably would have had. A good enough motive.

The reports sounded a little odd to Gage. Though Oliver
Prescott was a member of the city's most prominent Mardi
Gras Krewe, no one really called him a close friend. And despite the publicity surrounding the case, its active stage had
ended fairly rapidly. Too rapidly, Gage thought.

He'd wondered then, and wondered again, whether it was
because of the public figures involved. Prescott's family was
one of a tight group of city leaders, including city officials,
prominent political donors, judges and attorneys. Any cop
who pursued the case would probably open closets some
wanted kept closed.

Gage didn't give a damn about offending anyone. He'd
made a career out of it.

He would poke around, see what could be stirred up. Perhaps it would take his mind away from Meredith Rawson. He was damned if he knew why she aroused such strong re- actions in him. Although her blue eyes were striking, she was not his usual type. She wore her hair in a no-nonsense feathered haircut and her suits were severe. He liked long hair and casual clothes. He was a beer guy. He suspected she was a champagne woman.

One detective wandered over and peered down at the files. "I got those last year," he said. "Apparently they give them to the new guy in the division."

Gage raised an eyebrow. "Or people they don't like. Did you have any luck?"

"Broke my ass on the Cary case, but nothing. At least nothing I could take to the DA."

"What about Prescott?"

"Couldn't find a damn thing. No one would talk to me. Maybe you being from here . . ." He held out his hand. "Name's Wagner. Glenn Wagner. They call me Wag."

Gage took his hand and studied him. Wagner was a big man, probably about forty. He had the cautious eyes of a cop and his cheeks told Gage that the man probably drank too much. "You might as well know I'm bad news around here," Gage said.

"You also have a great rep in solving cases."

"That's one reputation," he said dryly. "The other is why I have these cases rather than current ones. I expect the lieu- tenant intends to get rid of me as soon as possible."

"Then he's a fool."

Gage didn't answer. He was suspicious of such an obvi- ous overture.

"Wanna grab a bite? I haven't had time for lunch."

He was hungry, so why not? He also wanted to know why Wagner was making an effort toward a man most other cops steered clear of.

"Sure," he said.

They went to a sandwich shop not far from the station and ordered at the counter before finding seats.

Once seated, Gage started his own interrogation. "Why the welcome?"

The other man shrugged. "I'm an outsider, too. It's a closed shop here."

Gage could understand that. The department had always been insular, self-protective. Newcomers were regarded as threats to the old way of doing things.

But he was a loner. He didn't want pals, particularly in the police department. Years ago it had led him into compromises that still haunted him.

"The Prescott case," he reminded Wagner. "Who did you talk to? I didn't see any update in the file."

"Nothing to update," Wagner said. "I found zero. Nada. But I can give you a list of people I talked to."

"Your impressions of them?"

"Mainly impatient that such an old case had been revived. Nothing that made me suspicious."

"I'd like that list this afternoon."

"Why that case?"

"It just interests me."

"Well, you're a hell of a lot better than me if you get anywhere." He changed the subject. "You married?"

"No."

"Smart guy. I'm in the middle of a divorce. She couldn't take the hours."

So that explained the approach. Wagner was probably lonely.

Gage finished his sandwich and rose. He didn't want any more confidences. "Time to get back."

"If I can help . . ."

"Thanks," he said, his mind already going back to the pages in the Prescott file. He wanted to study the case files more thoroughly, then make a list of possible interviews. One particular name had emerged from the file. Charles Rawson. He'd been the last person known to see Prescott alive.

Charles Rawson. Prominent attorney. And father of Meredith Rawson.

KANSAS CITY, MISSOURI
THREE WEEKS EARLIER

Holly held her son's hand tightly as she roamed among the sentiments engraved on plaques in Baby Land.

Although the section was only a small part of the cemetery in Kansas City, it had to be the most heartbreaking. What must it be like to lose a child?

All her emotions seemed to pound against the dam that had held them back during the week since she unbelievably killed a fellow human being. It didn't matter that he apparently had intended to kill her. She felt as if she had lost a part of her soul.

She was going to lose even more now. She was about to steal the identity of the most innocent of victims.

But she had to elude her husband and his resources. She needed a completely new identity. She hoped—prayed—she could find one here.

A dead child left behind a bronze marker, a birth certificate and little else but love in the hearts of those who mourned. Nothing that could be traced. She could request a birth certificate and use it to get a Social Security card and other forms of identity, including a badly needed driver's license. It would take weeks, but she *had* to have those documents. In the meantime, she would obey every speed limit sign in the country.

She'd grabbed her son that horrifying night and little else: a few clothes, what money she had saved from the small sculptures she loved creating, two sculptures, and a few of her sculpting tools. She hadn't taken them all. She didn't want Randolph to notice she had taken any. Randolph called it her "little" hobby. He'd had no idea that she'd secretly sold her works to a craft shop and had been hoarding the money they brought.

She'd wanted to leave him long before, but knowing his power and his alliances, she'd been terrified of losing her son. She knew Randolph would find a way of getting custody. He had warned her over and over again that he would.

She could never leave her son under his control and influence.

He had threatened her into inertia. Still, she had been saving and hiding money. She'd built a fantasy escape, had researched places to go.

Bisbee, Arizona. That had been her Mecca. She'd read about it in a magazine, then researched it on the Web at the library. A haven for artists. She could lose herself there and make a living for herself and her son.

She never would have had the courage to do it, though, if not for the intruder. Then she'd had no choice.

She made herself look at the small bronze markers. She couldn't linger here. She'd carefully laid a trail to Florida, having driven east for four hours. She had cashed out her credit card in Mobile, then continued across Alabama. In Pensacola, a navy town, she'd abandoned the Mercedes in a bad-looking section of town, hoping it would be stolen or looted of parts. She didn't dare try to sell the car. It was in her husband's name, not hers.

She'd hocked her engagement and wedding rings for a fraction of their worth and bought bus tickets to Miami, then cut her long, blond hair and dyed it a dull brown. She dyed Mikey's sandy hair the same brown color.

The dye and ragged haircut made a difference. Randolph had always wanted her to look her best. She'd been what so many called a trophy wife, always impeccably groomed and dressed. She couldn't change the high cheekbones, the heart-shaped face or the wide blue eyes, but she could downplay them by scorning makeup and wearing a pair of cheap glasses.

After the transformation, she purchased two more bus tickets from a separate ticket agent for Mobile. In Mobile, she bought bus tickets for Chicago. They had been wandering since. No, not wandering. Running in sheer terror.

Until they'd reached Kansas City. She felt they were far enough away from New Orleans and had taken enough twists and turns to throw off the most determined follower. Despite all her precautions, though, traveling with a child on a bus might be traceable. She couldn't go farther before getting a car and starting work on a new identity.

She planned to search the auto ads in the local paper. Cars for sale by private individuals. They wouldn't require identification, not if she offered cash.

But first . . .

She continued her search, among the small graves. She finally found one that met her needs. *Elizabeth Baker.* It even had the day of birth and death. And a sentiment: *Our Little Angel.*

Everything she needed. She felt like the worst of villains. An opportunist benefiting from a death.

But then she looked at her son and knew she would do anything for him, anything to protect him.

She wrote down the dates from the plaque, said a small prayer for the child, then took a city bus back to the small motel where they were staying.

Once there, she settled Mikey down for a nap. "Why did we go there, Mommy?"

"To visit a friend," she said, giving him a tight hug.

"Do I know her?"

"No," she said.

"Was it a girl or a boy?"

"A girl."

"Is she in heaven?"

"Yes."

"Why?"

For once, she wished he wasn't so precocious, so curious. "I don't know, love. I think she was sick. Now I want you to go to sleep for me."

"I'm not sleepy."

"But Henry is," she said, putting his battered and much beloved stuffed dog next to him.

" 'Kay," he finally acquiesced.

She waited until he was asleep, then started to call the sellers who'd listed cars in the classifieds. She explained that her own car had died on the road and the mechanic said it wasn't worth saving. She needed a car. Would he be interested in bringing it to her?

On the third call, the seller agreed to bring the vehicle to the motel. The car was dark and eight years old. But she drove it around the parking lot and, though not smooth like her Mercedes, it appeared to run well. The seller swore by its condition. New tires. Recent tune-up. The odometer said a little over eighty thousand miles. It was a lot, but it convinced her he hadn't turned it back.

Desperate people couldn't be choosy. She couldn't stay here.

"You said it was forty-five hundred. Will you take thirty-seven hundred in cash?"

"It's worth every bit of my price," the seller said.

"I don't have that much. And I compared that model to other advertised cars. I think my offer is fair." Desperation was making her stronger.

He eyed her speculatively. "Would you like to talk about it over supper?"

"My son is with me, and my husband is overseas in the army."

He looked down at her hand. No wedding ring. *Damn.*

"I sold it to buy the car. I have to get home. My mother is ill." She felt as if her nose was growing longer.

He looked as if he saw it, too. She wondered if he saw, or felt, her desperation. Perhaps he did, for after a moment, he nodded. "You can have it," he said simply.

She smiled for the first time in three days. "I have the money with me. Do you have the bill of sale?"

He looked at her curiously. "You don't want a mechanic to check it out?"

"Do I need to?" She opened her eyes wide.

"No, but most people—"

"I really do have to get home," she said. She was using every acting skill she had, even forcing—or perhaps not forcing—a tear.

"Are you sure I can't take you and your son to supper?"

"We'll be leaving very early in the morning," she said. "But thank you."

In minutes, she had the bill of sale and had given him half of her money. She felt both victorious and apprehensive. She had accomplished something on her own. But her money was very short. And once it was gone . . .

She had a glimmer of satisfaction that Randolph paid for her escape. The sale of her rings had made it possible.

If only the fear didn't linger inside like some deadly snake ready to strike.

three

Holly and Mikey reached Bisbee three days after leaving Kansas City.

She found a cheap but clean motel where she paid cash. She explained that she was a new widow and had not yet had time to get her own credit cards.

This time she was prepared. She'd bought a ring at a discount store along the way. A ring was protection. A ring verified her story of being a bereaved widow.

Bisbee was everything she'd expected, and more. She and Mikey walked through the old town and Brewery Gulch, a once blue-light district now filled with funky restaurants and craft shops, the kind that might carry the type of work she hoped to sell.

Mikey was obviously bewildered and delighted by the odd town, where houses perched on hills and tiny lanes meandered among them. "Mommy, look at that funny house," he kept repeating.

She stopped in a small cafe where he happily ordered tacos and she started to order a salad. Then she changed her mind. Her husband had always noticed when she gained a pound and let her know about it. She had lived on salads and skinless chicken.

"Three tacos," she said. She felt like a kid playing hooky,

but this was a moment's indulgence that she could, and would, enjoy.

After they finished, she wandered into a real estate office. Bisbee, she already knew, was where she wanted to stay.

The agent on duty was a loquacious middle-aged man dressed casually in blue jeans. She soon learned he was a California banker who'd migrated to a simpler life in Bisbee.

She quickly caught his enthusiasm for the area. "Bisbee is a way of life," he explained. "Once you've been here awhile, you'll never want to leave." He rattled on. "Bisbee was a thriving mining town—billed as the largest town between St. Louis and San Francisco. It all but became a ghost town when the mines closed in the fifties."

Then what he termed "the aging counterculturalists"—hippies, she thought with a smile—discovered it and quickly moved into homes they bought for a song. "Now it's attracting craft people and retirees, along with us Californians looking for something more relaxed and inexpensive.

"Unfortunately," he added as he showed her some listings of rental properties, "it's not as inexpensive as it was even two years ago. Newcomers are moving in, transforming old homes into bed-and-breakfasts and deserted buildings into art galleries."

Still, compared to most places, Bisbee offered cheap housing. The real estate agent showed her a tiny furnished frame house for four hundred fifty dollars a month. Best of all, it had a fenced yard and the landlord allowed pets.

Worst of all, it was little more than a slum. Even her son looked dubious as they were shown the two small bedrooms, the small bathroom, the small living room and the even smaller kitchen. The furniture was cheap modern.

But it was the only property within her budget that allowed pets. And that was one promise she'd made to her son. "Can I paint it?" she asked.

The agent grinned at her. "I'm sure the owner will be delighted at any improvements."

"He lives here?"

"She," he corrected. "Marty Miller. She owns Special Things, a gallery off Main Street. She'll probably come over to see if you need anything."

Holly paid two months rent in advance. She did not want any credit checks.

She used the name from the cemetery—Elizabeth Baker—on the application. She'd used another alias when she'd purchased the car. She'd also asked Mikey to pick a name he liked. A game they were playing, she told him. What was his favorite name in the world? After long deliberation, he'd decided on Harry, from Harry Potter. Harry went on adventures, too.

An adventure. She had been able to convince him thus far that this was a grand adventure. But eventually he would start asking about his father. He would want his toys and his preschool and his friends.

She tucked that thought away as she checked out of the motel, purchased some groceries and moved them both into the tiny house. Then, following the agent's directions, she took her son—now Harry—to the animal shelter. That, she knew, would both distract and cheer him.

There were twenty dogs. Harry went from one cage to another, enchanted by all of the mostly nondescript mongrels who eyed him longingly. "I want them all," he said.

The volunteer smiled. "I think I know the perfect dog for a young man."

Harry beamed at the description.

She went to the next to the last cage and unlocked the door, coming out with a scruffy-looking, half-grown dog. The dog squirmed in her arms until she put him down. He walked over to Harry, wagged his tail, sniffed him briefly, then sat in front of him as if to say, "You're satisfactory. I pick you."

"He's been house-trained," the volunteer said. "The woman who had him became ill and went to live with a relative who turned out to be allergic to dog hair. It broke her heart. I would have taken him myself, but I've already adopted four dogs."

"Does he have a name?" Holly asked.

"Caesar."

"A noble name for a . . ." She stopped for fear of hurting her son's feelings. He obviously thought the dog very handsome. She'd had a puppy in mind, but Mikey—no, Harry—was on his knees, his arms around the animal as it slurped its tongue against his cheek.

She'd never had a dog and always wanted one. Her parent said no, and so had her husband when they were first married. She should have left then. She should have realized . . .

But then she wouldn't have Mikey. She caught herself. She *had* to start thinking of him as Harry.

"We'll take him," she said.

"He's had his shots. You need to bring him in next month to be neutered," the volunteer said, then paused. "You've had a dog before?"

Suddenly afraid the woman might jerk the dog away if she said no, Holly nodded. Maybe nodding wasn't as big a lie as actually mouthing the words.

Moments later she had paid the fee, filled out the form with her new address and received a free leash, a pamphlet advising how to be a good dog owner, as well as a voucher that was good for neutering.

"By the way, my name is Julie," the volunteer said, peering at the address. "I see you're new in town and I know how lonely that can be. I give a free obedience class once a month. Please come if you're interested." She wrote down a time and place.

"Thank you."

"And call me if you have any problems with Caesar. We take them back if they don't work out. No blame. Don't just abandon him."

"No, I won't. I wouldn't."

"Perhaps I can visit and see how he is doing."

"I . . . don't have a phone yet." Holly suddenly realized for the first time that she might not be able to get one. She supposed they *did* check credit ratings or at the very least require a Social Security number.

So many things to consider. Despite all the small accomplishments she'd made today, her heart sank. How could she do this? She was sure to make a mistake.

How many mistakes had she already made?

She forced herself to push that thought aside. She thanked Julie and invited her to stop by the house they had rented.

The dog sat primly beside Harry in the car seat she'd toted across half the country. Her son was not going to let Caesar get more than an inch away from him. Caesar seemed content as well, occasionally putting one paw on his lap.

She had to buy some dog food, but it was too hot to leave the dog in the car while she shopped for it. Caesar would eat human fare tonight.

Human. She suddenly realized she felt human for the first time in years. Perhaps fear made her feel alive. Or was it the freedom? Yet she wasn't really free. She had killed a man.

The pleasure of the day faded. She was reminded of something else she needed to do today once they got the dog home. She wanted to go to the library and check the Internet for Louisiana newspapers. There would be news stories about her disappearance. A lot of them. She was, after all, the daughter of a judge, the wife of a rising state senator.

However, she had seen nothing in the newspapers she'd purchased when traveling from Florida to Arizona, nor had she heard anything on the television. She'd held her breath every time she'd turned it on.

But now she had to get to their new home and make it theirs. She had to find metal for her work. If she didn't sell something soon, they would be in trouble. Perhaps tomorrow she would take the two sculptures she had brought from home to the various galleries and gauge their interest.

She had to earn a living. Something she'd never done before.

She wouldn't let herself think it could all come to a screeching halt today, tomorrow, next week, next year.

She wouldn't think about it. She couldn't, and keep going.

NEW ORLEANS

Meredith rang the doorbell of her parents' house at six-thirty in the morning.

She didn't just barge in. Never had. Doubted that she ever would. Once she'd moved out on her own, she'd never again considered the house on Chestnut Street her home. If, indeed, it had ever seemed like home.

Built in the early 1800s, the house now resembled a museum. There had never been a newspaper lying around or a cup of coffee left on a table for more than a moment. A book left in the living area might well disappear forever.

Her father did not like disorder.

Mrs. Edwards, the housekeeper, opened the door. She was always "Mrs.," never Maude, although she had been with the family for nearly ten years. Her father hated change and was willing to pay a premium price for consistency.

The housekeeper's homely face wreathed into a smile. "Miss Meredith. Good to have you home."

"Thank you. Is my father here? I'd hoped to join him for breakfast."

"Six-thirty sharp, just like always," she said. Then the smile slipped from her face. "Almost like always, 'cept Mrs. Rawson isn't here." She hesitated, then added, "Any news about Mrs. . . . your mama?"

"Not good, Mrs. Edwards."

"I should go to see her."

"She wouldn't recognize you," Meredith said. "It's all right. My father needs you here."

"I'll bring you breakfast. Two eggs over light?"

"You know me well. Thank you."

"The griddle is still hot. It will just take a few minutes."

"I'll go with you and get my coffee."

She followed Mrs. Edwards into the large kitchen, poured herself a cup of coffee, then went into the dining room.

Her father was reading the newspaper as he ate. He looked up when she came in. "Meredith. This is a surprise." His eyes regarded her critically. "You look like hell."

"Probably because I stayed with Mother last night."

"I hear accusation in your voice."

She was startled. He usually didn't hear anything he didn't want to hear. "Probably," she said. "Don't you want to know how she is?"

"I know. I talked to the doctor this morning. For your information, I also talked to him last night. He said she was in a coma. She wouldn't know I was there."

"She might."

Some emotion crossed his perfectly blank face, surprising her.

"Are you going to see her today?" Meredith couldn't keep the question from her tongue.

He gave her the piercing look she had seen him give opposition witnesses.

"She was awake yesterday," Meredith said, wanting to startle a reaction from him.

He frowned. "I thought she was in a coma."

"That was later," she said.

"Is that why you came this morning? To instruct me on my husbandly duties?" His voice had taken on a decided frost.

"No. Not exactly."

"Then what exactly?"

Meredith was not easily intimidated, but she had to admit her father still made her nervous. Old habits died hard. Especially after thirty years of seeking his approval.

Mrs. Edwards appeared with a plate loaded with two eggs, croissants, and fruit, and disappeared just as discreetly.

"Mom asked me to do something for her," Meredith said.

His head snapped up. "What?"

"Did . . . did you know she'd had a baby? Before me?"

His face paled. She realized immediately he *had* known. It was like a blow in her stomach. Secrets. So many secrets in this house. Was that why it was so cold, so . . . empty? Even when filled with people?

"Don't rummage around in the past," he said.

"She asked me to find her. She wants me to share the trust fund she saved for me, for us."

"That doesn't give you pause?"

She knew exactly what he meant. "No. I earn all that I need."

He shook his head as if he could not imagine how she came to be his daughter. "Your mother is full of drugs. She doesn't know what she's saying."

"Are you telling me that it didn't happen?"

"You know your mother. Can you believe . . .?"

"I'm beginning to think I don't know either of you," she said tightly. "I realize you don't love each other, but—"

"You know nothing, miss," he said sharply. He very carefully folded his napkin and placed it next to his plate, then rose. "I have to go to the office before court."

"We haven't finished talking."

"I have."

"I'm going to find her."

He spun around. "The hell you are! You want to ruin your mother's reputation, everything she worked to build? She cared about what people thought."

"Did she? Or was that you?" she asked quietly.

"You've thrown away everything I've tried to give you," he said. "Don't lecture me."

She knew what he was doing. By attacking her, he could avoid her questions. "What do you know?" she persisted, her anger rising. He knew something. His eyes told her he knew something. The way he avoided her questions told her he knew something. He wasn't the only attorney in the family. She knew the techniques as well as he did.

He turned away without another word. She heard him walk down the hallway, his steps not quick and determined as they usually were. The door opened and shut behind him.

She had more questions now than before.

•   •   •

Once in his office, Charles Rawson picked up the phone.

He didn't bother with the niceties. "Meredith knows about her half sister. She's going to try to locate her."

"There's no trail. I made sure of that."

"She's persistent. She can be obstinate."

"Stop her."

"I'm not sure I can."

"I'm not asking you to try. Just do it."

Charles felt trapped. "She promised her mother."

"Marguerite?"

"She's very ill. She asked—"

"You assured me your wife would not say anything. To anyone."

Charles didn't answer that. At one time, he could make that assertion. But now . . .

Up until now, he'd had a threat. He'd had a control that he had used mercilessly, partly because his wife had never loved him. He had loved *her*, enough in fact to sacrifice all his ambitions. But she had spent years telling him in so many ways that she was with him out of necessity rather than love. Perhaps she'd even stayed to punish him.

And she had. Nearly every day of their lives.

Never once had she told him she loved him. He couldn't bear to see her now, a shadow of the vibrant girl she'd once been. He knew he had been responsible for the fading of colors. And now she was dying, withering away as a malignant disease rampaged through her body, and still the rejection was in her eyes.

"She's dying, for God's sake."

"Fix the problem," came the voice with the chilling threat.

The phone went dead.

Charles replaced the receiver in the cradle and sat still for a moment. What if he had told Marguerite years ago where her daughter was? He knew the answer only too well. She never would have stopped trying to get her back.

He'd sold his soul to the devil a long time ago, and it was far too late to repent.

Now he had placed his own daughter in jeopardy. Unless he could stop her from continuing this damned quest.

A knock on the door.

"Come in."

His young associate entered. "It's time, sir."

Charles looked at his watch. He pasted on his confident smile for the benefit of young Hart. The case had not been going well. He knew it. His firm was defending a chemical company that had taken shortcuts in a small community east of New Orleans and dumped dangerous chemicals near a stream. People had sickened. One child had died.

He could read juries. It had always been his strength. He saw the verdict already in their faces—the way their expressions tightened when they looked at him and softened as they looked at the defendants.

The defense was that rogue employees had done the illegal dumping on their own. Two men even admitted it and had been arrested. The question was the company's culpability.

The company was his law firm's largest client. He'd been steadily losing clients, and the loss of this one would mean he would have to dismiss several associates.

He wasn't going to let Braden Hart know that. The young man was the brightest of his associates. Charles had even once hoped that Meredith might become interested in him.

But neither Meredith nor Hart had seemed interested in each other.

Dammit, but Meredith had become one hell of a stubborn woman, totally unlike the girl who had craved his approval as a child. He had wanted a son, but a complication with Meredith's birth had prevented Marguerite from having another child even if she had been willing. He'd then tried to make Meredith into his son. She had been compliant until a few years ago.

He still didn't know why she'd turned away from his tutelage.

In recent years, she had discarded all his plans for her. She'd quit her position with the DA's office. The DA's office was the fastest way to be noticed in legal circles. But just as she'd acquired a reputation as a real comer, she'd quit. Her clients now included the down and out, the dregs of society.

He suspected she did it to spite him. He had pushed too hard.

He'd lost her.

"Let's go," he said to Hart, turning his thoughts to the next few hours. He would be cross-examining one of the men who said he had, on his own, dumped the chemicals. That he had been told to take them to a regulated site.

If the man was to be believed, it would put the onus on him. He would be liable, and he had nothing.

If was a big word.

As he strode from his office, he tried to concentrate and not think of Marguerite. There was nothing he could do for her. The doctors said she would probably not come out of the coma.

Even so, he hesitated to visit. He was, he knew, the last person she'd want to see.

Why had she opened Pandora's box now?

Revenge? Had what happened so many years ago festered inside even more than he'd ever wanted to believe?

He only knew he had to do something to stop his daughter before she destroyed them all.

four

Sarah, Meredith's paralegal, was in her own cubicle when Meredith arrived at her office.

Sarah's face creased with concern when she saw her. "You look beat."

"I slept on a cot in my mother's room last night and stopped to have breakfast with my father this morning."

Surprise widened Sarah's eyes, but thankfully she made no comment about the breakfast. "How *is* your mother?"

"She slipped into a coma yesterday. The doctor doesn't seem to think she'll come out of it."

"What can I do to help?"

"A personal favor?"

"Anything. You know that, boss."

"What about robbing a bank?"

"Un-huh. Miss Law and Order asking that? I don't think so. So what can I do?" A widow and the sole support of two children, Sarah had previously worked in the district attorney's office. Meredith had stolen her when she left.

An attorney on her or his own needed a great paralegal, and Sarah had been the best one in the DA's office. She'd given up a safe job with health benefits to go with Meredith. In turn, Meredith had given Sarah the flexibility to be with her children when necessary.

Sarah would sometimes work at home, and that was fine with Meredith. The electronic age made it possible.

The kicker in wooing Sarah away had been Meredith's promise to make law school possible for Sarah through flexible hours, salary advances and recommendations. She intended to see that promise kept.

The only other permanent member of her staff was Becky Thomas, who served as bookkeeper and general secretary.

"Where's Becky?"

"She called in. A flat tire. She'll be late."

Meredith nodded. Becky, too, was a jewel. She had been one of Meredith's first clients and had testified against her boss. She'd lost her job, and Meredith had snatched her up. They were both very happy with the arrangement.

"The favor?" Sarah prompted.

Meredith didn't answer directly. "Any calls this morning?"

"Nothing urgent. You have the women's shelter this afternoon. I cancelled everything but that."

Meredith nodded. The shelter was a commitment she intended to keep. "And you?"

"Mrs. Evans's will. I wanted it ready for you to look at, then we can call her in. I'll work with Mrs. Abbot on compiling a list of marital assets. She believes her husband is hiding some. Mary Golden called to say she won't press charges against her husband. And we need more information on the wife in the Keyeses' custody battle. Want to call Doug in?"

Doug Evers was an investigator they used now and then. He was a former cop who was competent enough, though she continually had to warn him not to use illegal means in her cases. He'd never learned to recognize the line he shouldn't cross.

"I'll talk to Robert Keyes and see if he can afford it," Meredith said.

She hesitated, then added, "The favor . . . it's a personal matter."

Sarah waited.

Meredith started hesitantly, "Before she lapsed into a coma yesterday, my mother told me that she'd had another child. A girl. She was born in Memphis in February 1970. She asked me to find her."

"My God," Sarah said. "You didn't know?"

"I had no idea."

"But why now?"

"She wants the two of us to share the trust."

"Wow. That must have been a blow."

"Not the way you think. I inherited my house from my grandmother and I have a fairly good income from this practice. The blow came in discovering that she cared so much . . . and never let me know. I could have helped her then. Now there is so little information."

"What are you going to do?"

"Try to find her."

A pause. Then, "What can I do to help?"

"Search for a birth certificate for a daughter born of Marguerite Thibadeau."

"The father?"

"I don't know," Meredith admitted. "I'm hoping this will be easy and something helpful might be on the birth certificate. Try to find any records of an adoption. If you can't locate any, give me a list of adoption agencies in and around Memphis as well as attorneys who were known to handle private adoptions."

"I can do that," Sarah said.

"I know you can," Meredith said, looking down at her hands. They were clenched. She hoped Sarah didn't notice. "You're a treasure."

Sarah grinned "You pay me to be a treasure. What does your dad know about the baby?" Sarah asked, suddenly changing the subject.

"He says I shouldn't 'rummage around in the past' and destroy my mother's reputation. He also says it's none of my business, that I should let it go. He thought I should worry about my own inheritance."

"Most people would," Sarah said.

"I would rather have a sister."

"So you think we can eliminate your father as the father of the child?" Sarah said.

"Most definitely."

"But he knows something about it."

"Yes."

"Would your grandfather have been involved?"

"Most certainly. She was only seventeen. She said she was sent somewhere in Memphis."

"Do you have any relatives in that area?"

"A great-aunt used to live there. She died three years ago."

"Was she married?"

"Yes, but I think her husband died before her."

"Do you have an address?"

"I can probably find it in my mother's address book or . . . somewhere." She stopped suddenly, realizing that she had no idea how her mother kept that kind of information. "The name was Warren, I think. Sylvia Warren. I think her husband's name was Bob."

"Probably Robert then. What did he do?"

"I think he was a builder. I never met him. I met my aunt when she came to my grandmother's funeral."

"That's a little strange, don't you think? That you didn't see more of her. New Orleans isn't that far from Memphis."

"I never really thought of it. I remember liking her when I met her, but I never questioned why we didn't see her again. It was my mother's aunt and I had the impression my father didn't care for her. In any event, he was never strong on family or sentimentality."

Sarah nodded. She knew Charles Rawson's reputation. And her employer's reticence on the subject spoke volumes.

"Did they have children? If so, they might remember something if your mother did stay with her aunt."

"I don't think so."

Sarah raised an eyebrow but didn't say anything.

"Mother never talked about her," Meredith said defensively.

"Did you two ever talk about anything?"

"No, I guess we didn't. Not really. She was always busy. And even when she was home, she wasn't. Not really. Not in spirit." Pain and anger filled her again. Why had her mother waited until now to confide in her? How could her mother care so much about the child she'd given up and care so little about the one she'd kept? She swallowed past the lump in her throat. It was too late. Everything was too late. Too late to realize her mother *had* loved, that she had suffered. Too late to discover that her mother *did* feel emotion and maybe felt some for the daughter she *had* raised.

Or had the lack of emotion been because she'd lost the daughter by a man she loved and was burdened with the one by the man she hated? That thought was excruciating.

She was numb. She realized she had been numb ever since her mother had revealed her secret. The numbness had cloaked an anger so deep she could barely contain it. She looked at her hands and saw that they shook.

She willed them to still.

Sarah looked away.

Meredith changed the subject. It was still too raw. "You've heard nothing from Nan?"

"Nope. I think no news is good news."

Meredith agreed. The longer the time passed after a court order without contact, the better. Then she recalled the odd encounter in the courtroom. "Do you remember Gage Gaynor? He was a witness in a cop murder case I helped try."

"He's hard to forget. Big. Brooding. Honest, I think."

Meredith hadn't quite made up her mind about that yet. There had been rumors. Perhaps because he'd testified against a fellow cop. Or perhaps it was because of his cool green eyes that had been so difficult to read or the odd warm feelings he'd aroused in her. She hadn't trusted them.

"He was at the hearing."

Sarah looked surprised. "Did he say why?"

"Just that it was official business. He got in a dig about L.L. and Tommy's case."

"They were just kids."

"According to him, they were lowlifes unfit for a second chance."

"They were carrying drugs for a pittance. I think they learned their lesson." Despite having worked for the DA, Sarah was the original bleeding heart. It was at her behest that Meredith had taken the case. She'd been moving more and more toward family law and farther away from criminal practice.

The phone rang, but it stopped suddenly, and she knew Becky must have come into the office.

Meredith went to the door and looked out. Becky gave her a short wave and silently mouthed to her, "Are you here?"

"Who is it?" she mouthed back.

"A Detective Gaynor."

"Speak of the devil," Sarah muttered.

For a moment, Meredith thought she must have conjured him. It was an unwelcome thought. But she nodded and went into her office. She picked up her phone. "Detective?"

"I wondered whether Mrs. Fuller has had any more problems."

"No. Why?"

"He had a warning. If he goes near her, let me know."

"Thank you. I'll pass that on to Nan." She paused. "Will there be departmental charges?"

"No."

"May I ask why?"

"If he were fired, who would he blame?"

She was silent for a moment. He was right. A man with nothing to lose could be very dangerous. "And if he attacks someone else?"

"As far as we know, he hasn't. No complaints. He has a good record."

"Except for beating his wife."

"Look, Ms. Rawson, I don't like it any more than you do, but he'll be watched carefully now. One wrong step and he's out. He knows that. But I think he would be far more dangerous to your client if he lost his job. He wouldn't be able to find another in law enforcement. He would go after her for ruining his life."

"You sound as if you know that firsthand," she said.

"I do. A lady I liked a lot was killed that way."

She heard, or thought she heard, emotion in his voice. "Is that why you were in the courtroom?"

"I was the one who recommended that he not contest the charges, or the divorce. I told him I'd better not be wrong in not pressing for departmental action. If he so much as calls Nan, let me know."

"Thank you," she said. "You could have told me that then."

"Yep," he said cheerfully.

"Why didn't you?"

"Because you were glaring at me."

She probably had been. She had been so sure he was there to support Fuller.

"Just thought you should know." He hung up.

She stared thoughtfully at the phone in her hand. One question answered.

She didn't think she would be as lucky on the others.

Why in the hell had he done that?

Gage seldom explained himself, especially to an attorney.

But he had seen the suspicion in her face and for some reason he wanted to explain. He had no idea why he mentioned April, the wife of his first partner.

He hadn't been able to save her, but perhaps he could save Nan Fuller. Perhaps his call would give Nan a little reassurance, and Gage intended to keep an eye on her soon-to-be ex-husband, even though it was no longer officially his job. He certainly hoped he had made a believer out of Rick Fuller.

He had another reason as well. He had not been able to resist picking up the phone this morning. She had stayed in his thoughts last night. Meredith Rawson had the cool demeanor of a society belle, but the sparks in her blue eyes were those of a true crusader. He had never cared for either. Yet the combination appealed to him. As did the wide mouth and firm chin. They kept her from being a traditional beauty but gave her an intriguing quality that lingered in his mind.

He replaced the phone in its cradle. Gorgeous eyes or not, she was not for him.

So why had he bothered?

He told himself he did it because of the Prescott case. She would have been around fifteen when the man died, and Prescott was a friend and acquaintance of her father. She might know something, even if she didn't realize it.

A leap in logic.

An excuse.

Dammit.

He didn't need the kind of grief he was tempting by even thinking of the woman in any way but a professional one.

He picked up the phone again and called Dom Cross. Cross was one of the few people he trusted, perhaps because he was a maverick like himself. Cross ran a shelter for runaway and troubled boys in New Orleans. He was an ex-convict and made no secret of it. His background was one reason he'd been so successful with his young charges. He related to troubled kids far better than any establishment type could.

Dom had tried to help Gage's brother years ago but it had been too late. Clint had been too deeply involved in a gang to extricate himself. Because he'd had a cop as a brother, Clint had been given several passes by police who had found minute amounts of drugs on him. But then there was one time too many.

Gage wished Clint had never received a pass on the first offense. Perhaps that lesson would have stopped the progression of drugs and gangs earlier. It was one reason he said what he had to Meredith Rawson about the release of L.L.

"Gage!" Dom's hearty voice boomed through the receiver. "Haven't seen you for an age."

"Three weeks," Gage corrected.

"That's an age."

Gage ignored Dom's somewhat cavalier sense of time. "What about a pickup game this afternoon?"

"I think I can round up a few of the usual suspects."

"Good. I'll be there at six."

"Loser buys the drinks."

"A little confident, are you?"

"I know which kids to pick."

"So do I."

"I have a surprise on my side. Some new kids. Pretty damn good. It's what you get for finking out on me."

Gage chuckled. Dom had conned him into the pickup games two years ago. The kids needed a righteous cop as a good role model, he kept saying. Problem was Gage had doubts about his own righteousness.

But he'd owed Dom for what he had tried to do for Clint. And damn if he didn't just like the man. He was the most persuasive charmer Gage had ever met. And Dom genuinely cared about boys who had no one else who cared. And he made other people care.

Gage also enjoyed athletics, particularly basketball. In high school, he'd played both basketball and football, then football in college until an injury had ended his pro hopes. And his scholarship.

Those pickup games at the shelter were the only competition he had these days.

"I'll be there," he said with some relish. He always enjoyed tromping Dom.

five

Meredith stayed at the women's shelter longer than she intended. She devoted at least one afternoon a week there to counsel the women on their legal options. Some, like Nan, she represented pro bono.

The questions were always the same. Custody. Protective orders. The return of personal property. Marital and child support. The husband almost always had been the dominant member of the family and had controlled all finances and purchases. The wife rarely had any resources of her own.

Today the list of questions was particularly long, and she hadn't left until nearly eight.

She headed for the hospital again.

Her mother was the same. The private duty nurse was the same one who had been there the night before.

At Meredith's unspoken question, she shook her head. "No change, Ms. Rawson."

"She hasn't been conscious at all?"

"No."

"Is there any way we can wake her? Any stimulus?"

Her expression gave Meredith the answer. Her oral answer, though, was more cautious. "You might discuss it with her doctor."

"Does she know I'm here?"

"I don't know," the nurse said honestly. "There's a theory that comatose patients feel the presence of loved ones, but no one really knows."

The answer didn't comfort, or absolve, Meredith. Everyone should have someone with them. Someone they loved. Someone who loved them.

Now it was only her.

"Why don't you go out to supper?" she asked the nurse. "I'll stay with her until you get back."

"Why, thank you," the nurse said, then hesitantly added, "If you think it'll be all right with your father?"

Meredith wondered whether her father had bullied her like he bullied so many others. "Of course it is," she said. "I'll ring for a nurse if there's any problem."

"Then I'll do as you suggest. I'll be back within an hour."

"Take longer if you like." Meredith waited until the woman disappeared out the door before she took the chair next to her mother. She needed the time to think, to grieve, even to vent her anger. She had been given a task by a mother who'd barely acknowledged her existence, and then disappeared into a coma without giving her the information she needed.

"Dammit," she said to the still figure. "Don't do this to me. Give me something to go on."

But the figure on the bed did not move.

Meredith wanted to scream at her. *Why now? Why wait until it's too late?*

"Why didn't you care about me?" That question escaped her lips. She heard the plea in it. One that had echoed in her mind for so many years. The area at the backs of her eyes felt heavy with moisture, tears she was determined not to shed.

"Why?" she asked again. "If you care so much about losing a daughter, why didn't you love the one you had?" The pain was intense, the anger so powerful she could barely contain it. She wanted to shake her mother until she regained consciousness, until she could get some explanation. And yet she felt compelled to do this one last thing for her mother, despite the seeming hopelessness of finding someone lost thirty-three years earlier.

Had her mother agreed to an adoption, only to regret it later? Or had the baby been taken from her? If so, how? There had to be paperwork somewhere. She couldn't imagine her grandfather not making sure his grandchild went to someone safe. He'd always been possessive of everything in his life. He never threw anything out. The attic of her parents' house, which her mother had inherited from her father, was filled with his papers.

Perhaps she could find something there. Meredith decided to search her parents' house on Friday. Her father would be in court, and the housekeeper usually did her shopping then.

Meredith looked at her mother's face. Peaceful now, but thin. And aged. She was only fifty. This shouldn't be happening to her. If only she hadn't waited so long to go to their doctor. But there had been this meeting or that meeting, this project or that charity ball.

Meredith looked at the cards the nurse had handed her. Some had come with flowers. Other people had stopped in the room briefly. The cards included one from the mayor, several from members of the city governing board, one from the president of the symphony guild.

Meredith knew them all. She'd met them at various functions hosted by her mother. She stopped at one card. Judge Samuel Matthews, a member of the Louisiana Supreme Court and one of the state's most distinguished citizens. Some called him a kingmaker. Meredith had seen a photo of his daughter and her husband, a state senator and probable candidate for Congress, in the paper just a few weeks ago.

"You were loved," she whispered to her mother even as she wondered how someone so well-respected could have been so reserved with her own family. Perhaps it had just been her mother's nature to give to strangers. No emotional price that way.

She closed her eyes, trying to think of instances that would give her more insight into her mother. Meredith had known for a long time her parents' marriage was a loveless one. They slept in separate rooms. They were always scrupulously polite to each other. She couldn't remember an affectionate gesture between them.

She knew about abuse. Her father had not been abusive, at least not physically. He just lived in his own world, totally absorbed by his practice. He had given her mother everything she wanted. Unlimited funds. Household help. Contributions to all her favorite projects.

Everything but love. At least Meredith had seen little evidence of love.

And her mother in turn had given her daughter everything, everything but the warmth and affection she'd craved. It had made Meredith tough. She'd built her own shell.

To divert her mind from self-pity, which she hated, she made a mental list of things to do. Search her grandfather's records first. Her mother's room next. There might be a diary or records of a list of the steps her mother had already taken to find her missing daughter.

Then Meredith would try to locate neighbors and friends of her great-aunt. Perhaps she had told them something. And she would try school friends of her mother. Perhaps they might know who the father was. He might know something. *Someone must.*

Her eyes were trying to close, and she looked at the clock. Midnight. The nurse had returned and quietly taken a chair in the corner. The machines clicked on, one pouring drugs and nutrients into her mother as another recorded her heartbeat. Steady.

A lump caught in Meredith's throat.

She finally rose.

"Good night," she said to the nurse. "You will call me if there is even the slightest change?"

"Of course."

"I know my father is paying you but . . ."

"I'll call you."

"Thank you." She left the room blindly and leaned against the wall outside. She hated to go. But her mother had asked one thing of her. It was doubtful she would ever wake, but if she did, Meredith wanted her sister next to her.

She left the hospital. A few staffers were visible but nearly all the visitors were gone. She went down the eerily silent corridors, out the door to the covered parking decks a short distance away.

Clouds shrouded any light from the moon and stars. Rain drizzled in the oppressive heat, cloaking the city lights. The covered parking lot had been crowded when she'd arrived earlier, and she'd had to take a place in the third tier near the back.

For some reason she felt a tingling along her backbone. Her mind issued warning signals.

There were no people and few parked cars. An eerie silence magnified the sound of her footsteps on pavement.

She glanced uneasily over her shoulder, then told herself to relax. She'd been on her own too long to frighten easily. She followed all the safety tips. Have keys in hand, walk swiftly and with confidence, be alert. Still, she felt a prickling at the back of her neck.

The sound of a motor and the squeal of tires broke the silence. A car appeared in the curve leading from the level above where her car was parked. She backed up into an empty space. Unaccountably, her heart raced faster. She felt like a fool when the driver passed her without a look and drove toward the exit.

She was almost to her car when she heard an odd sound, like a muffled whistle, followed by the shattering of glass. An overhead light went out. Before she could react, the sounds were repeated, and the area was plunged into darkness.

Stunned, she didn't move for a second. She heard a different noise, the sound of a car revving up.

Meredith didn't have time to think. She leaped backward just as a car roared toward the spot where she'd been standing. She rolled under a car as the other sped away. She stilled completely, her heart pounding so loudly she thought anyone could hear it.

The sound—it had been like gunshots stifled by a silencer.

A gun? Fear threatened to strangle her, paralyze her.

Who had shot out the lights? Had he been in the car? Or was he still here, waiting to see whether she had been injured?

Whether she was dead.

It couldn't have been an accident. Someone had aimed the car at her. She was certain about that. And the shattering of the lights was a deliberate action. A planned, calculated action.

Her blood ran cold and she shivered in the hot humidity. Her arm burned and she realized she had scraped it as she hit the ground. The smell of gasoline nauseated her. She lay still, trying not to even breathe, willing her heart to slow.

After several moments of complete silence, she slid from under the car and hunched at its side. She sneaked a quick look, even as fear crawled up her spine. She'd never known exactly how some of her stalked clients had felt. Not really. No one could unless she'd felt terror herself.

Now she knew.

She remained unmoving for what seemed a lifetime. Listening . . . wishing she had a weapon with her.

Then she stood, slowly, painfully. No one in sight. The garage looked empty except for the shadowed cars. Apparently no one had heard the silenced shots that had shattered the lights, nor wondered about the sudden darkness on the third level.

She'd dropped her purse when she had jumped out of the way of the car. She stooped again and felt for it as her eyes gradually became accustomed to the darkness. She finally found it. Her hands shaking, she called hospital security on her cell phone.

She wasn't going to move away from the protection of the car. The shooter could still be out there. Or he—or she— might have an accomplice.

A robbery? Or something more sinister?

The thought that someone might still be in the parking

decks made her skin crawl. But if he were, wouldn't he be hunting for her? If she were the target, why hadn't they made sure they'd hit her?

Or was it a dangerous prank? Meant only to scare, not to kill?

She ran through her mind a list of people who might want to hurt her. Rick Fuller was one. Several other ex-husbands who had lost their wives to the women's shelter or divorce. Criminals she had sent to prison as an assistant DA. As she waited for security, the list grew uncomfortably long.

Shouts and flashlights. Finally. She released a deep breath she hadn't realized was bottled in her throat. "Over here."

In seconds she was surrounded by uniformed men. One stepped closer. "Ms. Rawson?"

She nodded, afraid her voice might come out as timorous. *Never show weakness.* Something drummed into her by her father.

"The police are on their way." He aimed the flashlights at the broken lights. "What happened here?"

"I'm not sure. I heard the shattering of glass and the lights went out. I think it might have been a silenced pistol. As soon as the lights went out, I heard a car tearing toward me. I just managed to jump out of the way."

"You think the driver was trying to run you down?"

"If not, he was giving a good imitation of it," she said. "He couldn't have missed seeing me."

"What were you doing here so late?"

"My mother is a patient. She's very ill."

"Next time, call for a security guard to accompany you," he said briskly but with a hint of sympathy. "Can you tell us anything about the car?"

"Big and dark."

"Not much help."

"Sorry, I was busy rolling under a car."

He flashed his light over her. She'd left her suit jacket in the car, and her plain white short-sleeved blouse was stained and torn. Her arm had scraped along the pavement and blood trickled from it.

"I need to get you inside to Emergency."

"It's a scratch," she said.

"But it's a scratch on hospital property," he said with a wry expression. "Lawsuits, you know."

"You know I'm an attorney?"

"I recognize the name."

"Don't worry, Mr. . . ."

"Adcock. Head of security."

"Mr. Adcock. Right now I just want to get home. I have no intention of filing a lawsuit."

A police car arrived, then a second.

She repeated everything she'd said to Adcock, then reluctantly went into the emergency room with him. The wound was cleaned, swabbed, then bandaged. She was even given several pills "for pain," though she said they weren't necessary.

Police reports were taken. A detective—Cliff Morris—arrived, and she told the story for the third time.

He offered to follow her home and check out her house, and she accepted. She didn't like being frightened. She didn't like asking for help, either, but she wasn't a fool. If the attack *had* been aimed at her personally, then there might be another attempt.

From now on, she vowed to herself, she would carry a weapon with her.

It was nearly four in the morning before they arrived at her house, a small historic home near the French Quarter. It had been her inheritance from her grandmother. Both her parents came from old New Orleans families.

Morris took her key from her but tried the door first. It was unlocked. She knew she'd locked it.

He looked at her.

"I locked it," she said.

"Get back," Morris said. His gun was immediately in his hand and he slowly opened the door.

"What can I do?" she asked.

He hesitated. "Do you know how to use the police radio?"

She nodded.

"Go to the car and call headquarters. Ask for backup." He stepped inside, holding his gun in both hands.

She ran to the car. It took her thirty seconds to make the call and give directions. Heart thumping, she went back to the front door of her home. Listened. Once again, she knew what terror truly was.

It made her damned angry.

The sound of wailing sirens rent the air, then flashing blue lights were visible through the rain.

Two uniformed officers sprinted out of the car and up on the porch. "Ms. Rawson?"

"Detective Morris is inside. The door to the house was open when we arrived. It was locked when I left. I was attacked just hours ago in a hospital parking area."

The officers already had guns in their hands. One man yelled out, "Police." Then the two went inside.

She waited, then heard voices, and all three came out. Morris holstered his gun. "All clear." He stepped in front of her before she could go in. "It's a mess in there. The whole place has been tossed."

He moved aside, and she entered, only to stop in astonishment and outrage. Sofa cushions had been slit open and tossed on the floor. Volumes from the bookcases lay strewn around the floor, spines broken in some cases. A vase was shattered. Tables upturned. It wasn't just a simple burglary. It was damage for damage's sake.

"All the rooms are like this," Morris said grimly. "It appears that someone doesn't like you."

"I've concluded that," she said, barely holding back tears. But she had learned never to cry in public. Tears were strictly private.

She walked around in a daze, first through the living room, kitchen, and dining room on this floor, then through the two bedrooms and office on the second, careful not to touch anything. All had been trashed. Her computer was gone from her office. Her printer and copy machine had been smashed to the ground.

Morris followed her soundlessly. She was aware of him standing at the door as she regarded what was left of the office.

"We need a list of anything that's missing," he said.

Still speechless, she simply nodded as she looked at the shambles. All she wanted was a drink and bed. She couldn't cope with any more tonight. No, she numbly corrected herself. This morning.

"The beds are pretty well torn up. I would suggest a hotel or another residence until you get those locks fixed. I would also recommend a security system." He paused. "You have anywhere you can stay?"

She could go to her parents' home. But she wasn't prepared to tell her father what happened tonight. He would tell her it was because of the type of people she had as clients and once more demand she join his corporate law firm. She simply wasn't up to it. Not this morning. And Sarah's apartment was too small for a guest.

"A hotel," she decided.

"I'll take you to one. Do you need to get any clothes?"

She nodded. Then a thought struck her. "I want to call the night watchman at my office building. I want to make sure no one has tampered with my office computers."

She dialed the emergency number at the office. All her backup files had been in her home computer. There were records and memos in there that she wouldn't want in the wrong hands. Addresses. *Dear God that was the real disaster.*

Archie was the security guard who was usually on duty overnight. She knew him well, since she often worked late. He answered immediately.

"This is Meredith Rawson," she said. "My home has just been ransacked. Will you check on my office?"

"No one here but the cleaning people, Ms. Rawson."

"Just go look for me," she said.

In a few moments—they seemed like hours—he was back. "Nothing disturbed there. Least not so I can see."

"Keep a special eye on it for me . . . please, Archie."

"You bet, Ms. Rawson. You can depend on me."

"I know I can, Archie. Thanks." She hung up the phone and turned to the detective. "I'll have to warn some people. I had files on my hard drive that included addresses. Clients hiding from their spouses."

Morris waited patiently as she called four women, waking them up and warning them that their addresses might be compromised. She suggested they either keep someone with them or move to a different location.

There were no protestations. They had all been through the kind of fear she felt tonight.

When she finished, Morris looked at her steadily. "Could it be one of their husbands?"

"I don't know."

"We'll need your client list."

She hesitated. "I can't give you that without their permission."

He looked exasperated. "At least a list of anyone who has threatened you. That wouldn't be privileged."

She nodded. "I'll get some clothes."

She entered her bedroom. It looked as if a tornado had hit it. The painting she loved had been slashed. The mattress was cut open and linens littered the floor. Drawers were pulled out, her clothes scattered.

She swallowed hard. Despite the weariness that almost overwhelmed her, she yearned to start the cleanup process, to cleanse the room—her room—of a foreign, malevolent presence.

Suitcases. She needed a small suitcase. Three of various sizes were in the back of the closet. When she opened the closet door, a new shock ran through her.

Her clothes had been torn from the hangers. Some had been slashed. One suitcase had been ripped. She grabbed the smallest one. It was intact. Apparently her intruder had tired of his destruction.

Frissons of new fear ran through her. Someone really hated her to tear up her clothes like that. She tried to dismiss the thought as she found a pair of good black slacks that had survived the carnage, along with a cotton shirt and a silk blouse. They were wrinkled but whole.

The next stop was her bathroom for a few toiletries. It was the least ransacked, probably because there was little of value there. She located necessities—toothpaste, toothbrush, deodorant—and threw them into the bag. She always carried makeup in her purse.

Shutting the bag, she returned to the living room, where she had left her purse. She met the gaze of the detective.

"The lock . . ."

"Didn't keep anyone out. I'll return after I get you to a hotel. I have some work to do here anyway. I've ordered a crime scene technician." He hesitated, then offered, "I know a locksmith who is on call twenty-four hours a day."

"Please call him."

He nodded. She looked at him for the first time. He had that rumpled, overworked cop look. He was older, probably nearing retirement age, yet he had not hesitated to go inside her apartment to look for an intruder.

"Thank you," she said. "You've been more than kind."

He gave her a long, searching look. "I don't think I have to tell you to be careful."

"No," she said.

"Most women would be in hysterics after being nearly killed and seeing a mess like this."

"I've never been good at that."

"I know. You had a reputation in the DA's office."

She wasn't surprised. Though she'd left the office two years ago, she was very aware that the police often discussed members of the district attorney's office. Some they liked. Some they dreaded. She'd been told she had been put in the "dreaded" category. She'd always been hard on the police officers. She hadn't liked losing cases because they didn't dot the i's and cross the t's. Or worse.

"I'm surprised you didn't let me come home alone," she said wryly.

"I was on your side," he said with a slight smile. "You didn't plead out cases as others did."

"That was usually the DA's decision."

"And that depended on how well the case was prepared. Some of us appreciated it."

It was a brightener on what had been the worst night of her life. "Thank you."

"I'll bring the key to the new locks over to the hotel and leave it at the desk," he added.

"I'm forever grateful."

He just nodded and opened the door for her to leave.

She walked outside and turned to look back. All the lights were on, though they looked diffused by the rain. She swallowed hard at the thought of the destruction inside.

Tomorrow. Like Scarlett, she would think about that tomorrow.

But tonight she knew she would think about who hated her enough to try to run her down and then destroy everything dear to her.

And when would he, or she, strike again?

six

Despite its small size and seedy condition, Holly took pleasure in the small house. It was *hers*. Sort of. More, certainly, than any other place she'd lived.

She loved the desert sunrises and sunsets. She loved taking Harry for walks, carrying with her a book of flowers and plants she'd found at the library. She didn't have to meet anyone's expectations but her own.

Still, fear was never far away. She flinched at the sight of a large car and dreaded what was becoming her daily pilgrimage to the library to check Louisiana newspapers. Her heart always pounded faster as she searched for her name in headlines.

Nothing. She could find nothing about a murder in her house. Nothing about a search for a murder suspect. Nothing about the missing wife of a prominent politician and daughter of a state supreme court judge.

The silence convinced her that her husband had indeed planned her murder and was now covering the murderer's death.

She knew he wasn't protecting her. Having a wife as a murderer would hurt his career. So might embarrassing questions.

How had she ever thought him charming?

She shivered in the hot air as she sat on her stoop and watched her son play with Caesar. The two were inseparable.

She'd bought him some jeans, shorts and T-shirts, clothes he'd never been allowed to wear before. He'd been particularly delighted with the jeans. He was a cowboy now.

Holly took a flyer from her pocket and smoothed it out. It advertised riding lessons for children. She wished she could afford them, but money was too tight at the moment. Perhaps later, when she sold some of her sculptures. She'd already been able to place two on consignment in a small Main Street gallery.

To make enough to support them, though, she had to increase her output.

To her relief, Harry was so intrigued by the dog and his new surroundings that he had not asked for his father. But then Harry had been more a possession to Randolph than a person to be loved unconditionally. Approval had been based on exemplary behavior.

But the questions would come. Like any little boy, he loved his father. He wanted his father's praise and approval, though she knew he sensed that something was lacking. She wished she could give him an easy world with a dad who adored him. She wished he could have more than she would be able to give him. She was a fugitive, and their lives would be peppered with lies and deceptions.

If they managed to evade Randolph.

For the briefest of moments, she wondered whether her son would be better off with someone else. But that thought quickly fled her mind. There was no one. Her mother had died five years ago, still believing Holly had a fairy-tale marriage. Her mother had never seen what she didn't want to see. Her father was as controlling as Randolph. She did not want her inquisitive, generous and kind little boy growing up to be like his father, to have those kind of values. Nor did she want him to grow up as she had grown up: a hothouse plant protected from everything real in life.

If she hadn't grown up that way, she might have recognized Randolph as the monster he was.

She sighed, then called Harry, delighted when he immediately ran into her arms and gave her a hug. Caesar jumped around them, wanting Harry's attention back.

"Go inside," she said. "You can draw while I work."

"Cookie?" he said with a four-year-old's penchant for blackmail.

"Yes, indeed. Maybe even two," she said, pleased that he wanted them. She had baked her first batch of cookies two days ago. They had been terrible. This batch, though, was edible. More than edible.

He beamed. "Caesar wants one, too."

"Caesar can have a dog cookie."

"Okay." Harry followed her into the small kitchen and waited patiently as she poured him a glass of milk and handed him two cookies. Caesar frantically wagged his tail until she gave him a dog biscuit.

She turned on the television. The combination TV/VCR was new, one of her few purchases. She'd taken enough from her son. She couldn't take his favorite cartoons, too. Besides, it gave her a link to the outside world, even though the local channels didn't offer much in the way of world news.

She watched as Harry settled on the lumpy sofa. Caesar followed him, lifting first one paw, then another before crawling up as if he were putting something over on her. She had no objections. She gloried in the sight of the two of them cuddled together, a happy smile on her son's face.

Once Harry's attention was glued to a cartoon, she started to work on some pieces of copper sheeting she'd purchased at a home improvement store in Tucson. A ladybug this time, she thought, designing it in her head before she started cutting the metal. Then a dancing pig. She'd sold two turtles this past week, an event to celebrate.

They hadn't brought in that much. Only sixty dollars each, and out of that she paid for materials, along with a commission. But it was a start toward independence. Toward a new life.

She wasn't sure how long she could stay here. Not long,

she feared, even though she was becoming attached to the odd little town where houses perched on a mountainside.

She'd found a poem at the library that kept running through her head.

> *We realize fully we've a very queer town,*
> *Where it's not up, it's certainly down,*
> *Our houses all perch on the sides of the hill*
> *There's no building laws, we place them at will.*

She smiled whenever she thought of it. The town was an outlaw, a little like herself. Remnants of its old, somewhat seedy history remained in Brewery Gulch, once the home of free-for-all bars and houses of prostitution. Bars remained but they were of the more sedate kind, attracting tourists rather than minors.

Bisbee was both charming and quietly seductive. The sunsets and sunrises were glorious, and the nights so clear she could see a million stars.

She had gone out each night and sat on the porch, gazing upward. She was always reluctant to go to bed. Nightmares haunted her. She often woke up wringing wet, cringing. Even worse, she woke one night to hear her son calling for her. Apparently her cries had awakened and frightened him.

The sound of creaking stairs, the image of the intruder crumpled on the floor were with her always. So was the fear that her husband would find them and take Harry away from her. He was the dearest person in her life. He *was* her life. . . .

The ladybug, destined for someone's garden, took shape under her fingers.

The doorbell rang and she froze as the now familiar terror seized her. She had to force herself to go to the window. She looked outside and saw Marty, the woman who owned both her house and Special Things, the craft shop that displayed her work.

She unlocked the door as Caesar jumped off the sofa and barked.

"Too late, pal," she told him with disgust. "Hi," she greeted Marty warily.

"Hi yourself. I wanted to call you but you said you didn't have a phone yet."

"You mean one of those newfangled machines that interrupt your every waking hour?"

"Ah, that's the one," Marty said with a grin. "I thought you would like to know I sold the last of your sculptures."

Relief—and pride—rushed through her. She waited for Marty to continue.

"I want as many as I can get. They've sold better than any item I've carried." Marty paused. "And I want to invite you to supper. A barbecue with a few of my friends. It's time you started to meet other people."

Panic seized her throat, clogging it with questions. What would she tell them? About Harry's father? About her past life?

"I'm sorry," she said, her voice hoarse with anxiety. "I haven't felt well all day, and Harry—"

"There will be other children there," Marty interrupted. "It would be good for him."

"We have a new dog. I don't think Harry . . ."

"Dogs are welcome, too. And no wonder you don't feel well. You look like you haven't eaten in weeks."

Did she look that bad? Did the sleepless nights show in her face?

"Please, Mommy, can we? Can we go?" Harry was by her side. Pleading.

"You can walk there," Marty said, tempting her. "I promise you can leave anytime. No questions asked."

But what if Harry slipped up and mentioned his real name? What if he talked about his father to other children when she'd told everyone she was a widow?

"Please?" Harry said again.

But wasn't this what she wanted for him? Normal relationships with normal people? Friends?

Should she take the chance? Perhaps she could make a game of it. Challenge him to remember that he was Harry from Chicago. If he said anything wrong, they would flee again. But, darn it, he needed friends.

"We would like that," she said.

A broad smile transformed Marty's weathered face. She was one of many aging flower children who had found their way to Bisbee years earlier. Holly had already discovered the older woman had a tendency to mother everyone she met.

"Around six," Marty said.

Feeling trapped, Holly just nodded. She needed Marty's goodwill.

"Just bring yourselves," Marty said. "Very casual." She handed Holly a little map. "No parking up there, I'm afraid."

"We'll walk."

"Good. And remember, I'll take as many of those garden creatures as you can give me. Don't take them anywhere else."

Marty's enthusiasm was contagious. Someone actually liked her art. "You might regret that."

"I don't think so." Marty looked down at Caesar. "Ah, you have Caesar," she said with a lilt in her voice. "I'm glad he found a good home."

"You must know Julie at the animal shelter then?"

"Live here long enough and you know nearly everyone and everyone's business," Marty said. "She'll be at supper, too."

Know nearly everyone's business. A shudder ran through Holly. Perhaps a large city would have been more anonymous. She had second thoughts, and third, about accepting the invitation, but there was no way to retreat now.

Marty gave a little wave and walked down to what must have been the most ancient Volkswagen Bug on the roads. The paint was rusted, but the car started immediately.

Work. She had to get back to work. She had a son to support. She wouldn't think about tonight, except to warn him about "the little game." Still, she felt the growing web of lies strangling her.

NEW ORLEANS

Gage heard about the attack on Meredith Rawson from another detective.

Any violence against a former assistant district attorney was news. It could be payback from a bad guy she'd put away. That was something a police department could not tolerate.

Those attacks always received special attention.

But she was also in a legal specialty that attracted threats. There was nothing more dangerous than a bully husband who'd lost his favorite victim. But it wasn't murder, and he wasn't involved.

Or was he?

He did not believe in coincidence.

All of a sudden, Ms. Rawson's name—or her family's name—was appearing a little too often. His instincts were prodding him, and he trusted those instincts. Even a mental warning that none of the events seemed connected didn't subdue them.

Because he didn't want them subdued?

He soaked up all the rumors, all the talk flying around the offices.

She'd not been hurt. She'd used her head. Her home had been practically destroyed. She was staying in a hotel. She refused protection.

It's not your case.

He knew he would be on thin ice if he approached her. The case was in someone else's hands, and poaching was not appreciated. But her father's name *had* surfaced in one of his cases.

He took the files from the Prescott case and looked at them again, though he knew them by heart. The investigators obviously had not wanted to annoy New Orleans's powers-that-be. Charles Rawson had been asked very few questions. Yes, he was a friend of the victim. Yes, he had dined with Prescott the night of the murder, then Rawson had gone home after an argument. There was no folllow-up, no note as to whether the wife had been interviewed to verify the statement or even what the argument had been about.

He was going to start with Rawson's wife. A surprise visit might shake her.

He looked up the phone number and called, only to learn that Mrs. Rawson was in critical condition at the hospital. So that was why Meredith had been there. When he had heard she'd been attacked in a hospital parking lot, he'd assumed she'd been visiting a client, or a friend.

Gage sat there for several moments, weighing his next move. It obviously was not Mrs. Rawson.

Meredith Rawson? Or her father?

He called Rawson at his law firm, only to discover that he was in court. He hesitated, then tried Meredith Rawson's law office. He wanted to know more about the burglary as well, and whether Rick Fuller could be involved. More than once, a husband had gone after the wife's attorney.

To his surprise, she answered the phone.

"Ms. Rawson, Detective Gaynor."

"What can I do for you, Detective?"

"I would like to talk to you."

"About Rick Fuller?"

"No. Another matter."

"This is not a good day."

"I heard about the attack and burglary. I'm sorry."

A short pause. "Is that what you want to discuss?"

"No. I'm looking into an old case. Oliver Prescott."

"I remember that," she replied cautiously. "Is there something new?"

He chose to ignore that question. "You knew him. I hoped you could tell us something about him."

"I was in school at the time. I knew him, of course, but not that well. He was much older. I don't know how I could help you."

"Just a few questions, a few moments of your time. Perhaps you know more than you think."

"My mother is very ill. My house has just been ransacked

and my computer stolen. I simply don't have the time. If I knew anything—"

"What about lunch? A quick sandwich."

She paused, then, with an audible sigh, said, "If you'll bring it to my office. We're backing up all our files. I have to be here."

"Done. What will it be?"

"Comfort food. A muffaletta."

"You have it. Noon okay?"

A pause. He feared she was reconsidering.

"I have two people working with me."

"I'll bring enough for all."

"I still don't know how I can help—"

"I'll be there at noon," he said, and hung up before she could change her mind.

As soon as Gaynor hung up, Meredith wished she hadn't agreed. In fact, she didn't know exactly why she had.

She'd had three hours' sleep at most. And what sleep she'd had had been restless. Her life seemed to be in free fall.

She'd risen at seven as she always did and called the hotel's front desk to see if anything had arrived for her. It had. The new key to her house was in an envelope. Then she'd hurried to her office to see for herself that her office was untouched.

Sometime today, she had to return home and start cleaning up the mess. She had to see her mother. She'd promised the police she would make a list of people who might want to do her harm. She wanted to get started on finding her sister.

There was no end to this day. And now this. She definitely should have said no. She should never have picked up the phone, but she often did when they were all busy. Most callers wanted her.

She didn't know if she was alert enough to go head-to-head with Gaynor. Why in God's name would he want to talk to her about a fifteen-year-old murder? At least, she thought it had been that long.

She went to her computer. Sarah was using her computer to back up files. This time the compact disks would go into a safe deposit box.

She looked up Oliver Prescott on the Internet and found dozens of stories about the murder. The number had dwindled as time had passed without any apparent progress in the investigation.

Now she remembered more. She'd been sixteen at the time and attending accelerated classes at a respected Catholic school. She'd been on a class trip to Washington, D.C., that weekend. The murder had been the main topic of conversation for weeks.

Meredith read all the accounts she could find.

Prescott and her father had dined together at the Court of Two Sisters, where they apparently discussed some business matter. Witnesses saw the two separate outside the restaurant, each taking his own car.

Prescott's body was found the next morning in his home. He had been shot. There was no indication of a break-in, but his wallet was missing. So was a very expensive painting.

Clues had been scarce.

She realized why Gaynor wanted to talk to her. Her father had been the last known person to be with the victim. The police always started at that point.

But why did the detective want to see her? Why not her father?

She returned to backing up her files, then went into Sarah's office. "How's it going?"

"Another hour."

Meredith looked at her watch. "Someone's bringing us lunch."

Sarah raised an eyebrow, even as she replaced one CD with another and carefully marked the one she had just ejected. When Meredith didn't immediately answer, Sarah asked, "Who? And more important, what?"

"Muffalettas."

"I can deal with that," Sarah said. "It's far better than my tuna salad. Should I ask who again?"

"A detective."

Sarah waited again, then pressed, "Who?"

"Detective Gaynor."

Sarah started to grin. "The Lone Ranger strikes again. You must have made an impact at court."

"Lone Ranger?"

"Some of us at the department started calling him that after the Teller case."

"Why the Lone Ranger?"

"He took on the blue wall of silence by himself. Believe me, he suffered for it."

"Didn't appear to be suffering to me."

"He did," Sarah said. "I have a friend who was a secretary in his division. He was completely shunned. Except by the secretaries. The unmarried ones. They all thought he was hot."

"Do you?"

"Not my type. I lean toward the safe accountant type."

"Well, he's not my type, either."

"Who is?" Sarah asked after she clicked the mouse again, saving more files.

Meredith shrugged. "I just wish he'd picked another day. I'm not thinking well today."

"You have reason. Why don't you go home? I'll back up the info on all the computers here and get the compact disks to the safe deposit box."

She wanted to. God, how she wanted to.

No, she wouldn't. She *said* she would be here. She *would* be here. She hated the good little girl who always did the right thing, but neither could she shake it off because it *was* the right thing. She would backtrack ten miles if she discovered she received more change than she should. She sighed and mentally devised a game plan. She would cut the discussion short, take the CDs to a safe deposit box, and head home to start the cleaning process. She would stop by the hospital later. The list for the police would have to wait.

She wouldn't take any guff from Gaynor this time. He would answer her questions before she answered his. She paced the floor, waiting for him, too restless to be of any value to Sarah or Becky. Her mind could not sort the events, much less prioritize what needed to be done.

Nor could it conquer the lingering fear, the sense of being violated. She'd been trying to forget it, to bury it, to cloak it all day. But the bandage on her arm continually reminded her of last night's terror.

She would *not* let it take over her life.

The door to the office opened, and Gaynor entered, carefully balancing two large sacks. The impact of his presence was more than she had expected. He'd made her feel that way before, but then she'd been armored by the rumors circulating about him.

She detested crooked cops, and some officers had pointed fingers at Gaynor during the Teller investigation. That had been her first introduction to him, and she'd never learned the truth of it.

He was still with the department, though. And now he dominated her small reception area with his presence. Perhaps it was his sheer size. He had to be six-foot-three or more, and had a wide-shouldered, rangy body. But it was the confidence she'd noted before, the self-assurance that was in every movement, that seized her attention.

He had immediately filled the room, crowding it with male energy. His eyes assessed her openly, frankly, and a dizzying current raced through her. Dammit, she didn't know why—or how—he always affected her in such a sensuous way. It was . . . disconcerting. More than that. Maddening.

"Five muffalettas as ordered," he said after a brief pause. She wondered whether he felt that same odd electric awareness.

"Five?"

"Two for me."

The sandwiches were huge. She could usually eat only half of one, if that much.

"I burn a lot of fuel," he said, obviously reading her mind. His gaze went to the bandage on her arm. "From last night?"

"Yes."

"I'm sorry."

"Why? You didn't have anything to do with it."

He shrugged. "It's my city."

"Mine, too."

"You're not protecting it any longer." It was a little bit of an accusation.

She was mesmerized by those green eyes. They weren't icy now. Something flared in them, and she suddenly knew he felt the same infuriating attraction. And didn't like it any better than she.

She forced herself to take one of the bags, place it on the table in front of the sofa and start taking out sandwiches. He took six tall cups from the second bag. "I have three of ice tea and three of cola."

Meredith called Becky and Sarah to get some food, then took an iced tea and muffaletta. "My office?" she suggested to him.

"Sure."

He took two of the sandwiches and a cola and followed her down the short hall into her office, his gaze sliding past the law books, the license and the degrees hanging on the walls and lingering on her untidy desk.

"Sit down," she said, clearing off a space for the food. "Sorry about the desk." She'd been going through recent cases, looking for names, as requested by the police.

"I have a theory about that," he said with a grin.

Several seconds went by. She wondered whether he was baiting her. "What?" she said.

"If a cluttered desk suggests a cluttered mind, then what does an empty desk suggest?"

She smiled at that. She'd needed a distraction, and he'd apparently known that. She suspected he was a very good interrogator. Despite their earlier sparks, he had immediately put her at ease.

At least he would have, had the attraction not radiated between them. His very presence shrunk the room and raised the temperature considerably. At least for her.

She forced her attention back to the food. She was hungrier than she'd thought, and the muffaletta looked wonderful. She loved the things, but seldom indulged. The huge freshly baked loaves, still hot from the oven, held layers of ham garnished with a spicy olive dressing.

She took a bite and sighed with pleasure, then put it down. "Can we get on with it? I want to get home, then to the hospital."

"You're not going home alone?"

"The detective last night had the locks replaced."

He shrugged. "There's not a lock that can't be breached by someone who really wants to get in. I could probably break into any house in this city. And I'm not nearly as good as some of the burglars who operate here."

"That's encouraging," she said dryly.

"The detective should have explained the facts of city life.

"Perhaps he thought I should have realized them."

"I'll have to have a talk with Morris."

She raised her eyes and met his. "How did you know it was Detective Morris?"

"I checked," he said equably.

"Did he meet your approval?" she said, unable to prevent a twitch of a smile.

"He's okay."

From the sound of his voice, that was probably his highest praise.

"I'm glad you approve."

It was a snippy reply, but she reacted to the arrogant assumption that she couldn't take care of herself. She'd always prided herself on handling her own problems. Mixed with that was a traitorous jolt of pleasure that he had taken the trouble.

Faint amusement crossed his face. "Except I would have explained about the locks," he added.

"I didn't give him a chance. I was somewhat rattled."

"I would have been more than rattled," he replied.

That unexpected admission really *did* rattle her. "I'm sorry. I'm really tired and—" It was intended as a brush-off.

He didn't take the subtle invitation to leave.

"Why don't you stay with a family member? Or a friend?"

Because she didn't have anyone? She wasn't going to admit that to him. "That's not your concern."

He raised an eyebrow and she wondered why she was so short with him. Possibly because his presence was so strong, even overwhelming.

"I'm sorry," she said. "I'm tired. In any event, I thought you wanted to talk about the Prescott case."

He took a big bite of sandwich, chewed slowly, then sat back in his chair. "Do you remember him?"

"Barely. He was a friend of my father."

"Do you recall where you were when he was killed?"

"I was on a class trip to Washington, but I don't understand why—"

"I'm just talking to everyone who saw him during the days before his murder," he said. "Your father couldn't see me today. I thought you might remember something."

"I was only sixteen."

"Sometimes you don't realize that you do know something."

She didn't reply, choosing to take another bite of sandwich instead.

"Was Prescott at your home frequently?"

"I truly don't know. I was usually studying and avoided most of the social gatherings at my house. I remember seeing him. I don't remember anything more than that."

"Your impressions of him?"

"I didn't like him," she said flatly, "but then, to be honest, I didn't care for many of my father's friends."

A startled look crossed his face, then a slow, appreciative grin that sparked a frisson of pleasure in her before he continued, "Did you hear your father say anything about his murder?"

"No. He didn't talk to me about things like that."

"What *did* he talk to you about?"

"I think that's between him and me," she said tartly, wishing he would smile again. It transformed his stark face. She remembered when she had questioned Gaynor years ago and realized how he'd probably felt—like a butterfly on a pin—even though there was nothing to hide.

She knew he was fishing. She also knew that's what detectives did on cold cases. And it was logical to start with her father, who had been a close friend of Prescott's and seen him last. Still, she couldn't imagine her father having any knowledge of a murder. He was too rigid about proper behavior, and murder certainly wasn't proper behavior. He was also too concerned with his public image.

Yet in the back of her mind there was a seed of doubt. It was around that time that he had dropped his attempts to win a federal judgeship, a position she'd known he wanted. Badly.

She dismissed the disloyal thought, took another bite, then rose. "I have to go, Detective."

"Are you going home now?"

"Yes."

"I'll go with you." His gaze dueled with hers, warming her with the attention, the perusal that seemed to peel her layers back one at a time. Wanting to study him in the same way—too much—she dragged her gaze away. She distrusted the sparks that streaked between them. He was everything she disliked, a macho man who felt he should always be in charge.

"No." She wanted to be alone when she surveyed the ruin again. She wanted to replace the underwear and bring some semblance of order to her home before anyone saw it. It was her life that lay in shambles there.

Or perhaps she didn't want Detective Gaynor in particular to see her vulnerability. Of all people, he was the last one she wanted to see the house as it was.

He rose with a lazy grace that belied his size. "Thanks for the time. If you think of anything else—"

"I'll call you," she said quickly. "Why is the Prescott case being opened now?" she asked after a pause.

"I'm the low man on the totem pole now," he said. "I get what they assign, and right now it's a few of the cold cases. I'm sure you know that many of them are being reopened because of technology advances."

"But isn't there a separate cold case unit?"

"There is. Apparently someone wants to keep me out of trouble," he said with an affable grin.

She tried to tamp down the little jerk in her chest, stronger than it had been the last time he'd smiled. "But why Prescott?"

"Why not?" he replied, and ambled out of the office.

She stared at the empty doorway, suddenly wishing she'd not turned down his offer. Somehow the "Why not?" didn't answer her question. It only piqued her curiosity.

She should have pushed him more. And maybe . . . she should have someone with her when she returned home.

But her refusal was not entirely because she didn't want him to see the shambles at home. She didn't want to admit her fear. Not to him. Not to herself.

She wouldn't give anyone that victory.

She could protect herself. She'd practiced at the police shooting range and had a gun permit, though she hadn't carried a weapon since she'd left the district attorney's office.

She planned to remedy that today and felt it was something she needed to do on her own. Between the attacks on her and her home and the effect Detective Gaynor had on her, she'd lost enough control over the last few days.

seven

Charles Rawson closed the door to his luxurious office and picked up his phone. He was so angry that his fingers shook as he pushed one number and the memory on his phone did the rest.

"Are you responsible for what happened to my daughter?" he said before any pleasantries were exchanged.

"She wasn't hurt."

"She might well have been. A friend from the police department called me. Dammit, you didn't have to destroy her home."

"There was no question of 'might.' The orders were quite clear. It *will* keep her busy for a while, won't it?"

Charles sat back in his chair and drew a long breath, trying to cool his anger. He had not expected this violent reaction to his news that his daughter had found out about her half sister and intended to try to find her.

"Leave her alone," he said.

"I will, if you do your part. Control her, Charles."

But Charles wasn't sure he could do that. He had guided her for twenty-five years and then she had started to turn against him. She said it wasn't against him, but for her. He hadn't accepted it then. He still didn't accept it.

The silence must have spoken loudly.

"I mean it, Charles. I cannot guarantee her safety if she continues to meddle in this."

Charles exploded. "It's your damn fault. If you hadn't . . ."

"Hadn't what, Charles?" came the silky smooth voice.

"I wish to hell I had never agreed to your bargain."

"But you did, didn't you? And now, if you want your daughter to remain well and happy, you know what you must do. We gave you time last night. Use it."

The receiver went dead.

He slowly replaced it in the cradle.

The sins of his past wouldn't go away.

Somehow he had to stop Meredith.

If he didn't, he knew someone else would.

BISBEE

If Holly hadn't been worried about making mistakes and even more so that Harry would, she would have enjoyed the evening.

She'd never attended a party in blue jeans and a casual shirt before. Yes, there had been barbecues, but they had usually been big, elaborate affairs or small, intimate fund-raising events. Both called for expensive, elegant clothing.

Neither her father nor her husband had ever had neighbors over for hot dogs and hamburgers.

She felt herself relaxing for the first time since she'd left her home. The first time in years. In addition to Harry and herself, she counted ten adults, four children and four dogs. But people came and went, wandering at will into the house set high on the hill. Tubs of iced beer sat on the porch.

She tried to remember names, and was fairly good at it. It was one of the requirements of a politician's wife and she had been a good student.

One of the women was a painter, another a sculptor. Both were accompanied by husbands, one of whom wore a long gray braid. There was an older man who was a guide for city sightseeing trips, and a bearded man who had once worked as a miner and now conducted tours in the now closed mines. Russ, a man who looked to be in his late forties, was a rancher. Julie, the woman from the animal shelter, was accompanied by a teacher at the high school. And there was, of course, her hostess, Marty.

It didn't take long to discover that Marty was a self-appointed matchmaker. Holly had been there only minutes before Marty had asked her to join Russ in cooking the hamburgers on one of two grills.

"What brings you to Bisbee?" Russ asked as she carefully followed his directions on moving the hamburgers from the center of the grill to the side.

"An article in a magazine. It sounded like a good place to raise a child."

He glanced at where Harry was happily entertaining three dogs. An amused look came over his face. "He likes animals."

"He loves animals," she corrected. "He never had a chance—" She caught herself saying too much. She had to watch that.

He looked at her, waiting for her to finish.

"We lived in an apartment in a large city. Having a pet wasn't practical."

"What city?"

"Chicago," she said, wishing that lying came easier to her. She was sure everyone present saw a big L on her shirt.

"Marty said you were a widow. I'm sorry."

He didn't look sorry at all. He looked interested, and she could not return that interest. She was still married. Not only that, but her trust in men had reached an all-time low. Most important, she had a past she couldn't share. Perhaps he was just being polite. She'd thought her now mousy brown hair and store-bought glasses would quell any interest.

"Thank you," she said. "It wasn't very long ago." She hoped he would get the message.

"How long ago?"

How long ago? Marty had asked the same thing. Not nosy, just interested. Sympathetic. Holly had brushed it off then, but she couldn't do that any longer. She'd decided on three months. That would be recent enough to still be grieving and have an excuse to avoid relationships, yet long enough to be a reasonable time to resettle. "Three months," she said.

It worked. He started paying more attention to the hamburgers. He would have been an insensitive clod not to get the message and, thank God, he wasn't that.

"This is a friendly community," he finally said as he put fragrant hamburgers on a plate. "If you need anything, call one of us. Marty calls me all the time if she needs something fixed, and Jim's our computer guru."

She released a long, grateful breath. Friendship. He was just offering neighborly friendship, as the rest of them were.

Then reality struck again. Would they do that if they knew she was a murderess?

She and her son were here on borrowed time. Was it possible for either of them to have friends . . . to have any sort of normal life? Was tonight a mistake?

Looking at her son and hearing his laughter as he played chase with the dogs and another small boy, her heart warmed. He needed this. He didn't need expensive day schools and formal clothes and a demanding father. He needed play and fun and friends and warmth.

He took that moment to give her a wide grin of sheer delight.

Her heart broke. For him. For her.

"Elizabeth?"

She heard the name but for a moment it didn't register. She turned back to Russ and saw his puzzled look. "I'm sorry. Everyone calls me Liz."

"Liz then," he said easily.

The hamburgers were ready. Marty insisted she and Harry go to the head of the line. "The cooks are always first. That's the only way we can get them."

Holly fixed a plate for both Harry and herself, then searched for a place to sit. The one table on the front porch was already filled with people talking to one another. She found a step, happy to be alone with Harry for a few minutes. Others also found steps or a swing on the porch. Marty came over. "There's room at the table."

Holly smiled and shook her head. "We're settled now. Thank you."

Marty gave her an understanding look, then retreated.

Holly was grateful. No more questions this way. She was happy to be with her son, to know that he was safe.

The hamburger was delicious, far more delicious than a steak at one of the famous New Orleans restaurants she'd frequented with Randolph. Perhaps the flavor came from the mesquite wood or the smoke rising up into a clear night, or the unconstrained laughter or the dogs chasing one another around. She did not have to worry about saying something that her husband would dislike and let her know about later.

The hamburger suddenly lost its taste. She placed the remainder on the plate and looked at the others. Laughing. Talking easily. She was the outsider, would always have to be the outsider. How she longed to be one of them.

A car parked at the road in front of the steps—a sheriff's car. Her heart stopped as a uniformed officer stepped out.

She wanted to run, or hide.

The officer was alone. Tall with a solid teddy bear build. Black hair. Dark brown eyes. Certainly part, if not all, Hispanic and about the same age as Russ the rancher.

Marty went down to meet him, and they both climbed the steps to where she sat. Terror spiked in her chest. She tried not to let it show.

But there was no sternness in his eyes. Instead he knelt in front of Harry. "Hi, young man," he said.

Harry looked at her, then back. " 'Ello," he said noncommittally.

Marty broke in. "Liz, this is Sheriff Doug Menelo. Doug, Liz Baker."

"Marty showed me your sculpture of a frog," he said. "My niece fell in love with it."

Niece. Not daughter. Or wife. Evidently Marty had dragged out every single man in Bisbee to meet her.

"Thank you," she said.

"Thank *you*. It solved my birthday present problem." His smile crinkled his face, especially around the eyes. If it hadn't been for the uniform, she would have been charmed.

She stood. "Which reminds me, I should get home. Marty has ordered more."

"Indeed I have, but all work and no play—"

"Work satisfies me," Holly broke in. "And it's getting to be Harry's bedtime."

"Did you drive?" Sheriff Menelo said.

"I walked."

"That's a fair distance," he said. "Can I drive you both home?"

How did he know where she lived? Or did everyone know that a widow and her son had moved into town?

She wanted to take Harry and flee. Yet then she might not be able to sell her sculptures, and money was imperative. Her little creatures were one of the few things she could do to raise money without needing a Social Security card. She had been waiting daily for the birth certificate to arrive in the mail. Until she had that, she couldn't apply for a Social Security card.

And Caesar? It wouldn't be easy to find another place that would take pets. She could never take the dog away from her son. Not after seeing the pure joy on his face whenever they were together.

But now she had caught the attention of someone in the sheriff's department. What if photos of her or Harry were circulated to various law enforcement agencies?

"Thank you," she said again, "but we need the exercise. And it feels safe here."

"It is for the most part," he said. "I'll leave you then to finish. If you change your mind . . ." He gave her another warm smile, then took a plate and filled it with food before sitting in a chair just vacated by someone else.

Ride in a police car? The very thought made her tremble. She hoped he didn't notice her shaking hands. She looked down at Harry's plate. The hamburger was gone. So were the pepper-flavored beans and spicy cole slaw.

Harry's attention was focused on several cakes sitting on the serving table.

She was not going to get away until he had a piece.

She only wished her gaze didn't continue to go toward Sheriff Menclo as someone picked up a guitar, sat on a rock and started strumming.

Harry went to get a piece of cake and returned. Night had settled around them and the sky filled with a million stars, far more than she'd ever seen in New Orleans. The plaintive Mexican music made her ache with loneliness. There was no one she could trust. There might never be again.

New Orleans

Gage didn't give a damn what Meredith Rawson wanted. He sat in his car in the parking lot until he saw her leave. Then he followed.

He was not going to let her go into her house alone, not after what had happened earlier.

He wondered whether he had been partly responsible. Could it have been Rick Fuller? Had his intervention turned Fuller's anger in another direction? If it had, Gage would see the man buried under the jail, regardless of any support he had in the department. Too often it had turned a deaf ear to spousal abuse.

After seeing that Meredith Rawson was safe, he planned an interview with Fuller.

He kept her car in sight as she drove home, and parked down the street when she turned into a driveway sheltered by giant oaks. He quickly got out of his car and reached her side as she opened the front door.

She gave him a hostile look. "You weren't invited."

"I invited myself."

"That's arrogant."

"I've been told that before."

"I bet you have."

"Do I detect petulance?"

"It's daylight, Detective. Detective Morris had an alarm system installed this morning." She looked down at the paper in her hand and darted inside, punching numbers in a new alarm detection box.

He looked at it. "Good choice."

She turned and glared at him. "Are you satisfied now?"

"Nope." He went inside and looked around. It was as bad as he'd ever seen a home ransacked. "Wow," he said.

"An elegant observation," she said.

He was going to retort but saw her slump against a wall. She looked vulnerable and tired.

"Hey, did you get any sleep?"

"Would you have?"

"No. I think you're gutsy as hell for doing as well as you have."

She looked at him then, and he saw tears in her eyes, saw the way she was trying to hold them back.

"I'm just so . . . angry," she said.

He didn't intend to do it, but his hand cupped her shoulder, and then somehow she was in his arms.

He held her for a moment, his arms tightening around her as he felt her body shake. "It's okay," he said. "Just let it go."

"I don't want to," she said. Her tone had the sound of a small child protesting an adult's demand. Well, she was entitled.

Regardless of the circumstances, she felt damned good in his arms. She had the slightest scent of lilacs. Her short hair was silky and her body was rounded in just the right places. Yet despite the momentary weakness, he sensed her spine of steel. Sensed, hell. He felt it.

Just as he felt the heat rise between them. The air in the small space separating them crackled, threatening to ignite. His right hand moved to her left arm, his fingers running up and down in slow, caressing trails.

He'd always recognized the attraction between them, had thought it might be the attraction of opposites—he the product of a New Orleans slum and she the product of New Orleans society. There had been a wall between prosecutor and street cop as well. While they were not exactly enemies, the success of the prosecutor depended on the competence of the cop, and vice versa. Too many times, their respective translations of procedure were at odds.

None of that mattered at the moment. He had a need to comfort, but he had another need as well.

He bent down, his lips barely skimming hers, but that fleeting touch was enough to ignite the sparks. Warmth spread throughout his body, then centered in his groin.

He hadn't known what to expect. Maybe ice that would cool the damned heat burning him inside out.

But there was no ice. Instead she stood on tiptoes, offering her lips to him.

As he deepened the kiss, he tightened his arms around her. The storm gathering around them became explosive, filled with hot expectancy. Her lips yielded, yet it was not a surrender. More, he supposed, like astonishment and curiosity at the currents that raged between them.

Like his own feelings. How long had it been since he'd felt this alive?

Her mouth opened hesitantly under his, greeting him with an unexpected need that he felt straight through to his core. Trapped by the range of emotions, he looked in her eyes. The blue he always thought so cool was now more like the color in the heart of a flame.

The kiss took on a wild, fierce quality given and reciprocated, blocking out the world around them.

The blaze ignited deep within him and spread. He knew she felt it too as she pressed closer to him, clinging to him with a need that equaled his own.

He knew how unwise this was. Her life had been jeopardized, her mother was near death, and her private world had been tossed. Desperation born of fear was part of her response. But that was the logical, civilized part of him speaking.

He had no interest in being a gentleman at the moment.

His hand automatically reached for the top button of her shirt as his mouth moved from her lips and up the side of her face. He tasted salt and felt moisture. Reluctantly, he raised his head. One tear, then another, wandered forlornly down her face.

He may not be a gentleman, but neither was he a cad.

She was too vulnerable now. Much too vulnerable. Too much had happened too fast, and he knew the drugging effect of one disaster after another.

He also knew she hated those tears.

He gently kissed them away, hesitated for the slightest fraction of a second, then stepped back, ignoring—or trying to—the urgent condition of his body.

The cool and controlled Ms. Rawson looked thoroughly bewildered.

Well, he was damnably bewildered himself.

He reached out and touched her face, brushing away the last of the visible tears. He thought about making a wisecrack about never having made a woman burst into tears before, but he knew it would fall flat.

"I'm sorry," he said. "I shouldn't have done that."

"Why not?" she said, surprising him. "I think I needed that. It reminded me how . . . interesting it is to be alive."

He raised an eyebrow. "Interesting? I think that might be an insult."

She had the grace to look embarrassed. She had obviously sought a noncommittal word. "No insult intended," she finally said. "It was . . . very nice."

"Nice? We're going from insult to injury."

She had to smile. "What about mind-boggling?"

"Better," he conceded.

She studied him for a moment. "You're trying to distract me. You're a kind man, Detective."

He chuckled at that. "That's a rare observation, and I'm no such thing. I didn't want to stop."

"But you did."

"To my regret."

"Why don't I believe that?"

"Believe it, lady."

She stared at him for a long time with those blue eyes, and he wondered how he had ever thought them cold. "Thank you."

He decided right then he had to keep away from her. There was something about this woman. An honesty he liked. A passion he liked even more.

He dropped his hand from her face, which he'd continued to caress. To comfort, he realized. He couldn't remember when last he had done that with a woman. When last he'd wanted to.

An agonizing loneliness coursed through him.

He turned and purposely looked at the disaster that had once been the very nice interior of a very nice home. The type of home that was beyond his means.

He tried to think of that rather than of the ache deep inside him.

Meredith Rawson was as far beyond him and his world as a star in the sky. He would hurt both of them if he allowed himself any involvement.

"Let me help you clean up," he said, hoping that physical exertion would quiet the need raging in him and satisfy his sudden need to protect her.

"You've done enough," she said in a voice just a little ragged. "Thank you."

"You can't get rid of me that fast."

"I think it's a good idea."

"Do you now?"

Their voices were low, almost like those of lovers exchanging secrets. It was all he could do to keep from moving closer to her. From her eyes and body language, he suspected it was all she could do not to take a step forward.

He didn't want to leave her alone. Not here. Not after all she'd been through in the past few days. He'd seldom seen such wanton destruction and he wondered whether the rest of the house was like this. There was a twisted maliciousness in it.

But someone had obviously tried to kill her last night. There was nothing more malicious than that.

"Did Morris offer you protection?"

"I doubt whether New Orleans's finest has time to protect everyone whose home has been burglarized."

"This is more than that. You know that. Not to mention the fact that someone tried to run you down last night. You're a former prosecutor. That could be the reason."

Their gazes clung. He wondered whether his voice was as sensuous as hers sounded to him. They were courting in every word, every inflection.

Courting? Such an old-fashioned word. Yet it fit in some strange way.

Stop! End it now.

He didn't know if he could. He didn't know whether he ever could in her presence. They were like dynamite and fire together. He'd suspected as much before, which was why he'd been defensive with her.

She pulled away this time, stepping back and looking at the room again.

"Let's clean it up," he said.

"You don't have—"

"Do you have a weapon?" he interrupted.

"No, but I have a permit. It's on my agenda after finding a cleaning service."

"Know how to use one?"

"Cleaning service?" she asked with a weak grin.

He frowned at her feeble attempt at humor.

"I trained at the police academy after receiving some threats as a prosecutor," she added after a moment's silence.

"When is the last time you practiced?"

"Three years ago."

"Time for a refresher course."

"I realize that. I'll do it soon."

"Very soon," he emphasized, then changed direction. "You're not planning to stay here alone tonight, are you? Or am I taking something for granted?"

"That I live alone?"

"Yes." He wanted to bite back the word, eradicate the sudden jealousy that rose up.

"I do. Except I might be getting a very large dog."

"I have one of those. I would certainly suggest a gun as well."

She stared at him. "You have a dog?"

"That's so surprising?"

"I don't know. I've never given it much thought."

He grinned at that. "Touché." Then he looked at the room. "Call the cleaning service. Then we can see about a gun and start cleaning up."

"Do I have any choice in this?" A chill had crept into her voice.

"No," he said.

She stared at him for a moment. "I let someone rule my life for more years than I want to remember. I won't do it again. Thank you for bringing me home, but I really need some time alone."

The tears were gone. Pure determination and defiance were in her eyes, in her voice. All the passion he'd felt in her moments ago was now rallied in defense of her independence.

It was a dismissal. Royally made.

Well, he'd known better. He should have followed all his instincts and left her alone.

He nodded. "All right. Good day, Ms. Rawson."

She bit her lip, an oddly vulnerable expression.

He opened the door and left. He strode to his car and got inside. He didn't start the engine.

He was angry. Angry at himself for not knowing better. For letting his libido get out of control. For trying to comfort someone who didn't want comforting. He'd known she was poison for someone like him.

Hell, he was just plain angry.

But damned if he was going to leave. Someone had wanted to hurt her. Someone who did that kind of damage wasn't going to quit.

Dammit. He couldn't follow her forever. Why hadn't Cliff Morris provided some kind of protection?

Hell, he would call Morris and make sure she had it. It just wouldn't be him.

He tried to tell himself his only interest in the Rawsons—father and daughter—was the Prescott case, the case that could repair his career in a department that still didn't quite trust him.

That was his interest.

He kept telling himself that.

eight

Meredith closed the door softly behind Gaynor and leaned against it.

She'd overreacted. She knew that the moment the words left her mouth, but she hadn't been able to take them back.

Fear. Grief. Lack of sleep. They had made her strike out at the nearest target. She couldn't remember ever doing that before. She thought she had mastered self-control.

But her need to lean against him, to linger in his arms, had frightened her, stunned her into defensive mode.

She had been unfair. He'd only tried to be kind.

But she knew the dangers of getting involved with someone when emotions were running amok. And hers were certainly doing that at this moment.

She straightened. *Priorities. Think priorities.* A cleaning service. A new computer. Bedding. A weapon.

Meredith tried to look at the damage dispassionately. She couldn't. This was her home, each piece of furniture and every accessory selected carefully by her, not a decorator. Upholstery stuffing littered the floor. Her paintings had been cut, and pages had been ripped from her books. It was as if her life had been torn apart.

Thank God, her law books were at her office.

She peered outside. Detective Gaynor's car was still parked at the curb.

A rush of air left her lungs with relief she didn't want to feel. Perhaps she had been foolish to try to return here alone. Yet she refused to live her life in fear, and she had to begin the cleaning process.

First she had to take inventory and decide exactly what could be salvaged and what should be discarded. Keeping busy might wrestle the detective from her mind. It might cool the warmth lingering deep inside her. It might remove the memory of sensual tingling in every part of her body.

She forced herself to turn away from the window and not look outside. Instead she put torn pillows on the torn upholstery of her comfortable sofa, replaced salvageable books on shelves and placed damaged ones in a box.

She made a path through the living room to the kitchen. Items from the fridge had been splashed on the floor and thrown against the wallpaper. She straightened the room as well as she could, then sat down on a chair and considered her next move.

Meredith couldn't stay here, even if she wanted to. She would stay at the hotel tonight. No court appearances tomorrow. Her one appointment had been cancelled.

Yet there were a dozen things that needed to be done with current cases. Witnesses to be interviewed for one of her cases, motions to be prepared for another, and a proposed court order for a third. Most important of all, she had to start her search for her half sister. If only she could find her before her mother died . . .

If only.

If only pigs flew. She knew adoption laws well. She knew how difficult it was to open a closed adoption.

She used her cell phone to call cleaning services. She actually reached a human being to whom she explained her needs.

She made an appointment for the following day, then turned off the phone and stood. Enough today. She would get here early in the morning, supervise the cleaning, shop for new mattresses, purchase a new computer and start the search for her sister.

And visit her mother.

One more item. She went through her desk. Her pistol permit was in a file with her passport, the mortgage and other important documents. She prayed that it was intact.

All documents were in a manila envelope labeled "Stuff." She found it on the floor. Apparently "stuff" hadn't received much attention from the intruder. For once she admired her less than professional techniques. The envelope was untouched.

Had whoever had done this been constrained by time? Had the burglary been timed to coincide with the attack in the garage? Certainly they must be connected.

Had they meant to kill her? Or had they meant only to delay her while they went through her files? If it were the latter, they came damn close to making a mistake. If she had not been so quick in dodging the car . . .

An abusive husband bent on destruction was still the most likely prospect.

She looked at her watch. Nearly six. She looked outside. Summer light was still with her. Detective Gaynor's car was gone. Loss—and loneliness—settled deep inside her. Yet hadn't she wanted him gone? Hadn't she told him to leave?

She'd felt safe, knowing he was outside.

She couldn't blame him for leaving. She'd welcomed that kiss, and then she'd acted like a raped virgin. *Dammit.*

Her heart jumped as the doorbell rang. He had come back. She wished she didn't feel an unexpected anticipation. She opened the door.

Disappointment filled her as she looked at Detective Morris's tired face.

"You shouldn't be here alone," he said.

"Who told you I was?"

"Didn't tell me. Gaynor ordered me to get my ass over here."

"Can he do that?"

"Officially, no. But he's pretty damned good at making me feel I'm not doing my job very well."

"I know the department is undermanned," she said. "I didn't expect protection."

"I can make an argument for it," he said. "You were one of our prosecutors."

"It probably doesn't have anything to do with my prosecutions," she said honestly. "It's probably the husband of one of my clients."

He shrugged. "Still, Gaynor was right. You shouldn't be alone here right now."

"I plan to stay another night at the hotel. I'll be safe enough there."

"Good. That will give us time to check out a few people. Make out a list for me yet?"

"I can give you a few names."

"Do that, and we'll pay a few visits."

She shivered in the air-conditioned room, but she knew it wasn't from the chill. She went to the ruined kitchen, rummaged around in a drawer and found a pencil. She jotted down some names and handed them to him. "I'll have some more tomorrow. You'll keep me informed?"

"Of course. Gaynor is going to talk to Rick Fuller. He told me about the protective order."

"Do you think . . . ?"

"I don't like to think any officer would be involved in something like this, but we'll be checking on all your recent cases as well as any individual you think might carry a grudge from your prosecutor days."

"Fingerprints?"

"We took all we could find. We need to get a list of people who have been here." He hesitated. "This was obviously well-planned. I doubt whether they left any clues."

"Then you think the attack and the burglary are related?"

"I don't think there's much doubt about it."

"Then there must be more than one person involved. One in the car, and one here."

"Not necessarily. Whoever attacked you would have known you would probably be tied up for hours afterward."

"Would they take that kind of chance? What if I hadn't had a scratch that needed tending? What if I just told the officers I wanted to go home?"

Frustration lined his face. "It doesn't make sense to me, either. But until we know why and who, I want you to be very careful."

"I will. I've decided to get a handgun."

"Gaynor told me. He also told me to make sure you get one. He threatened all that was dear to me if anything happened to you."

She could see Gaynor saying just that. So he hadn't just left her. He'd apparently put the fear of God in his fellow detective. Some of the chill left her.

"I know a good gunsmith," Morris continued. "They have a range, too. I can check you out right away."

She simply nodded. She went back upstairs to her office, retrieved the permit and put it in her purse, gathered several pieces of clothing together, then set the alarm and locked the front door.

"I want to take my car and go to a hotel afterward. Can you give me the location and I'll meet you there?"

"I'll follow you," Morris said. "I want to make sure no one is tailing you."

She nodded gratefully.

She backed her car out of the drive. Morris was already in his car. She passed him and saw him fall in behind her.

For a moment, she wished it were another detective behind her.

That thought was almost as frightening as the past few hours.

Gage was waiting for Rick Fuller when he returned from patrol with his partner.

The man's face tightened as soon as he spotted Gage and he swerved away from his companion. "What do you want?"

"Ms. Rawson was attacked last night. Her home was tossed."

"I was on duty last night."

"Your partner can verify this?"

"Yes," Fuller said shortly, anger smoldering in his eyes. "I didn't go near the—" He clamped his mouth shut. "You have no right, anyway. I hear you went on homicide."

"You might say I have a special interest in this particular case," Gage said. "If you're lying to me . . ."

"I'm not, Detective. I have to go. I have a date."

Fuller tried to push past him, and Gage grabbed his arm. "I hope to hell she knows what she's getting into."

"Leave me alone, Gaynor, or I'll—"

"You'll what? Report the fact that you have a protection order filed against you?"

"Leave me alone."

"I'll have an eye on you for a long time," Gage said. "And if anything else happens to Ms. Rawson, I'll come looking for you. So you'd better start praying nothing does."

He turned abruptly. He had done what he could. From now on, Meredith Rawson would have to take care of herself. He didn't need the aggravation.

He would try to interview her father for the Prescott case. He had sent all the evidence that still existed, including the victim's clothes, to the lab to check for DNA. If none of it produced anything, he would move on to another case.

Charles Rawson opened the door to his home and entered. He glanced at the grandfather clock just inside the foyer. After nine. He neatly laid his briefcase on the table at the front of the hall. Mrs. Edwards would take it upstairs.

It had been one hell of a day. The case would go to the jury tomorrow after a four-week trial. He doubted that the jury would deliberate more than a few hours before returning with a verdict in favor of the plaintiffs. He expected to lose the company's retainer shortly thereafter.

He headed for the library and the scotch. Pouring himself

an unusually large glass, he sat down in the chair in the corner and took a long swallow, wishing the warm liquid would dull his senses.

Everything in his life was going to hell.

He knew he should visit his wife. Part of him wanted to. But she wouldn't recognize him, according to the doctor, and if she did, she wouldn't want him there.

He would honor one last wish.

He thought back to the day he had first seen her. *Really* seen her. She was only seventeen, but he'd thought she was the most beautiful vision in the world.

She was the daughter of the senior partner of the law firm he'd joined three years out of law school. She'd been only fifteen when he'd started, and he'd dismissed her as a child. But two years later, she appeared at one of the Mardi Gras balls he'd attended, and he hadn't been able to take his gaze away from her. She'd been breathtakingly lovely.

He'd known then he had to have her. And he would do anything to get her.

He had.

He swallowed hard and shifted his mind from pointless regret. His secretary had taken a call from a Detective Gaynor who wanted an appointment with him. When his secretary had refused to relay the message without a reason, the detective mentioned reopening the Oliver Prescott case.

Charles thought he'd buried that years ago.

He could avoid the detective for several days, but that might arouse suspicions. A quick interview with responsive answers should end the matter.

Charles would call him tomorrow.

And then there was Meredith. Dear God, how could he slow her down? Convince her that her search was quixotic? And if he couldn't, would he lose her completely, too?

He took another long sip of scotch. He didn't like drinking by himself. He always feared he would become like his own father, who drank himself into stupors. *Discipline. That was what was important.*

A drink of scotch when he arrived home. A glass or two of wine with dinner. He usually drew the line there.

Tonight he could drink the entire bottle.

He looked at his right hand. His fingers were clenched in a tight fist. He tried to relax them and was immediately sorry. They were shaking.

BISBEE

The library staff now greeted her as an old friend.

One reason, of course, was the common love of books. Her son could already read the simplest of books, and he did so vigorously. And since she still didn't sleep well at night, she ran through books at a fast rate.

But though she checked out books for both herself and her son, she had another, more urgent reason to haunt the library. She wanted to search the New Orleans newspaper for news of a murder and her disappearance.

Worried that someone might check the computer to see why she used it so frequently, she also turned to papers in Chicago, Kansas City, Atlanta and Washington, D.C. She would occasionally visit papers of Los Angeles and even Detroit. She was, she told the librarian, a news addict.

Once she reached the New Orleans paper, she skimmed through the front page, the local news and the society section. She stopped at a story about a symphony function. Among the attending dignitaries was her husband.

How had he explained her disappearance?

She saw nothing else of importance. Her gaze went again to Harry. Her son was sitting at a table not far from her, reading a book.

He was such a good little boy. Curious and loving. He had asked about his father last night. How long could she continue to put him off?

She visited the website of another newspaper, then closed the browser and rose. She held out her hand to her son. "Let's go. It's time to eat."

"Tacos," he said happily.

"I think I can manage that."

She checked out several books for herself and a pile for Harry.

One of the librarians smiled at her. "I saw him with the books. He's reading already?"

"Some. He knew his alphabet four months ago."

The librarian beamed at both of them. "Did you find everything you wanted?"

"Yes, thank you."

"I hope you like Bisbee. We're always delighted to have new residents, especially nice ones who love books."

There was a sincerity in the woman's voice that warmed Holly. She had always been admired because of her looks, because of her family's position, then because of her husband's career. She realized now how pleasant it was to be liked for herself, to be an individual rather than a mere adjunct of someone else. She had married far too young. She'd had no chance to explore the world on her own.

She was startled now at how much she wanted to do just that, especially this region. She was fascinated by the history, by the stark beauty of her new environment, by the courage of the settlers who had defied any number of dangers to live here. It gave her heart.

"I do," she said. "I like Bisbee very much."

Holly and Harry left the library. The small diner where she planned to get tacos was next to Special Things. She would stop in there and see how her sculptures were doing. She also wanted to thank Marty for including them in the gathering of friends.

The sun was hot and she was grateful for her comfortable clothes. She wore mostly T-shirts and shorts or jeans purchased at a discount store.

They walked to Marty's store. The gallery owner smiled as Holly entered with her shopping bag full of books. "Hi. When are you going to have some more sculptures for me?"

"I have some ladybugs and a dancing pig."

"I'll send someone to get them," Marty said. "And by the way, I'll need your Social Security number."

The simple comment was like a slam from a sledgehammer. She hadn't thought that would be necessary.

"Why?"

"You're an independent contractor but I'm responsible for reporting any money I pay out."

"I'm sorry. I never can remember the number. I'll get it for you."

"No hurry," Marty said.

"I never worked. My husband did the taxes. I . . ." She knew how stupid that sounded.

Something flickered across Marty's eyes.

Suspicion?

Holly wished she was quicker on the uptake, that her mind was more facile.

Marty shrugged. "We'll let it go for now. I really don't need it until the end of the year." Then her gaze searched her face. "You need a phone, you know. In case of an emergency."

"Money is a little tight right now and—"

Marty cut her off. "Tell you what. You live in my house. I'll get one there in my name. You shouldn't be without one."

Gratitude flooded Holly. "Thank you. I'll pay the bill. . . ."

"You need a phone. Just keep supplying me with your garden creatures," Marty said, waving aside any additional explanations.

Holly could only nod wordlessly.

"Liz?"

Holly looked at Marty.

"If you need anything, I'm here."

Holly nodded, moved beyond words at the conditions-free offer. She wanted to stay in Bisbee. She wanted it more than she could remember wanting anything. Somehow, she would do it. Both she and Harry needed roots. Friends.

"Let's go get those tacos," she urged Harry, who was investigating some carved birds.

As she left the shop, her quickened heart slowed. She took a deep breath. She had just decided. She wasn't going to run again.

nine

NEW ORLEANS

The newly purchased S&W .38 revolver was a hefty weight in Meredith's purse as she entered her mother's room. But she felt safer, more in control.

This was her last stop before returning to the hotel for badly needed rest. She was exhausted. Physically and emotionally.

The private duty nurse put down the book she was reading as Meredith entered and shook her head to Meredith's unspoken question.

"No change."

The room was full of new flowers. Mostly from her father, she supposed. He seemed to think that flowers were a substitute for his presence.

"I heard what happened," the nurse said.

"It seems no place is safe these days," Meredith said.

"Do they know who did it?"

"No."

"It makes me nervous to be in the lot."

Meredith didn't say that she didn't think the attack in the hospital parking lot was a random crime. "I would suggest calling someone from security when you leave at night."

"I plan to do that from now on," the nurse replied.

"Good." It was a good policy any time. She looked at her mother. *No change.* "I want to be alone with my mother."

"How long?"

"An hour."

"I'll get my dinner, then," the nurse said.

"Thank you."

The door closed quietly behind the nurse, and Meredith sat and took her mother's hand in hers. "I'm here," she said.

Her mother's face remained expressionless, her body still, various tubes running in and out of her arms. Did her mother have a living will? Meredith hadn't discussed using extraordinary means with her father. He would make that decision. He had the legal right.

She had to talk to him about it. She wished she knew what her mother wanted, but they had never talked about death.

They'd never talked about life, either.

Loneliness attacked her again, but this time she expected the dull, ragged pain. She wondered how many families were like hers. Cool. Detached. Uninvolved with one another.

"I'll find her, though," she told her mother. "Sarah is looking for birth certificates, and I'll be talking to your friends here. Someone has to know something."

She paused. "What does Daddy know?" The term "Daddy" slipped out unconsciously. She hadn't called her father that for many years.

"Please wake up," she pleaded. "I need you."

And she did, more than she believed possible. She needed to know unqualified love. She wanted to talk to her mother one last time, to express her anger and bewilderment and deep sense of loss.

She had to know the whys of so many things.

But there were no answers from her mother. She doubted there would be.

So she just sat there, hoping her mother knew she was there. Hoping her mother knew she was loved.

She leaned over and kissed her mother's cheek. She felt guilty for leaving.

Dammit, but she was tired of guilt.

"Good night," she told the returning nurse, then went to the security office and asked for an escort to her car. Revolver or not, she had no intention of walking alone in the parking lot.

Morris had followed her to the hospital tonight and left only after she promised to have security walk her to the car. He'd also arranged for her to park in the doctors' lot not far from the hospital's front door. Probably still afraid of a lawsuit, the security staff had readily agreed.

She would use valet parking at the hotel.

She would be safe tonight.

And tomorrow?

She wouldn't think about tomorrow.

Gage took the call on his home phone. It was a collect call.

Clint. His younger brother.

"Gage?"

"Yeah."

"You coming on Sunday?"

Guilt coursed through him. He *had* almost forgotten about it. "I plan to. Just been transferred back to homicide. I never know—"

"I understand," came the resigned reply. "Just wanted to ask you to bring a couple of books." A pause. "I'm in a computer technology course."

"That's great," Gage said, trying to interject some enthusiasm in his voice. His brother often joined self-improvement programs in prison. They never lasted long.

"I got a clerk's job."

That *was* progress. His brother's first years in prison had been disastrous. He'd rebelled constantly. A clerk's job meant good behavior.

"That's good news"

"I'm good at it, Gage. Really good."

"I'll try to be there," Gage said.

His brother gave him the names of two electronics books, then paused, "Thanks, bro."

Gage closed the phone. His brother was the only family he had left. The familiar feeling of failure filled him. He had tried to be father, mother and brother to Clint. He'd succeeded at none.

He wanted to hope now. But he'd hoped too many times before. Still . . . perhaps.

He *would* make it Sunday.

Sheer exhaustion dictated sleep. Even so, the sleep was restless, and Meredith woke early. She didn't feel refreshed.

She drove home. The cleaning firm would be there at nine. She took photos throughout the house for the insurance company, straightened up what she could downstairs, then climbed the stairs to inspect her closets in closer detail.

Most of her good suits had been destroyed beyond repair. Something else to do in the next few days: shopping. She had a court appearance at the end of next week. That required suitable clothing. She had a few blouses that had survived the carnage. Some slacks. A dress. Her shoes were untouched. Perhaps whoever did this ran out of time.

She looked at the underwear. She couldn't bear the thought of putting them back in the drawers after they had been touched by the intruder. She put them in a basket and took them to the washing machine. Even then, she knew she would never feel entirely comfortable in those garments. She wondered whether she would wear any of it again.

After she started the wash, she used her cell phone to call her insurance company and ask for a form to list destroyed items, then called the office. Sarah was already there.

"Ask Becky to come over to my house," Meredith said. "I have some shopping to do, and I want someone here with the cleaning crew."

"You plan to move back home?"

"Yes."

Silence. Then, "Do you think that's wise?"

"I now have a state-of-the-art alarm system, a revolver in my purse, and constant visits by the police. I think I'm safe enough. I will *not* live in a hotel the rest of my life."

"I prepared a list of people who have expressed some displeasure toward you, both in the DA's office and in your private practice," Sarah said.

"Tell me it's a small list."

"Well, it's not that long."

That reminded Meredith that she had not made out her own expanded list yet. "Thanks. I'll add to it and call Detective Morris."

"What about Rick Fuller?"

"He's at the top of mine."

"You know how they protect their own."

"I don't think they will here."

"Okay," Sarah said. Meredith heard the doubt in Sarah's voice.

"I'll be in the office later. I want to discuss the next steps to finding my sister."

"I'll be here."

"You're always there. Have I ever thanked you?"

"All the time, boss."

Meredith hung up, then called the hospital. No change. "Critical but stable."

She leaned against the wall and waited for the cleaning service to arrive. The same wall she had leaned against yesterday when Detective Gaynor kissed her. Why had she allowed it?

More important, why had she responded in such a wanton, needy way? Because she *was* needy. She felt as if she were holding up the Empire State Building on her shoulders. Her Empire State Building of conflicting loyalties and duties. Her mother against her father. Her practice against both of them. Her duty to clients against the chaos in her own life.

Had that made her so susceptible to a kind word? A gentle touch? An offer of help? Was that why Gaynor ignited a passion she'd never experienced before?

Could she trust that help?

The doorbell rang and a small covey of women crowded inside with brooms, pails and other cleaning equipment. She showed them through the house and explained what she wanted done, then provided them with huge trash bags she'd had in her garage for leaves.

Even though she had cleaned up some of the mess, the women gasped at the sliced upholstery, the stains on the floor, the destroyed clothes on the bed and the pieces of glass in her office.

She worked with them, answering questions, until Becky arrived. She told Becky what to do, then left on a shopping expedition. She didn't expect it to take long. Only the necessities—computer, mattress and at least one suit—now. She would see to everything else in the next several weeks.

Feeling a little more in control, she checked the revolver in her purse. The tossing of her home was a stumbling block, nothing more. It would not interfere with what she had to do.

"Nothing," Sarah said. "No birth certificate on record with the Memphis and Shelby County Health Department or with any other surrounding counties—at least not with your mother's name on it. I also checked with local hospitals. None has records dating back that far."

"I need the names of medical facilities and OB practitioners near my aunt's home in February 1970. The doctors we can contact. I'll visit the medical facilities."

Sarah nodded.

"Any other emergencies?" Meredith asked.

"Nothing I can't handle."

"Have you spoken to Nan Fuller?"

"She hasn't heard from her husband. Becky took a copy of the protection order to her yesterday."

Darn. She should have done that. But yesterday had been volcanic.

"A Mrs. Fellows called today for an appointment. A divorce case."

"Can she wait until next week?"

"Yes."

Meredith went into her office, checked her calendar, then reappeared. "A week from Monday at two. Tell her it's tentative. I have an illness in the family."

"Are you sure?"

"We still have a practice to maintain."

"Okay. I'll set it up. Did you add any names to my list of people who might want to do you harm?"

"You did a very thorough job. I never would have listed some of them. But no, no one else."

"Nothing I wouldn't know about? Anything personal?"

"I have no personal life, Sarah." The words escaped Meredith's mouth before she considered them. She suddenly realized how sad they sounded. But she didn't have a personal life. Work had been her balm for years, her reason for being.

Now she realized how few friends she really had. Professional acquaintances, yes. But little else. What social life she'd once had had disappeared when her friends' lives evolved and she had no children about whom to exchange stories, no time for social lunches.

She didn't even have a family. Not really.

"You should remedy that, boss."

"Some day," Meredith said lightly. "But now my calendar is full. Do you have everything under control?"

Sarah nodded.

"I'm going to drop the list at police headquarters, then go to my parents' home. It's Mrs. Edwards's afternoon to shop. Some of my grandfather's records are stored in the attic. My father always expected a case might come back to haunt him, so he kept all his records. There could be some personal stuff there as well. I'm also going to look through my mother's things for a diary. Address book. Anything that can give us a clue."

"I'll call your cell phone number if I need you."

"Good."

Meredith decided to go to Morris's office with the lists. She could call him, ask him to meet her, but . . .

She might see Gaynor. Perhaps he would have talked to Rick Fuller, who was still at the top of her list.

Let Morris take care of it.

She couldn't. Drat it. She wanted to see Gaynor. She tried to keep thinking of him as Gaynor. Not Gage. She wanted to convince herself that yesterday's encounter was the result of sleeplessness, of fear, of grief. She had her emotions in check today. She wanted to prove to herself that the attraction between them had been fleeting.

Certainly not because you just want to see him.

Meredith picked up her purse. "Thanks, Sarah."

"Good luck."

"You, too. After thirty years, it will be a miracle if the doctor in Memphis is still around."

"We'll find something," Sarah said.

"I would like to do it before . . ." She couldn't quite say the words. She knew them in her head. Her heart had not quite accepted them yet.

"I know," Sarah said softly.

"Talk to you later."

"Be careful."

"Oh, I am," Meredith said.

No one was going to make her a victim again. She'd spent the better part of the last eight years comforting victims, knowing she didn't fully understand their trauma.

She was beginning to understand now. She didn't like it. She wouldn't tolerate it. Of that much she was sure.

Gage threw all his efforts into the Prescott case. In lieu of an immediate interview with Charles Rawson, he sent evidence—clothes worn by the victim and the bullet that killed him—to the FBI lab to see whether they could find something the local crime lab had not years ago.

Then he started extensively researching everyone mentioned in the case files.

He started with Prescott's uncle. He had the strongest obvious motive. His nephew had been groomed to assume the chairmanship of one of the largest banks in Louisiana. Now he held that position.

Gage knew the man's reputation as a builder of consensus.

He moved next to Charles Rawson, the last man known to have seen Prescott alive.

Rawson had an alibi, and no physical evidence linked him to the crime. Still, it apparently had hurt his career. He had been an assistant district attorney, then a municipal judge. He was a big political contributor and was known to be angling for a federal judgeship.

After Prescott's murder, the talk of a judgeship faded. Rawson resigned as municipal judge and never ran for office again. Instead he returned to a law firm in which he was now senior partner.

That appeared odd to Gage. Why the sudden lack of interest in a judgeship? Rawson certainly had the political connections. Gage made a note to investigate that aspect further.

He turned his research to Mrs. Rawson. Like the older Prescott, she had been active in nearly every cultural and charitable organization in the city.

He compiled a list of her interests, looking for patterns. She seemed to stay away from anything political as well as causes that called for more effort than raising money. Charities such as United Way, the American Cancer Society, and the Heart Fund all received her attention. But nothing personal like local women's shelters, boys' clubs, or children's hospitals.

Meredith Rawson's mother. Was that where Meredith learned that cool demeanor that locked people out?

The daughter hadn't been cool a few hours ago.

He still felt that kiss. Hell, he'd felt it all evening.

He stretched. He thought about going home but he doubted he would sleep. He was haunted by her face, by the kiss, by how much he'd wanted her.

He swore at himself and turned back to the file on his desk. He'd scrawled out a number of questions raised by the case.

It was interesting that Meredith had been out of town the weekend of Prescott's death. Or was he simply tying her to the case because he wanted to see her again?

He wanted to breach those walls she'd built around her. He wanted to know if that moment of passion was a fluke or whether it was a small glimpse into a very complicated, very passionate woman.

Gage worried that the intriguing idea might blind him to the case itself. To the evidence.

"Hey, Gaynor, the captain wants you." Gage looked up to see a uniformed officer in his door.

He looked at the clock. A little after seven.

Surprised that the brass was here so late, he nodded and stood. Time to give it up, anyway. He walked down the hall to the captain's office. "You wanted me?"

"I'm told you're looking into the Prescott case."

"The lieutenant gave me ten cold cases to review. That was one of them."

"It was a mistake," Captain Adams said. "We set up an office elsewhere to review cold cases. Bennett didn't realize that Detective Wagner had already gone over the case. He's damn good. If he didn't find anything, there's nothing to find. It's a waste of your time. And ours."

"I've already started and—"

"We need you on active cases," Adams said. "We don't have enough experienced men. Bennett should never have given you cold cases. I've spoken to him about it." He paused. "You'll partner with Wagner from now on. You can start tomorrow."

"Tomorrow is my day off."

"Okay, the next day then."

Gage wanted to protest, but his superior's face didn't encourage it.

"You can return the case files to records when you come back in."

Gage nodded.

"Go home, Gaynor."

There was nothing left to say. He turned toward the door. Why was the captain working so late?

Certainly not to tell one of his detectives that he had a new assignment. That could have waited until the next day.

He told himself he should feel relief. But he had thrown himself into the Prescott case. There was something there. He knew there was.

And now he was sure of it.

ten

A car's tires crunched on the gravel outside.

Holly glanced out the window and saw the sheriff's car pulling up. Her heart stopped, just as it had when she'd seen the uniform at the cookout.

Harry was napping. She had been working and stopped long enough to get a glass of water. Her hair was messy. She had no lipstick on. Her feet were bare.

The man she'd met at the picnic the other night—Sheriff Menelo—stepped out of the car. No one was with him. Surely there would have been if they had come to arrest her. She started to breathe again; she had to concentrate to keep her hands from shaking.

What could he want? She thought about pretending not to be home, but her car was in front. She could not postpone trouble forever. She had discovered that with Randolph.

And if there was any suspicion about her story, perhaps she would see it in the lawman's face. Then she and Harry *would* have to disappear again. She kept their things ready.

She approached the door and opened it just as Sheriff Menelo was about to knock. His hand was in midair, and he looked at it sheepishly when there was no place to knock.

"Sheriff?" she said.

"Hello," he said awkwardly. "Russ, well, he told me your

boy liked animals and might want to go riding. I board a couple of horses at his place, and I'm taking Jenny, my niece, out there now for a ride. I wondered if you and Harry would like to go. Russ has several ponies."

No!

Yes.

Once more her head was telling her one thing, and her heart something else. She knew how much Harry wanted to ride.

She'd promised him a great adventure. She had encouraged his interest in cowboys. But how long could she pretend to be something she wasn't with a man trained to detect deception?

"I don't think—"

"If you're busy, I can take him. The whole city will vouch for me," he said, with a slow, easy smile. "I'm mighty careful with children. Been looking after my niece since her father left her and her mother."

"I'm sorry," she said. And she was.

"I'm not. He was a sorry—" He stopped suddenly.

She had a pretty good idea of what he would have said if she had not been standing there. "How old is she?"

"Seven, going on thirty."

She smiled at that. Harry surprised her at times as well.

"You should do that more often, Mrs. Baker."

"Do what?"

"Smile. It's very nice."

Not beautiful. Not elegant. Not lovely. All adjectives she'd heard before. Just "nice." It was the best compliment she'd ever received.

"Mommy." She heard Harry's voice behind her.

She turned. A sleepy-eyed midget stared up at her with confusion.

"Hi," she said. "Do you remember Sheriff Menelo?"

Harry looked up—a long way up, Holly noticed. He nodded.

She waited. She expected Sheriff Menelo to make the

same offer to her son, to make her the bad guy if she refused. That's what her husband always did.

But this man didn't. "Hi, buddy," he said.

"'Ello," he said as he had last night, then looked at her. She had emphasized over and over again not to trust strangers, especially not to talk to adults without her being present.

"He wants to know if you want to ride a horse," she said.

All the sleep left his face and he looked as if someone had handed him the world. His face was so full of hope that her heart broke. "Mommy, can I?"

She nodded.

"Good," the sheriff said. "I'll take the patrol car back and pick up my niece. I'll be back here in, say . . . an hour."

She wondered what she was doing. Yet there was a shy sincerity about the man that disarmed her. Several hours of being very careful would be worth seeing pleasure on her son's face. And maybe feeling a few moments of pleasure herself.

Yet deep down, she knew she would regret this. She knew it to the depths of her soul.

NEW ORLEANS

Fingering her rarely used key to her parents' house, Meredith rang the bell first and waited.

No Mrs. Edwards. After several minutes, she put the key in the lock and let herself in.

The house was like a tomb. Big and silent. She went into the kitchen. It was spotless. Then she stopped by her father's study. The room was large and wood-paneled. Certificates lined the walls. The desk was completely clear, the mahogany gleaming in the light drifting through the windows.

A computer was on a computer stand to the right of the desk. She resisted the urge to go over to it and turn on the power.

She looked at her watch. She thought she had several

hours before Mrs. Edwards returned. Meredith didn't want her father to know she was snooping and didn't want to put Mrs. Edwards in an awkward position of choosing between two loyalties.

Meredith went up the stairs, then opened the door that led to a second set of stairs. She reached for the light overhead, wondering whether it still worked. No one came up here. Relief flooded her when it illuminated the dim stair area. She climbed the steps to the attic door and turned the knob. It was unlocked.

The room was lit by sun streaming in through two windows.

She looked around, stunned.

The attic was empty. The file cabinets were gone. So were the boxes that had been piled against the walls.

She stood there for several moments, then ran her finger along the floor. No dust. The boxes had been removed recently.

Very recently.

What was her father trying to hide?

She left, turning out the light. She descended the stairs and walked to her mother's room. Her mother and father had had different bedrooms for as long as she could remember.

The room was large and, like the rest of the house, looked as if it waited for visiting royalty. The walls were of a sky blue, and the floor covered by a rich, deep royal blue. Lovely delicate bottles lined the dresser.

Meredith looked in the night table. A recent bestseller. A notebook and pen.

She looked in the notebook, feeling a little like a Peeping Tom. This was her mother's world, one she'd never quite been allowed entrance. But the pages were blank, or they had been torn out.

Undeterred, she looked in the dresser, then a large chest, and finally the closet.

The walk-in closet was filled with clothes neatly separated into casual and dressy. Built-in drawers were filled

with lingerie. Shoes lined racks. Sweaters were neatly
folded on two shelves.

She sighed, then spotted a shelf in the back. Books. She
reached back and found three yearbooks for the private
girls' school her mother had attended. There was also a
book of poetry.

They were out of sight but not hidden. She took all four
volumes, feeling as if she'd caught the golden ring on a
carousel. Her mother had cared enough to keep them. Perhaps they held some secrets.

She took the stack to the small antique writing desk and
sat down. She picked up the book for the year her mother
was a senior. Her mother was in the class photos and some
group scenes, but there were no scrawled messages as there
usually were in yearbooks. No writings from classmates.
She picked up the second book. She found her mother's
photo in the junior class. Fellow classmates had written all
over their photos.

Her glance rested on the photo of her mother. She had
long blond hair and looked at the camera with a huge
smile.

Meredith couldn't remember ever seeing that smile.

An observer could see the energy and life in the girl,
even in a black-and-white photo. Meredith looked through
the group photos. Drama Club. Choir, Art Club. Homecoming court. In the latter, she looked like a princess.

Meredith thought how different her mother and she had
been. She had gone to a different private school where she
excelled in scholastic activities and not much else. She had
been in the Latin Club and Honor Society, on the debating
team. She'd been editor of the school paper.

And her sister? Was she more like their mother?

Meredith suspected she had been a disappointment to
her mother. She had her father's analytical mind and intro-
spective nature. She'd never liked parties and fancy dresses
and dancing classes.

Then she turned her attention to the book of poetry. A
collection of romantic poetry.

She looked inside for an inscription. There was none. So it probably wasn't a gift. It certainly wasn't something her father would have given her. At least Meredith didn't think so. But then nothing was as she had thought.

She put the book of poetry down and rifled in the drawer of her mother's desk. The contents were spare and neat. Stationery. Pens. Envelopes. An address book. She flipped through it and recognized the names of many of the city's social figures. Nothing that caught her attention.

She picked up her purse and the books. It would soon be time for Mrs. Edwards to return, and she would rather that neither she or her father knew Meredith had been inside. Not now.

There were too many puzzles. She needed more information before she confronted her father again.

She would start with some of the girls in the yearbook, particularly those with more personal messages. Surely her mother had confided in one of them.

It was, at least, a place to start.

Gage woke to the sound of heavy panting. Beast was standing on his bed, exhaling dog breath on him in an effort to get his attention. He obviously wanted his breakfast and this was his way of making an offer that Gage couldn't refuse.

He'd had damn little sleep. Despite the captain's warning, he'd spent his day off going over the Prescott files. He was missing something. He knew it. Then, frustrated after failing to find anything, he'd gone to a blues bar and stayed far too long. He wondered who had gotten to the captain. He had wondered that when he went to bed and again now as he reluctantly put feet to the floor. He looked at the clock. Seven in the morning. It had been three when he had arrived home, and he'd been unable to sleep.

Beast nudged him and Gage scratched his ears. Beast sighed with delight.

Gage had named him Beast for lack of anything better.

Beast was big, probably part Doberman and God knew what else. He had been a watchdog for some drug dealers Gage had busted. The animal had been pacing the interior of a fence surrounding a house suspected of being a lab. The dog had bared his teeth and growled, and one of the officers had taken out his pistol. Gage had a soft spot for animals, though, and had shook his head. Instead he'd started talking to the beast, and the damn thing stopped growling and started wagging his tail. He followed Gage to the door and knocked him down just as a bad guy fired at him. Gage wasn't hit. The dog was.

Hell, that damned animal saved his life. He couldn't let him go to the dog pound after that.

And so he had taken the dog to a vet, then home. The sixteen-year-old son of his neighbor loved dogs, and he and Beast had taken to each other immediately. When Gage worked late, Foster would feed Beast and play with him.

But Gage was his person, and Beast was ecstatically happy when Gage was home. He would crawl up in the king-size bed one leg at a time. Slyly. As if he were invisible and putting something over on his person. At first, Gage had tried to discourage the practice but Beast would stand there, looking at him with heartbreak in his eyes.

Beast had been Gage's first impression and Beast he had remained. The dog seemed perfectly happy with the name.

"Okay," he said as a huge red tongue darted out and licked his forehead. "I get it. You want to eat."

He rose, still feeling the effect of two days without much sleep, and grabbed the pair of jeans that always lay next to the bed. He was getting too damned old for these kind of hours.

He went into the kitchen, started a large pot of coffee and poured dry food into the dog dish. Then he went to his bathroom and stepped into a shower.

He thought best in the shower.

He especially thought best as steaming water poured over

his body. So many questions echoed in his mind. Who had called the captain about his reopening the Prescott case? Someone had. That much was for sure.

Who had the kind of power to stop an investigation, to bring out a captain late at night to remove a detective from a case? That alone would raise questions. So why had it been risked?

Was there something to be found?

The only people with whom he'd discussed the case were Glenn Wagner, the homicide detective who'd previously looked into the case, Meredith Rawson and her father. The father was the most likely person to intervene.

He turned off the shower and stepped out. Beast was sitting there, waiting.

Beast barked.

"Okay," Gage said. "I know. You want to get the paper." The tail wagged frantically.

Gage dressed in a pair of jeans and a T-shirt, then opened the front door. Beast raced out, picked up the newspaper lying in the driveway and raced back in, plopping the paper into Gage's outstretched hand.

"Good boy," he said, giving Beast dessert—a giant size dog biscuit—as the smell of coffee permeated the kitchen. Gage poured himself a large cup of coffee, took a donut from a box he'd bought yesterday and sat down at the table to read the paper.

He found little of interest, probably because his mind was wandering. It kept returning to Meredith Rawson and the Prescott case. Why had he been told to leave it alone? And did either the father or the daughter have anything to do with it?

He'd never liked being told to leave something alone once his curiosity had been piqued. It was certainly piqued now.

Perhaps he would go into the station and talk to Morris, the detective handling the attempt on her life. Or had it been an attempt? Had it only been a ruse to try to find something in her home? If so, what?

The questions wouldn't go away.

He thought about piling his canoe into his pickup and paddling through the swamp. The quiet beauty usually cleared his head.

Or he could visit Angola Prison to see his brother today rather than Sunday. He looked at the clock. He would never arrive in time for visiting hours. And he had to get the books.

He also knew he was stalling. He loved his brother, but God, it hurt seeing him in prison. It always made Gage feel that he had failed, and that Clint was paying for that failure. He would find those books this afternoon and have them ready Sunday.

He and Beast went outside for a few moments to play with a Frisbee.

But he couldn't get Meredith Rawson off his mind. Nor the Prescott case. Instinct told him they could be related. He didn't believe in coincidences.

"Okay, boy," he said. "That's enough." He tried to ignore Beast's mournful look as the Frisbee hung forlornly from his mouth. "Foster will come and play with you later."

Beast was not placated. He tried to push the Frisbee back into Gage's hand. Gage threw it one last time and the dog jumped high in the air to catch it, then proudly trotted back.

"Now that really is enough," Gage said, scratching an ear.

He went back in, Beast at his heels. As he mentally plotted the day, Gage picked up the file that he'd happened to take home.

The bookstore first for Clint's books. Then he would find an office supply store and copy some of the Prescott files. He didn't know whom he could trust in the office, and he had the feeling that if caught copying the file, he would be told in no uncertain terms to leave it alone. Then he would have no choice.

He would also drop in to see Morris and see whether he knew any more about the attack on Meredith Rawson.

A question. Just one question to ease his mind.

eleven

It took until Saturday night before her house was habitable again.

Meredith unboxed her new computer after the cleaning crew left and sat down at her desk, one of the few undamaged pieces of furniture remaining in the house. Other pieces were being reupholstered and repaired.

She hadn't had time to replace the paintings or even the ruined drapes in her bedroom. That would have to wait. Other things couldn't, like the mattresses she had purchased on the condition that they be delivered immediately.

But enough was completed for her to go home.

She was tired of the hotel room and had thought she would like nothing better than to be home again. She wasn't prepared for the fear that accompanied her homecoming.

A tremor shook her body. Would she ever feel safe again? She double-checked the locks on both the windows and doors but the sense of violation remained. Every time she looked around, she saw something that needed to be done. A rip along the wallpaper in the dining room. An obviously empty place on the wall that was formerly occupied by her favorite painting.

After completing all the computer connections, she went

out to the kitchen, made a sandwich and heated some hot chocolate, then sat at the kitchen table with her mother's yearbooks in front of her. Hot chocolate was her comfort food, an indulgence she rarely indulged. But she needed indulgence tonight.

She was tired, on edge. She'd decided not to go to the hospital tonight; the private duty nurse promised to call if there was even the slightest change. She needed tonight to go through the yearbooks and identify people she knew. Then she would use those people to find others.

Someone had to know whom her mother had been seeing at the time. Once she had her sister's father's name, she could find out what he knew. Surely her mother had told him something. Perhaps he had agreed to the adoption, or had raised the baby himself.

She sipped the chocolate as she studied the yearbook from her mother's junior year. She recognized some of the students as current pillars of New Orleans society. That made sense. They had attended the city's most exclusive private school. By the time she'd finished the chocolate, she had identified nearly a third of her mother's class. Then she studied the photos of the classes directly ahead and behind her.

She was totally absorbed when the phone rang. She picked it up. "Meredith Rawson," she said.

No answer. Heavy breathing. Then *click*.

She had started to feel safe again. Now she stood next to the phone, the receiver quivering in her hand. She looked at her Caller ID but she knew what she would see. *Unknown*.

A chill permeated the room. Someone wanted to terrify her.

She wouldn't give them the satisfaction. She sat back down and called the cell phone number Morris had given her. He answered immediately.

"This is Meredith Rawson. I just received an anonymous call. Ordinarily I wouldn't be concerned but—"

"Was anything said?"

"No. Just heavy breathing." She paused, then continued, "It could just be an annoying sales call, or a wrong number. I probably shouldn't have called but—"

"You did the right thing," he broke in. "I'll send a car over now to search the area and I'll see if we can't have someone there overnight."

She didn't protest this time. The call had sent icy fingers up her spine.

"When the car gets there, the officer will knock at your door. Don't open it unless you see the uniform and badge. I'll be over in the morning."

"Thank you."

"No need, Ms. Rawson."

She hung up. This was a two hot chocolate night.

She put more milk and powdered Dutch chocolate in the pan and carried it back to the range. The phone rang again, the shrill sound now threatening. Meredith dropped the pan, splashing milk over the top of the stove.

She hesitated, then went to the phone and picked it up. "Meredith Rawson."

Silence.

"You don't frighten me, you coward," she said. Then hung up.

Brave words. But it did frighten her. Now she was convinced.

Someone was intentionally trying to terrify her. Doing a darn good job of it, too.

Why?

Dammit, why?

For the first time, she wished she didn't live alone. She wished there was someone with whom she could share her fear. Her father? No. He hated weakness of any kind, and now she didn't trust him. He wouldn't hurt her, but she couldn't stop feeling that he was hiding something she should know.

For a moment, her thoughts went to a tall loose-limbed detective with a shock of sandy hair and piercing green eyes.

Her fingers itched to call him. But he wanted something from her, too. Something she wasn't prepared to give.

She was alone. Completely and utterly alone.

Holly felt liberated. Pure joy bubbled inside her as she rode Miss Mary alongside a creek bed.

She hadn't ridden a horse in years. She'd taken riding lessons at an exclusive camp when she was ten. But that was the last time she'd mounted a horse. She had almost forgotten her yearning for the freedom of being on such a magnificent animal.

Harry wasn't the only one who wanted to be a cowboy. She'd just suppressed all those longings.

She hadn't meant to ride. She had gone along with Sheriff Menelo to give Harry a treat. She had added just a touch of lipstick and had not changed from her T-shirt and jeans. After all, it wasn't a date.

When the sheriff had driven up in a dusty Jeep, a young girl dressed in jeans and a T-shirt jumped out. "I'm Jenny," she introduced herself.

Holly had liked her immediately. Her dark hair, a shade deeper than the sheriff's, was worn in a long ponytail, and she radiated energy. She regarded Holly and Harry with interest and a quick smile.

"This is Mrs. Baker," said the sheriff, who'd been a little slower in getting out of the Jeep. "And Harry."

"Like Harry Potter," her son chirped, obviously impressed by the older woman.

"Neat name," Jenny said.

Holly was incredibly grateful. Now her son would probably never forget the name.

"You sit in the back with me," Jenny said to her son. Harry immediately crawled into the backseat.

The sheriff opened the Jeep door for Holly. "Sorry for the transportation," he said. "But I like going up into the hills. My only other vehicle is a pickup truck."

"It's fine," she said, tucking herself inside. "How far is it?"

"Ten miles," he said.

"Does Russ know you're bringing us?"

"I called," he said. "He boards and rents horses there, so people are often coming and going. I wanted to make sure he had a pony available for Harry."

"And he does?"

"Uh-huh." He glanced toward her. "Would you like to ride, too?"

"Me?" It was a foolish reply, but she had not considered it. It had been a long time since she had indulged in a pleasure just for her.

"Yep, you. Ever ridden before?"

"Ages ago," she said slowly, afraid to give away even that small piece of information. "At summer camp when I was a child."

Didn't every child go to summer camp? No need to tell him that it was a very expensive, exclusive summer camp.

"It's a little like riding a bicycle," he said. "You don't forget. But you might be sore if you haven't used those muscles in a while."

The idea of riding—even with a minion of the law—gave her a rush of anticipation.

Still, caution ruled. "My shoes—"

His glance went down to her loafers. "They'll do. Russ has some gentle mares."

Excitement rose in her. She had loved riding that summer. She had wanted to ride when she'd returned home, but her mother said it was only a phase and promptly enrolled her in dancing class. She'd hated that class, mainly because it was a substitute for what she'd really wanted.

After fifteen minutes, he turned down a dirt road. A small sign saying HORSES BOARDED was all that marked it.

They drove up to a cluster of buildings backed against a hill. The house was adobe and modest-looking; the stables looked far more elaborate.

Several cars were parked in the front of the house. One had a horse trailer attached.

She stepped out of the Jeep, and Jenny followed with Harry. Russ came out of the house, gave her a brief wave, and headed for the stables. In minutes he was leading a pony and a small horse into the yard.

"Thanks for letting Harry ride," she said.

"My pleasure," he replied as he leaned down and ruffled Harry's hair.

"Sheriff Menelo said you rent horses. I want to pay for Harry's."

He shook his head. "That's for tourists," he said. "Not for friends."

Friends. It had a nice sound. Still, despite her now frugal existence, she pressed the point. "I would rather pay."

He sighed. "You have to get used to our ways, Liz. That's not the way it works."

She flushed. She suddenly realized she was being ungracious. But she had been so determined to pay her own way and remain aloof. She didn't realize how difficult that was going to be here.

"Then I accept with thanks."

"Good," he said.

She and Sheriff Menelo watched as Jenny used a mounting block to climb into the saddle. Russ handed the reins of the pony to Sheriff Menelo and moved over to the side of the fence. Jenny walked the horse into a large fenced area that held a number of barrels placed at intervals. She increased the pace to a canter as she started to maneuver around the barrels.

"Russ is teaching her," Sheriff Menelo said. "She wants to be a barrel racer."

"Rodeo?"

"Russ is a former rodeo cowboy."

Startled, she looked at Russ again. He had the lanky build of a cowboy but still she was surprised. And intrigued. "When did he quit?"

"About fifteen years ago. A bull nearly killed him. He

decided raising cutting horses would be safer, but it's a hard way to make a living, so he boards horses and gives lessons as well."

Sheriff Menelo looked down at Harry, who was gazing at the pony in rapture. "Ready, cowboy?"

"Yes, sir."

The sheriff threw her an approving look for her son's manners. If only he knew it was a habit born of fear, not courtesy. He leaned down, picked Harry up and settled him into the saddle, then walked the pony, his right hand securely on the reins.

She could hear the sheriff talking to her son. "Relax but straighten your back. Move with the horse."

The smile left her son's face, replaced by a look of total concentration. He so obviously wanted to do well. After about twenty minutes, the sheriff handed the reins to her son but walked alongside, his hand on the bridle. For a moment, her mouth went dry, but Harry's expression was a combination of joy and pride. He loved it.

The sheriff stopped and lifted Harry down. Her son stumbled a moment, then looked up at her, beaming.

"Thank you, Sheriff," she said.

"Doug," he corrected.

She wasn't sure whether she wanted first-name intimacy. But she nodded.

"Now you," he said. "Jenny and Russ will be busy for another hour. There's a creek not far away."

"But Harry . . ." She almost said *Mikey*, but stopped just in time.

"He can ride in front of me," Doug said. "Russ has a mare called Miss Mary." He grinned. "She's a perfect lady . . . just right for you."

Was he implying that she was a perfect lady? If he only knew . . .

Run. Run like the devil is after you.

But instead she nodded. She waited as he went into the barn.

"Did you see me?" Harry asked. "I was riding all by myself."

"I saw," she said. "I was amazed."

He grinned. "I like it here, Mommy."

"I do, too."

"I wish Father could have seen me."

Her heart skipped a beat. What if he had said that in front of the sheriff?

She looked down at her suddenly clammy hands. Would the fear and doubt never end? How could she possibly think she could live a normal life or provide one for Harry when she panicked over every word, every question, every answer she could not give?

Sheriff Menelo returned, leading two horses. One was a bay, tall and obviously anxious for the ride. The other was a smaller horse, a chestnut mare. More delicate, if you could call a quarter horse delicate. Yet that was the word for her. Miss Mary. A perfect lady.

Doug tied his horse's reins to a post, then helped her up into the saddle. "Just relax," he said as he showed her how to hold the reins. "She'll do all the work."

He put Harry on his horse and swung up easily behind him. Very easily and very gracefully for such a big man. He directed the horse toward the dirt road, then looked at her. "Are you okay?"

She was and she wasn't. The new Holly—no, Liz now—loved the horse, the company, the day. The old Holly kept warning her to be careful.

"Have you known Russ long?" she asked Doug.

"We went to high school together. Bisbee High."

"Friends?"

"We played football together. He was a quarterback and I was a tackle but neither of us was good enough to get a scholarship. He went to the rodeo and I went to the army."

"And you've remained friends all these years?"

"Pretty much," he said.

Despite her fears, Doug Menelo was an easy companion. He did not demand conversation. Nor did he try to pry.

The sky was as pure a blue as she could remember and she enjoyed the heat of the sun. She tried not to think of the future or the past, even as she knew the latter was never going away and the former was perilous.

But she wouldn't allow those thoughts to spoil this afternoon.

Doug guided his horse toward her and motioned to the left, where golden flowers colored the starkly beautiful desert. "Mexican gold poppies," he said.

"I know," she said. "I've been reading about the desert."

"Hmm. Does that mean you're staying?"

"It means I haven't been here before and I'm curious."

"Do you like Bisbee?"

"It's hard not to like it. It has character."

"Have you been to Ramsey Canyon?"

"Ramsey Canyon?"

"It's not far from here. It's a preserve, and they have hundreds of hummingbirds. Jenny loves it."

"I'll have to take Harry there," she said.

She knew she was precluding the invitation he'd probably meant to issue. She regretted it. More than regretted it. She liked Doug Menelo. She liked him very much. She liked the way he appreciated his surroundings and the gentleness he demonstrated with his niece and her son. He was a man meant to have children. She wondered why he didn't.

If he was anyone but who he was, she might have even taken a chance in building a friendship with him. But a sheriff? Eventually he would want more information. More answers. More answers than she could ever give him. And she could never forget she had a husband.

They stopped at a creek bed. Although it was dry now, cottonwoods had soaked up enough moisture to flourish. They contrasted with the cactus and the landscape that rose up to meet the sky.

"Want to get down?" Doug asked her.

"If I can get back up again."

He grinned. "You might be a bit sore, but I think we can get you back aboard. How do you like Miss Mary?"

"Are all horses this easy to ride?"

"No. Miss Mary is unusual. Russ always gives her to novice riders. She seems to understand that she has to take care of them, rather than the other way around."

"She's wonderful."

"I'm sure Russ will let you and Harry ride any time."

She nodded, although she had no intention of doing it again. Next time, she would take Harry to a public riding stable. She could not feel obligated, nor could she dare the intimacy that friendship demanded.

Doug leaned over and lowered Harry to the ground, then dismounted. She did the same.

He pointed to a mountain in the distance. "That used to be an Apache stronghold," he said. "This whole area was a battleground. It took guts to settle it."

"You love it," she observed.

"I do. You either love it or hate it," he said. "It has a pull on those who love it."

"You said you were in the army. What did you do?"

"Military police. That's how I came to be in law enforcement."

That was one subject she didn't want to pursue. She took several steps, then stumbled. He reached out to steady her.

Involuntarily, she flinched.

He removed his hand immediately. "I'm sorry," he said.

"I . . . was just startled."

"Mrs. Baker . . . Liz . . . I know you were recently widowed. I wouldn't take advantage of that. I just thought you and your son needed to get out."

She felt her cheeks darken. She swallowed. "I didn't think that you would. It's just that—"

"I know. I lost someone years ago. It's not easy." The sincere sympathy in his voice made her feel worse. She was a cheat.

"No it's not," she said. "Harry and I should be getting back. I have work to do, and we have supper early."

"Okay," he said easily. "Here, use my hands." He interlocked his hands and she stepped into them, then up into the saddle. This time, she felt more confident.

She waited until he and Harry were mounted, then she turned back in the direction from which they'd come.

They rode back in silence. His face was emotionless, but his hands were protective of her son. Harry kept glancing up at him, apparently finding something he had never found in his father.

She fought to keep tears back.

twelve

Gage waited at least thirty minutes in the visiting room before Clint arrived.

In the meantime, Gage watched other prisoners and their families, feeling a little like a voyeur. How many times had he been here? At least once a month for nearly eight years. Sometimes more often.

He swallowed hard. These visits were soul crushing. So was the eager, hopeful look on his brother's face when he saw him.

Despite eight years in Angola, Clint appeared impossibly young. Gage knew the look belied the experience. In the first three years, Clint had been disciplined repeatedly. He'd been in one fight after another, establishing his reputation in a prison that demanded toughness.

And Gage couldn't help. He'd felt the bitter frustration of being unable to make things better for someone he loved.

The two brothers gave each other a bear hug.

"You look good, kid."

Clint gave him the funny little half grin that had charmed girls when he'd been younger. "I have a parole hearing coming up."

Gage should have known that. He hadn't. "What can I do?"

"I need a job waiting."

"I'll talk to Dom. He might have some ideas."

"I've been studying computer technology. I'm good at it, bro. I didn't tell you before because, well . . . hell, I know how many times I've let you down. But I graduate from the course next week." His gaze went to the books on the table and his eyes lit. "These books will help me go beyond what they're offering here. The instructor suggested them."

"You've always been smart as hell," Gage acknowledged. "You just never tried."

"I'm trying now. I don't want to be here."

Gage nodded at the books. "If you need any more, let me know."

"Thanks. I won't disappoint you this time."

"When's the hearing?"

"Next month."

"You need an address, too. You can move in with me," Gage said.

"Won't that affect your job?"

Gage shrugged. "It's no one's business. Not if you keep clean."

"I will. Thanks."

"Until you get on your feet."

"You'll come to the hearing?"

"I'll be there."

Clint sighed with relief.

"Did you think I wouldn't?"

"You're a cop, bro. One of them."

Listen to me, Clint. I didn't have anything to do with your arrest. You did all that by yourself. I'll help you now, but by God, if you get involved in drugs again, I'm out. I'll turn you in myself."

"I know," Clint said. "Believe me, I've learned my lesson." He gave Gage that crooked smile again.

But Gage had stopped believing it years ago. He'd believed Clint too many times. He wasn't going to offer him money. A place to live if he stayed clean, yes. He would help find him a job. He would pay tuition for college. But he knew he wasn't going to give Clint money.

"I'm going to make it," Clint said.

Gage merely nodded.

"You still on internal affairs?"

"Public Integrity," Gage corrected. "No. I've been transferred to homicide."

"That's good, isn't it? For you, I mean."

"That's very good."

"I'm glad then."

"You still getting grief here because I'm a cop?"

"Nothing I can't manage. You got a girl yet?"

"Nope."

"I appreciate your offer to stay with you, but I don't want to cramp your style."

"Nothing to worry about there," Gage said wryly.

"You still canoeing?"

"When I can."

"Maybe we can go together."

"You never used to be interested."

"I've gained a new appreciation of the outdoors." Clint was talking about parole as if it were a natural conclusion.

Gage warned, "Don't be disappointed if the parole doesn't happen, Clint."

"I won't," he said. "But you have to have hope in here."

They talked a few moments longer, mostly about acquaintances they knew. Unfortunately, most of Clint's were either dead or in prison. He had gotten involved with drugs when he was sixteen and had never been able to overcome them. He'd turned to burglary to pay for his habit, as well as selling drugs himself. Small amounts, but enough to get him a long sentence on his second offense. A fight during his first year had sent him from a medium-security institution to Angola.

Gage finally rose from his seat. "I have to get back."

"Have a big case?"

"Just got on the squad," he said.

Clint rose, too, and held out his hand. "Thanks for the books. And for coming."

"I'll see you at the hearing."

Gage left, not quite sure how he felt. He wanted freedom for Clint, yet he was afraid to hope. To trust. There had been too many promises in the past.

The sun was hot. The sky cloudless.

He drove faster than usual. He wanted to get back to New Orleans, where he had some control, where he wouldn't feel so much a failure. He wanted to make sure Meredith Rawson was safe despite Morris's assurances that she was. She had purchased a pistol. She'd had no more attacks. The police were driving by her home every few hours.

It was all they could do. He knew it. The police department was understaffed, like police departments across the country, and Morris had promised to keep an eye on her. At any rate, it was no longer his business. She had made that clear. So had Morris.

Yet something kept prickling him about the break-in and the attack on her in the garage. Something wasn't quite right.

It hadn't been mere anger. It was too well-planned. The destruction had been methodical. There had been purpose behind it.

Was it simply revenge?

Or could it be something else? A hunt for information, disguised by the destruction? Or an attempt to distract her?

Then the question would be, Distraction from what?

He pressed his foot on the gas pedal.

New Orleans

Meredith started dialing numbers she'd found for those members of her mother's class that she could identify.

Machines answered at two of them. She didn't want to leave a message. Her errand was too personal. She was luckier on the third call.

Mrs. Robert Laxton, formerly Pamela Cannon, answered on the second ring.

Once Meredith had identified herself, she related part of her errand. "My mother is very ill," she said. "I want to notify her old friends but I'm not sure who they are, and she's too ill to give me a list. I understand you two were friends. I was hoping you could help me."

"Oh, my dear," Mrs. Laxton said. "I had heard she was ill but I didn't know it was that critical. Of course, I would be happy to help you. Could you come for tea tomorrow?"

"That would be very nice," Meredith agreed. "What time?"

"Four?"

"Perfect."

"I will look forward to it," Mrs. Laxton said, and clicked off.

Mission completed, Meredith slowly put the receiver back in the cradle. She picked up the insurance claim papers she'd filled out earlier and tucked them into her briefcase. It was seven. Time to go to the hospital.

Forty minutes later, she entered her mother's room. There was no change in her condition, though her mother's skin looked pasty and her face seemed to have shrunk even more.

Still, she felt as if her mother knew she was there. She ignored the nurse after greeting her. Instead she talked to her mother. She didn't say anything about her own problems. "It's a pretty day, and the symphony is holding a concert tonight. I know how much you like music. I'll bring a CD player next time.

"I'm going to tea with Mrs. Robert Laxton. Remember Pamela Cannon? Of course, you do." She paused. "I wonder if you know how much I hated those teas you made me attend. I know your friends always looked at me and wondered how I could be your daughter." She had been expected to be the perfect lady, but she had always been bored with the talk of this party and that, and the gossip that flowed so easily.

"I used to look at you," she continued. "And your face

was always so attentive, but I always sensed you were some-where else." The memory had never been so clear as it was now. Perhaps because she had never probed beyond her mother's facade before.

The hurt had always been too strong. The gulf between them too wide. Now she felt her mother's reticence wasn't due to disappointment in her daughter, but a wound so deep inside her that she had closed herself off. Until Meredith knew more about that wound, she could never decipher the puzzle.

"I'm going to find my sister for you. And for me. I keep thinking that if I do that, you'll wake up. But you have to fight. You have to keep fighting." She looked down at her hands. They had curled into tight fists. The area behind her eyes squeezed. She fought back tears.

Later.

Not now.

Carrying her mother's yearbook in her briefcase, Meredith knocked on the Laxton door promptly at four. The door was opened by an attractive woman who looked far younger than her early fifties.

"Hello," she said. "I'm delighted to meet Marguerite's daughter. I'm so sorry to hear about her illness."

"Thank you for seeing me," Meredith said.

Mrs. Laxton led the way into a lovely sunroom. "If you will wait here, I'll tell Enid to bring the tea."

Meredith looked around. It was a lovely room, the walls all glass and the interior filled with flowering plants. The windows looked out over a garden highlighted by a foun-tain.

In seconds, Mrs. Laxton returned, a woman in a maid's uniform following with a tray laden with a tea service and plates of small sandwiches and even scones and cream. She poured the tea into delicate china cups.

"Thank you," Meredith said, taking a cup in both hands.

She waited until the maid left. Then she turned to her hostess. "Thank you for seeing me."

"You're welcome. Now tell me how Marguerite is."

"She has cancer and is in a coma. I'm afraid . . ."

Mrs. Laxton leaned over and patted her hand. "I'm so sorry. What hospital is she in?"

Meredith told her, then said, "I hoped you could tell me about when she was in school."

"Or course, you know she left before graduation. An opportunity in Europe. After that, I didn't see much of her until the last few years when we served together on the board of the Symphony Guild. She had changed so much."

"What do you mean?"

"She was, well, a little headstrong—a rebel, you might say—but now she's a pillar of the community. I never would have thought it," Mrs. Laxton said. "I hope you don't mind my saying that, dear."

Her mother? Her very proper mother? But she was discovering how little she really knew about her mother.

"Can you tell me more?"

"It's not really for me to say."

"Please."

"She was always breaking rules. Staying out past curfew. She liked to go to . . . well, undesirable places. Then her father sent her to Europe. There were whispers of an unsuitable liaison."

"Do you know who it was?"

"No. We weren't that close. Now tell me about yourself, my dear. I saw in the paper that you had been attacked. I hope you weren't hurt."

"Mostly scared."

"Crime these days is just terrible. I won't go anywhere at night without my Robert. I don't even like going out alone during the day. And the police? They don't really care. A friend of mine was burglarized a month ago. The police didn't even take fingerprints."

Meredith tried to steer the conversation back to her mother. She handed her hostess the yearbook. "I wondered if you could tell me the married names of some of your classmates."

"Certainly. I was hostess of our thirtieth reunion a few years back. I'll get my list. You enjoy your tea."

When Mrs. Laxton returned, she carried several sheets of paper. "I copied them on my husband's copier, so you may take them."

"Do you know who was closest to my mother?"

"Lulu. Lulu Green Starnes now. The two were always together."

"Does she live here?"

Mrs. Laxton nodded. "I had a hard time finding her. She's a widow. Her address is on the list, though she didn't come to the reunion. Out of town, I believe."

"Thank you," Meredith said, rising. "You've been a tremendous help."

"You are very welcome. If you need anything else . . ."

"I'll call," Meredith said.

Meredith returned to the office. Sarah and Becky were still there. Using Mrs. Laxton's addresses and phone numbers, she called Lulu Starnes. No one answered. She left a message.

Meredith had never heard her mother mention anyone named Lulu. She was sure she would have remembered a name like that. It was unusual enough, especially among her mother's crowd.

Sarah was having no luck in finding a birth certificate. There simply wasn't one in the state of Tennessee that had her mother's name on it. She'd also tried Louisiana and Mississippi. No birth certificate issued for a girl born to Marguerite Thibadeau. But Sarah did have names of doctors and hospitals in the area near her mother's aunt's home.

Frustrated, Meredith turned to the business of her practice. Lord knew she had been neglecting it.

"There's a call from another potential client on a divorce case," Sarah said.

Meredith wanted to turn it down, but she had an office and two employees to support. "Why don't you talk to her. Determine what she needs and whether she can wait a few weeks." She planned to fly to Memphis on Thursday and interview neighbors of her aunt's and obstetricians who might have delivered the baby. After thirty-three years she thought it unlikely she'd find the right doctor, but maybe some records would still exist.

It was the longest of long shots, but . . .

She tried Lulu Starnes again. Not even an answering machine replied.

Well, she would try tomorrow.

The phone rang. Becky buzzed her.

It was Nan Fuller. Terror was in her voice.

"I saw him," she said. "He was watching me when I picked up the children from school."

"Did he say anything to you?"

"No, but he wanted me to see him. He didn't try to hide."

"Did he get within five hundred feet of you?"

"No. But his face . . . It was scary."

"I'll contact Detective Gaynor. He might be able to do something."

"I'm thinking about moving out of town but I don't have any money, not until the divorce is settled . . ."

Meredith knew the court had given Rick supervised visiting rights with the children. "You will need a court order to leave unless you want to become a fugitive and give him more leverage against you."

"I know. I had hoped to go home. . . ." Nan said. She had been staying at the women's shelter with her two children. Neither Nan nor Meredith had any doubt that Rick knew exactly where it was, but she'd be safer there than in the house she'd shared with her husband.

"Let me see what I can do," Meredith said. "I'll call you back."

Meredith sighed. Rick would only claim he wanted a glimpse of his children. He hadn't violated the protective order. There was precious little she could do at this moment. But she knew from Nan's voice that she was terrified.

She didn't want to call Gage Gaynor. She hadn't heard from him since that unfortunate kiss . . . that she still felt deep in her bones every time she allowed herself to think about it.

But if she did call him, and he talked to Fuller, would it even further enrage Nan's husband?

Had she underestimated the officer's anger? Had he been the one who destroyed her home?

Her hand went to Gaynor's card he'd left with her when he'd inteviewed her, then reached for the phone. Hesitated. The detective disturbed her in more ways than she wanted to admit. She lost her disciplined composure with him. Darn it, she lost her wits.

It's for Nan.

She dialed Gage Gaynor's cell phone.

Gage sat back in a chair in his new office and looked at Wagner. "Okay, what do we have?"

"Too much," Wagner replied. "I'm more than happy to have you here. I liked Tom, but he was really slowing up." Wagner's old partner—one of the veterans in the department—had just retired.

"These are our active cases," Wagner said, giving Gage several files. "Most are routine. A domestic murder. A homeless man found dead in an alley. A robbery homicide.

"We have a confession in the first, but we need to do follow-up work on evidence and the perp's background. The homeless man . . ." He shrugged. "We have damned little there. Probably another homeless man. I have some snitches nosing around. The robbery? We think it's the same two men that have committed a series of robberies. The pattern and description is the same. Except they haven't killed before."

"That's it?"

"The current ones."

"Okay. Where do we start?"

"The robbery. Go back and interview all the other robbery victims. See if we can't get something new."

"Car?"

"A dark sedan. One person got a license plate number, but the car turned out to be stolen. No prints. They're careful."

"What kind of stores do they like?"

"Fast food, just before closing."

"A lot of kids work those places."

"That's probably why they choose them."

"And the killing?"

"Older woman. A manager."

Gage's cell phone rang. He took it out and pressed the talk button. "Gaynor"

"Detective Gaynor, Meredith Rawson."

He felt surprise. And a flicker of unexpected pleasure.

"What can I do for you, Counselor?"

"Nan Fuller."

The pleasure died. "What happened?"

"She saw Fuller watching her at the school. He's stalking her. She's terrified."

"I talked to him. He didn't like it."

"What can we do?"

"He didn't violate the protective order?"

"No. He didn't approach her. But he wanted her to see him."

"Unless he goes near her . . ."

"I know." He heard the weariness in her voice. Had she gotten any sleep lately?

He hoped she'd gotten more than he had. He had spent the past day worrying about his brother. He had compiled a list of possible employers but he dreaded asking them to do him a favor. He hated asking favors. Especially when he couldn't vouch that his brother would be a responsible worker.

He dismissed the thought and concentrated on the conversation. "Do you want me to talk to him again?"

"I don't know. I just thought you should be aware of it."

"You're right. Morris have any luck with your case?"

"No, not yet. Do you think Fuller . . .?"

"I checked his schedule. He was on duty that night."

"That lets him out, then."

"Not entirely. He could have friends. I'll have another little talk with him."

"Thank you."

There was something in her voice that alerted him. "Has anything else happened?"

A short silence, then, "Two anonymous calls. Silence, then heavy breathing. It wasn't just a wrong number."

He swore to himself. "Morris doing anything about it?" He knew how impossible it was to trace calls, especially with today's throwaway cell phones.

"He's doing what he can. I take it there isn't much."

He knew he should hang up. He wasn't sure why she intrigued him as much as she did. And God knew he had enough problems in his life without someone like her. *You're forgetting a hard lesson.*

"Have you moved back to your home?"

"Yes."

"Morris aware of that?"

"He's having cars drive by, and he checked the alarm system himself. And I have a revolver now."

Wagner eyed him curiously. He wondered whether his voice had changed. It was time to hang up. More than time to go. She had let him know the other day that she had no interest in him. Yet he found himself loath to do so.

"I'll get back to you on Fuller."

"Thank you."

"Are you okay?"

"No."

It was a confession he was sure she hadn't meant to make.

"Look, can I take you to dinner tonight? We can talk about Fuller and what steps we should take." Just as she probably hadn't panned to admit a weakness, neither had he planned to set himself up for rejection again.

Hesitation on the other end of the line, then, "Yes."

"Where would you like me to pick you up?"

"At my office."

"When?"

"Seven?"

"I'll be there." He hung up.

Wagner raised an eyebrow. "Counselor?"

Gage debated whether to answer or not, but they were working together. Partners shared. He'd always been reticent but this was no big deal. It was business.

"Meredith Rawson. Her house was broken into, and she was attacked a few nights ago."

"I heard. It's not your case."

"We were working together on something else."

"She's the legendary ice queen," Wagner said. "Or so rumors go."

"Right now, she's a lady in trouble," Gage retorted. "Nothing more."

"Okay. Just a friendly warning."

"Let's get back to work," Gage said.

"It's your life, pal."

"Exactly."

Meredith held the receiver for a moment. The invitation had been as unexpected as her reply.

She didn't date cops.

She never had. It wasn't snobbery. She respected the dangerous job they did. Perhaps she understood too much. She knew the pressures on them, on their wives and children.

She didn't have time for relationships. Occasionally she went to the opera or symphony with a male friend, but she had not been involved in a relationship for a long time. Her practice was her life right now.

Truth was, she wanted to avoid entanglements. If she was attracted to a man, she usually ran in the other direction, and as fast as possible. Her parents' marriage of icy courtesy was something she never wanted.

She admitted she was attracted to Gage Gaynor. She'd never believed in the looks-across-a-crowded-room type of attraction, but she'd felt a connection the first time she met him. Perhaps that was why she had given him a really bad time.

He obviously didn't hold grudges. He had tried to help her, and she had practically shoved his help in his face. At the very least, she owed him an apology.

And she did want to talk about Fuller. She wanted to know if he might be her attacker. She wanted Nan safe and free from fear.

Excuses. She wanted to see him.

She felt safe with him. She liked his easy confidence. And she wanted to know . . .

Know what that kiss might have led to.

Just remembering it made her nerves react with anticipation.

She would run a brush through her short hair. Add some lipstick. Nothing else. It was a business engagement.

Yes. A business engagement.

Gage figured he had enough time before dinner to drop by Dom Cross's shelter for teenagers.

The shelter was located in one of New Orleans's less desirable business communities. The rent was cheaper there but the shelter was still accessible to the runaways who had escaped wretched home lives to come to New Orleans and found only more misery.

Dom was an ex-con himself. He'd been convicted as a teenager of car theft and served time in Angola. He'd been befriended by a priest and had been recruited by him upon his release to help at his shelter. When Father Murphy had died, Dom had taken over.

Because of his record, some police officers were wary of the man, but Gage had met him through Clint. Someone had suggested Dom Cross might be able to help Clint when Gage had found him high on drugs. It had been too late.

Though the two had met and Dom had tried to get Clint involved in the center, Clint's friends—and their drugs—were far more tempting to a rebellious young man than what Clint called a "do-gooder."

Yet after Clint's arrest, Dom had visited him in jail and the two had connected in some way. Perhaps because Dom had been there himself.

Dom was playing basketball in the gym with some of the kids. The Cajun influence in his family tree was obvious. He was not as tall as Gage and carried more weight. But though his black hair was graying, he moved with an agile grace as he dunked a ball in the basket.

Then he apparently saw Gage, and a broad grin spread over his face as he said something to one of the boys and left the floor.

He held out his hand to Gage, then pulled him to him in a bear hug. "You're a sight for sore eyes."

"Maybe not when I tell you what I want."

Dom immediately sobered. "Should we go into my office?"

Gage nodded and walked alongside the man whom he respected as much as anyone he knew.

When they were seated in the small cubbyhole Dom called an office, Gage studied him. "You look well."

"I feel well. Just got a new grant. It means we can finally expand. One of my boys also offered to give us that new roofing we need."

One of his "boys" meant a New Orleans businessman who had gone through Dom's center.

"Let me know if I can help." Roofing had been one of Gage's various jobs as a teenager.

"I would rather you spend time with the boys."

"Work . . ."

"I know. I didn't mean to lay a guilt trip on you. God knows we need as many honest—and understanding—cops as we can get. Now what can I do for you? It's none of my boys, is it?"

"My brother. Clint thinks he has a good chance for parole, but he needs a job. I know you're miraculous at finding them."

"Now that *is* good news. I'll see what I can do. Where is he going to stay?"

"Probably with me for a while."

"I'll go up and talk to him."

"He's into computers now."

"Good. That should help." He studied Gage for a moment. "Something else going on?"

"Do you know anything about the Rawson family?"

Dom didn't move, but a muscle throbbed in his throat. Then, "I know of them, of course."

That casual answer contradicted the sudden tenseness of his body.

Gage tried not to show his surprise. Dom was one of the most open men he knew. Yet it was obvious that he was keeping something to himself.

He decided to probe. "I think the daughter, Meredith Rawson, might be in danger. She was nearly run down at a hospital and her home has been trashed. She's also received threatening phone calls."

Dom didn't say anything.

"Her father's name also came up in connection with an old murder. A man named Prescott."

Dom sighed heavily.

"If you know anything . . ."

"Why would I know something?"

"Your reaction a few seconds ago."

Dom leaned back in his chair. "Prescott was the reason I went to prison," he said. "I was still there when he was killed."

"I've never known exactly what happened."

"He loaned me his car. He later said I stole it."

"And you spent how long in prison for that?"

Dom smiled slowly. "A long time."

"Why would Prescott do that?"

Dom shrugged. "A friend of his wanted something I had."

"What?"

"Now that, my friend, is between God and me."

"Maybe it was connected with Prescott's death."

"Not many people liked Prescott. He was a liar and a cheat," Dom said in a calm voice that belied his words. "Now tell me more about your brother."

It was obvious Dom wasn't going to say more.

They talked about several of Dom's boys for a few moments, then Gage rose. "Thanks for looking into a job for my brother."

"Any time. You know I always liked him."

Preoccupied, Gage left the center. He had another item on his agenda now: a search back through the police files concerning Dom.

thirteen

Meredith tried to work as she waited for Gage Gaynor. She had been hungry earlier, but now her stomach was full of butterflies.

She'd been an awkward child, more comfortable with books than with people, and she'd never been popular as a teenager. Her stomach always churned when she had to confront people or when attention centered on her. It had taken her years on a debate team to conquer her fear of speaking, and she was never entirely at ease in social situations.

She'd always known she wasn't the beauty that her mother had been. Not even close to it. She was tall and awkward. Her face was lean and sharp like her father's, not oval and symmetric like her mother's.

The comparison had always wounded her. She would see a visitor's double take when she was introduced. She had refused to participate in the Krewe parades, feeling as if she would stand out as the ugly duckling.

She'd grown out of that feeling of inferiority. Her face had filled out a little and she'd learned how to dress to suit her figure. Confidence had been hard-earned.

But now she felt like that schoolgirl again. She hated that feeling. Another strike against Gage Gaynor for bringing all that insecurity back. She needed to feel secure and confident now. She needed to control her own life. She did not need the anticipation bubbling inside despite her best efforts to quench it.

Meredith glanced back at the computer. Between calls to Lulu Starnes, she'd tried researching the woman on the Internet, using some sources she shouldn't. She could find nothing. Lulu Starnes must be the most law-abiding citizen in Louisiana. Meredith couldn't find so much as a parking ticket.

The woman certainly wasn't social as Meredith's mother had been or Meredith knew she would have seen the name. That was unusual behavior for a graduate of the school she'd attended. Most of the students were the daughters of the New Orleans elite and then became the New Orleans elite.

From the address Meredith had, it appeared that though Lulu had attended St. Agnes, she'd not gone on to marry among the city's elite. The address was in a working-class neighborhood of fifty-year-old bungalows.

She tried the number she had again. No answer. Frustrated, she decided to run home and change clothes. Once there, she slipped into a new pair of slacks, then tried to call again.

This time a woman answered.

"Mrs. Starnes?"

"Yes."

"My name is Meredith Rawson. My mother is Marguerite Thibadeau."

"Maggie?"

Meredith had never heard her mother referred to as Maggie. "Yes, I think so."

"How is she?"

"She's ill."

"I'm sorry to hear that."

"She asked me to do something for her. I need some help. Could you possibly see me?"

"Anything for Maggie. I haven't seen her for years but I owe her a lot."

"Why?" Meredith asked. "If you don't mind my asking. If you do, just tell me it's not my business."

"She didn't tell you?"

"She's in a coma. I got your name from her yearbook."

"Oh, God," Lulu Starnes said. "I'm so sorry. I haven't seen her in thirty years, but she was my friend then. Probably the only one I had at school."

Meredith was silent, allowing the silence to ask questions for her.

"I was a scholarship student," Lulu said. "Maggie befriended me, insisted I was invited to parties, made me one of her crowd. Then she dropped out. I didn't see her again. But I'll never forget her."

"I wonder if we can meet tomorrow. I would like to hear more about her then."

"I teach at a high school. I'll be home at five. I had a meeting this afternoon."

"Would six be all right? That will give you some time unless it's your supper hour."

"It's just me and Nicky, my dog. My husband died a year ago."

"I'm sorry."

"Thank you. I would like to hear about Maggie."

"At six then," Meredith said.

"I'll be there. Do you need directions?" She went on to give detailed directions.

Meredith finished dressing, wishing she didn't care so much about tonight, then left for the office.

Lulu Starnes had given her a completely new perspective on her mother. *Maggie.* Someone who took an outsider under her wing and obviously protected her.

Where had Maggie gone? When had Marguerite taken over?

She looked at her watch as she arrived at her office. Ten to seven. Sarah had gone home early to attend a junior high basketball game. Becky had left an hour ago.

The building was nearly vacant and had that lonely feel that buildings often did after their occupants disappeared into their other lives. Meredith's world had changed in the past few days. She once would never have had a second thought about walking down the hall alone. But now a flicker of apprehension ran down her spine.

I'm not going to live in fear. She kept reminding herself of that as she said hello to Reggie, then walked to the rest room before heading to her office. As she emerged, she saw Gaynor strolling toward her.

He was early. Not much. Just a few moments. She appreciated people who were on time. She was the next thing to obsessive about being on time herself.

"Hi," he said.

He looked terrific. He wore a sports jacket over a light blue shirt that was unbuttoned at the neck. His sandy hair had been tamed and his eyes held a hint of a smile.

"Hello. You're early." She meant it as a pleasantry but it came out more as an accusation.

"Sorry," he said.

"Don't be. I was . . ." She started to say *apprehensive*, but she didn't want to show weakness. That was a no-no in her world. "I was just putting on some lipstick."

His lips parted into a smile that was seductive and teasing. "You never do what you're told, do you?"

She gave him a questioning look.

"You're alone here."

"Just for a few moments. My paralegal left not too long ago and there's a guard downstairs. I also have my revolver with me."

"What is it?"

"A Smith and Wesson Titanium .38 Chief's Special."

He nodded. "Do you know how to use it?"

"Yes. Cliff Morris checked me out, in fact."

"Good. Ready to go?"

She nodded.

"Do you have your car here?" he asked.

"Yes."

"Then we'll eat near here. I can bring you back and follow you home."

"That's not necessary," she protested. She remembered what had happened the last time he'd followed her home. She was resolved that it would not happen again.

"Yes, it is."

He placed a hand at the small of her back as they entered the elevator, a small courtesy that sent electricity through her system. The elevator seemed smaller than usual when the doors closed. Warmer.

His hand stayed at the small of her back. The electricity between them sparkled little internal blazes. Three floors later, the doors opened too slowly. Or too quickly.

Dammit. She never reacted like this. Never.

Nonetheless he guided her out, his hand still protectively on her. She nodded at Archie.

"Are you gone for the evening, Ms. Rawson?"

"Yes. Thanks for looking out for me," she said.

"Any time."

She turned toward Gage. "Archie takes very good care of me. Archie, this is Detective Gaynor from the NOPD."

Archie held out his hand. "Ms. Rawson is one of my favorite tenants."

"I'll take good care of her, too," Gage said.

As they walked out of the door, Meredith basked in the protectiveness. She had never asked for it or even wanted it before. She had always taken care of herself. She took great pride in that fact. But her world had been turned upside down these past few days. For the first time in several days, she didn't feel she had to have eyes in the back of her head. She didn't have to keep touching her purse to reassure herself that the revolver was still there.

"Any place special you would like to eat?" he asked.

The question startled her. She had no idea what he liked. She really had no idea as to who he was. The only time they had eaten together was when she had suggested muffalettas. She had no idea of his budget or even whether she should split the bill with him.

"You choose," she said.

"Do you like Cajun or American?"

"Both."

He turned and gave her a wry look. "Neither of us are being much help, are we?"

She had to smile at that. They were like two people on a first date, which couldn't be further from the truth. This was a business meal. Hadn't she spent the last few hours convincing herself of that?

"What about Deanie's, if it's not too crowded?" she suggested. The restaurant was a moderately priced neighborhood eatery on Lake Pontchartrain and famous for its seafood. It was light and airy, not particularly romantic.

He nodded his approval. "Good."

He led her to a plain blue sedan with a rack on its roof and opened the door for her. She was used to the courtesy and yet there was something extraordinarily sensual in the way he offered his hand to help her into the seat. The touch was electric. For a second her legs felt boneless as a warm longing spread inside her. She froze, afraid he might feel her reaction, hear the increased tempo of her heart, of her breathing.

His hand lingered, his fingers splaying against her skin.

She breathed deeply, forcing air from her lungs. She sat down abruptly, jerking her hand away from his.

He looked at her with veiled eyes and a small twist of his lips as he shut the door and strolled to the driver's side. Once inside, he started the car, all his attention on backing up and driving out of the lot. She saw his quick glances to the left and right and to the rearview window.

The glances reminded her too much of the last few days, of the terror and the fear. She turned her thoughts, instead, to the car. The interior was clean and neat. She'd noticed a briefcase in the back as she'd stepped in.

He reached over and turned on the CD player, and the low, soft sound of plaintive blues filled the interior.

The sultry music flowed through the car, increasing the intimacy levels substantially.

She didn't need more intimacy. His proximity was intimate enough. His large frame dominated the vehicle as did his sure, confident control of the straight shift. A tangy scent told her he had recently shaved. Darn, but it was enticing.

She sat closer to the door than to him. The better to observe him, she told herself. But really it was cowardice. She didn't want that electricity to grow any stronger.

She looked outside. Dusk was settling around the city and traffic was moving steadily. She checked behind them.

"No one is following us," he said, as if reading her mind.

"I wonder if I will ever stop looking back now."

"When we catch him, you will."

"Are you so confident?"

"It's not my case, but yes, I am. Your intruder wanted something. If he or she wanted something, then there's a clue."

"You don't think the attack on me was just anger?"

"It could have been timed to delay you. Someone might have wanted to search your house. He certainly wanted to make an impression. The more I think of how your house looked, the less I think it was personal, committed out of rage against you specifically."

"Why?"

"It was mechanical destruction. No passion in it. No writing on the walls or mirrors. Things were sliced neatly, not in the jagged stabs that usually accompany rage. There was a purpose. A sane purpose."

She shuddered slightly. "And the anonymous calls?"

His shoulders shrugged. "Perhaps someone is trying to tell you to stop doing something you're doing. Do you have any active cases that you think might irritate someone?"

"Every legal case irritates someone," she observed dryly.

He grinned. "Dumb question on my part," he admitted. "What about more irritating than usual?"

"That's hard to judge. I do a lot of domestic violence cases. I also volunteer at the women's shelter and advise women on their legal rights. I suspect you know how insane some of their husbands or boyfriends become."

"A volunteer?" He sounded so surprised that she took it as an insult.

"You didn't think I would volunteer?"

"No, ah, I know your mother did. But you have a legal practice and . . . hell, I'm just digging a deeper hole, aren't I?"

"Almost to China, Detective."

"Maybe I should be quiet."

"Maybe you can tell me something about yourself."

"What?" Suspicion punctuated his word.

"Where do you live?"

"I have a camelback house in the Garden District."

Camelback. She smiled at the term and the fact that he lived in one. It was a housing style unique to New Orleans. Tucked among the Garden District's mansions were more modest streets with camelback and shotgun houses. The camelback featured a second floor but only at the back of the house, a design that at one time helped residents finagle out of a tax levied on homes with complete second floors.

Somehow she had imagined him in a cabin on stilts in a bayou rather than a camelback in the Garden District. He must have purchased it in the early 1990s when the city was in a housing slump. Those houses were expensive now. Anything in the Garden District was.

"Any family?" she asked. The question had plagued her. He didn't wear a ring but . . .

He threw her a quick glance, taking his gaze off the road for only a fraction of an instant. His gaze immediately turned back to the road. "Only one brother now. I suppose you know about that."

So he remembered their conversations. "Yes. Is he still—?"

"In prison? Yes. He's up for parole in the next few weeks."

She had her answer. *Only one brother now.* She wasn't sure whether the fact that he had no wife or children was comforting or not.

"That must be difficult for you."

"More for him," he said shortly, his tone cutting off the conversation.

She said nothing else until they drove into the restaurant

parking lot. The restaurant was crowded but she was recognized. She often brought clients here. The atmosphere was comfortable and nonthreatening, and the food was good.

In a few moments they had a table. "Influence," he remarked. "I like it."

"I come here often."

They both ordered barbecue shrimp.

"Tell me what happened with Rick Fuller," he said after they each ordered a glass of wine.

"Nan saw him at her children's school. He parked where she always picks up the boys. She thinks he made sure she saw him. Of course, he would just say he wanted to see his sons. But it terrified her. She took precautions driving back to the shelter, though she believes he knows exactly where she is. She's agreed to file for divorce but she doesn't want the house because she's afraid he will come after her."

He worried with his glass of wine. "I talked to him. He didn't like it. I'm not sure how far I can push him without his taking it out on Nan and the children."

She knew the same fear. Perhaps she'd hoped he had a magic bullet to solve the problem. "Surely his job—"

"If I talk to him again, he might well think his job is in jeopardy. He has to know that chances of promotion are slim now."

She remembered what Gage had said a few days ago. *If Fuller lost his job, he might well snap.* For the first time, she saw some uncertainty in his eyes. She liked it far more than a bluff assurance. It meant he cared about Nan Fuller. Really cared. It wasn't just his job. That, she knew, was over. He was off Public Integrity. But he still cared. Something shifted inside her. "Perhaps you shouldn't do anything now," she said. "Nan is going to move. We're asking the court to limit his access to the children. I'll talk to his lawyer."

He nodded. "Go through him. Don't talk to Fuller on your own."

"Why? Do you think he's the one—?"

"He's not the one who tried to run you down or tossed your home," he said. "I checked again on his movements that night. He was on duty. In fact he was booking a suspect at the time of your attack." He hesitated, then added, "But he might have taken advantage of the attack on you and made the anonymous calls. And if he's taken that first step, it could lead do something else. He could take his rage out on either you or Nan. He has a lot of it inside."

"Should he be on the force?"

"No," he said.

"Then why is he?"

"Years ago, I partnered with a man. I often went to his home. I liked his wife tremendously. I never saw the signs. Not until I visited her in the hospital and realized he'd badly beaten her. I told my superior and advised his wife to press charges. He was suspended. The next day he killed her." His fingers fumbled with his glass, and when she met his gaze, she saw a hint of dampness in his eyes. Gage Gaynor. *The tough cop.* So that was why he had been at the hearing.

"You're that worried about Nan?"

"Yes," he said shortly.

She took a sip of wine. "There has to be something. . . ."

"I'll watch him. Perhaps we can get something on him that has nothing to do with Nan."

That was obviously the best he could do. Much more than she had expected. She changed the subject. She had to, before she became lost in those green eyes that were no longer cool, or icy, but intense with emotion.

"How is the Prescott case coming? Have you contacted my father yet?" Then she realized how telling that question was. She should know. Her father should have told her if the police had contacted him.

If he caught the implication, he ignored it. "I've been taken off the case," he said. "I'm now on active homicides."

"You weren't on it very long, were you?"

"Nope."

"Can you tell me why?"

"No. Not because I won't, but because I can't. I really wasn't given a reason other than I'm needed elsewhere."

"Why didn't someone realize that earlier?"

"That's an excellent question, Counselor."

At first, she'd been annoyed by his use of "Counselor," almost as if it were an insult. Now it sounded more like respect. "I don't understand."

"I was given the case by one superior and it was taken away by another," he said. "Not only that, I was taken off cold cases altogether and moved to active homicides. That's not only unusual, it's unheard of. It has to be the shortest tour of duty in departmental history."

He was telling her something other than the main recital of facts. "Someone called you off."

"Looks that way."

"Who?"

His gaze bore into hers.

"No," she said. "My father wouldn't do that." But even she heard the doubt in her voice.

"But is it possible?"

She searched his face for a long time. "He was never implicated in the slightest way."

"He was the last person known to see Prescott. The case was closed too quickly and was never investigated thoroughly. And now this closure. Could your father have that kind of influence?"

She shook her head, sharp edges of disappointment cutting into what had been a growing pleasure at being with him. "My father would not be involved with anything as messy as a coverup," she said. "Much less a murder. I suggest you look elsewhere."

He took a roll from the basket just delivered to their table. "Well, I'm off it anyway. Tell me more about Meredith Rawson."

She was cautious this time. "Not much to tell."

"What do you like to do in your spare time?"

"What spare time?"

The left side of his lips turned up slightly. "A workaholic?"

"A private practice with one attorney requires it."

"Okay, what about the rare occasions when you do have time?"

"A good book. Good music. Theater."

"No significant other?"

"That's a personal question."

"Maybe I have a personal interest."

His voice had lowered, his drawl deepened. The air of expectancy thickened between them. She had to keep telling herself he had just practically accused her father of conspiracy. He wanted something from her, just as her father had always wanted something from her.

"No," she said.

"That's hard to believe. You're a very attractive woman."

Not beautiful. Not lovely. Both terms that applied to her mother. Yet his gaze told her he did think her attractive. And desirable. She felt as if she could get lost in those eyes. How had she ever thought them cold? They were green fire now.

She was saved from having to reply by the server who delivered two steaming plates of barbecue shrimp, a Louisiana delicacy that required extremely indelicate eating. The shelled shrimp rested in a butter barbeque sauce. Several packages of wet towels accompanied the meal.

Directing her gaze toward the food and away from the very disturbing man across from her, she picked up a shrimp with her fingers, sauce dripping from it, and tasted it slowly, savoring every flavor.

Then she made the mistake of looking up. He was watching her with amusement in his face though his eyes still glittered with something close to lust.

She licked her lips and met his stare head-on. "Gage," she said, using his name for the first time, her tongue playing over the sound of it. "Where did the name come from? I never heard it before."

"My mother loved movies. She told me it came from one, but I've never been able to find it."

"And your brother?"

"Clint. The movie star."

"And your mother?"

"She died years ago."

"I'm sorry."

"It was a long time ago." No emotion now. But she knew he rarely showed emotion.

His reply reminded her of her own mother. She had planned to go back tonight.

"How is your mother?"

So he had read her mind again. He had a habit of doing that.

"Holding her own. I'll stop over there later."

"I'll follow you," he said in that deep, sexy voice that caused her heart to beat a steady tattoo in her chest. There was obviously to be no discussion. She could no more stop him from following her than she'd been able to the other night.

Her appetite left her, fading in the intensity that had deepened rather than lessened with the delivery of the food. She watched as he tackled the slippery, buttery shrimp with his fingers, the only way to eat them. His expression of unabashed pleasure made her pulse speed up.

She took a sip of wine and concentrated on her own meal. She tried another shrimp, licking the butter sauce from her lips. Sinful and messy, they were delectable.

Then she made the mistake of looking at him again. He was smiling, a dimple she hadn't noticed before indenting his chin. She felt riveted by his attention, as if a force field enveloped them, shutting out every other person in the room.

Somehow she finished the shrimp. They both declined dessert and he paid the bill, despite her protest. He quieted it with one look, then pulled out her chair in a courtly manner that she had not expected. His hand rested on her shoulder, his touch burning straight through to her soul.

He took her hand as they left the restaurant. Natural. It felt so very natural. Her long fingers fit his large hand perfectly and she found herself drawing closer to him. An almost palpable tension leapt between them, filling her with a raw need so strong and deep that it was like a body blow.

They reached the car, but instead of opening the door for her, he put his arms around her, pressing her back against the door. He leaned down and his lips slowly lowered to meet hers, skimming more than pressing, as if posing their own question. Her mouth caressed his, assenting—no, more than assenting. Asking. Wanting. Demanding, even, in some primitive way she couldn't control. Her mind warned, but her body responded as their lips explored and teased, and liking the taste, ventured further.

Laughter interrupted like a splash of freezing water. Obviously reluctant, he drew away slightly and looked at her. "I'm afraid we're making a spectacle of ourselves."

Meredith felt like a teenager in love for the first time, and the thought terrified her. She straightened, trying to gather her wits about her. "We had better go," she said, hearing the hoarseness in her own voice.

He raised his right hand and touched her cheek. "I could . . ."

But he stopped himself and his hand fell. He lowered the other arm that had held her against the car, and opened the door. She noticed his hand had a slight tremor. Did hers, too?

Her body still reacting to the feel of his, her lips slightly swollen from his kiss, her blood racing from the unexpected explosion of sensations, she stepped inside.

Dear Mother in heaven but she wanted him.

He got in his side of the car. "A nightcap at my house?" he asked as his gaze met hers.

The invitation was too beguiling to refuse. She wanted to know more about Gage Gaynor. Much more.

She swallowed hard, fighting conflicting needs.

"Yes," she finally said.

fourteen

It was all Gage could do to keep his gaze from her.

He knew the dangers of allowing his attention to wander from the road. God knew he'd seen enough disaster that resulted from distraction.

It was equally difficult to keep his hand from reaching for hers.

He couldn't quite believe the intensity of his feelings, of the need resounding inside. It wasn't all sexual, though he would be lying if he said that wasn't part of it. Sexual wouldn't be dangerous.

This *was* dangerous. He liked her. He was intrigued by her. He wanted to be with her. Worst of all, he knew he would rather be with her than paddling the bayous in his canoe.

He caught himself smiling at that.

"Hey," she said.

He glanced quickly in her direction.

"You're smiling."

"Is that so odd?"

"No, I like it," she said.

He liked it, too. He felt more relaxed than he had in years. Relaxed yet energized at the same time. Expectant.

Damn.

He stole another glance at her. The hot humid wind had ruffled her short hair, making her look more approachable. Her cheeks were flushed and her usually guarded blue eyes sparkled.

He drove to his house, which was not far from her office, and pulled into the drive. A canoe was visible in the fenced backyard, as well as a patch of roses that always embarrassed him when someone else saw it. Gaynor and roses. He'd always imagined he saw amusement in the eyes of his visitors.

As she stepped out of the car, even before he could get to her door, he saw her gaze turn toward the roses, then the canoe. "Is that why you have the rack on top?"

"Yes."

She smiled at his short and relatively uninformative answer. "I have never been canoeing."

His own words startled him. "I'd like to take you. I usually keep it at a small place I own but it needed some mending."

"Where?"

"A bayou south of here. It's peaceful there."

"And you like peace?" An element of surprise shaded her voice.

"If you had grown up where I did, you'd like peace, too."

She was silent. He knew she was probably aware of where he grew up. It would have been in the background information she'd gathered when he had testified.

The silence served to emphasize the difference between them. She had grown up in the mansions of New Orleans, he in the slums. She had probably gone to the best private schools; he had attended the worst public schools and had gained a scholarship only because he'd realized athletics was the fastest way out.

The fact that he'd once thought that skill would equalize him with her kind had proved a fantasy.

Remember that.

Then he heard Beast, who tore out of his dog door into the fenced backyard, racing around and barking furiously until he saw Gage. The dog came to an abrupt stop, tipped his head to regard the newcomer and let his long tongue loll out.

"This is Beast," he said. "He won't hurt you. Truth is, he wouldn't hurt a flea, but he scares the hell out of everyone."

She went to the fence and held out her hand. Beast first sniffed, then licked it with embarrassing eagerness.

She knelt. "Hi," she told the animal.

Beast palpitated with happiness.

"I'm going to sue you for alienation of affections," he said.

"But you need a witness," she retorted.

"One look at Beast slobbering over you would convince a jury."

A sly, mischievous smile curved her lips. "I can't help it. He's very charming."

"I've never heard that particular term used for Beast," he said with amusement. "Are you insinuating he's more charming than I am?"

She raised an eyebrow. "I can't answer on the grounds it might incriminate me."

He gazed down at her with an odd sense of contentment settling deep inside him. What was it about her that made him feel comfortable?

"It's hell to come in second to something that looks like Beast." He turned toward the front door, taking her hand as he did. She didn't resist, and her fingers curled around his.

Gage unlocked the front door and led her in, wondering what she would think about his odd little house.

Thank God, the housekeeper had been there three days earlier and he hadn't had a chance to trash it over the weekend. It was acceptable, though not, he knew, what she must be accustomed to. He knew where she lived, where her father lived. It was only a few miles away but it might as well be another world.

She stepped in, and Beast was there, having made his way through the dog door. He panted heavily but sat down in front of her and offered his paw.

She took it solemnly and gave Gage a look of delight. "He has very good manners."

"He thanks you," he said, inordinately pleased and at the same time displeased at that pleasure.

"Did you teach him that?"

He shrugged. "He's a smart dog."

"How did you find him?"

"A drug bust. Apparently, he was supposed to intimidate. He tried his best, but his heart wasn't really in it. He took one look at me and came over to the good side."

"You told me to get a dog. If I do, will you train him?"

"He shrugged. "I don't want to mislead you. I didn't train him. He trained himself."

Damn, if she kept looking at him like that with those blue eyes, he would take her right on the hall table.

He forced himself to stop looking and led the way into the living room. It was a man's space. A large leather sofa and two leather easy chairs were situated in front of a large television set. Bookcases surrounded a sound system.

He saw her gaze travel over the room, just as he had done with her office. "What's your pleasure? I have beer, scotch, bourbon, red wine."

"Beer."

He'd expected the red wine. But as usual, she surprised him. She was making a habit of that.

"Coming up. Make yourself comfortable."

He went into his kitchen. Small but functional. A bachelor, he'd been forced to learn to cook.

She followed. Beast followed her.

Alienation of affection, indeed. The damn dog had fallen in love.

He opened the fridge and pulled out a beer. "Glass?"

"Nope."

He must have looked startled because she chuckled and added, "You didn't think lady lawyers drank beer from the bottle? It's colder that way."

"I didn't think daughters of New Orleans's most prominent families drank beer from a bottle," he corrected.

She grimaced. "Don't tell me you're a reverse snob."

He probably was. He didn't want to admit it. Instead he reached in and grabbed a beer for himself. As he closed the door, he stepped back.

Into her.

Awareness shimmered between them. Thundered like a sudden Southern storm. A craving such as he had never known gnawed inside him. She looked up at him. He saw himself in her eyes and he was suddenly stronger, better than he was. He put the beers down and then reached out and touched her face. Soft. He trailed his thumb across her cheekbone and down to the small of her throat. He felt her pulse. Fast. Like his.

Gage lowered his head, though not much since she was tall, and his lips met hers. He lost himself in the feel of them, the receptiveness, the welcome. The passion that met his.

The kiss exploded into something else, something stronger, deeper. He ached for her. He ached for what he wanted from her, for what he wanted to give to her.

His arms went around her. He'd known when he brought her here that he'd be opening a part of him he'd shut off for years. Yet there hadn't been a choice. Like the tides of the ocean, her pull left him helpless to resist. All the dikes he'd built after his engagement had collapsed were crumbling.

He pulled back. "We're like water and oil," he said.

She gave him a crooked smile. "Who is which?"

He didn't answer for a moment, then muttered almost to himself. "I tried this before."

"And what happened?"

"Nothing good."

Her gaze never faltered. "*I* haven't tried this before."

He took a long breath. "Water and oil?"

"More like falling off a cliff."

Dammit. She looked so vulnerable. He knew she was anything but that. Yet in this moment, he understood her uncertainty. They had nothing in common. They had been adversaries. They would be adversaries again. She was a defense attorney. He was a cop. They were terrible for each other. Worse than water and oil.

But then he looked into the sea blue eyes again and was lost. To hell with reservations. Or consequences.

He kissed her again, felt her body lean into his, and he responded. Damn, but he responded. The building warmth was becoming an inferno, the ache in his groin intensifying. He felt the swelling and braced for the need he knew was coming.

Gage buried his fingers in her short curly hair that smelled like flowers. It was as soft as silk and twined around his fingers.

He touched her cheek, and the fire in her eyes seemed to smolder. The blue was like the hottest part of a flame, not the cool clear blue of the ice queen. He leaned over and his lips brushed hers, lightly at first.

Her lips were yielding, welcoming. Eager. His kiss deepened, his tongue entering her mouth. Teasing. Then engaging in a primitive mating game. She stilled for a moment, then responded with a passionate curiosity that kindled a recklessness he couldn't control.

Nothing mattered then except the need they created as they fed on each other, tasting, exploring, reacting. He wanted her. God, how he wanted her.

He pulled her tighter to him, his hands caressing her back, the nape of her neck. He slid his lips from hers and trailed them along the side of her cheek.

The desire within him was near explosion. He took a step away but he didn't take his hands from her. Instead they moved to her blouse and deftly unbuttoned it. Her breasts strained against the silk of her bra. He pulled down the straps and leaned down and nuzzled first one breast, then the other, feeling the nipples harden as her hands explored the back of his neck.

She uttered a small cry, and he sensed she was consumed by the same wild yearning as he.

"Meredith?" he asked, seeking permission.

She nodded. He took her by the hand and led her down

the hall to his large bedroom, dominated by his king-size bed. He turned on the small lamp that overlooked his desk and reached inside the top drawer of his nightstand, pulling out a small package. He halted there, uncertain. But he wanted everything to be right.

This time she took the lead. She unbuttoned his shirt, then helped him pull off the T-shirt he wore. Her hands roamed his chest, her fingers playing with the short crinkling hair.

The craving deep inside him proliferated with every touch, spreading like wildfire until every nerve end tingled with need.

He took her bra off, then unzipped her slacks and watched as she stepped out of them, standing only in a pair of flimsy panties. She was beautiful, her body taut with just the right curves.

He cupped her breasts, and he felt them swell. His gaze went to her face. Her lips were slightly damp and crooked into a small uncertain smile. Tenderness washed through him. "You're beautiful, you know."

She looked startled, as if she had never been told that before. Then she smiled, and it was as if the sun had suddenly paid a visit. She stood up on tiptoes and her lips skimmed his. "Thank you."

"A fact doesn't call for a thank-you," he said, putting his arms around her again, this time feeling her skin against his, relishing the warmth that played between them. His lips found her ear, nuzzling the lobe gently, and he enjoyed the sudden tenseness in her body.

His hands skimmed up her body. He familiarized himself with it, memorized it. He kicked off his shoes, then unzipped and pulled off trousers that were becoming unbearably snug.

He watched her eyes study him, then she held out her hands to him. He took them and together they sank down onto the bed.

Gage made himself go slow. He slipped off her panties,

then leaned over, his mouth seducing hers, his tongue inviting her to join with him.

Meredith had never felt this wild abandon before, had never been so bold with a man. She had never felt so at ease while at the same time so consumed by need.

Gage's mouth moved hungrily on hers, spreading a honeyed, wheedling warmth throughout her body. The warmth became heat, then a fever as her body melded into his.

She heard his heartbeat. It raced as rapidly as her own. Her hand moved instinctively to the back of his neck, teasing with whisper-soft strokes. As her hands coaxed forth reaction, so did her lips, meeting his with equal hunger until they were both caught in frantic eddies of desire that she knew couldn't be stopped.

His lips released hers and brushed over her cheek, then traveled down her body to her breasts and across her stomach. Surges of physical pleasure swamped her as his fingers explored farther. As her expectation climbed to an unbearable summit, he rose up over her, his manhood touching, teasing, playing against her. Craving overwhelmed her. She wanted him as she had never wanted a man before.

All the time, his hands caressed, soothing while burning, reassuring while inciting.

He turned away for a moment, and she heard the rustle of cellophane. Then he turned back to her and slowly entered her, the physical sensation causing her to gasp. It had been a very long time since she had been intimate, and even then it had been nothing like this, nothing like this . . . gnawing hunger of her body.

His movements became more urgent, and something wild and primal surged through her. She gasped at the growing intensity of the swells of pleasure rocking her as he plunged deeper and deeper, each stroke sending waves of ecstasy billowing through her.

Meredith reacted in a way she had never expected. Her body instinctively moved in an intimate exotic dance, her body melding with his in a kind of equality in which they both gave and took. The sensations built and built until, shuddering, he exploded in her, and she collapsed in hundreds of tingling vibrations.

He turned her so they lay side by side, breathing heavily. His lips touched hers in almost awed reverence as both their bodies shuddered with tremors from the aftermath.

His hand inched over and took hers. "Wow," he said.

That was a understatement as far as she was concerned. She'd never understood the glory of lovemaking. Now she did.

And it *was* glory. She relished every lingering reaction, every twinge. She hadn't realized that loving could be a gentle thing as well as a needy one.

He cradled her head with his arm. She snuggled next to him, feeling no need for words. There was a comfort in his presence, a sense of belonging in his arms.

It was Beast that interrupted the reverie. He placed his large head on her knee and started licking.

Gage chuckled. "Go away," he said.

Beast looked stricken but obediently stepped away and sat down, never taking his eyes away from them.

"I think he's jealous," Gage said in his slow Louisiana drawl. The sound of his voice rumbled through her.

Reluctantly she glanced at his bedside clock. Eleven.

"Stay with me," he said.

"I can't. I have to go by the hospital and . . ."

And she wasn't ready to stay with him all night. That would be a commitment of sorts. She had to think about this.

His eyes seemed to tell her he knew exactly what she was thinking. "All right," he said. "I'll take you to your car, or would you rather go to the hospital first? Either way, I'm sticking with you until you get home."

"You don't have to—"

"I do, Meredith. And not just because of tonight." He hesitated, then added slowly, "You don't owe me anything, and I don't owe you. It was chemistry, and . . ." His voice trailed off.

"And?" she prompted.

"You've been under a lot of strain."

"An easy mark, you mean."

"No, dammit."

"You want to see me home because of duty?"

"Well, there is some pleasure involved," he admitted wryly.

Chemistry. It was certainly that. But it had been more, and she sensed he knew it as well as she did, regardless of his denials. "And you?" she asked when it was very clear that he was not going to continue. "What is your excuse? Have you been under pressure?"

He sat up, swung his legs over the side of the bed and gave her a crooked grin. "Except for tonight, this has not been my best week."

"Why?" She couldn't turn her gaze away from him, from the firm, hard body that was so tanned and fit. Her body still tingled from his lovemaking. She thought the memory would always be in every fiber of her body.

He didn't answer. But as he had said, neither of them should expect anything from the other. A one-night stand, so to speak.

Had she hoped for anything else? She certainly hadn't wanted any entanglements. She had eschewed those long ago.

She watched as he stood and pulled on briefs, then jeans. He looked incredibly sexy as he stood shirtless and with his hair messed.

He held out his hand. "You never had that beer."

"No," she said.

"Now?"

"No." Her comfort zone was gone, lost in the indifference of her host.

He drew a T-shirt over his head, and gathered her clothes and handed them to her. He was taking her at her word after she said she had to leave. No argument. No discussion.

It was what she wanted. Why did she feel so betrayed? She disliked people who played games and now she was angry because he hadn't. Not angry. Disappointed. Frighteningly disappointed.

She wouldn't let him see it. She put on her bra, then her blouse. She needed the armor it provided her. She concentrated on that. Then she reached for her panties and finally her slacks.

"Bathroom?" she asked.

"On the left," he said.

She went down the hall and turned left into a large bathroom. Definitely remodeled. Older houses did not have elaborate bathrooms. This one had both a tub and large separate shower. Several clean towels were folded beside the wash basin.

She wondered whether it was the one he used, or a guest bath. If so, who were the guests? And he'd had protection in a drawer of his nightstand beside the bed. She didn't like the obvious answer to both observations.

Meredith looked at herself in the mirror that stretched across one side of the wall. Her hair was totally mussed. She ran her fingers through the curls, trying to bring back some semblance of order. But she could do nothing about the flush of her cheeks or the glazed look of her eyes.

She looked guilty as hell and felt guiltier. She had not participated in the sexual freedom of her generation. She didn't make love unless there was a long-standing relationship of some kind. She never just "hopped" in bed with someone.

Until now.

Weighed down by the fact, and by apparently how meaningless it had been to Gage, she washed her face to erase some of the telltale color, the tears that glimmered in her eyes.

Dammit.

She summoned a smile, then left the room. He was standing in the kitchen, watching a coffeemaker brew.

He turned. "I thought you might like some coffee first."

She would. She wouldn't sleep tonight at any rate, so she might as well indulge her love for caffeine. But that meant staying in his presence longer. She didn't want that. She feared she would reach out and touch his face again, and take his hand in hers. She feared the charged air that was still between them, and detested the fact that the need she had for him had been fed but not sated.

She looked around the house for more hints about its owner, but strangely she picked up few clues. The furniture was comfortable, the television big. But other than that the interior was bland, without character. Then she thought of the roses outside and Beast, who'd padded alongside her and now sat perfectly still at her feet.

The dog looked up at her pleadingly, and she leaned over and scratched his ears. She'd never had a dog though she had always wanted one. Her father wouldn't hear of it, and then she was in college and later was simply gone from home too much to be fair to an animal. She wondered how a cop managed to have time to care for him.

Gage handed her a cup of coffee. Black. He'd noticed her preference at one time or another. Or perhaps he didn't have cream and sugar.

He looked at her for a long moment after she took the cup in both hands. Intimacy was in that look, and something else she couldn't identify. She thought he was going to say something but he seemed to stop himself.

He waited until she'd finished her coffee, then turned toward the door. "Let's go."

BISBEE

Holly looked through the on-line New Orleans newspaper with special interest. Today was the day her husband had planned to announce his race for the U.S. House of Representatives. He had to file with the state within the next three weeks.

There was no mention of any announcement.

Because she and her son would not be standing with him?

She had sat in on strategy sessions although she'd always been silent, just as she had been meant to be. She was there as an ornament, not for any meaningful contribution.

She was the daughter of one of the most powerful judges

in Louisiana, and she was deemed a distinct asset, along with her precocious, photogenic son.

Had Randolph delayed the announcement until he could find her? Was he afraid of questions as to her whereabouts?

One thing she knew for sure, her existence was a decided threat to Randolph now. Yet it was a weapon as well. She knew he had gotten rid of a body, and that endangered his reputation—and possibly his freedom.

He would not want her to surface. He would far prefer that she died in some fabricated scheme, like a botched kidnapping. But what about Harry? Their son was smart enough to know they had not been stolen away. Would that knowledge condemn him as well?

Was Randolph really that evil?

When she returned home she would write some letters, send them to people she felt she could trust, though they were few in number. Incredibly few, in fact. Still, she would do that. Then she would let Randolph know that others knew she was alive and well. If he let her disappear, then he could continue his life, perhaps even his political career. A tragedy could be an asset. He would milk it for all the sympathetic votes he could get.

Feeling a little better now about her prospects and her hopes for a new life, she left the computer and went over to where Harry was flipping through a picture book.

At last, she was taking a little of her own life back. It might be one small step at a time, but at least she'd started.

fifteen

Meredith sat in her car outside of Lulu Starnes's home.

She was early, and she'd been taught that it was just as rude to be early as it was to be late.

She also needed a few moments to think.

Her world seemed to be disintegrating ever faster. All that precious control she thought she had was crumbling.

She had made a fool out of herself last night. She'd lowered her barriers and then run.

She never ran.

Or had she been running all her life? Now she was uncertain whether she had been running from or to something.

After they left Gage's house last night, he had driven her to her car, then followed her to the hospital and waited outside while she went up to her mother's room.

There had been no change. Except her mother seemed paler. Her breathing even more shallow.

How much time did her mother have? How long before it was too late to let her mother know that her daughter was found? And safe?

Meredith had allowed herself to be distracted. She was still distracted. Her body glowed while her mind scolded. Guilt roiled inside. She'd leaned over and kissed her mother's cool face, then left.

She'd averted her face from Gage's car as she reached her own. Yet she couldn't control her body or even her thoughts as she drove home, knowing he was behind her.

When they'd arrived, he insisted on going inside and checking her house. She stood outside, afraid to follow. Afraid of the heat that they generated together. Then he returned to the door and stood there, his green eyes searching hers.

She ignored the question in them, though her heart beat erratically. "Thank you," she said awkwardly.

"You're welcome," he said, equally polite though a muscle twitched in his throat. "Good night."

She nodded, wanting to stretch out her hand to him yet knowing if she did, she would not want to let him go. He was a loner. That fact radiated from him.

He obviously disliked commitments as, she told herself, did she.

He walked away, and she quickly shut and locked the door, locking him out as well. Still, she went to the window and watched him leave. She'd never felt quite so lonely and inadequate before.

Why couldn't she accept what he was offering? Friendship. Wonderful sex.

She knew exactly why. A lifelong fear of relationships.

A wave of loneliness gushed through her. Had she made a terrible mistake?

She willed away thoughts of last night and the confusion she felt and checked her watch again.

Six P.M. exactly.

She left the car and knocked on Mrs. Starnes's door. A dog barked with frenzied excitement.

No answer.

She knocked again, then rang the bell. Still no answer.

She knew she had the time right. And the correct address.

Unlike the Laxtons' near-mansion that she'd visited, this house was a small but well-kept bungalow. The front was ringed with flower beds. It was a house that looked loved.

She waited a moment, then tried the bell again. Again she heard the frenzied, even panicked, barking.

Meredith went around to the back of the house. Another garden filled the yard, along with a patio. Comfortable-looking lounge chairs were arranged around a glass table.

She knocked at the back door, then feeling a little like a Peeping Tom, peered through the window. The room was obviously the kitchen. She saw a fridge, its front covered with photographs, but couldn't see much else.

Meredith slumped into one of the chairs. She didn't know whether to wait or not. Then her gaze went to the detached garage. The door was closed but there was a window at the top. She walked over to it, stood on tiptoes and peered through the glass. A car was parked inside.

Did it belong to Mrs. Starnes? Was she visiting a neighbor or had she decided not to see Meredith? Perhaps the woman was sitting inside waiting for her to leave.

But Meredith had a bad feeling about this. Perhaps it was the frantic barking that hadn't stopped, as if the animal was trying to tell her something.

She decided to wait a few more minutes. Maybe Mrs. Starnes was simply late.

She sat on the porch. If the anxiety in her hadn't been deepening, she would have enjoyed the interlude. A bee buzzed among the flowers. Huge white blooms from a magnolia tree scented the air. Peaceful. Except for the barking.

Meredith looked at her watch. Thirty minutes past the time of the appointment. She stood and went to the front door. She tried the doorknob. To her surprise, the door opened easily.

"Mrs. Starnes?" she called out. "Mrs. Starnes?"

A dog—a small black-and-white Sheltie—jumped against her, dashed around her legs, demanding attention, bumped its nose against her legs, then ran toward another room and came back again. *Follow me.*

Apprehension flooded her, then outright fear. She followed the animal down the hallway. She stopped, and the dog barked again, treading back and forth until she took several more steps in the direction he indicated.

The hall led to the kitchen. Meredith stopped suddenly.

A middle-age woman lay motionless on the floor, her clothes stained with blood. Her eyes were wide open.

Meredith knew before she stooped and put her fingers to the woman's neck that she was dead. Horror chilled her. Disbelief. She knelt there, paralyzed by both.

Her mind started working again. *What if someone is still in the house?*

But she had been waiting outside for thirty minutes. . . .

Dear God, what if she had gone in then? *Perhaps the woman would still be alive.*

The dog stood as close as he could to Mrs. Starnes and made soft noises. Crime scene, she reminded herself. This was a crime scene.

"Come on, guy," she told the dog.

He wouldn't move. When she leaned down to pick him up, he growled and inched closer to his mistress. Her heart ached for the woman and the distressed animal.

Dammit. She was doing everything except what she knew she should do. *Call the police.*

Because of shock. She had been on the scenes of murders before, but this woman, who must be Mrs. Starnes, had known her mother, had been a friend. She had been waiting for Meredith, to give her answers.

Call the police!!! She looked around for a telephone, but long training stopped her. She knew the need to maintain the integrity of a crime scene. Her cell phone!

She took the revolver out of her purse and placed it on a table within quick reach, then found her cell phone and called 911 to report a murder.

Gage looked over his notes as Wagner drove. The two of them were returning from interviewing street people in the area where a homeless man had been stabbed nights before. Henry was the only name they had for the victim. The dead man had been wearing faded and torn fatigues and was in his fifties. Vietnam vet age. Had he been in the army and, if so, had his tour led to what he'd become? Gage had seen too much of that.

They were running fingerprints now through the FBI. They'd also sent them to the army.

Both he and Wagner were silent on the way back to head-quarters.

When they were ten minutes from the office, his cell phone rang.

"Gaynor," he said.

"Cliff Morris," the caller identified himself. "Miss Rawson called me. She had an appointment with an old friend of her mother's. When she arrived, no one answered. She tried the door and went in. The woman was dead. She called 911, then me. This is a homicide and out of my territory, but I thought you would like to know."

"What's the address?" Gage jotted it down. "Is she still there?"

"I think so."

"I'm on my way." Gage hung up, then called the desk. "I just heard about a murder in the Garden District. It's not far from where I live and I'm out there now. Do you want me to pick it up?"

A pause on the phone as someone went to check with an officer. Gage knew it was logical for Wagner and him to get the case. Because he was new, they had a reduced caseload. He had no intention, though, of mentioning the Rawson name. That could wait until he officially had the case.

The sergeant was back in several moments. "The lieutenant said go ahead."

Gage closed the phone.

Wagner glanced over at him. "What murder?"

"A woman in the Garden District. A detective just called. The lieutenant gave us a thumbs-up." He gave his partner the address. He didn't say more. Why in the hell had Meredith called Morris rather than him? And why was she wandering about the city without protection? What if she had arrived earlier and walked in on a killing?

His blood ran cold at the thought. This murder couldn't be a coincidence. Not now. Too much was whirling around Meredith. She was the eye of a hurricane.

"Step on it," he said.

Gage put the light on top of the unmarked departmental car as Wagner maneuvered through the crowded streets. They arrived at the address within minutes.

Uniformed police had beat them there. Two cars, lights still flashing, were in the driveway. An ambulance was parked on the street.

Gage barely waited for the car to stop before jumping out, badge in hand. He went past two officers, who nodded him inside. He followed voices to the kitchen.

Meredith was sitting in a chair next to the kitchen table. Her face was white, her jaw clenched, her expression grim. Her arms clutched a furry dog that looked like a miniature collie.

A woman lay on the floor several feet away. Two paramedics stood by. A uniformed officer was talking to them. Gage showed them his badge while casting a look toward Meredith.

Then he turned to the paramedic. "How long has she been dead."

"Hard to tell at the moment," he said. "At least an hour. The medical examiner will know more."

Gage turned back to Meredith. "What happened, Meredith?"

"You know each other?" one of the officers said.

"Ms. Rawson is a former assistant district attorney," Gage said.

The officer turned back to her. "You didn't say that."

"I didn't—" she started.

"What happened?" Gage broke in.

The officer shrugged. "What you see is all I know. We just got here a few moments before you, about the same time as the paramedics. It looks like a bullet wound. "

"Call the crime scene people," Gage said. "Then secure the scene and keep anyone else from coming inside." The paramedics left. The body couldn't be moved until the crime scene unit did its work. He turned to Meredith. "We should go in the other room."

Once he got her out of the kitchen, he asked Meredith gently, "Who is she?"

"Are you the lead detective?"

"I'm not sure yet," he said. "Probably."

"I didn't think . . ."

She was in shock. He knew that. A few days ago, he would have been surprised. She must have been at similar scenes. She'd certainly seen thousands of photos.

But this was different. This was the latest in a succession of threatening incidents. Attempted murder. Her home trashed. Threatening phone calls. All aimed at her.

"It probably didn't have anything to do with you," he said.

"Didn't it?" Her voice was a cry for help.

"What is her name?" he asked again.

"Mrs. Starnes. Lulu Starnes. She was a widow. A teacher." Tears glittered in her eyes.

"Did anyone know you were coming here?"

"I don't see how . . ." She stopped suddenly. "I called from my house and my office. Several times."

"I think we should have someone check your phone and house for bugs," he said.

Her face paled even more. "But I have a new alarm system. Wouldn't someone have discovered listening devices?"

"Not if they weren't looking for them," he said. "Did you know her? Before coming here today?"

"No," she whispered and sat down on the edge of the sofa.

The dog tried to get loose from her hold, but she held him tighter.

"Why did you come to see her?"

"My mother. She was one of my mother's friends when they were younger. I wanted her to know—"

She stopped in mid-sentence, leaving something unsaid. Why?

"Gage?"

He turned around at Wagner's voice. He had almost forgotten the man's presence.

"Glenn, this is Meredith Rawson. Meredith, my new partner, Glenn Wagner."

"I've heard of you," Wagner said.

Her blue eyes appeared luminous as they turned toward Wagner. "Detective Wagner," she acknowledged. "I don't think I've met you."

"I joined the department after you left the prosecutor's office," he said. "What happened here?" His voice was gentler than Gage's voice had been.

"I had an appointment with Mrs. Starnes," she said. "She seemed pleased about meeting with me, but no one answered the door. I waited a while, then tried the front door. It was unlocked." She glanced away. "The dog was pretty frantic," she continued. "Running back and forth as if there was a problem, as if he wanted me to follow him. I went inside. He led me to her."

"You didn't see anyone around the house?" Wagner was asking the questions Gage should have asked. But he was watching her face, the bewilderment and fear in her eyes. He sensed she wasn't saying something. Something important.

She had made it clear the other night that she was busy with her practice and her mother. Why would she take time to visit someone in her mother's past? Why not just call?

And why would anyone target someone from her mother's past?

A pattern was developing.

It was clear she saw it, too, and it terrified her, though she tried hard not to show it.

He longed to reach out to her. But she had signaled the

other night that she didn't want more than a professional relationship, that their encounter had been born of desperation and was not to be repeated. Hell, this was a murder scene—and no place for personal feelings.

Wagner's gaze moved from Meredith back to Gage.

Had he been that obvious?

She looked helplessly at the dog. "He keeps trying to go back to the kitchen. I'm afraid . . ."

Gage looked around for a dog leash, finally found one, snapped it on, and handed it to her.

"His name is Nicky. Mrs. Starnes mentioned him when we made the appointment," she said in a small voice. Grief was embedded in it. He heard it. He felt it.

He looked around the room. It was neat except for dog toys. Photos of a man and a woman together were scattered around. There were no photos or portraits of children.

The dog was still agitated, standing alert. Gage sat down in a chair near Meredith, leaned over and scratched the dog's short ears. "It's okay," he crooned.

"What will happen to him?" she asked.

"There might be family," he said.

"Now. I mean now."

"We'll be canvassing the neighbors. Perhaps one of them can take him in."

"She loved him. I heard it in her voice when she talked about him." Her voice cracked. She was obviously fighting back tears.

"Meredith," he said.

She looked at him.

"We have to get details." He was insistent.

"You know everything I do."

He didn't. He would bet on it. "You may not know what you know," he said.

She nodded. She knew the drill.

"Did you see anyone around the house when you arrived?"

"No."

"What time did you arrive?"

"About five forty-five."

"Your appointment was for that time?"

"No. It was at six. I waited. . . ." She stared at him again. "Maybe if I . . . hadn't . . ."

"The paramedics said she had been dead for more than an hour," he said. "It wouldn't have mattered if you hadn't waited."

But her expression didn't ease.

"How did your mother know her?" he tried again.

"They went to school together."

"Which school?"

She named New Orleans's most expensive and exclusive private school. He looked around the modest home, remembered the appearance of the woman on the floor. A lined face. A plain, practical haircut. The dark hair touched with gray that had probably never been tinted.

"And you haven't seen her before?"

"No. Apparently they lost touch when . . ."

"When what?"

"After graduation."

He knew she was withholding information now. He had gotten to know her well last night. It had been only a few hours, but it might as well have been much more. He knew by her carefully phrased words that she knew more than she was saying.

"When did you make the appointment?" he asked.

"Yesterday. When I reached her, she told me she was a teacher."

"Anything else? Did she sound worried or upset?"

"No. She didn't know about my mother's illness and she expressed sympathy about that. But that's all."

"Why did you want to see her?"

"I told you—"

"No, you didn't. Most people don't go to so much trouble to seek out old friends of their parents."

"My mother is dying. I wanted her friends to know."

It was more than that. Much more, dammit. It had to have

something to do with what had happened to her this past week.

He knew Wagner was listening intently. He saw from the corner of his eye that his partner was taking notes.

The front door opened again, and a man and a woman from the crime scene unit entered.

"Wag, will you show them the crime scene and tell them what we have so far?"

Wagner had seniority at the moment. Still, he shrugged and went to the door, ushering in the newcomers and taking them into the kitchen.

"Now tell me why you were really here," Gage told her. "And don't tell me it's privileged."

She gave him a hostile stare that slowly faded. She looked lost for a moment.

"There are too many violent incidents around you for them to be coincidences," he pressed. "And now someone has died," he added brutally. He had to shake her loose from whatever she was withholding. "What was your connection with Mrs. Starnes? It's more than you've told us. Hell, you've been a prosecutor. You know better than this."

"My mother," she whispered. "She told me a few days ago that I have a half sister. She had a daughter that was taken from her. She asked me to find her. There wasn't anything to go on. I thought I would start with her friends at that time."

Her face was strained, her eyes pleading. "I didn't want it public," she said. "I didn't think it was anyone's business but ours."

"The attack on you happened after that?"

"Yes."

He had been sitting across from her. Now he stood. Tried to think. Damn, he wished she had told him last night. But then they had both been occupied with each other, with the obvious hunger they'd had for each other.

But it showed an obvious distrust of him, and he felt a stab of disappointment, even hurt.

He knew it was unreasonable. He hadn't shared any of his past with her. Why should she have poured out her guts to him, especially with something so personal and private?

"Have you talked to anyone else about your mother?" Gage asked.

"Mrs. Robert Laxton. She gave me Mrs. Starnes's name. I wish to God she hadn't."

"We'll send someone over there to talk to her," he said.

"She didn't really have any information, other than some names of my mother's friends. She said Mrs. Starnes was close to her, but I never heard my mother mention Mrs. Starnes's name."

She was in control again. Her face was still pale, her eyes sad, but she was in complete control. Still, her back was stiff with tension, and he wondered exactly how much emotion she was holding in.

The dog whined and she leaned over and hugged it, sharing some of that emotion, and sorrow over a death, with the dog.

"I want to take him until someone claims him," she said. "I don't want him to go to animal control or wherever you usually take them."

"I don't see a problem there," he said. "We will notify the next of kin and tell them where he is."

She looked stricken again. "I wonder who the next of kin would be." She looked around again. He did as well. No pictures of children. Yet Mrs. Starnes must have loved children if she was a teacher.

He hated what would come next. Finding someone to contact. Then the message itself. It was the part of the job he despised.

"Who else knows about your mother's daughter?" he asked.

"My father. My staff. No one else."

"How much do you know about your sister?"

"Only that she was born somewhere around Memphis and was taken away from my mother. I don't know how, or why, or even who. I know the approximate date. Nothing more."

"An informal adoption then?"

"I think so. I don't know. We can't find a birth certificate."

"When your home was trashed, was anything taken pertaining to this mysterious daughter?"

"No. I hadn't had time to do anything."

"It might have been an attempt to distract you," he said.

"But why? Who would care about an adoption thirty-plus years ago?"

That was the question that kept ringing in his head.

But he knew from long experience that the immediate questions were probably not the right questions.

"Anything else?" he asked. "Anything you can remember that might have even the slightest relationship to the events of the past few days?"

She shook her head.

"What was your father's reaction to your sister?" He kept coming back to Charles Rawson.

She shook her head slowly. "He would never hurt my mother or myself. We've had differences. More than one. But I am sure of that." She paused. "He would be mortified if this came out about my mother."

"I would think he would be more concerned with his daughter's safety."

Her face flushed. Her eyes glinted. She was becoming defensive.

Because he'd hit a sore spot.

"Can I go home?" she asked.

"I'll talk to Wagner." His emotions were reeling. Her terror came through, even though she was very good at hiding it. And her grief about her mother's friend. He'd wanted to take her in his arms. Tell her that he would help. That he would be there.

It had taken all his willpower to remain cool and professional. Yet that had been what she needed now.

Today showed she continued to be in danger. Mrs. Starnes's death proved someone would stop at nothing.

How much of a catalyst was Meredith Rawson?

And how much a target?

sixteen

Meredith struggled to keep her composure as she hugged the dog to her. He whined to get away, to check on his mistress. How long had the two been together?

She rubbed her cheek against the dog's fur. She would not cry, even though grief wrapped around her heart. She couldn't shrug off the guilt, no matter what Gage Gaynor said.

The only way to help now was to care for the dog.

She glanced at the front door. She wanted to leave this house. She wanted to go home. But that, too, had been violated. Despite the new alarm system, she hadn't really felt safe at home. She wondered whether she ever would again.

Get over it. She was an attorney. She prided herself on her toughness and control. She had seen horrendous situations both as a prosecutor and as a private attorney.

But she had never before been the focal point of violence.

The dog licked her hand anxiously.

"It's okay, Nicky," she said softly. "I'll find someone for you."

But *someone* wasn't his mistress, and she was fully aware of that.

Gage returned. "You can go for now. I'll drive you home."

Not "May I?" Or "Can I?" An order. Like her father always gave.

"My car is here," she argued.

"I'll have a patrolman drive it to your house later."

She didn't want to capitulate. Didn't want to need him. Didn't want to need anyone.

But she did. She needed someone now. Not to protect her. But to share her sorrow for a woman she didn't know.

A warning voice told her that someone shouldn't be—couldn't be—Gage Gaynor. She didn't want to break down in front of him, and she was frighteningly close to that point right now. Her mother's illness, her mother's secret, the attempt on her life, the trashing of her home, and now this.

Emotional overload. She recognized it. She'd seen it too many times in her clients. She knew there was a breaking point, and she wanted hers to come in private.

"No," she said sharply. "You have things to do here."

He sighed heavily. "Meredith. Someone died today. It may or may not be connected to you, but it's a hell of a coincidence if it isn't. I'm not going to let you go home alone to an empty house. If I have to follow you, I will."

"Then you will have to follow me," she said. It was better than being in the same car with him, seduced by the sight and sound and scent of him.

He nodded curtly. "Ready."

She stood, still holding the dog. He was an armful. A furry armful. He squirmed, protesting, and she whispered to him. He quieted and drooped forlornly against her.

Gage reached for him, but she shook her head. "I'll take care of him."

Gage shrugged.

"You *will* tell the relatives about him?" she asked him again. She had no time in her life for a dog. Her hours were horrendous.

"Yes."

"If no one wants him . . ."

"You can take him to the shelter. Or keep him." He was looking at her with a raised eyebrow. Quizzically.

She knew she would never take the dog to the shelter. She owed Mrs. Starnes. Outside, she lowered the dog to the ground and he walked with her to her car. The house now was surrounded by police cars and uniformed police. She saw that several were at doors up and down the street, obviously canvassing the neighborhood for possible witnesses.

She reached her car and held the door open while the dog reluctantly got in. She was blocked by one police car, and she saw Gage talking to several officers. One moved the car behind her while Gage got into an unmarked car.

For a moment, she regretted her decision. She remembered how at ease she'd felt with him last night, how comfortable because of, or in spite of, the attraction that spiked between them.

She drove slowly, touching the dog occasionally. Talking to him. He sat upright in the passenger seat, his eyes seldom leaving her, as if she would help him fathom what was happening to him.

Fifteen minutes later, she parked in the driveway. It was the later part of dusk, and the air was hot and thick, laden with moisture. The sweet smell of hibiscus and magnolia permeated the air. She got out and opened the gate into the back, then returned to the car and drove inside. Gage parked outside.

He joined her at the door and took out his revolver. With the other hand, he took her key and opened the door, stepping inside first. She followed, punching in the code numbers of the security system.

"Stay here," he said, and moved forward without giving her a chance to say aye or nay.

She remained at the door, clutching the leash. Nicky stood still, panting nervously.

In minutes, Gage returned. "Everything looks okay. You might want to look through it before I leave, make sure no one has been here."

She had no argument left in her. She took the leash off Nicky and went to her office, the dog plodding behind her. She turned on her new computer. No one had used it since her last log-on. Her desk looked undisturbed. She returned to the living room, where he was inspecting her telephone.

Then she remembered his comment that her home and phones should be checked for listening devices.

"Anything?" she asked in little more than a whisper.

He didn't answer. His attention was fixed on the parts of the telephone receiver he'd separated. He took out a tiny piece of metal and balanced it in his hand, then carefully replaced it. Then he led her out to the back porch.

"The phone is bugged. I'll check the one in the kitchen and the one upstairs as well. Your burglar must have installed them between trashing your home. Perhaps the vandalism was just a cover for that."

She tried to tamp her growing anger. A malevolent presence had been listening to her every word to friends, associates, clients.

"What do you want to do?" he asked. "It might be better if whatever did this doesn't know you've discovered it."

"All right." She hesitated. "Do you think any of the rooms . . .?"

"I doubt it. That's harder to monitor than a phone line. But I'll have someone sweep the house. Just be careful what you say on the phone." He leaned over and touched her cheek. "Be careful, period. It could be dangerous."

"As opposed to what?" she asked.

He smiled. "That's the Meredith Rawson I know."

But she didn't want to be diverted. "You think Mrs. Starnes died because I tried to reach her?"

He shrugged. "It's a possibility."

"We still don't know if there's any connection other than the fact I found . . . her." Even she knew how weak that comment was. The person found at the scene of a crime was always the first suspect. Ironically, Meredith had probably told the killer through the bugged phone how to find Mrs. Starnes.

His gaze met hers. It did not allow self-delusion. "Tell me more about your half sister. Everything that has happened to you follows too closely your attempts to locate her."

"I planned to go to Memphis this week and see what I could find out."

"Alone?"

"Yes."

"I have some vacation coming. I'll go with you."

She knew she should say no. He had a way of distracting her. "I'm leaving Thursday. I want to check area obstetricians practicing at the time of my sister's birth. And attorneys. I doubt whether anyone is still in practice but . . ."

"I can manage that."

"I don't think it's a good idea."

"Going alone is a worse idea."

"Perhaps Sarah . . ." But she knew neither Becky nor Sarah could go with her. They both had families of their own. And he was right. Danger seemed to lurk around every corner.

She didn't consider herself a stupid person. And she would have to be quite stupid not to realize she was in the midst of a situation she didn't understand. A deadly situation.

"All right," she said.

"A little more enthusiasm please." A small crooked smile accompanied the words.

"I'm *not* enthusiastic. You and I . . . we are like gunpowder and fire."

"And you object to fireworks?"

"When they're uncontrolled," she replied. "Don't you?"

He studied her for a moment. Then shrugged. "I'm not sure," he admitted wryly.

At least he had some of the same doubts that haunted her.

"I don't like leaving you alone here."

"I'm not alone. I have Nicky."

"I'm not sure Nicky is such a good watchdog. Remember Mrs. Starnes. . . ."

She did. She remembered every second of the last few hours. She wondered whether the image of Mrs. Starnes on the floor would ever leave her.

"I'll keep my cell phone and revolver with me," she promised. "I know you have to get back to the scene."

He bent his head and his lips touched hers. Gently, yet with the spice of passion underneath. She sensed his reluctance as he drew away. "We'll probably be working all night. I'll send someone over to check the house for any more bugs. His name is Daniel. He's a deputy sheriff as well as a wire expert. He'll show his credentials from outside. You're not to let anyone else in unless you know them. In fact . . ."

"I'll be careful," she said.

He took her hand and held it for a moment, his fingers tracing the palm in a way that caused erotic shivers to run up and down her spine.

"I'll call later."

She liked that idea. Far more than she should.

BISBEE

The birth certificate came in the mail.

Holly looked at it for a long time. It was one of the necessary steps toward freedom. To a Social Security number. A driver's license. And a measure of safety.

Until this moment she'd feared that someone would discover that Elizabeth Baker had died years ago.

During her trips to the library, she'd found a book on how to disappear. She knew now that she had done everything wrong. She'd thought herself so smart.

The biggest mistake, it said, was settling in a small community. According to the book, she should have chosen a large city like San Francisco, or Chicago, where one could become an anonymous face in a crowd. It was far more difficult to hide in a small town where people knew one another and had a collective curiosity about newcomers.

Well, that certainly was true.

She'd thought about running again. That thought sent chills through her. She didn't think she could do that again.

Neither could she uproot her son again. She just couldn't

do it. Harry liked it here. He loved Caesar and what he called the "funny" town. He liked the sheriff and the pony he'd ridden.

He was leading a normal life for the first time in his life.

But she did have to obtain a driver's license and Social Security number.

Neither, she'd discovered, would be easy to obtain. You needed a Social Security card for a driver's license. But there might be other kinds of identification she could produce.

She decided the Social Security card was the most important. With that, she could obtain a driver's license and open a bank account. The bank account would allow her to build credit. A history.

She had considered opening a bank account with someone else's Social Security number. But her Internet research told her that facade could last less than a year. Banks reported transactions to the government. If she had any idea of staying here that long, she could be discovered.

And she *did* want to stay. It frightened her how much she wanted to stay. She had real friends now. Friends who liked her for herself.

In a very short time, she'd grown to love the desert and the odd little town with so much character. A town that refused to die. A town that valued the lesser of its residents. One that persisted but still refused to conform.

Staying posed a risk. Trying to get a Social Security card posed a risk. But she knew to stay here—or wherever she went—she would need identification. She was terrified every time she drove a car. If she was ever stopped, her house of cards could tumble.

She'd spent hours trying to devise a reason why she didn't have a Social Security number. Most people today had a Social Security card almost since birth. The best scenario, she decided, was that she was a daughter of missionaries and had lived outside the country most of her life, had married overseas and had never held any job but that of housewife. Under those circumstances it had been easy to overlook the need for a card. . . .

She looked at the birth certificate again. A beginning. But there were so many traps out there. One mistake, and she could die. And then what would happen to her son?

"Mommy?" Harry sensed something. His eyes were riveted on her.

"Want to go for a walk?" she asked.

He leaped to his feet, dislodging Caesar, who had crawled up on the sofa with him, and fetched the dog's leash. Caesar jumped down from the sofa and followed him, obviously eager for his evening constitutional.

Holly regarded what had become a ritual with a pleasure only slightly tinged with apprehension.

She'd established a routine. She worked all morning while Harry watched television or read, then at noon she would visit the library in her daily search for news from New Orleans. Then she and Harry would go somewhere for an inexpensive lunch. After lunch, it was home again to work the rest of the afternoon.

They would walk the dog after the worst of the heat faded, then she would fix a simple supper. She usually read to Harry unless there was something suitable on television.

Both Russ and Sheriff Menelo had asked her out. She'd told both she wasn't ready to date again.

She was feeling safer and safer as each day passed.

That was scary in itself.

Caesar barked with excitement as they left the house.

As always, she looked around for any vehicle that shouldn't be there, for any person who looked out of place. But she saw only the usual, and she allowed herself to relax, to enjoy the evening breeze and the softness of the desert colors.

They had walked two blocks when Harry looked up at her. "When is Father coming?"

Not Daddy. He was four years old, and the only word he knew for Randolph was "Father." Still, there was a yearning in his face.

"I don't know," she said.

"Does he love us?"

"Of course he does," she said, wincing inwardly again. She looked down. His small, beloved face was pinched with concern. She knew suddenly that he had been worrying for days, though he'd said nothing. Something he'd learned from her?

Her heart cracked. She'd chosen unwisely, yet if she had not married Randolph, then there would not have been solemn, bright little Harry.

"You know how busy your father is," she said.

He nodded. He'd been told enough times.

"He wanted us to have this adventure."

"But I want to tell him about it. I rode a horse. All by myself." He was puffed up with pride, obviously eager to announce his accomplishment to the one person whose attention he craved.

She ached for him. For his need for a father who had never cared about him beyond his value during a photo opportunity.

How much should she lie? Promise? When was it going to backlash? When would he not be quieted by her assurances? When would she be forced to tell him the truth . . . or make up an elaborate lie?

She tried to divert his attention, even while knowing that it was a problem she couldn't wish away.

"Do you want to go riding again?"

"With Sher'f Doug?"

"Yes."

His face brightened.

"Let's stop here," she said as they came to a park with swings.

That would take his mind away from his father.

But for how long?

NEW ORLEANS

Charles Rawson called his daughter.

She should be on his speed dial. But she wasn't. He didn't call her that much.

A pang of regret ran through him. They had never been close.

He loved her. Just as he loved his wife. But his love had never been enough for Marguerite. And he had feared rejection from his daughter as well. Hell, he hadn't known how to talk to either one of them.

He had never been good at relationships. He'd always taken what he wanted, and now he looked at his life and saw what a failure it had been. Even his law career was crumbling. And that was the only thing he had left.

No one answered the phone.

His hand shook.

A friend in the police superintendent's office had called him to tell him of a murder. His daughter was a witness.

He recognized the name of the victim.

Meredith apparently had not taken his advice or paid any attention to his plea that she leave the past alone.

He knew how dangerous her crusade was.

He knew because there was blood on his hands.

He hurriedly left the office. Although it was late, some associates were still working, as was his secretary.

"Go home, Virginia," he said.

"But I have a few more letters. . . ."

"Go home," he said, more gently than he had ever spoken to her before, and he saw the surprise in his eyes. For some reason, that reaction hurt.

His car was suffocating inside. In seconds, the air-conditioning sent a blast of cool air through the interior. It did nothing to cool the anxiety that clutched at him as he drove to Meredith's home.

Nothing looked disturbed at the house that once was his mother's home. As always, it was as peaceful as its garden shaded by magnolia trees and colored by flowers.

He parked in the front and opened the gate, surprised to hear barking from within.

He rang the bell. Nothing. Rang again.

Then he saw Meredith peer outside before opening. Good.

Except being careful wouldn't help against a determined enemy. And there was no question she was making enemies. She had made herself a target.

The door opened, and she stood there, surprise in her eyes. The same kind of surprise that had been in his secretary's eyes.

Then he realized this was the first time he had visited her at this house. He'd always summoned her to his own.

"Father?" she said.

"Meredith. I heard about what happened earlier. I tried to call."

"I was at Mrs. Starnes's house, talking to detectives," she said. "I just got home a while ago. I haven't had a chance to check messages."

"Are you alone?"

"Except for Nicky," she said, looking down at the dog next to her.

"I didn't know—"

"He's not mine," she interrupted. "He belongs—belonged—to the woman who was killed."

He soaked in that information. "May I come in?"

She stepped aside. "Of course. I was just . . . surprised to see you."

He realized how sad that was. It was, it seemed, a day for realizations.

He followed her inside.

"Can I get you some coffee? Or a drink?"

"A drink," he said gratefully.

He accompanied her into the kitchen. The house was much more comfortable than he remembered. Victorian furniture had been replaced by sofas with plush cushions. Fresh flowers filled vases but they weren't as carefully arranged as those at his home. Instead there was a profusion of clashing colors that was somehow more appealing than the sedate pale blooms at his house.

He hesitated at the door of the kitchen as she opened a cabinet door. "Scotch?" she asked.

He nodded. "Straight."

She poured some in a glass.

"You don't drink scotch," he said.

"How would you know?"

"I remember that you rarely took anything but wine."

"As well as an occasional beer," she said.

He found himself smiling at her. Despite what had happened the last few days, she was challenging him again.

"I like one, too, now and then," he said.

"Would you rather have that?"

"No. Scotch is fine."

She found a bottle of wine in the fridge and poured herself a glass, then led the way to the living room.

"To what do I owe the honor?"

"I'm worried about you," he said, watching her face tighten as he said the words.

"Who told you?"

"A friend in the police department. He called me about the shooting, the burglary and now this latest incident."

"It wasn't an 'incident.' A woman died. Probably because of me."

His first impulse was to agree. If she hadn't probed . . .

"It wasn't your fault," he said instead. "But I wish you would stop whatever you're doing."

"Looking into my mother's request, you mean?"

"Yes."

"I doubt if the attacks had anything to do with that," she replied. "The perpetrator could be the husband of one of my clients. You know I volunteer at the women's shelter."

He nodded, and again saw the surprise in her face. "I keep up with my only child," he said.

"And your wife?" It was a bitter accusation.

"She wouldn't want me there," he said. "I am doing what I can from afar."

"Why? Why wouldn't she want you there?"

"Do you want all the details?"

"I want to know what you know about Mom's past."

"I don't know anything," he said. He wondered whether his eyes conveyed the lie. He was a superb liar. He'd even been proud of the fact. Now he wasn't.

"Do you know who she dated before you?"

His mouth tightened. "Is that why you visited the Starnes woman? To find the dirt in your mother's background?"

That wasn't what he meant to say. But fear suddenly overtook him. If she discovered what had happened thirty years ago, she would despise him. He wouldn't have even the little of her he had now. He had to be careful or he would lose her entirely.

She took a sip of wine, then another, obviously trying to control her emotions. "What do you really want, Father?"

"I want you to stop looking into the past."

"Why?"

"For me, Meredith. I want you to do it for me."

She was silent for a moment, and he wished he knew what she was thinking.

"I can't," she finally said. "Mother wants me to do this."

"And I don't."

He knew when he threw out the words that he had lost. It was a foolish thing to say. He was asking her to choose between two parents, one of whom was dying. It was an impossible, selfish request. But he had been selfish all his life.

"I'm sorry," she said in a toneless voice.

"You can get hurt," he pleaded. "You've obviously stepped into something you don't understand."

"But you do, don't you, Father?" The accusation was in her voice.

"No. I just know everything that has happened to you has occurred since you talked to me that morning."

"I don't believe you."

The simple statement was like a sword in his gut. That it carried truth only made it more painful.

He took a gulp of scotch, something he seldom did. He was always very careful.

"Help me," his daughter said.

He couldn't. If he did, she would be even more of a target than she already was.

"I'll pay for protection," he said. "I want you to have it on a twenty-four-hour-a-day basis."

"That's not what I need."

A wave of helplessness passed through him. It was an increasingly familiar feeling.

"I'll have someone over here tomorrow."

"No," she said.

"With or without your cooperation," he said through gritted teeth.

"Please," she said. "Please tell me what you know. I need you to do this for me."

It was the first time in years she had asked anything of him. The answer could send him to prison, and place her into even more danger.

"I don't know anything," he said. "Nothing that can help you."

"Or the police?"

He looked at her sharply. "You haven't discussed . . ."

"Of course I did," she said. "They wanted to know why I was at Lulu Starnes's home."

He felt the blood drain from his face. He had thought she would keep it within the family.

"Do you realize what you have done?"

"No. Tell me."

He finished the rest of the scotch. This had been a disaster. He had to make some phone calls. He had to fix things.

Inflict some blackmail of his own, perhaps.

He stood abruptly. "I have to go."

"Tell me, Father," she pleaded again. "For once, talk to me."

"There is nothing to say."

He turned to go but not before he caught a glimpse of her face, her expression frozen into a mask. He realized now how often she had donned that mask.

He couldn't remember the last time he had touched her, given her a hug.

It was too late now. He had done too much damage. To her and to her mother. The heart that had gone into deep freeze years ago wept.

He turned back to her. "Good night."

"Have you seen Mother?" she asked.

"Yes."

She looked surprised.

"I know you've been disappointed I haven't sat by her bedside," he said. "But she wouldn't have wanted that."

"Maybe you're wrong. She loved you. . . . She must—"

"Never," he said. "She never loved me." Almost blindly, he left the house.

He drove a half block until he was out of her view, then parked the car on the side. He had to regain some composure. He buried his head in his hands, trying to think.

The office. He had to go to the office. He would write letters containing details of decades-old events and mail copies to several attorneys he knew. It could mean his daughter's life.

And his own.

But the latter no longer mattered.

seventeen

Gage sat in his office and put the phone back in the cradle.

He'd had Meredith's house electronically swept by a friend of his. There'd been no bugs other than the one on the phone downstairs. Perhaps there had been no time, no opportunity after the trashing of her home.

"Gaynor!"

He looked at the lieutenant who stood at the door.

"Where's Wagner?" the lieutenant asked.

"Checking out some leads on one of our cases."

"Well, I want you to concentrate on a floater we found." He handed Gage a location. Gage looked at it, then up at the lieutenant.

"They found his body in a bayou."

Gage swore. If there was one thing he hated, it was floaters. Usually bodies that turned up in the water were dead-end cases. Impossible to identify.

Still, he was the detective on duty. Wagner was following a lead on the homeless man murder.

It shouldn't take long. Gage would check the body before it was moved. Make sure the photos were made and that it was treated as gingerly as possible. Then send it to the examiner to find any identifying markers.

He would check to see whether the general description—

sex, height, age—matched the description of a missing person.

It was routine, but he begrudged the time.

Yet it was someone's son, husband, father, brother. He owed it to the victim to provide some closure.

BISBEE

Holly stared at the photo in the New Orleans paper.

Her father and her husband stood in front of campaign headquarters. Randolph was announcing his candidacy for the U.S. House of Representatives.

No mention of his wife.

She couldn't believe his audacity.

But then he would never consider her a challenge. He'd apparently rid himself of the body she'd left. All he needed now was to rid himself of a wife.

How on earth was he explaining her absence?

Or had no one asked?

Her only close relative was her father. But he had always been closer to Randolph than to her. Randolph was the son he'd never had. His legacy.

She stole a glance at Harry, who had a small pile of picture books in front of him and was engrossed in one of them.

She finally forced herself to move away from the article and on to the society pages. A photo stopped her. Randolph stood next to Sylvia Sams, a well-known socialite in town. The caption identified them as co-chairmen of one of the city's largest fund-raisers.

He looked totally at ease. A confident smile sat comfortably on his patrician face. Randolph had always wrapped himself around good causes. Sylvia Sams, sleek and always impeccably coiffed, was legendary for her manhunting. They looked like the perfect couple.

Holly wished her well in this instance. Anything to keep her husband's efforts focused on something other than finding her. And her son.

"Mrs. Baker?"

She looked up from the computer, turning it slightly so the woman could not see the screen.

"Your son. I helped a customer and when I came back, he was gone."

"Oh my God," Holly said as she leaped up so abruptly the chair fell. Her gaze went around the interior of the main room. No little boy.

"I'll look in the rest rooms," the librarian said.

"I'll start out here," Holly said, her voice rising in panic.

Two other patrons overheard and also started searching, going through each aisle of books.

Her heart pounding, her breath caught in her throat, Holly ran through the room, hunting behind shelves, every corner. She could barely breathe. What if her husband . . . ?

Panic exploded in her. She prayed even as she searched. *God, don't let anything happen to him.*

The rest room. Maybe Louise had found him. . . .

But the woman came out of the men's room, shaking her head. "I'll call the police," she said.

Outside. Maybe he went outside. She ran for the door, almost tripping. *Please, God,* she begged again. *Let him be there.*

She threw the door open. Her gaze swept the street in front and she dashed outside. Praying. Hoping. The street was empty.

She ran around the side of the building. "Mikey," she called.

Then she came to an abrupt halt.

Doug Menelo was on one knee, talking to her son. Both looked up, obviously startled by the sound of her voice.

Mikey!

She sped across the distance and grabbed her son, hugging him so tightly he yelped.

She released him only slightly. "Why did you leave?"

"I looked out the window and saw Sher'f Doug outside," he explained, his eyes wide. "I wanted to ask to ride again."

"Don't ever run off again without telling me. Ever."

His eyes started to fill with tears. She was almost never severe with him. Her own cheeks were wet. She put her face next to his and their tears intermingled.

After a moment, she stood, looked at the sheriff who was watching her every move. She had called out "Mikey," not "Harry." Her stomach seemed to fall away.

"I'm sorry," she said. "I'm not usually hysterical." She was afraid to say more, to explain. It would only draw attention to the error. Maybe he hadn't even heard her.

"I've noticed," he replied. "I should have brought him inside immediately. I was just going to do that. I didn't realize that you didn't know he saw me."

"He disappeared so . . . quickly. I was watching, then . . ."

She was stuttering, the panic lingering in her voice.

"I know how frightening it is to lose a child," he said in a gentle voice.

Had she overreacted? Did he think her reaction too extreme for a mother who had misplaced her child for a few moments?

"There are so many stories about—"

"I know," he said. "I would feel the same way about my niece."

She picked up Harry and hugged him again. She didn't care what Doug thought. She just wanted to hold her son. Forever.

"I'd better let the librarian know," she said. "Everyone is searching for him."

"I'll go and tell them," Doug Menelo said.

"Thanks, but I have some books to pick up."

"Is your car here? Can I take you home?"

Did she look that spooked? She and Harry had walked to the library. She wouldn't use the car any more than she absolutely had to until she received her driver's license.

Had he noticed her reluctance to drive? Would he put two and two together?

The fear in her deepened.

Doug Menelo was looking at her with concern. "Liz?"

She suddenly realized she hadn't answered his question. She also knew that this moment showed the disaster of becoming involved, even on a friendship basis, with anyone.

"I'm all right, truly I am," she said. "It was just . . . I had a fright."

"I can get those books for you. Louise can show me—"

"No!" The word was sharper than she intended. Still holding her son, she turned and hurried up the stairs. She didn't look back as she opened the door and rushed to the checkout desk, where Louise was dialing a phone, evidently calling the police.

"I found him," Holly said.

"Thank God," Louise said.

The few other patrons crowded around, visible relief on their faces, and she thanked them all for their efforts in looking for him.

People cared here in Bisbee. People cared, and they wanted to know their neighbors.

She closed her eyes and hugged Harry again until he wriggled in protest. She never wanted to let him go.

Holly lowered him to the ground but clutched his hand as she hurried to the computer. The monitor still showed the article about the fund-raiser. The photo of her husband. She quickly clicked off the website. She should visit another site or two, but right now, she wanted nothing so much as to get home with Harry.

Home. The small shabby cottage had become that in these past few weeks. It was more than home. It was her refuge.

"Let's go," she said to Harry.

"Where?"

"Home."

He looked disappointed. "I want tacos."

"Tacos are not for little boys who wander off."

"But . . . Sher'f Doug . . ."

"I don't care who it is," she said. "Please don't do that again."

"You're crying, Mommy."

She reached up and wiped away the tears. "I was frightened for you."

"I'm a big boy."

"You are a very big boy, but I love you. I worry about you."

"I'm sorry," he said earnestly.

She hugged him again. Her hand tightened around his as they started walking. It tightened even more as she saw Doug Menelo leaning against his patrol car, his gaze following their every step.

Her stomach was still tight, sick with lingering fear for Harry.

Every mother's nightmare.

But she wasn't just every mother. And her nightmares were all too real.

In that one moment of complete terror, she'd learned what it would be like to lose a child.

NEW ORLEANS

Charles Rawson left his daughter's home and went to his office. It was still lit. One associate was in the library when Charles walked by. A paralegal was sitting at her desk, staring at a computer screen.

Charles passed both without speaking, went into his office and closed the door. He sat down and started typing.

When he finished, he looked at the clock. More than three hours had passed. He printed out four copies of the document he'd typed, placed one copy of each into individual envelopes and sealed them. He then placed each of the envelopes into a larger one, carefully adding a cover letter and a check to each before sealing the outer envelopes and addressing them.

He turned off the computer, placed three envelopes into his briefcase and tucked the remaining copy, addressed to

Meredith, into a file for a case under appeal. He would take that copy to his safe deposit box in the morning.

He would drop the envelopes into a mailbox on his way home.

In the morning he would make several phone calls, relating what he had done.

As he left the office, he noticed the paralegal was gone. So was the associate, but a light still shone in one of the offices. An eager beaver. He'd been one years ago. Now he was just tired.

He nodded at the night watchman and headed for the underground parking garage. It, too, was patrolled on a regular basis.

He had just about reached his car when a car gunned behind him. He turned around and saw two headlights coming directly at him. He braced for the impact.

Pain struck, ripped through him, then he felt nothing.

The sound of insistent knocking on her front door and loud barking woke Meredith.

She woke with a start, having finally sunk into a deep sleep after a restless night. Gage's friend had swept the house earlier, finding only the bug in her telephone. Still, she felt uneasy. More than uneasy. Mrs. Starnes's death combined with her father's visit haunted her.

When the knocking persisted, she reached for an old robe she kept at the foot of her bed and pulled it over the large T-shirt she slept in.

She went to the window and looked outside. A generic car that screamed unmarked police-department issue. Gage? What would he be doing here again?

The knocking became more urgent.

She hurried downstairs, Nicky keeping pace beside her. At least he was a good barker if not defender.

She looked through the spy hole that had been recently installed. Two men. And neither was Gage. They both looked grim.

One of the two—Max Byers—was familiar. A detective. He'd been a witness in one of the cases she'd prosecuted. The other also had the look of an officer.

She opened the door.

Byers couldn't meet her gaze. "Ms. Rawson," he said politely. "May we come in?"

"Why?" she asked, instinctively knowing it was something bad. His eyes told her that. So had the insistent knocking at this hour in the morning.

He didn't have to say anything. She knew their message before they opened their mouths. Her head knew it. Her heart wouldn't accept it.

She couldn't bring herself to ask the question.

After a few seconds of silence, Byers repeated his request, "May we come in?"

Wordlessly, she opened the door for them, then went around the room, turning on the lights. Doing something kept bad news at bay. It delayed what she knew was coming. Someone had died. Someone close to her. If it had been her mother, a call from the hospital would have sufficed. There was only one person whose death would be announced to her this way.

She looked at the sofa where her father had sat several hours ago. In her mind's eye, she saw his worried face, the desperate plea in his voice. A plea she'd ignored.

Finally, she asked the question. "My father?"

Byers nodded.

"Is he dead?"

"I'm afraid so."

She slumped against a wall.

"Are you alone, Ms. Rawson? Is there anyone you can call?"

"No. My mother is in the hospital." She padded across to a chair and sat down. "What happened?"

"Hit-and-run in the parking lot of his building."

Her heart thudded so loudly she thought they must hear it as well.

"When?"

"He was found two hours ago. The paramedics think he had been there less than an hour when they were called. So the best guesstimate as to time of death is one to two A.M."

"There's a guard on duty in that parking lot. How—"

"We don't know. He says he didn't hear anything, but he also admitted he might have taken a nap. He's the one who found him."

She was numb. Too numb to think. Except of her father's words.

Do you realize what you have done?

She hadn't then. She was terribly afraid she did now.

The impact of those thoughts were like a boulder hitting her.

"Did your father have any enemies?" the second detective asked.

"I imagine he had quite a few. Attorneys usually do. There are losers in every case. But I can't think of any who would want to kill him."

"Do you know why he was in his office so late?"

She wanted the questions to end. She didn't want to think that perhaps something she'd done had cost her father his life.

Do you realize what you have done? The words echoed over and over again in her mind.

"Ms. Rawson?"

"I'm sorry," she said. "What was the question?"

"Do you know why he was in the office so late?"

"He often worked very late."

"Do you know what he might have been working on?"

"You'll have to ask his associates," she said slowly. "I'm not that familiar with his cases. There has been a big corporate case but that's drawing to an end."

"When did you last talk to him?"

The question she dreaded. "Earlier tonight."

"Did he seem worried about anything?"

She hesitated, then said, "I need coffee."

She really needed time. To think. To decide what to say.

Byers nodded. Nicky, who hadn't wandered farther than

a few inches from her feet, went with her to the kitchen.
Byers followed.

Mechanically, she started the coffee.

The phone rang, and Gage rolled over to his bedside table.

He had been up until three this morning, following up on
the Starnes case. He looked at the clock and groaned.

Five.

Less than two hours' sleep.

He picked up the phone receiver.

"You left too early, partner."

"What do you mean?"

"Charles Rawson was just found. Dead."

Gage sat up with a jolt. "What did you say?"

"Prominent New Orleans attorney Charles Rawson just
bit the dust. A hit-and-run in his building's garage. Strange
that his daughter was a murder witness yesterday, huh?"

"Christ," Gage said. "Who has the case?"

"Not us. It's high profile now. I suspect we'll be taken off
the Starnes case. I'm not sure if the captain knows the connection between the cases, but he sure as hell will soon."

"Thanks for letting me know."

"Hey, we're partners."

The line went dead.

Gage hurriedly took a cold shower to wake up, then
stepped into a pair of Dockers and found a clean blue
shirt. Beast waited impatiently, obviously eager for a
meal. He poured some dry food into a bowl and filled the
water dish.

The impact of the news slowly sank in. Meredith would
be devastated. Her mother dying. The Starnes murder. Now
this.

Had she been notified yet?

Surely she had.

He wished she'd called him.

Would she want him near? Did she have anyone?

Surely yes.

Still, he would stop by her house, make sure she was all right.

Then he would start his own investigation. To hell with the department. Meredith Rawson was involved in something extremely dangerous. And he was damned well going to find out what it was.

From the time the phone rang to the time he stepped inside the car, only fifteen minutes had passed. He had not taken the time to shave.

Her house was lit. An unmarked department car was in front of the house.

He hurried up to the porch and tried the door. It opened.

Meredith was sitting in the living room, wrapped in a robe. Her hair was tousled. Her face was pale but under tight control.

She glanced up and a look of relief crossed her face.

The detective in a chair opposite her looked annoyed. "I didn't know you've been assigned to this case."

"I wasn't. I'm an acquaintance of Ms. Rawson. I thought she might need someone."

Max Byers shook his head.

"Her father has just been killed, for God's sake," Gage said. "She's not a witness."

"But she was yesterday, wasn't she? That's one hell of a coincidence."

Gage ignored him and sat down next to her. "Are you all right?" he asked softly.

"No."

Gage turned to Byers. "Can she have some time?"

"She should identify the body."

"Later today."

Byers nodded. "Call me and I'll send over a car."

"I'll take her."

Byers raised an eyebrow but handed her a card and left, taking his partner with him.

Gage turned to Meredith and held out his arms. She went into them, her body shuddering against his.

"I'm so damned sorry," he said.

"Thank you for coming. I know they're doing their jobs but . . ."

He ran his fingers through her hair, then down to her neck, massaging the muscles.

He didn't say anything, just held her close, wishing he could absorb some of her pain. He knew how he'd felt when his mother died. She'd never had time to be much of a mother, but she tried. God knew she had tried. He had been twenty-two and devastated.

"Cry," he said.

"I can't," she whispered into his shoulder. "I can't even comprehend. . . . He was here last night. Just a few hours ago."

For a moment, he felt as if his breath had been knocked from him. Death was following her like some dark shadow.

"Did he say anything? Was he worried?"

"He wanted me to stop looking for my sister."

"And you said . . .?"

"No. We argued. I didn't say good-bye." A tear rolled down her cheeks.

Her body was tense. Rigid.

"Some coffee? Tea? Or rest?"

She gave him a wan smile. "Maybe some coffee. There's some already made."

"I'll get it," he said, gently unwinding from her.

"I have to tell Daddy's housekeeper. She . . ." She looked back at him. Tears hovered in her eyes. They were held back, he thought, by sheer determination. "I'm sorry. I didn't mean to . . ."

"Hell with that," he said, resting his hand on her shoulder. She'd just been orphaned. Her father was dead, her mother was dying, and someone was killing people around her. Perhaps they had even tried to kill her. And missed.

She was being uncommonly strong. Nearly anyone else—man or woman—would be on their knees after the past few days.

"Tell me about him," he said, hoping that talking would help.

"He was a hard man to know. Distant." She started talking, and the words flowed out. "Demanding. For years I did everything I could to get his approval, but nothing seemed good enough. He was furious when I left the district attorney's office. He had plans. A judgeship was the least of them."

"I heard he'd been a prospect for a judgeship."

"It was something he always wanted."

"Why didn't he run for state judge?"

"He wanted the federal bench."

She needed to talk. He felt a little manipulative that he encouraged her to do so. Charles Rawson had been one of his suspects in the murder of Prescott fifteen years earlier. He should warn her. And yet . . . the closer he came to answers, the safer she would be.

She suddenly went quiet but her eyes searched his as if she knew exactly what he was thinking.

Telepathy? He had never before felt the kind of connection he felt with her.

"Why did you come here this morning?" she finally asked.

"I thought you might need a friend."

"Are you that?"

"I think so. I'm a good listener."

Emotion swirled in those gorgeous eyes. "Neither of my parents would be nominated for mother or father of the year," she said. "But they were all I had. The only family. Except . . ."

"The sister you've been trying to find."

"Yes."

"Which makes it all the more important."

"Yes."

"Everything began after you learned about her."

She looked at him, her eyes huge. "Why didn't I pay attention when my father told me to leave it alone?"

"You said he warned you last night. Had he done it earlier?"

She nodded. "After my mother told me about my sister, I confronted him. I asked him if he knew about it."

"Did he?"

"He didn't really answer. He just said it would soil my mother's reputation. And his. I really thought that was the only reason. . . ."

He read the guilt in her face and hated Charles Rawson. The man had been her father, for God's sake.

"How was he acting last night?"

"Nervous. It was unusual because he usually kept his emotions to himself. He asked me if I'd told anyone about my half sister."

"And you said you had. To me?"

"Not you specifically. To the police."

"Then what?"

He asked me if I had any idea of what I'd done. Then he left." Tears were in her eyes. "Mrs. Starnes. My father. It's my fault. Why didn't I just leave it alone?"

He wrapped his arms around her again and kissed the area around her eyes. "Because your mother asked you. Because someone is trying to keep a deadly secret. And secrets have a way of surfacing."

"It's my fault," she insisted.

"No, Meredith, it's not. Your parents made choices years ago. I suspect they weren't the wisest choices. I think that's why your father died. Not because of anything you did."

Her body trembled.

He held her against him, then asked the question he had to ask. "Is there any chance your mother might wake from the coma?"

"The doctors don't think so." Then she sat straight, pulling away from him. "Do you think someone might try to kill her, too?"

"Not if she's in a coma. They've already taken too many chances. Perhaps they hoped your father's death would be considered a simple hit-and-run. Your mother's death . . ."

"It wouldn't be that difficult, though. She's dying. An extra shot of morphine or—"

"There wouldn't be a reason," he assured her. "Not unless she regains consciousness. And even then she may not know any more than she told you."

"When is it going to stop?" Her voice trembled. The words were more a plea than a question.

"I don't know," he said. "This sister seems to be the reason behind everything. We can't keep it to ourselves any longer. I have to tell my partner. You have to tell Byers."

She knew he was right. And now it couldn't hurt her father. Or her mother.

She nodded. "Then I have to find my sister, don't I? That's the only way we can unravel this puzzle."

"Yes, but not alone. I don't want you alone from now on."

"That's something else," she said suddenly. "My father said he was going to hire protection for me. He knew something. He wouldn't tell me what."

"Perhaps he left something at his office."

"I'll . . ." She'd started to say she would go by the office later in the morning, but there were so many other things to do. Visit the coroner's office, for one. Make funeral arrangements. Notify people.

Her mother.

She closed her eyes against the enormity of it all.

The best gift she could give to both of them was to find the person who had killed her father, and to find the sister she hadn't known existed. The two must be linked.

But would it result in more deaths?

What had Lulu Starnes known that was so dangerous? Was there a clue in her home? In a scrapbook?

And her father. She knew how meticulous he was about his cases. He was a compulsive note taker. Had he left information somewhere?

She knew she was asking the questions to keep other emotions at bay. Her father had never been warm. He had never been much of a father.

But he'd been *her* father.

She had loved him.

And her mother, for all practical purposes, was gone.

It frightened her that no tears fell. She didn't want to be as cool and detached as they had been. At one time, she had wanted that. It was protection from hurt. Now she wanted to feel sorrow, grief. Instead there was a great chasm inside. Black and fathomless.

"Cry," Gage said. "Let it go."

But she couldn't. She couldn't until she knew why.

Still, she leaned back in his arms and warmth crept into her.

Not the warmth of passion, but the warmth of comfort.

eighteen

Trying to keep her nervousness from showing, Holly entered the Social Security office in Tucson.

A friend of Marty's was baby-sitting Harry at her house. Holly had not wanted to leave Harry in their own rented cottage. She still lived in fear that her husband would find them, snatch her son, then lay in wait for her.

She was loath to leave him at all. But a Social Security card was now urgent. She had to have one to get a bankcard, then a driver's license. Holly had rehearsed her story over and over again. If it sounded implausible to her, how would it sound to a clerk? But the book she read said that if you failed at one office, try another. Some clerks asked questions; others just accepted the fee and gave you a card.

She had her story together, the birth certificate, a baptismal certificate, a library card, and a rent receipt.

She'd practiced an accent for days. She had been excellent in French in high school and had continued her French studies during the two years she attended college.

She took a seat and waited for the first available clerk, then approached, holding an envelope with her pitiable documents.

"*Mademoiselle*, I hope you can assist me," she said with a slight accent.

The woman looked surprised and she gave Holly a smile. "I'll try."

"I have just returned to the States after living abroad since I was a child. My father was American but my mother was French. She left him when I was a child and I grew up in France, even married there. But like my mother, I was unlucky with love, you see. My husband took all we had and ran away with another woman. It was very sad, and I decided to come home. But now I need a job. I was told I must have a card."

The woman looked sympathetic. "You've never had one?"

"*Non,* I think not. We left America when I was a child."

"Do you have identification?"

"*Oui.* I have a birth certificate, a baptismal certificate made before we left this country and my library card. I am trying to relearn English again. I hope you will forgive my . . . poor—"

"You speak very well," the woman said, glancing over the documents. "We really need something with a photo on it, but . . ."

"I tried to get a bankcard, but the people at the bank said I need one of these numbers, and so does the driver's license office. I have been going around and around, and I am so . . . desperate."

"How did you happen to come to Arizona?"

Holly gave her a bright smile. "I read books about . . . your cowboys. And cactus. I thought, This looks a fine place to live. Not so much rain as France."

The woman hesitated, then nodded. "I think this will be enough."

Holly sighed with gratitude. "*Merci.* I mean, thank you."

"*Merci* will do nicely," the woman said. She gave Holly forms to fill out, then took them back when Holly had completed them.

"Bring by your driver's license when you receive one, and I'll add it to the file," she said.

"You are very kind, *Mademoiselle* . . ." Holly peered at the sign on the desk. "*Mademoiselle* Mackay."

"It is Mrs.," she said. "Welcome back to America."

"I will be very happy here if everyone is like you."

Holly took back her documents. The birth certificate. The baptismal certificate she had purchased at a Christian book and gift store, then aged by leaving it outside in the sun.

And was handed her Social Security card.

Her lifeline.

BISBEE

Liz Baker's reaction to her son's brief disappearance had raised a warning flag for Doug Menelo.

She never talked about her past. Never mentioned her husband's name or anything about him. At their first meeting, she'd been more than a little skittish around him. Wary. Even scared.

He had chalked it up to recent widowhood and the uncertainty of facing the dating world again. Now he wondered.

She had started to relax with him at Whitaker's ranch. Perhaps, he realized now, because he had done all the talking. He'd enjoyed teaching her about the land he loved. But he also remembered how reluctant she was to repeat that ride. Or go with him for supper.

He wasn't vain enough to think a woman should fall into his arms. But he would have been stupid not to recognize the attraction that had sparked between them. Something held her back. He'd thought it was her loyalty to a dead husband.

But there were small things . . . like Harry's unusual silence about his father, and his mother's worried expression when anyone talked to him.

Doug didn't like the thoughts. He liked her more than any woman he'd met for a long time. He had begun using cologne and dressing with more care. He'd smiled more since meeting her.

She was unquestionably a very pretty woman, although

she seemed to try to hide it. She rarely used lipstick and dressed in oversized shirts and loose jeans or slacks. But the bone structure of her face was exquisite and she had a shy smile that lit all of the outdoors.

Now he recalled her expression when she'd first met him. He'd seen echoes of it since. Fear. It had been fear. The kind of fear that an abused wife usually harbored. He had seen it far too many times to mistake it.

Could she be running from an abusive husband?

His protective instincts couldn't quite shroud a warning: If she was running from a husband, what about Harry? Had she violated a custody order?

He was jumping to conclusions, but they were conclusions reached from years of experience in domestic disputes. It would explain much that had puzzled him.

He rifled through a pile of bulletins for missing women and kidnapped children. As he discarded each one, he breathed easier.

Still, his instincts were usually right. She was afraid of something.

He would go by her house tomorrow. Perhaps take some offering. Candy. Cookies for Harry. His niece loved making chocolate chip cookies and he could drop off a package. Perhaps he could get Liz to confide in him.

He would also continue looking. A fugitive wife or not, she might well need help. He was damn sure going to try to give it to her.

NEW ORLEANS

Meredith woke up in Gage's arms. They had not made love, but he had accompanied her upstairs and had lain down with her, his arms around her. Comforting. Protective.

She'd been cold. So very cold. She had lain awake for a long time before drifting into a listless sleep. Questions. So many questions.

Who killed her father and why?

And Lulu Starnes?

And had whoever tried to run her down in the hospital garage really meant to kill her? If so, why hadn't they used the gun that shot out the garage lights?

Nothing made sense.

Her mother! Should she tell her about her husband's death? Would some subconscious part of her mind understand? Meredith was suddenly aware that her mother's care was now in her hands. Guilt twisted inside that she had not stayed at her mother's side nor had she had any success in finding her sister.

Did her mother understand on some level that Meredith was trying to fulfill that one last wish, trying frantically to do so before her mother died?

Why did one thing seem to be connected with the other? A lost daughter. Death.

She'd finally slipped into sleep. She didn't know how long she slept but when she woke, Gage's arms were still around her. She turned and looked at him. He was awake and looked as if he had been for some time. She wondered whether he'd slept at all.

"Hi," he said in the low lazy drawl that had so attracted her from the beginning. He was still fully clothed except for shoes, and his hair was tousled. Golden bristle covered the lower part of his face. His eyes were fully awake.

"Hi," she said as a wet nose bumped her arm.

Nicky.

He chuckled. "Get use to it. The perils of having a dog." He rolled over to the side of the bed. "I'll take him out, then make some coffee," he said. "Why don't you stay here and get a little more rest?"

"I can't." She looked at the clock. It was nine.

"All right."

She liked the way he accepted her comment. He didn't push. Didn't baby her. Didn't try to manage her. She left the bed and went into her bathroom. She stared at what she saw in the mirror. Her eyes were red-rimmed and swollen. Her hair stuck out in all directions. Her T-shirt looked as if it had just emerged from the bottom of a clothes bin.

Funny she could regard herself so passionlessly when the only world she knew was collapsing around her. She imagined she was still in shock. She supposed that was one of the mind's protections.

She took a quick shower, shaking the cobwebs from her mind. She pushed away grief by making a mental list of things that had to be done. First was a visit to the police department. She would tell them everything she knew, including the information about her sister and how it might be related to two deaths.

She would have to formally identify the body, make funeral arrangements, prepare information for the obituary. She shuddered. His death wasn't really real to her. She suspected it soon would be.

Her search for her sister would have to wait.

She went back to her bedroom and changed into a dark blue linen suit she'd just purchased for court. She added just a hint of lipstick and went into the kitchen where the smell of brewing coffee met her. Nicky was contentedly eating a piece of toast.

She would have to get food for him. She added that to her growing list.

Two slices of toast popped up from the toaster. A glass of orange juice was on the table.

"I was going to make an omelet," Gage said, "but your fridge is dismally empty. It's obvious you do not have growing boys in your household."

"And you're a growing boy?"

"Damn, I hope not. But I am a hungry one. What about breakfast on the way to the police station?"

She wasn't hungry. But she hadn't had anything to eat since a quick bite at noon the day before. She needed her energy, and her wits. She took a cup of coffee. "Before we go to the police department, can we go by Lulu Starnes's home?"

He raised an eyebrow.

"You're the detective on the case," she said.

"Probably not for long. I called my partner just now. I am

being sought by my superiors, probably so they can inform me that the case is being turned over to the detectives involved in your father's case."

"But you haven't been told yet."

He eyed her with bemusement. "Nope."

"Have you reached Mrs. Starnes's family yet?"

"Yes, a sister. She's in Detroit. She should be here later today."

"Then we should go to the house now. Will you get in trouble if you take me there?"

"As you said, it's still my case. What are you looking for?"

"Photos. Memorabilia. A diary. Anything that might tell us who the father of my sister is. We should do this now, before you get taken off the case."

"Okay. Then Byers's office. I told him you would be there this morning."

Her mind sorted through what she needed to do today. "I'll make some calls on the way." She paused. "What about Nicky?"

"I can take him home with me. Beast likes other dogs."

"In what way?" she asked suspiciously.

He grinned. "Not for dinner, if that worries you. I feed him well. And there's a kid next door who feeds him when I'm gone."

"Just until I go home," she said. She wanted someone with her tonight. She couldn't expect Gage to hang around. He had been kind last night, but . . .

She nodded. "Thank you."

"We'll go by my house first to drop off Nicky, then Mrs. Starnes's home."

Anything to delay visiting the morgue. Anything to delay reality. She had never considered herself a coward but now she felt like one. Only Gage kept her from falling apart and she wouldn't crumple in front of him.

Lulu Starnes. Concentrate on Lulu Starnes.

She waited while he fetched a leash and attached it to Nicky's collar. Though the dog had eaten the slice of toast, his tail was between his legs. Well, he had lost someone he loved. And so had she.

At Gage's home, Beast greeted Nicky with enthusiasm. The dog wagged his tail for the first time since she had taken him from the crime scene. Then the two dogs did what dogs do. Sniffed each other as they continued to wag tails. She decided he would be fine with Beast.

Five minutes later, Gage and Meredith reached Mrs. Starnes's home. The crime lab people had obviously left. Yellow tape indicated a crime scene. A police car sat in front.

A chill invaded her. She really didn't want to go inside again.

"Are you sure you want to go in?" he asked gently.

Once again he'd read her mind. "Yes," she said. "How?"

"It's my case and my crime scene until I'm officially relieved," he said.

There was quiet anger in his voice. She got out of the car and waited until he went over and talked to the officers, then returned.

He led the way to the door and stepped aside for her to enter.

She couldn't move for a moment. She remembered yesterday—or was it an eon ago?—when she'd walked in.

She felt Gage's hand at her back, bracing her.

She took a deep breath and went inside. She avoided the kitchen and started her search in a small room obviously used as an office. Bookcases stuffed with books lined three walls.

Meredith checked the desk. She knew that Wagner and Gage had probably already checked it. But she knew what to look for and they hadn't. A large calendar filled the surface of the desk, and she saw her name written neatly on it. A pile of what looked like bills were on one side. There was no computer.

Strange. She would have expected one.

Photos. Lulu Starnes must have photos somewhere.

Meredith went through the drawers but found nothing. Gage joined her, shaking his head to her unasked question.

Had the person who killed Mrs. Starnes already searched the house?

She forced herself to return to the kitchen. A tea kettle sat on a burner of the stove. Two cups were on the counter, along with tea bags. Had Mrs. Starnes started to prepare for her visitor? For Meredith? In her horror over finding the body, she hadn't noticed yesterday.

The breakfast nook was furnished with a small oak table. Two places had been set; a creamer was filled with soured milk. Was this where Mrs. Starnes had planned to talk to her?

If she had anything to show Meredith, perhaps it would be in this same area.

Meredith spied a pile of cookbooks on a baker's rack, along with some flowering plants. She went over to them. As she picked up the top volume, several photos fell out.

She sat down and studied them.

Her mother was in two of them. So was a younger Lulu Starnes.

Meredith gazed at the girl who had become her mother. Marguerite Thibadeau smiled through the decades, a mischievous grin spread across her face. She looked as if she owned the world.

Lulu Starnes, on the other hand, looked out of place. Only a forced shadow of a smile crossed her face. A young man stood between the two young girls, his arm draped lazily across her mother's shoulders. His face was turned toward her mother, and she saw only his profile.

It was not her father. The man was tall, lanky, with his dark hair in a ponytail.

Meredith stared at the photo for a moment. She had never seen that particular expression on her mother's face. Nor that consequences-be-damned set of her chin.

There was no question that the young man would never have met Meredith's grandfather's standards.

She looked at other elements of the photo. The three

young people were standing in front of what looked like a tavern. The sign said PAULE'S.

She knew she had never seen it before. It looked as if it were located in some rural area.

"Find something?" Gage's voice broke her concentration.

"I don't know. Did you?"

"No. I called my partner. We're still on the Starnes case, although they are trying to take it away. They are talking about your father's death as an accidental hit-and-run."

"No!"

"The detectives aren't happy about it, either."

"After what happened to me?"

"Someone is pulling strings, and whoever it is has to be powerful. I trust the chief—it's not him."

"Then how . . .?"

"It could be anyone. The medical examiner. Some judges. Even the mayor. But any rookie cop would know it's a murder."

"What can I do?"

"Make noise. Demand answers. Publicly, so you're no longer a target. Another suspicious death won't fly." He hesitated. "Continue to search for your sister. I don't think the police will help. Someone's putting the damper on it."

"But it doesn't make sense. Why would anyone care?"

"Think about it." He was pushing her. "Think of reasons."

"Someone—whoever adopted my sister—doesn't want anyone to know it was a back door adoption."

"And?"

"Crimes were committed," she said.

"Crimes serious enough to warrant murder thirty years after the fact," he added. "I don't think it was just because of an undocumented adoption. Perhaps someone had a motive not to let anyone know his or her child was not a child of their blood."

"I can't do any more looking until after I bury my father."

"I realize that. And I plan to stick to you like glue."

"What about your job?"

"If I can't protect you on the city's nickel, then I'll take leave."

"But if they are as powerful as you believe . . ."

"No one is as powerful as they think they are. We *will* find them."

Gage was looking down at the photo, a puzzled look on his face.

"What is it?"

He shrugged. "There's something about that boy but thirty-plus years makes a lot of change in a person."

"Perhaps we can find the tavern," she said. "If he went there often . . .?"

"I doubt whether it still exists but I'll try. I think Memphis might be a better bet."

"You could be in danger, too. If they would kill someone as well-known as my father . . ."

"I know how to take care of myself."

"I expect my father believed that as well."

"I'll be careful."

She turned her attention back to the photos. There was one other photo.

Her mother dancing with the same young man. Again his face was only in profile. They were in a crowd that looked more like families than young people.

"I'll have Sarah start researching a bar named Paule's in the New Orleans area."

He nodded. "Let's go see Byers," he said. "Perhaps with what you've told me we can change the decision on your father."

She felt a little better. They were doing something. She wasn't just being a victim.

She only hoped it didn't lead to another death.

nineteen

Identifying her father's body was the hardest thing Meredith ever had to do.

Even though she knew the police had identified him, she—as a member of the family—had to do it as well.

She had watched before as family members had identified their loved ones. She had often ached inside for them, even while trying to maintain an objective but sympathetic exterior.

Peering through the window as a tech uncovered her father's face, she knew she would never again watch such a procedure with any objectivity.

It was like being hit in the heart with a sledgehammer.

His face was gray. There were bruises on his cheek where he had fallen, but other than that he looked . . . just still. The real damage, she knew, was underneath the sheet: catastrophic injury to every major organ.

Byers, who stood beside her, was silent and patient. He, too, had been witness to this scene often.

She nodded to him. Signed the papers. She took pride in the fact that her hand didn't tremble.

Then she turned and followed him out of the morgue. At her request, Gage had waited outside.

He reached out a hand to her in silent empathy. She held

it tight for a moment, then let go. That brief human contact meant everything, made the present tolerable.

Gage then drove her to the homicide unit and they went into the conference room. Gage's partner, Glenn Wagner, was already there. Byers would join them soon.

Wary, she paused at the door. Someone with a great deal of influence was trying to squelch the investigation. The fact that Gage might be taken off the Lulu Starnes case proved that. He hadn't known how far they could trust Byers. Or even his own partner.

Byers walked in several minutes later and eyed her speculatively. "Gaynor said you might have some information."

She attacked first. "Why is my father's death being considered a simple hit-and-run?"

"I wish I knew. The call came from above."

"How far above?"

"I don't know. It was relayed by the captain." Byers glanced at Gage. "Your lieutenant as well."

"Hit-and-run is still murder," Meredith said sharply.

Byers didn't blink. "Yes, but not with the same priority."

"Not even with the fact that my father was rather prominent?"

He gave her a wry look.

"Perhaps Ms. Rawson can change your mind," Gage said.

"It's not my decision," Byers said. "I'm convinced it was intended murder, particularly after the attempt on Ms. Rawson's life."

"There's a lot more."

"I know about the Starnes murder," Byers said.

Meredith broke in. "My father visited me hours before his death. He was worried. He told me . . . He said I didn't know what I had done."

"What had you done?" Byers asked.

"My mother recently told me she'd had a child out of wedlock. She wanted me to try to find her. As soon as I started searching, someone tried to run me down. My home was trashed. I received anonymous phone calls. Records disappeared from my father's home.

"I talked to my father, and he warned me not to search for my sister, that it would destroy my mother's reputation. I thought he meant his own. I was angry."

"Go on," Byers said.

"I started trying to contact my mother's friends. Mrs. Starnes was one of them. She was killed before I could talk to her."

"Have you contacted anyone else?"

"Mrs. Robert Laxton."

"When?"

"Sunday. And I visited her on Monday."

Byers looked toward Gage. "Has anything happened to her?"

"No," Gage said. "I checked on her this morning."

"Then I don't see a connection."

Meredith had a sinking feeling in her stomach. Byers was obviously going along with what had to be a cover-up. She had the photos from the Starnes home in her pocketbook. She decided not to show them. She was not going to put the young man with her mother and Mrs. Starnes in danger.

She gave Gage a warning look, hoping he would not mention the photos.

He didn't. "Let's go," he said.

She stood.

"I have more questions," Byers said.

"If you think it's a simple hit-and-run, why?"

"I didn't say simple."

"Look, this is a waste of my time. I have funeral arrangements to make, an ill mother to see."

"I may have questions later."

"Talk to me then."

She didn't have to stay. She was not a material witness.

He knew it as well. He stood. "Thank you for the identification. We will keep in touch."

"Only if my father's case is called what it is and treated as such," she shot back.

She stalked out, slamming the door behind her. She couldn't remember being so angry. New Orleans had once been notorious for its corruption. She had thought that era had come to an end.

Her father had been a part of it. She knew that now. It hadn't been only fear in his eyes these past few days. It had been guilt.

Guilt for what?

Something to do with what happened to her mother.

She thought again of the smiles on her mother's face in the photos she had inside her purse, then of the caution that had always shadowed her face. Meredith had believed her mother just had not loved her enough, that she had cared about her causes more than she could care about fellow human beings. Now she wondered whether it hadn't been lack of caring, but fear of caring.

Meredith had that fear.

She looked at Gage as they reached his car. "Thank you for not telling him about the photos."

"It's called withholding evidence, Counselor," he said as he quirked an eyebrow questioningly.

"We don't know that it *is* evidence. I do know I don't want anyone else to die because of my search."

"You can end it."

She stared at him.

"You can drop it. Forget it."

"But you said . . ."

"I was wrong. And anyway there's no trail."

"There's the photo."

"It's more than thirty years old. And the father probably didn't even know about the child."

"But maybe he did. Maybe his family took it."

"Then your mother would have probably known about it."

"I thought you were on my side." She heard herself and cringed. She sounded like a tired, whiney child.

"I am," he said. "But let me handle it from now on. Let

me investigate the Starnes case. I can't do that if you are going off on your own. Let it be known you've given up."

"And how do I do that?"

"Stop asking questions."

She looked up at him. "What about you?"

"I'll keep investigating. It's my case."

"You said you might be taken off it."

"Now that your father's death has been ruled a probable accidental hit-and-run, there's no reason to combine the cases."

"What if they come after you?"

"A cop? I doubt it. That's real trouble."

"My father should have been 'real trouble.' "

He didn't answer that observation. "Come on, I'll take you home."

"How can you investigate if you keep looking after me?" she persisted. She didn't like the direction of the conversation. She didn't like being sidelined. She didn't like trusting someone else. Particularly now when everyone she'd trusted before was turning out to be untrustworthy.

It would be a very long time before she believed anyone again. Even the man beside her. The man she had started to trust.

Now she wondered.

He had been nearby every time something had happened. He was part of a department that was trying to hide something. He'd encouraged her to find answers. Now he was steering her away.

She remembered that flicker of recognition she thought she saw as he'd looked at the photograph, yet he had not shared anything with her. From the beginning, she'd been the one giving information and he had been taking it.

And if he was not using her, then she was putting him in danger, just as she had put her father and Mrs. Starnes in jeopardy. How many more deaths could she have on her conscience?

Either way, she had to do what she had done in the past. Rely on herself.

She leaned against the car. "You can't do your job and mine, too."

He looked at her quizzically. "Is that a brush-off?"

"No. Someone is attacking people around me. Not me. They've tried to scare me, yes, but I'm alive."

"You don't think I can take care of myself?"

"I don't want you to be a target because of me."

He looked at her for a long moment. "Afraid?"

"Of course I'm afraid. I would be incredibly stupid not to be."

"I don't mean of what's happening around you. I mean what's happening between us."

She was silent.

He studied her face. "I'm not happy with it myself. I'm distracted when I should be sharp. I'm losing objectivity. That's not good for a detective."

"That's why we should separate."

"I'm afraid it doesn't work that way."

Darn those green eyes that always seem to see into her soul. She resented the invasion, even though she knew it was possible only because of the connection they had with each other. Had always had, though she'd tried to deny it.

"Ah, Meredith. Don't fight me," he said. He touched her chin with such gentleness and sweetness, she probably would have pledged him the moon and stars had he asked. Then he leaned down and kissed her, apparently oblivious to several passersby.

When Gage finished his kiss, she was giddy with his taste, his scent. She caught a glimpse of people getting into a car, amused expressions on their faces.

She had just identified her father's body.

But perhaps that's why she needed the tenderness of his lips, the heat of his body. She'd been so cold since learning of her father's death.

She forced herself to step back. She had things she must do. "Please drive me home," she said. "I'm grateful but . . ."

"I don't want gratitude, Meredith."

"What do you want?"

He looked her straight in the eyes. "Damned if I know," he said with a smile. "Except I want to keep you in one piece."

"I like that priority."

"But you don't intend to let me do it?"

"I don't intend to let anyone else get hurt." She reached for the door handle. "And I have funeral arrangements to make and . . ."

She closed her eyes at the prospect of the next few days.

He touched her cheek and she leaned her face against his palm for a fraction of a second.

She moved and broke the spell. "I have to go."

"I'll stay with you."

She shook her head. "I need some space right now."

"I'll make other arrangements for your protection then," he said. His voice had lost the warm drawl and was clipped. She looked into his eyes and saw a flicker of something like hurt.

Better that, she told herself, than to have his death on her conscience as well as the others'.

Still, the chill had crawled back into her heart.

BISBEE

Doug Menelo slammed down the phone in frustration. No record of an Elizabeth Baker.

She'd said she was from Chicago, but he had neither her address nor the name of her deceased husband. He hadn't realized until he started searching that she had never once mentioned the first name of her husband.

Still, he ran a check on her. There were any number of Elizabeth Bakers but none that fit what he knew about her. No traffic tickets in Illinois. No arrests.

He searched recent deaths in Illinois for a male with the last name of Baker. He found a number of them but none with a wife named Elizabeth.

He then turned to the driver's license bureau in Illinois. There were numerous Elizabeth Bakers, including ten in the

Chicago area, and three with a birth date that would equate with hers. He found the addresses and called. All were at home.

He tried Arizona. She had not applied recently for an Arizona license, but she still had time to do that.

The lack of information only piqued his curiosity further.

He checked missing children bulletins, mainly custodial kidnappings again. Nothing in the past two months fit Liz and her son.

An overactive imagination on his part?

He looked at his watch. Four P.M.

He didn't usually force his company on women. He knew he was no matinee idol. But his gut was telling him something. He prided himself on being a good judge of character. And Elizabeth had a sweetness and shyness that couldn't be disguised or feigned. She was also afraid. He hadn't missed that, either.

He was a sucker for a damsel in distress. But he couldn't help unless he understood the reason for her fear.

He decided to try Marty and headed for Special Things.

Marty welcomed him. "Hi."

"Hi yourself."

This part was going to be more difficult. He had established a good relationship with most of the merchants. Marty was on the town council and one of his greatest supporters. She was also a firm believer in an individual's privacy. She had protected many of the town's more eccentric citizens when others wanted them invited to leave because they might annoy tourists.

She looked at him closely. "This isn't a social visit."

"Not exactly."

"And you're not happy about it."

"You didn't tell me you were psychic."

She grinned. "I don't tell you everything."

"What do you know about Liz?" he asked abruptly.

The smile left her face. "Not much. Only that I like her."

"I do, too."

"Then . . ."

"Has she said anything about her husband to you?"

"No."

"Would you tell me if she had?"

"No."

He smiled at that, but it didn't deter him. "She's afraid of something."

Marty didn't reply.

"She might need help."

"Then she'll ask for it."

"You're a hard woman, Marty."

"I'm an old softie and you know it."

He sighed. "I won't hurt her."

"You may not intend to."

"You're right."

"Have you been asking questions?"

He nodded. "But in such a way it shouldn't attract attention."

"Good."

"Keep an eye on her," he said.

"I will."

Frustrated, he went down the street to a restaurant, where he ordered two large pizzas. He looked at his watch. Hopefully, Liz and her son hadn't eaten yet.

Thirty minutes later he was on her doorstep, ringing the bell.

Harry opened it, looked at the two big boxes in his hand and grinned. "Pizza," he exclaimed.

Liz reached the door then, wiping her hands with a cloth.

"Hi," he said. "I was getting a pizza and decided I didn't want to eat alone. I hoped you and Harry would share them with me."

"Them? That's a lot of pizza."

He shifted uncomfortably at the door.

"Where's Jenny?" she asked.

"At a sleep over."

She was not welcoming. Then she smiled, and it was as if the sun just entered the room. "Thank you. I *am* hungry, and pizza comes second only to tacos in Harry's opinion."

"I'm a taco man myself," he said, grinning down at Harry.

He stepped inside and looked over in the corner of the room where she'd established a work area. "I hope you don't mind. I don't usually barge in on people, but I was at the restaurant and I thought of Harry. I won't stay if you don't want. But—"

"I don't mind at all," she broke in. "It was thoughtful."

Relief. Maybe he was wrong. Maybe she didn't have anything to hide. Or anything to fear. He hoped to God not.

He took out the pizzas while she got some napkins.

"I got a pepperoni and cheese, and one with the works."

"They smell wonderful. What would you like to drink? Cola? Or water?"

"Cola sounds great."

They sat around a small wobbly table. Harry waited until he was offered a piece, then ate carefully. Too carefully for a small boy.

Liz's gaze met his. Damn, but her eyes were soft. Gentle. Her lips looked inviting.

He took a piece and decided it tasted a great deal better with company than without it. "I didn't know whether you would like pizza."

"Hmm. I love it. I haven't eaten today, either."

She looked beautiful with tomato sauce on her lips. He wanted to ask her about taking Harry riding on the weekend, but he knew how much a parent hated being put on the spot in front of her child. He would do it later.

"How are the sculptures doing?" he asked.

"Marty said they're selling out."

"Good. Does that mean you will stay with us awhile?"

She took another bite of pizza, not answering immediately.

"Or will you return to Chicago?"

"Why?" She met his question directly.

"Family?"

"I don't have any. My mother and father are both dead."

"I'm sorry," he said, feeling immensely uncomfortable.

He didn't want to interrogate her. He wanted to enjoy these few moments. Hell, he wanted her to enjoy them even more.

He refrained from asking more questions, hoping against hope that she might come to trust him with more answers than she'd given thus far. He paced his eating to theirs, and when he'd taken the last bite he pushed away from the table. "Thanks for letting me stay."

"I could hardly refuse a hungry man with pizza," she said with a hint of a smile. Since it was one of the few she'd gifted him with, he felt a fuzzy warmth inside.

He wanted to ask her out for a real date. Hell, he wanted to lean over and kiss her.

Most of all, he wanted to pierce the mystery that enveloped her. He put the leftover pizza into the box and followed her out to the kitchen as Harry munched on some cheese sticks that had been included.

Once out of hearing of Harry, he asked his question. "I'm taking Jenny to the ranch Saturday. Would you and Harry like to go?"

He saw the swift denial on her face but she never put it into words. Instead he watched desire war with caution. "We'd like that," she said almost defiantly.

"Good. I'll be here at nine. Perhaps some breakfast along the way?"

She nodded. "Thank you for not asking in front of Harry."

He suddenly realized that his decision in that one matter had opened her door to him.

But even while that thought pleased him, he felt a deeper disquiet. She was opening up to him. Ever so slightly. He felt traitorous. As low as he ever had felt in his career.

He decided to give up his queries.

NEW ORLEANS

Meredith looked around at the mourners. Her heart was numb. Nothing seemed real. It was as if she were an onlooker watching the drama and grief of others.

Was someone here a murderer?

Everyone was solicitous. But she sat alone in the second pew of the packed church. Sarah and Becky, she knew, were at her father's house, helping to supervise caterers for the gathering after the funeral. She'd invited Mrs. Edwards, the housekeeper, to sit with her but the woman declined. She wanted to sit in the back.

Meredith had always been alone but she was even more alone now.

She had looked for Gage, but he hadn't come. She had told him she needed space. He'd apparently taken her at her word.

She tried to listen to the service. Her father had once been an active member of the church and had, with his wife, continued to give tens of thousands of dollars although he seldom attended. She listened to her father's character extolled.

She'd declined to say anything. He was her father, and as such she had loved him. She had admired him even if she had not actually liked him. Now she realized his life had been full of secrets. So had her mother's.

Secrets dangerous enough to kill for.

Still, she mourned him. She felt infinite sadness for the man who had told her his wife had never loved him. He had uttered the words with such despair. She was beginning to feel that both her parents had lived in a hell of their own making.

But why?

So many questions. So few answers. All she could do now was mourn her father. She couldn't change the past. She could only try to understand it.

A hymn. "Faith of Our Fathers." She remembered when she had first heard that. Years ago when her mother had thought she should go to Sunday school and church. She had sat between them and felt the tension.

Images flitted through her head. Her father as a younger man. Even then he had been distant. Demanding perfection. She remembered his rare smile when she told him she'd been accepted into law school. There might even have been pride in his face at her law school graduation. She had relished that until she learned he had her life planned.

The last hymn. The coffin was carried out by six men in dark suits. She wondered if they knew him better than she did.

She had to endure the graveside service as well. She invited Mrs. Edwards, her father's housekeeper, to share the limousine with her, and this time she agreed.

Unexpectedly, the woman had tears in her eyes. Meredith felt guilty that she didn't have any of her own. Not now. They were locked inside.

She noted that the day was sunny. Not like those funerals in the films when the sky seemed to weep. When the group gathered at the graveside, she looked at every face. Most she knew. They came from the legal and political communities or were her mother's acquaintances.

Her stomach roiled as she wondered if one was a killer.

She tried to look into their eyes. But all she saw was sympathy.

When the service was over, she looked again for Gage. She knew detectives often attended the services of their victims. But the police department wasn't considering her father's death as a deliberate act.

She didn't see him. She had told him this was something she wanted to do on her own. She would be safe. Surrounded by people. And he needed to do his job.

She'd wanted to prove to herself that she could stand alone.

She realized she was fighting a losing battle. She needed him far more than she wanted to. The big question was whether those feelings were fueled by grief and her bewilderment about the violence swirling about her or by something deeper. Something more lasting.

After the graveside service, there was the reception at her parents' house. She had planned it there since her house was far too small for the crowd. She suffered through it, accepting condolences. Uttering words of thanks. All the time she watched for a tall, graceful detective with unruly blond hair and clear green eyes.

When he didn't appear, she made mental lists even as she urged more food on her guests.

She had to make an appointment to see her father's attorney and make decisions about his estate. He had named her trustee for the estate years ago. He hadn't thought his wife could handle it on her own.

First on her list, though, was that delayed visit to Memphis, to the neighbors of her great-aunt. Perhaps someone would remember a visit thirty-three years ago of a young girl with a big secret. With more information, she might find the doctor. And records.

The last guest left her parents' house. With grateful relief, she returned home and fed the dog. She took him for a walk, enjoying the uncomplicated companionship. Both Sarah and Becky had suggested coming over to keep her company, but she'd assured them she just needed rest.

She had Nicky. And the gun in her purse.

She also had things to do. Meredith had given Mrs. Edwards several days off with pay. She'd left immediately after the reception to stay with her sister for a few days.

Meredith knew she couldn't sleep. She had to do something. She invited Nicky into her car and drove back to her parents' house. It had been thoroughly cleaned by the caterers but she thought she heard the echoes of the people who were there just hours ago.

She would have to decide what to do with it. She didn't want to live there. Too many memories.

She pictured her mother and father in it, remembering all the times they had both been there. But not together. Rarely together.

The doorbell rang. Nicky barked loudly.

Another mourner. Perhaps a reporter. She thought about ignoring it, but Nicky was frantic. She looked outside.

Gage Gaynor's lanky form leaned against the outside wall. Another man was with him. She recognized him. He had swept her house for listening devices.

Relief flooded her. She opened the door.

Gage took one look at her face and pulled her into his arms. He held her for a moment, then stepped back and introduced the man with him.

"Hi. I wanted the house swept for bugs."

"You think . . ."

"Your telephone was bugged. I think it's entirely likely your father's might have been as well."

She stepped back as the two men entered. She was silent as Gage's companion checked the phones, then swept the entire house for listening devices. Gage shook his head. "Nothing."

She was confused. "Why me and not him? Why didn't they kill me but killed him?"

"Perhaps he told someone something they didn't want to hear." He hesitated, then asked, "No more mystery calls?"

"No. But then the phone hasn't stopped ringing. I finally turned it off."

"You haven't noticed anyone watching you?"

She shook her head. She wished she wasn't so glad to see him.

"Good. A friend of mine has been keeping an eye on you. I'm glad to know he's good enough not to be spotted."

Anger flashed through her for a second. He'd had no right. Then she realized how stupid that was. She would be a fool to allow pride to get in the way of safety. And he'd cared enough to see that she stayed safe. Some of the chill left her. "Do you think they'll come after me again?"

"I think it depends on what you find. I think whoever did this is probably wary of too many bodies turning up. Hopefully, they'll think you are too distracted . . . and too frightened to keep looking. I'm sure they know you're too smart not to have made the connection."

"I'm not distracted."

"I know, and that worries me."

"Where were you today?" She pressed her lips together, hating that she had asked that question as if the answer mattered. As if she had the right to hear it.

"A floater turned up this week. Fingers were cut off. No head. Bullet in the heart. Looks like a mob hit. We've been trying to get an ID on him. The lieutenant scheduled a meeting on it. I didn't have a choice." His gaze met hers and shifted. She suddenly realized he was holding something back.

Or was she just wary now of everyone?

Her cell phone rang.

She picked it up.

"Ms. Rawson?"

It was Nan Fuller's voice. Frantic. Hysterical.

"Nan?"

"I went home to pick up some things for the kids. Rick was supposed to be on duty. He's here. I think he's going to kill me. I locked myself in the bathroom but—"

"Have you called 911?"

"Yes, but—"

Meredith heard a loud bang at the other end of the line. Muttered curses. "I'm on my way," she said.

She looked at Gage. "Rick Fuller is attacking Nan at their house."

He headed for the door. "Let's go."

Meredith followed at a run. She had neglected Nan these past few days. She had neglected all her clients.

And now one of them might die.

How many more deaths could she bear?

And how much more guilt?

twenty

The siren wailed as the car careened toward the Fuller home.

Gage drove as fast as was safe. He was only too aware of the woman who shared the front seat with him.

He'd feared exactly what was happening. The last time he'd confronted Fuller, he'd sensed the seething fury in the man. He'd hoped he'd tamped it. Instead it appeared he'd ignited it. He was furious with himself.

He also wondered at the timing. Fuller must have heard about the death of the father of his wife's attorney. He was also fully aware of the attacks on Meredith. Had he been waiting for an opportunity?

Gage prayed silently that squad cars were closer than he and Meredith. He felt the tension emanating from her. He felt it in himself. He knew he shouldn't have brought her with him. But he'd also known she wouldn't have stayed at home. She would have driven herself to the Fuller home.

He pressed down on the gas pedal, jerking in and out of traffic. As they neared the location, he debated turning off the siren. Sometimes it would instigate even more violence. Other times, it would scare off the intruder.

He's a bully. Bullies want the advantage. They're mostly cowards.

Take a guess.

He kept the siren on.

The car screeched up to the curb in front of Fuller's home just as two squad cars arrived.

"Stay here," he told Meredith.

He bounded out of the car and went over to the first cruiser. Two uniformed officers left the second one and met them.

"A cop," Gage said with disgust. "There's a restraining order against him."

"Hell," said one of the officers, then looked to him for advice.

"I'll go in. I know him."

A shot echoed from inside the house and lingered in the humid air. Gage drew his weapon, told one of the officers to call for more backup. He looked around and saw Meredith leaving his car.

"Detective!"

At the shout of one of the uniformed officers, he whirled and saw Fuller running from the house. He was in uniform and had a gun in his hand.

Gage yelled, "Police. Stop."

Fuller turned around. He obviously saw Gage, then Meredith. He raised the gun and pointed it at Gage.

"Drop it," Gage shouted.

Instead Fuller turned the gun on Meredith. Fuller and Gage fired at the same time. It was like watching a movie in slow motion. His heart skipped as Meredith twisted around. Fell. In the periphery of his vision, Fuller dropped to the ground.

Meredith. He ran to her. Knelt. She clutched her arm and blood oozed between his fingers.

"Let me see." He pried her hand away from the wound. The fist around his heart unclenched. It was a flesh wound.

The officers had dived for cover when the shooting started. They rose and went over to Fuller, kicking away his weapon and checking for a pulse. "He's dead," one said loud enough for both of them to hear.

Gage went over to him, checked Fuller's neck for a pulse himself. Wordlessly, he returned to Meredith's side.

"Go and look after Nan," Meredith said. "I'm all right."

He turned and ran inside. He knew that paramedics were automatically dispatched on a 911 call. He directed two of the other officers to check the rest of the house . . . to check on the children.

"Mrs. Fuller!" he called out. He moved from one room to the other in the modest bungalow. Then he saw a closed door. There was a bullet hole in it.

From his one previous visit, he knew it led to a bathroom.

He heard a noise from behind and whirled around. *Meredith.* She was dripping blood. An officer behind her spread his hands in an expression of helplessness.

He wanted to rail at her, but he knew the sooner he found Nan Fuller, the sooner he could get Meredith to listen to reason.

He tried the doorknob. It was locked.

"Mrs. Fuller? Police."

Silence.

"It's Detective Gaynor. Meredith Rawson is with me. You called her."

The lock clicked. The door opened slowly and he saw Nan Fuller in front of him. Her face was pale and tearstained. Drying blood stained her dress.

"My kids," Nan said, her voice rising as she tried to push past them. "He said he would get them. He said he would get Ms. Rawson. He said he would finish the job."

"Where are the children?"

"At the shelter, but he said he knew where it is."

Gage was sickened that a police officer would cause such terror. "They're okay. Your husband is dead."

"Dead?" She looked dazed.

He hesitated, then said. "I shot him. He was threatening Ms. Rawson."

"Oh my God," she said, leaning against the wall, then her eyes focused on Meredith and the blood dripping from her arm. "I . . . It's my fault."

"It's not your fault," he said softly. "He made the decisions tonight, not you. Don't ever think differently."

"He shot through the door but I was against the wall. I thought he was going to break down the door. He tried. Then he heard the sirens."

She trembled all over.

Meredith stepped over to Nan, hugging her with her good arm. "He won't hurt anyone again."

He heard another siren. The ambulance. "Both of you should go to the hospital," Gage said.

"My children!"

"I'll have a car pick them up and take them to the hospital. Do you have someone who can stay with you tonight?"

"A counselor from the shelter."

Gage broke in. "I'm sorry, Mrs. Fuller."

"Why?"

"I should have recognized. . . . I thought keeping his job would keep him away from you."

She shook her head. "He knew his career was over. That he would never get a promotion. He blamed it on me. And Ms. Rawson. He said he would make her pay."

Gage looked back at Meredith. She was still bleeding. He went into the bathroom and grabbed a towel to wrap around her injured arm.

"You don't follow directions very well," he said more harshly than he intended. He had nearly lost her. "You should have stayed in the car."

"I know but I heard the shot. . . ."

He heard the siren of the ambulance cut off as it stopped in front of the house. "Come on," he said. "I want them to attend that wound."

"I don't want—"

"I don't care what you want," he said. "You need stitches."

She started to get that stubborn look, then nodded. "Will you come with me?"

God, how he wanted to. "There's been a shooting, Meredith. I have to stay here and I'll probably be tied up for hours. I'll make sure someone meets you at the hospital and takes you home."

"It's over," she said. "It was probably Rick Fuller all this time. I should be safe enough now."

He didn't like easy solutions. He suddenly realized how much he had come to care for her. He liked her. Admired her grit. Hell, it was a lot more than that.

He had avoided admitting that to himself but watching her fall had caused icy fear to twist around his heart. "We can't be sure of that."

"I'll be careful."

He reached up and touched her cheek. "Don't go home alone."

"I won't," she promised.

Despite her wound, she put her arm around Nan and led her to the door. It was obvious her concern was more for her client than for herself.

He wished he could follow them to the hospital. He knew he couldn't and he braced himself for what was coming. It was a righteous shooting. He had four other officers as witnesses and a wounded civilian. Still, he knew there would be endless hours of interrogation and a suspension with pay.

When they went outside, he saw that the neighbors had started to gather. Two paramedics were kneeling beside Fuller.

He went over to them and stared down at the officer.

Gage had wounded before, but never killed.

He tried to swallow the bile in his throat.

BISBEE

Using her new Social Security card, Holly opened a bank account, planning to deposit part of her money and keep the other half in cash. She might need some quickly without leaving any trail. She didn't want to think about that on this momentous occasion. She didn't want to think of leaving and building another identity. She had been very lucky so far, and she knew it.

But the bank account provided a bankcard. It was one more form of identification, as well as building credit.

She'd already obtained a temporary driver's license, passing the test yesterday with flying colors. For the first time, she felt secure in driving. It gave her a huge sense of freedom.

The bank account gave her a sense of equally strong accomplishment.

She was opening a bank account for money *she* had earned. She had become independent. For someone who had been told from childhood that she wasn't capable of being anything other than an ornament, it was heady stuff indeed.

Empowerment. She had been reading a lot about abusive behavior and empowerment. She saw herself only too clearly as a victim. She had thought about leaving Randolph, but she'd feared losing her son. It hadn't been until she was faced with her own death that she had been able to take the steps toward freedom.

She signed the bank papers and carefully counted out fifteen hundred dollars. Another fifteen hundred was hidden in various places in her house and in her car. And now her small sculptures were selling well enough to provide what little she and Harry needed to live day to day. Everything above that went into savings.

The assistant manager gave her a broad smile. "We're delighted to have you as a customer. Your bankcard should arrive in a few days. Here are some temporary checks until you receive the personalized ones."

"Thank you," she said, rising from the chair.

"If you need any investment advice or anything at all, please call me," the woman said, giving her a card.

Investment advice. The words implied a future, stability. Success. Permanence. Independence.

A future.

And it was *hers*.

A thrill of accomplishment ran through her, chasing away some of the dark shadows that had been hovering around every minute of every day. She warned herself she would still have to be cautious. But she had taken positive steps on her own, and had succeeded.

Now she had one thing left to do to try to secure her safety and that of her son.

She would have to record the recent events as they had happened. She wished she had kept the paper with the security code for her home written on it, the paper she had found in the pocket of the intruder. But she hadn't, and the least she could do was alert authorities in the event Randolph found her.

But who to entrust with her story?

She didn't know anyone she could trust in New Orleans. Not after what had happened. How long was her father's and Randolph's reach in New Orleans? She didn't know. She couldn't take chances.

But her new friends?

Would she be putting them in danger if she gave them information to forward in the event anything happened to her? An attorney here. That would be her best bet. Client-attorney privilege was absolute. She knew that.

With renewed confidence, she left the bank. She held Harry's hand firmly. Her son clutched a red lollipop, a gift from the bank, in his free hand.

Home. A phone call. Lunch. Then work.

Normalcy.

It felt good.

NEW ORLEANS

Meredith had to wait three hours at the hospital before the busy emergency room staff had time to swab her arm with antiseptic and stitch the wound.

The level of pain increased with each passing minute. Now it hurt like hell. She'd had a shot to deaden the area before the stitches were made, but it had worn off. Now she had to wait to be released.

Nan needed a simple bandage and had left with the counselor from the shelter. She would be all right.

Now.

Meredith was tired, exhausted from the emotional aftermath of the funeral and then the shooting. Too tired to consider rationally what had happened.

Nan had said Rick had pledged to get her. Could he have been behind everything that had happened? He had been on duty the night she'd been attacked, but he certainly had access to shady characters who wouldn't shy away from violence.

That seemed easier to believe than a conspiracy that reached back thirty-three years.

Had one bitter, deranged man who had wanted to terrify her and take away anyone close to her been behind the terrifying events of the last week?

If so, she was safe now. It was over.

She could return to normal.

Normal?

Nothing would be normal again. She knew she would never leave a door unlocked again. She would never walk in her city without fear again.

And she still had a sister to find.

She looked out the hospital doors. It was past midnight. Her limbs were weak, unsteady. Most of all she felt rootless. Rudderless. She thought about her mother lying in another hospital across the city.

She shouldn't die alone.

Or was doing as she asked more important?

Meredith didn't know any longer.

She didn't even have transportation. Her car was at her parents' house, where she'd left it when she and Gage raced to Nan's home. She imagined Gage was at headquarters, being grilled.

She could call Sarah.

She played with the idea, then dismissed it. She hated to put other people out, to ask her staff to do chores unrelated to the practice. She would call a cab. Go home. Have a pot of hot chocolate and a long, scented bath.

She allowed her thoughts to return to Gage, to the expression on his face as he had leaned over the body of Rick Fuller. For a man who usually kept thoughts hidden, it had been raw, naked. Devastated. The look had lasted only seconds. Then the mask had fallen back in place.

Perhaps two weeks ago that would have surprised her. Now it didn't. He cared far more about his job, and about people, than he wanted anyone to think.

In dying, Rick Fuller had hurt still another person who had tried to help her.

She only wished she didn't want to see Gage so badly. That she didn't wish he would appear at the door.

But she was only too aware of the procedures after a shooting incident. Add to the fact that the victim was a cop, he was likely to be tied up all night.

As she waited for the paperwork, including some prescriptions, she wondered again whether the violence was really over. She wished with all her heart she could believe that. But she couldn't dismiss the possibilities that something more sinister was at play. There was the sudden disappearance of everything in the attic to explain . . . and her father's last words to her. His fear and despair. Fuller had nothing to do with that.

Was she still a danger to everyone she met?

She wasn't going to take the chance.

From now on, she planned to proceed on her own.

She had two avenues left in her search for her sister. The photo. And Memphis, where neighbors of her great-aunt might recall something.

Both were long shots.

But finding her sister now was her driving force. She felt that in some way she had pushed certain people into action. Maybe it was Fuller. Maybe someone entirely different. She only knew she had to find out which.

She signed papers and dutifully accepted prescriptions for painkillers and an antibiotic, then used her cell phone to call a cab. For a fraction of a second, she wanted to cry. But tears wouldn't help.

She could think of only one thing that would. Her family

had been taken by disease and malice. But she still had a half sister somewhere.

No matter what it took, she was determined to find her.

Then perhaps she could reclaim her life. Get back to the practice of law.

BISBEE

Holly finished the letter. She wrote in longhand since she didn't have a computer, and what she had to write couldn't be done on the library computers. It was too dangerous.

Writing it in her own handwriting might be an advantage. *If* it was ever seen.

She had asked Marty for names of some reputable attorneys in the area. She needed a will now that she was Harry's sole parent.

Marty had given her several names but recommended one especially highly.

Holly called him and made an appointment in two days' time, the first slot he had available. It would give her time to perfect a story. Even with client-attorney confidentiality, she didn't dare trust too much.

She stared at the letter. This was her third try. The other two had gone into a wastebasket and would be later torn into tiny pieces and flushed down the toilet.

She was no writer. But she carefully detailed everything that had happened the day she had left New Orleans. She described the phone call she had overheard, then the intruder. She explained how the man had a gun in his hands, the code to the security system and a key to the house.

When she was finished, she had three pages. She took Harry with her to a store where she made three copies, then put the contents into envelopes and sealed each of them.

Then she went to see Marty.

She waited until Marty was alone in the store. She drew her friend aside to a place where she could keep Harry in sight, yet out of his sometimes too keen hearing.

"I have an appointment to see Mr. McIntyre," she said.

"I want to make provisions for Harry in the event anything . . ."

Marty nodded.

"I don't have anyone," Holly said starkly. "I know it's a great deal to ask but would you—could you—be my executor? Would you look after Harry's interests?"

Marty searched her face. "There's no one else? No parent? No sibling? Perhaps your husband's family . . .?"

Holly shook her head. "No direct relations, and those who aren't, well, I wouldn't want them near my boy."

"I'm sixty-five years old," Marty said.

"The youngest sixty-five I've ever known."

"Still . . ."

"I am not asking you to keep him," Holly said, her heart aching at the thought of an abandoned little boy. But she had thought and thought and thought. There was no one else she could trust.

Marty's eyes bored into hers, seeking to go deeper than Holly intended to allow.

"Nothing will happen," Holly sought to reassure Marty. "But everyone should have a will." She hated lying to Marty. She hated not telling her that there was a possibility that something *could* happen. If it did, her husband's family might get control of Harry after all. But at least she could try to do something.

Perhaps the desperation in her face reached Marty. She nodded her head slowly, then asked in a soft voice, "Is there something I should know, Liz?"

There was. There was a lot she should know. But Holly couldn't tell her. Not now. What if she disapproved of murder, even in self-defense? What if she didn't believe her?

She didn't know if she would believe someone with that kind of tale. Why not go to the police? That would have been her first reaction.

So instead she thanked Marty. She gave the shop owner one of the sealed envelopes. "It's not to be opened unless something happens to me."

Marty gave her a searching gaze, her eyes worried. Then she nodded.

One of the other two envelopes would go to her attorney. The third would stay in her possession.

Harry approached her, and his hand clutched hers tightly. His small earnest face reflected worry. Apparently her tension had seeped into him.

"Let's go someplace special," she said.

He looked up at her with big, round eyes. "Where?"

"It's a surprise."

"Can we take Caesar?"

"Not this time, but we'll take him for a walk when we get home."

She had been wanting to take him to a nearby town for days, but she'd been afraid to drive. Now, with her newly obtained license, she could give him some of the adventures he craved.

Work could wait until tonight when he was asleep.

She settled him into the car seat and looked around at the houses as she drove out of town.

Days were rushing by. She loved working on her sculptures. She loved the walks she took with Harry and Caesar. She liked her easy relationship with Marty and her growing friendships within the city.

She had even missed her morning trip to the library today. She had been intent on seeing Marty, yes, but she wondered whether it wasn't also a sign of growing confidence that she and Harry were safer. The visits to Marty and to the attorney were insurance. Nothing more.

Harry chattered as they drove. He saw a cow and exclaimed.

They reached Tombstone and his eyes grew even larger as he gazed at the Old West exteriors. The town had daily re-creations of the shoot-out at the O.K. Corral with Wyatt Earp. She wasn't crazy about the violence, but she knew Harry would love the actors in Old West garb. And the horses.

They had a sarsaparilla in a mock saloon, and joined the other tourists to watch the drama.

She flinched as one of the bad guys fell, and her stomach suddenly revolted.

For a moment she was back. . . .

She turned away.

"Mommy?"

Harry's face was confused. Uncertain.

She straightened up. *This is make-believe!*

"I'm okay," she said.

He stared at her for a moment, then seemed to relax and turned back to the action.

She glanced around at the other tourists. Families. Children. All enjoying the fictional re-creation of an American legend. Did any of the others have cold, clammy hands?

This is for Harry.

She forced herself to stand through the rest of the performance. The sound of gunfire. Blanks. She knew they were blanks, but . . .

Someone reached out and she found herself jerking away.

"Are you all right?" someone asked.

An older woman with a kind face and an elderly gentleman stood there with three children.

"Yes, thank you. The heat . . . " It wasn't heat at all. A flashback. It wasn't the first time.

They insisted that she and Harry accompany them into a restaurant, where she ordered iced tea for herself and Harry a root beer. She held her hands in her lap so no one would see them shake.

Mr. and Mrs. Dan Weston were taking a two-week trip with their grandchildren. They chattered about their adventures as she finally managed to steady the fingers of one hand enough to bring a glass to her lips without dropping it. Harry eyed the western hats the grandchildren wore with envy but thankfully he was unusually silent, awed probably by the older boys.

Thirty minutes later, they were going their separate ways.

She went into a souvenir shop and purchased a cowboy hat and sheriff's badge for him.

"Now I'm just like Sher'f Doug," he said, his small chest puffing out.

"Yes, indeed, you are."

"I wanna be a sher'f."

"A fine ambition." But her heart pounded a little louder. How would he feel if he ever discovered his mother was a fugitive? That some day she might even be charged with murder? She shuddered inwardly at the idea.

"I think we had better go home and see Caesar," she said. "He's going to miss us."

"I miss him, too," he said, putting his little hand in hers.

She looked down at him. He was bursting with excitement. He loved his blue jeans and his T-shirt that said "Little cowhand." And now he beamed from under the new hat.

She was glad for her son's sake that they had come here today.

But she hadn't realized how much it would affect her, how it would be a vivid reminder of something she wanted to forget. She knew now that she never could.

She felt a sudden relief from the sun and looked up at the sky. Dark clouds were moving in, one eclipsing the sun.

A shiver ran through her body even though the air was still hot.

A sense of foreboding filled her.

Because of the mock battle she'd just witnessed?

Or something else?

twenty-one

Meredith put her pain pills in the medicine cabinet and took several aspirin instead. After all that had happened, she didn't want to sleep too soundly.

Just before she went to bed, she tried to call Gage, but his cell phone was apparently off.

She left a message. "Thank you." If it hadn't been for him, she probably wouldn't be alive tonight.

She took the phone off the hook to avoid reporters who had been calling. Her friends could still reach her on her cell phone. Then she made sure her revolver was next to her. She invited Nicky up on her bed; she needed the comforting presence of the dog.

Gage's face was the last thing she remembered until the first light of dawn woke her. The moment she moved, Nicky started to lick her. He obviously wanted to go outside.

Meredith groaned as she moved and hit her wounded arm against the side of the bed. Then Nicky's tongue reached out and licked her again.

"Okay," she said reluctantly. She looked at the clock. Six A.M.

Then everything flooded back. Her father's death. Mrs. Starnes. The funeral. Rick Fuller pointing a pistol at her. The crack of gunfire.

For a moment, she wanted to sink back into bed and close her eyes. But she had things to do today.

First, she had to see her mother and make sure that the private duty nurses knew their services were to continue despite her father's death. She wanted to make sure someone was with her mother every second.

Then she would see Gage. She knew he would be exonerated from any fault but she also knew that suspension wouldn't be his biggest problem. She would never forget that look of anguish on his face when he almost willed Fuller to breathe again.

She rose, carefully protecting her arm. She looked outside and saw a car in front. Someone was sitting in it. Whoever it was wasn't trying to hide.

Meredith ran a brush through her hair, then pulled on a pair of jeans. She decided to forego a bra for the moment and put on a loose shirt. She went down to the front door, taking Nicky's leash and snapping it on his collar.

Then she walked him out the door and to the car parked in front.

The driver got out and met her. "Ms. Rawson?"

"Yes."

"Detective Gaynor asked me to look out for you today. I would have let you know earlier, but he said you'd had a bad night and I didn't want to wake you."

"And you are . . .?"

"Mack Thomas. Private investigator. Used to be a cop. Gage has helped us out several times. We're only too happy to return the favor."

"When did you talk to him?"

"Late last night. He told me to get my ass over here. He was stuck at headquarters."

"Do you know what happened?"

"About the shooting? Yeah. Bad stuff when a cop's involved on both sides."

He looked to be in his fifties but his body was hard and lean, and she would bet her practice that he worked out daily.

"How long did he employ you to watch me? I want to pay it."

"Hell, I wouldn't take his money. I owe him big time."

"I'd like to hear about it."

"Maybe later. Will you be staying here or going somewhere?"

"I plan to see my mother at the hospital, then I'm going out of town for a few days. I appreciate your help, but the danger may be over now."

"Gage doesn't think so."

In her heart, she didn't think so, either.

"How can I reach him?"

"I imagine he's tied up with his old friends in Public Integrity."

She nodded.

"Nice dog you have."

"He's not mine. I'm just keeping him . . . for a friend." She turned to go back in. "I'll be leaving in about thirty minutes. You can take off then. I'll be all right."

She went through the door before he could reply.

She didn't want anyone else involved with this. With her. Too many people were dying. She didn't even want to go near Sarah.

But she had to visit her mother. She still hadn't told her mother that her father was dead. Would she hear her? Would her mother care if she could hear?

She recalled what her father had said. The last words he had said to her. *She never loved me.* Why then had they married?

If only her mother could speak to her again.

If only . . .

She fed Nicky, then went into the bathroom. She brushed her teeth and awkwardly applied a touch of lipstick. She looked terrible. Her eyes were ringed with circles, and her face looked wan. Her arm still hurt like the blazes and she feared that anything she wore might soon be stained with the blood still oozing from the wound.

Not that it mattered. To even think about herself at this moment was self-centered. *She* was alive. Others had died.

She left the house and drove to the hospital, noting that Mack followed despite her dismissal.

At the hospital, she went directly to her mother's room. She said hello to the private duty nurse who stood when she entered.

"Ms. Rawson. We didn't think you would be in today." She looked down at the newspaper she was holding.

Meredith hadn't seen it. She hadn't even thought about the paper this morning. She looked now. Spread over the front page were photos of herself, Gage and Rick Fuller.

Former Prosecutor Shot In Domestic Dispute. Renegade Cop Killed By Fellow NOPD Officer.

She read the story, which was fairly accurate.

She handed the paper back, seeing the curiosity in the woman's gaze as it rested on her bandaged arm. "Should you be here?"

"It was just a graze."

"Well, then, would you like some time alone with her?"

"Yes. Thank you."

The woman started for the door. She turned. "By the way, someone stopped by here last night. I went to the desk and he was standing in the door when I returned. He left when he saw me."

A new frisson of fear ran through her. "Can you describe him?"

"In his fifties. Dark hair with gray on the sides. Blue jeans but they looked good on him. I only had a glimpse of his face. It was . . . arresting."

"Please don't leave her alone again. Even for a few moments. She might be in danger," Meredith said. She knew how odd that must sound. Her mother was dying. But she didn't want what time she had left cut short. She still hoped her mother would know a moment of lucidity.

The nurse started to say, "I'm sorry—"

"It's not your fault. No one told you or your service. But you know my father was killed by a hit-and-run driver. I don't think it was an accident. Someone might have a grudge against this family. I just want to be extra cautious."

The nurse nodded and left the room. Meredith sat next to her mother and took her hand. It was little but skin and bones now. Her pallor was more pronounced than ever.

"It's just you and me now," Meredith said. "Father died . . . was killed. I buried him yesterday. All your friends were there. They asked about you. You have so many." She choked as she remembered Lulu Starnes and the photo of three young people who'd looked ready to conquer the world.

She leaned down and kissed her mother. Tears dampened her face as she laid her cheek against the parchmentlike skin of her mother.

She heard a knock on the door. She wiped her cheeks as the private duty nurse returned, followed by her mother's doctor. She stood to meet him.

He gave her a look of concern. "I'm sorry about your father," he said. "I had hoped to attend the funeral, but I had an emergency."

"Thank you," she said. She drew him to the door. "I'll be taking over the responsibility for my mother's care. What . . . where are we?"

"You have some decisions to make. She didn't leave a living will. Your father ordered us to use all means to resuscitate."

"How much longer does she have?"

"Her organs are closing down. No more than several days, if that much; as little as a few hours."

"Is there any chance she will regain consciousness?"

He shook his head. "No."

"Can she hear anything? Feel anything?"

"I don't believe so," he said gently.

Meredith looked down at the shadow of her mother. She probably didn't weigh more than eighty pounds now.

"Then no heroic means," she said. "I don't think she would have wanted it."

He nodded. "I'm sorry, Miss Rawson. I liked her."

She noticed he used the past tense.

She went back to her mother's side. She hoped that on some conscious level her mother knew she was loved.

"I won't leave you," she whispered in a choked voice.

BISBEE

Holly watched the hawk circle above and thought life couldn't get better than this. She wouldn't allow the past to intrude. Not now.

She wished she could capture these moments and seal them in a bottle.

It was Saturday. Doug had arrived with his niece, who greeted Harry like a little brother. He basked in her attention.

When Doug had opened the Jeep door for Holly, his slow smile warmed her all the way through. Despite his office, she couldn't help but feel comfortable with him.

She liked the affectionate but firm way he treated his niece and the easy manner he had with Harry. She liked the feelings he aroused in her. She longed to put her hand in his, just as she'd watched so many other couples do.

She'd always missed that kind of intimacy with Randolph. She couldn't remember him ever just grabbing her hand or wanting her with him on any occasion other than a political or social event.

When they'd reached the ranch, Russ had cast her a rueful glance as Doug helped her mount the mare, his hand lingering a moment more than necessary. Her pulse quickened and she felt a jolt of electricity run through her.

She had to force herself to concentrate as he lifted himself into the saddle. She sensed Doug's gaze on her as they rode toward the mountain. Harry was riding in front of Doug, protected by strong arms. It was always Doug now. Not Sheriff. She had tried to think of him as the latter, but it was hard to equate him with a gun or violence. She knew it was a cliché, but he was more gentle giant than lawman.

He was both. She had to remember that. He might not want to do anything if he learned the truth, but he would have to. She'd known him long enough to sense his integrity, his strong sense of duty.

She did not want to be responsible for making him choose between his job—his vocation—and her. She sensed she would destroy him if she did.

She should stay away from him. She knew he cared about her and that those feelings ran deep. She saw it in his face, in his eyes; heard it in the way his voice lowered to a husky whisper.

Hers did as well. She cared more than she'd wanted to admit. She relaxed with him. He liked her for who and what she was, and not for her looks. She'd certainly gone to a great deal of trouble to make herself plain.

She must never forget that she was married to someone. Someone who had tried to murder her.

"Liz?"

She looked at him.

"That was a heavy sigh. Something wrong?"

"Just thinking of the work I have to do. My garden creatures are doing well. I really shouldn't be here, but Harry loves to ride. His ambition is to be a cowboy," she added. "A sheriff like 'Sher'f Doug.'"

"What about Liz?" he asked.

"Liz likes it, too," she admitted.

He continued to look at her. "Marty says your sculptures have been flying off the shelves."

Her stomach knotted. He had been talking to Marty about her. Had Marty mentioned her delay in giving a Social Security number or that the telephone was in Marty's name? She struggled to get back to the subject. "She also says that once the summer season is over, sales go way down. I need to sell as many as possible before then."

He didn't say anything but she saw the puzzled look on his face.

He was probably wondering why she didn't have insurance money from her husband's death.

She didn't explain. She couldn't lie in front of a son who knew his father was alive.

Once more, she told herself to stay away from Doug.

If only she could.

But she needed the sense of belonging that he brought to her life. The companionship. Harry needed it even more. Randolph was not the person she wanted Harry to emulate.

Doug's gaze kept coming back to her, though only in quick sideways movements. "There's a great movie for kids tomorrow night. I promised Jenny that I would take her. Perhaps . . ." His voice trailed off as if he knew her answer in advance.

A film. She knew the one he referred to. Magicians and magic and wonder. Harry would love it, especially going with Jenny. An older woman.

"You're smiling," Doug said with surprise.

Did she really smile so rarely that when she did, it caused comment? And how to answer? She couldn't tell him the reason—that her son had a four-year-old's crush on Jenny. Not with Harry within listening distance.

But she saw Doug's eyes light.

She nodded. "Harry would like that."

"And Liz?" he teased again, forcing her to make an admission.

"Liz would like it, too."

"I'm afraid to push my luck too far, but what about dinner as well? I make a mean steak."

This was spiraling out of control, and Holly knew it. Eventually, he would be asking more personal questions. And the more he knew her, the more he would be apt to realize when she was lying. And yet the invitation was alluring. She had been frantic about saving money in the event they might have to run again. She and Harry had been living on hot dogs, cereal, tacos and fifty other recipes for hamburger. The cowboy hat had been a rare treat for Harry.

Harry looked at her longingly.

But this invitation would lead to another and another. Dare she start something she couldn't end?

She couldn't completely isolate herself and Harry.

But a lawman?

She nodded. "Thank you, we would like that."

A broad grin spread across his face. Then he turned back to the trail they were following as if afraid she would take it back.

She should. She should call him tomorrow and cite a headache.

But she knew she wouldn't.

New Orleans

Meredith left her mother's side only when Gage appeared at the door. Mack must have told him where she was.

His gaze went to the bandage on her arm, then to her mother. He asked questions with his eyes.

"I'm all right. A little sore," she said. "My mother . . ."

She didn't have to say anything. The labored breathing, the color of her mother's skin said it all.

He didn't say he was sorry, and she appreciated it. She knew everyone was being kind but she'd heard the words entirely too many times lately.

Instead he held her for several moments, careful not to hurt her arm.

"I couldn't find my sister," she said. "Not in time."

His arms tightened around her. "Perhaps it's time to stop looking."

"I promised."

"Okay. How can I help?"

She wanted his help. She needed his help. She needed him and the light he brought to a now hostile world. But she'd already hurt him. Violence swirled around her like a whirlwind. She didn't want him to be in the line of fire again. She didn't answer that question but asked one of her own.

"Any news from the shooting board yet?"

"No. It'll take a couple of days."

"Thanks for sending Mack. I think he kept the reporters away last night." She tried to smile.

He studied her face. "Last night wasn't your fault. If anyone is at blame, I am. I should have realized how far he would go."

He looked exhausted. He hadn't shaved and light bristle shadowed his cheeks. She reached up and pushed back a lock of his hair. "I think you should go home and get some sleep."

"I'll stay with you."

Remember what happens to people around you.

"No," she said. "I . . . want to be alone with her."

He stared at her for a long time. "I want Mack with you then."

"This could be over," she said.

"It could. And it couldn't. You might still be a target."

"Thank you for saving my life."

He smiled. It was a tight smile but she liked it. Liked the pronounced dimple in his chin when he did.

She wanted to say more. She wanted to go home with him. She wanted him to go home with her. Just his presence made her world brighten, and right now it was in great need of the light.

"Go home," she said.

"You'll call me if you need anything? You'll cooperate with Mack?"

"Yes."

He put one of his hands to her cheek. It was a tender gesture and all the more meaningful since he so rarely revealed emotions.

A little like herself.

The thought was agonizing. That's what her mother had done. Kept her feelings and emotions wrapped in fire-retardant covering. Was she following her mother's example?

She didn't want to be like that. She didn't want to keep people at a distance. But she had. Learned behavior? Or simply a defense?

She stood on tiptoes and brushed her cheek against his stubbled one. It scratched her face but she didn't mind. "Thanks for coming."

"I really would like to stay."

"You need some rest. I'll be here."

"You promise to call?"

She nodded. That wasn't really a promise.

She watched him leave, then sat back with her mother as her breathing became more labored.

Five hours later, Marguerite Rawson expelled her last breath.

Meredith leaned over and kissed her. "I'm sorry I couldn't find her in time," she said. "But I will find her if I have to search all my life."

Meredith stood. Beyond tears.

Beyond feeling.

Both would come later. She knew they would come. But now shock dulled the pain. It was as if she were someone else. Watching from a distance.

She wanted to call Gage. She wanted to lean against him and borrow his strength. She wanted to share parts of her life with him. Feelings. Emotions.

She'd never wanted to do that before.

Instead she signed papers. She made phone calls.

The funeral would be in four days. She delayed it because she simply needed the extra time. She had just buried one parent. She needed time before burying this one.

Perhaps she could find her sister before that happened.

It gave her purpose.

It even gave her comfort.

But the pain lurked deep inside. She knew it was going to overflow before long.

twenty-two

Meredith called Sarah's cell phone from a pay phone in the hospital.

"My mother died this afternoon," she said.

"Oh, God," Sarah said. "What can I do?"

"Two things. Can you take care of Nicky for a few days? That's Mrs. Starnes's dog. I'm going out of town, and I'll be busy most of the time so I can't follow up on whether Mrs. Starnes's relatives want him. In the meantime . . ."

"Where are you going?"

"Memphis," she said. "I'll be back in time for the funeral. You can reach me on the cell phone if there's an emergency."

"Do you really think you should go alone?"

"Yes. It's all I can do for her now."

"You will call me often?"

"I'll try to, but I don't want anyone to know where I'm going, and our office phones might be tapped. My phone at home was."

Silence for a moment.

Then, "My kids would love a dog for a few days. What else?"

Meredith sighed with relief. She really hadn't wanted to take the dog to a kennel.

"Will you take a cab to a car rental company and rent a car? Bring it back and park it in the office garage? I'll add the amount to your next paycheck. I want to avoid the press and anyone who might be trying to follow me."

A pause. "Perhaps you should stay here where Detective Gaynor can keep an eye on you." Concern laced every word.

"I need to get away for several days before the funeral. I'll be safe enough if no one knows where I am. And I want you to be careful while I'm gone."

"Maybe it's all over now," Sarah said. "Maybe Rick Fuller was responsible for everything that's happened. In any event, there's no reason for anyone to try to hurt me."

Except you're close to me.

But her mother's death was a natural one, if you could call someone wasting away natural. Her father . . . well, that *could* have been a simple hit-and-run, not intended murder. And Mrs. Starnes . . . again, it could have been Fuller. Or a random burglary gone bad. "I still want you to be careful."

"I'm always careful. I worked in the DA's office, remember?"

"How are we on cases?"

"We've asked for continuances on our two court cases. You've just lost two parents. Becky and I can handle everything else."

"Thanks. I'll come in about four for the car."

"You'll keep in touch?"

"I'll only be gone two to three days. Maybe not that long. But I'll ring you every day at three on your cell phone."

"And seven every morning," Sarah insisted.

"And seven," Meredith agreed.

"Done," Sarah said. "And the dog?"

"I'll bring him up to the office. You can give me the keys to the rental then. Park it in a different part of the garage than where I usually park."

"Does Detective Gaynor know about this?"

"He has problems of his own, mainly because of me. I don't want him to get in more trouble."

"I'll continue working from this angle," Sarah said.

"No," Meredith said in a tone sharper than she'd intended. "The practice needs your attention. Let me take care of the other."

"Whatever you say, boss."

"I'll see you in an hour then?"

"Yes. And Meredith, I am so very, very sorry about your mother."

Meredith set the receiver back into place.

The two men met in the older man's library. Dusk shadowed the magnolia trees outside.

"We've lost the Rawson woman," the older man said.

"I thought you hired good men. They can't even find the stupid bitch that you talked me into marrying."

"I seem to remember a different scenario," the older man reminded him. "You wanted her."

Randolph glared at him. "Hire more men."

The older man looked at Randolph like he'd just grown two heads. "You want the world to know your wife has run away from you because she discovered you were going to have her killed? That would do a lot for your image among women. I trust the men who are looking for her now. They're the best in the business. And they know how to keep quiet."

"They can't be too good," Randolph said.

"They'll find her. And Meredith Rawson. As soon as she returns, we'll find a way to eliminate her as well. Perhaps a fire. Too many sedatives. A little carelessness after everything that has happened."

"Dammit, we have other problems. The police have found Carrick's body."

"They don't know who he is. They'll soon lose interest." The older man poured a glass of good brandy from a decanter, sat back and took an appreciative sip. "If you could have controlled your wife better, none of this would have been necessary."

"She's your daughter."

"The hell she is."

They glared at each other, each concentrating on the other's failings.

"Perhaps Meredith Rawson will lead us to Holly," Randolph Ames said.

"I made sure we covered all those tracks. I doubt she can discover who Holly is, much less find her. Charles can't help Meredith Rawson now. I thought he was frightened enough not to say anything, but I knew from our last conversation that he was becoming even more concerned about his daughter than for himself. We were lucky to recover those letters. I just don't know how much he told her that last night."

"We should have had her killed in the first place."

"We couldn't while Charles was alive. He would have sent us all to prison. His daughter was the biggest hold we had on him."

"But now . . ."

"Now all bets are off. But it needs to be an accident."

"You think anyone will believe an accident now?"

The man behind the desk shrugged. "Probably not, but it will be hard as hell to prove. Just as in Charles Rawson's death it is impossible to prove the perpetrator was anything but a drunk."

"And if Gaynor doesn't accept it?"

"Some planted evidence. People already think he's dirty. Killing that officer didn't help."

"He'll be exonerated on that. Too many witnesses."

"But it all adds up to trouble. I've already planted a few seeds."

"I hear Gaynor is no fool."

"He has enough problems with that shooting last night. That call telling Fuller that he was going to be bounced from the force because of Meredith Rawson was one of my better ideas."

Randolph chuckled. "Remind me not to get on your bad side."

"You're too valuable to me. I have plans for you."

They both had a second glass of brandy.

MEMPHIS

Meredith reached the outskirts of Memphis by midafternoon. She'd spent the night in Baton Rouge. She appreciated the anonymity of a hotel room after all that had happened.

She'd taken precautions. She'd packed a good pair of slacks and silk blouse in her briefcase along with a few necessities and her laptop. No suitcases to signal that she was leaving town.

She took some obscure roads leading out of New Orleans that she'd learned years ago, always keeping an eye on the rearview mirror. She stopped at a diner where she had a wide view of the road.

When she felt as if she had thrown off any potential tail, she started to relax. Driving always relaxed her. Something about the road and the rich green of Louisiana and Mississippi helped her clean the cobwebs from her mind.

Unfortunately, none of that diverted her thoughts from Gage.

She'd left a message with his office that she would be out of town for several days. She did not want to involve him in her personal quest any longer. It was too dangerous for him. Not only for him personally, but for his job.

She also knew he needed to stay in New Orleans while the shooting investigation continued. He needed to be available to answer questions.

She had caused him enough grief.

But he'd established a firm place in her consciousness. In her mind and in her heart.

She cared about him in a way she'd never cared about any man before. There was excitement and sensuality and physical pleasure, but he also attracted her in so many other ways. He did things his way, but he did them with an unconscious integrity.

She didn't want to damage him as she seemed to have hurt so many others in the recent past.

Meredith hoped that Rick Fuller's death was the end of the nightmare that had started only days earlier. It seemed liked eons. But she didn't fool herself. There might still be something else at play. She might still be a Jonah.

Her brain kept telling her that during the drive. How would Fuller have known about Mrs. Starnes? He might have tapped the phone but how would he have known the woman's importance to her? Or had he just wanted her to find a body?

Would someone really kill just to terrify?

When she reached Memphis, she headed toward Germantown, the community where her aunt and uncle once lived.

She had used the Internet to locate the exact neighborhood, and she'd found a hotel just blocks away. She would unpack, then start interviewing the neighbors and hope she could find one that had lived there thirty years earlier. In this mobile society, she doubted it. But she was quickly running out of options.

After locating the neighborhood and the hotel, she took a room under a different name. It was the kind of hotel that didn't ask for identification as long as you had cash.

Something to eat, then she would start canvassing her great-aunt's old neighborhood.

NEW ORLEANS

Gage hadn't been able to sleep after leaving Meredith and took the canoe down to his cabin. He'd grabbed a few hours sleep, then enjoyed a quiet dawn before heading back. Watching the rising sun change the colors of the sky had made him wish he'd brought Meredith. But then he'd needed this time to consider the last forty-eight hours.

He was not Meredith's keeper. She had made it clear she wanted no attachments. God knew, neither was he in a position to want them. He'd never been good at relationships, and now he had his brother to consider.

She could still be in danger. Rick Fuller may have been used. On the other hand, he might have acted on his own when he attacked his wife and made his wild threats. Either way, Gage didn't believe for a minute that Fuller had been at the bottom of all the attacks.

He trusted Mack, though, to keep her safe.

On the way back, his thoughts kept turning to the photo of Mrs. Starnes, Marguerite Rawson and the young man. The dark hair. The defiant yet proud tilt of his head. A sense of familiarity nagged at him.

Still restless when he arrived home, he changed clothes and went downtown to his office. Suspended or not, he wanted to know if there was any more news about the death of Charles Rawson.

Wagner approached him. "Are you all right?"

"Yeah. I feel naked, though, without my badge and gun."

"I'm told you'll be out for at least a week. You should just take it easy. Get some sleep. Enjoy life."

Gage gave him a disgusted look. "It's their idea. Not mine."

"We have a suspect in the homeless murder. An informant said another derelict was talking about it."

"Good. I'm more concerned about the floater. Someone went to a lot of trouble to hide his identity."

"We've gone through every missing person report for the last three months. Nothing fits."

"An out-of-towner?"

"Could be, but then why all the effort?"

"Do we have anything from the medical examiner on age or race?"

"No, but he sent a DNA sample to the feds. Maybe they have something." Wagner grinned. "Be glad to have you back next week. Cases are piling up. In the meantime, take it easy."

"I might do a little snooping on the Starnes case on my own."

"Keep me posted."

"I will. If you get anything on the floater, call me. Any time."

"Will do."

Gage hesitated at his desk, oddly reluctant to leave. He

had relived the shooting over and over in his head in the last twenty-four hours. He couldn't get the images from his head. Nor could he dismiss the notion that something was very wrong.

He was about to leave when Dom called him on the cell phone.

"I saw your brother. I think I can find him something."

"He'll need it for the parole hearing."

"I know. Working on it. He wants to know when you'll be up there."

"I'll try next Sunday."

"He said the hearing is two weeks from today."

"Will you be there?"

"I plan to."

"Thanks." Gage hesitated, then asked, "Dom, did you know Marguerite Rawson?"

A pause on the other side of the receiver. "I've met her, yes. I think everyone involved in charities has."

"Did you know she's just died?"

Another silence. Then, "I'm sorry to hear that."

Gage noted a catch in his voice. "Can we have a drink together some time?"

"With you, always," Dom replied. "By the way, I was sorry to hear about the shooting. But I've heard bad things about Fuller."

"I would like to hear more about that."

"When we get together," Dom said. "Speaking of the Rawsons, I see that Meredith Rawson was involved in the shooting." It sounded more like a question than a statement. "How is she?"

How much did he have the right to say? "There's been some other incidents. I think they might trace back to her mother. Something that happened years ago." He waited for a reaction.

There was a long silence.

"Dom?"

"Call me when you're available," Dom said.

"Thanks again for Clint."

"I think he means it this time."

"God, I hope so."

Dom hung up.

Gage held the phone for a moment. Dom's reaction to his questions had been so muted it was difficult to read. But Dom had always been difficult to read.

He looked at the photo again. The young man had been a teenager. He'd been clean-shaven with dark hair that needed a cut. Dom's face was fuller and he had a noticeable scar on one side, a souvenir of prison. He looked, in fact, a little like a prizefighter whose nose had been broken once too often. However, he had an intensity and charisma that drew people to him, and he certainly had magic with alienated youngsters.

Gage would have liked to explore the matter more, but Meredith was more important at the moment. He called Meredith's cell phone. He was invited to leave a message.

Frustrated, he found Sarah's phone number and called.

"Are you all right?" Sarah asked.

He wished everyone would stop asking that question. He wasn't sure of the answer and he didn't like that feeling. Not at all. "Perfectly," he replied. "I'm looking for Ms. Rawson."

"She'll be gone for the next few days. She said she had to get away."

"Dammit! Did she say exactly where she was going?"

"If she didn't tell you . . ."

"She might believe she's no longer in danger. I don't agree."

"Then you don't think Rick Fuller was involved in the other . . ."

"If he was, I don't think he was the only one. I knew Fuller. He wasn't that complicated a man."

Sarah hesitated.

"She told me about Memphis," he finally said. "Where in Memphis did she go?"

He waited patiently, letting her reach her own conclusions in her own time.

"I don't know. Just Memphis. She went to look for anyone who might have known her great-aunt."

"The address?"

Again she hesitated.

"Sarah, her life might depend on it."

Sarah gave it to him.

BISBEE

The steaks were wonderful.

Holly hadn't realized men could be such good cooks. Doug had grilled the steaks outside on the grill along with corn on the cob and kabobs of fresh vegetables. He had prepared tamales as an appetizer.

Harry was enthralled. He helped at the grill, occasionally squirting water on the fire.

"It's nice having another male in the house," Doug said as they all sat down at the table.

She couldn't remember tasting a better steak. But it might have been the company, and the knowledge that he had been cooking for her.

Jenny showed Harry her collection of stuffed bears, then took him out to see a garden where Doug grew a number of vegetables, including the corn they were eating.

Doug poured a glass of wine for himself and for Holly and they watched as dusk approached and shadows shaded the land with different hues. She felt more relaxed than she had in years. Perhaps more than she ever had.

She had been popular as a child, mainly, she knew, because of her looks. In turn, she had envied the studious girls who made good grades and served as president of the Latin club. At the urging of her mother, she'd tried out for the drama club but she'd been abysmal. Even she understood that. Her one talent had been her hands. And a whimsy that no one recognized.

Now she relaxed. She had merely run a brush through her hair and added a dab of lipstick. Her only concession to a "date" was a pair of slacks and a checkered short-sleeve shirt rather than shorts and a T-shirt.

Doug was relaxed as well. He stretched out in a pair of jeans and a blue cotton shirt with the sleeves rolled up. He looked masculine and confident and . . . sexy.

He took a sip of wine. She noticed he was very careful about how much he drank. He'd probably had a total of two small glasses. But then he was the driver.

"We had better go," he said reluctantly. "The movie's at eight."

It was going to be a late night for Harry, but this was a special treat. For both of them.

When they arrived at the movie, Doug spoke to nearly everyone. She knew several of the crowd and everyone eyed her curiously. Apparently, he was a prized bachelor.

The movie was excellent. Jenny sat on the outside with Harry next to her and Doug sat on Holly's other side. She was uncomfortably aware of his proximity, of his hand resting on the arm of the seat. She kept her hands clasped in her lap but at some time during the movie, his left hand inched over to take her right one.

Their fingers intertwined.

In a particularly scary part, Harry took her other hand.

She felt loved and secure and safe.

She wanted tonight to last forever.

MEMPHIS

Not one of the immediate neighbors of her late great-aunt had lived in the community more than fifteen years. Certainly none for thirty years.

Several remembered her great-aunt, who had been killed in a brutal robbery several years ago. But none knew of a young girl who might have lived there briefly decades ago. Neither did they remember her great-aunt mentioning one.

All of them had been horrified by her death. Apparently, they had truly liked her.

A brutal robbery.

Another violent death. There were a lot of them around. Coincidence?

The fact that murder may have been continuing for years was chilling. What secret was so desperate that it drove someone to kill again and again?

She couldn't even begin to answer that question.

Instead she asked the neighbors about doctors in the area, particularly obstetricans. She gathered a list of three that she would call first thing in the morning.

That evening she checked the yellow pages for local hospitals and used her laptop to find websites. Most included the hospital's history. She immediately discarded those that were less than thirty years old. The list was narrowing.

But that was a long shot and she knew it. Hospitals didn't keep medical records that old. Her only hope was to find someone who might have remembered a heartbroken teenager who gave up a child.

She had to eat, yet she had no appetite. She took a notebook with her and doodled as she waited for the ultimate comfort food she'd ordered. Hamburger and fries.

She noted every event that had happened since she learned of her sister, making a chart of them. Other than speaking with Mrs. Laxton and locating Mrs. Starnes, who was now dead, she had not gone further in searching for school friends, nor had she located the man in the photo.

She probably should have done the latter before she left. But she'd had to get away from New Orleans and the reporters and phone calls and sympathy. And her growing reliance on Gage. That reliance had cost him dearly.

If only she could find a clue here. One tiny thread. She knew how to pursue threads.

The comfort food was not at all comforting when it came. Usually she didn't mind eating by herself, but tonight she felt terribly alone. Terribly vulnerable.

Don't do that! Don't think of that! Think of your sister out there, possibly in danger.

She went back to her chart.

BISBEE

Holly paused at the door of the office of Daniel McIntyre, Esq., Attorney at Law. She looked at her watch. She had changed the appointment to a day when the local church had a "Mother's Day Out."

She didn't want her son to hear the conversation. He was much too bright. He would remember bits and pieces and pop up with a question about them at unexpected times.

She opened the door. A middle-aged woman with a quick smile sat at the desk. "You must be Liz Baker," she said. "You can go on in." She gestured to a door and Holly opened it.

A pleasant-looking man in his fifties stood up and came over to her. He reached out his hand and she took it. It was a grip meant to convey confidence. She liked the way his eyes met hers directly.

He sat down, inviting her to do the same. "What can I do for you, Mrs. Baker?"

"I would like to retain you first. What is your fee?"

"I take it you want the client-attorney relationship from the beginning?"

"Yes."

"Then fifty dollars will do for the initial interview. I charge a hundred dollars an hour."

Holly gave him the money. She sought assurance. "You can't say anything to anyone now?"

"Unless I know a crime is to be committed."

She nodded. "Two things. One is my son. I want to make provisions in case anything happens to me. I want a will naming a guardian for my son. Marty Miller, who owns Special Things."

He looked surprised. "No relatives?"

"No."

"That's easy enough. I'll draw up the papers and you both will come in and sign them. What else?"

She took the envelope containing the letter she'd written. "I want you to hold this. If anything happens to me, there are instructions inside."

His eyes sharpened. "Do you expect anything to happen to you?"

"No. But it's a letter to my son," she lied. "I would feel better if it were in a safe."

"I can do that as well."

"How much?"

He shrugged. "You've paid me fifty. I would say a total of two hundred would cover the will and guardianship."

It was less than she'd expected.

"Thank you."

She spent the next few minutes giving him lies about her son, and his name and birth date.

Then it was over.

She thanked him.

A small protection.

twenty-three

Meredith exhausted every possibility over the next three days.

She double-checked with the bureau of public records. No adoption records under her mother's name.

Next were local hospitals. None had records that reached thirty-three years back. A check of obstetricians proved equally as fruitless. The hospitals refused to—or couldn't—release lists of obstetricians on duty at the time.

She accessed the American Bar Association's Internet listing of Memphis-area attorneys. There were more than 2,800 listings. She narrowed it to Germantown. No downtown attorneys; those involved wouldn't risk large corporate practices for something like a black market adoption.

And that, she knew, was what must have happened.

It was the longest of long shots. She discovered that when she came up with forty candidates. She researched each firm. Three had been in practice thirty-three years ago in the general area of Germantown. One specialized in taxation, one in family law and the third was a general practice, which usually meant wills, estates and the like.

She called the latter office Monday morning, identified herself as an attorney in New Orleans and said she was looking for someone in a large inheritance case and there would be a substantial finder's fee. She said she would be in town only today—could they possibly squeeze her in?

A male attorney came on the line. She said she couldn't explain on the phone.

He finally agreed to an appointment at five P.M.

She hung up. It would be an amazing coincidence if that particular attorney had been involved, but then it would be amazing if she found the right attorney, regardless. At the very most, he might remember other attorneys active in the field of adoption.

Of course, there might not have been an attorney involved at all, though most people adopting a child would want some legal security.

The visit proved more fruitful than she'd imagined. It was a father-son practice, and while the older man was clearly just coming into the office, he'd been very active in the local bar association and never threw anything away.

William Hartley was in his seventies but had a spring to his movements that would put to shame most men decades younger. His gray eyes sparkled with curiosity and interest, and he obviously was a raconteur of stories about his profession. He wasn't shy about his assessments.

"I'm old enough not to give a damn about being politically correct, young lady."

"And I'm not old enough," she countered.

He sat back and laughed at that, and his son, William Junior, smiled. "Attorneys weren't as pretty as you when I first went into practice."

"I imagine you find plenty of them elsewhere," she said.

"Ah, but there was only one for me." The laughter left his eyes. "She died two years ago and I came back here to bedevil my son. Was going crazy by myself."

She was moved by the emotion behind the words. So there *were* happy unions. She knew that, of course, but her own personal experience and being an attorney who specialized in marital disasters sometimes made her forget that.

She explained that she had a client who had just died and left a very large inheritance for a daughter she'd given up at birth. There were no records. She was trying to find the attorney who might have handled it. As she'd said on the phone, there would be a substantial finder's fee.

It was the son who asked the amount.

"Fifty thousand dollars," she said. She'd already arrived at that sum. Any larger would be suspicious. Any lesser may not bring the cooperation she needed.

The father raised his eyebrows. "How much is the inheritance?"

"Several million."

That was a guess on her part. Her trust fund that had come from her grandmother through her mother was worth approximately a million. She assumed she would inherit most of her father's assets, including the house.

She was very prepared to spend whatever it took to find her sister, then to divide whatever was left. Part of what was hers would go to the women's shelter.

The son perked up at the sum. He looked at his father.

"I'll go through my lists. I have a pretty good idea of who might be involved in adoptions," the senior Hartley said. "If you like, I can hire an investigator to follow up on it. Or would you prefer to do that?"

"That would be extra, of course," the son said.

"Of course," she said, knowing that she didn't have much time. She had talked to the funeral home about plans for her mother's funeral, but some decisions had to be made in person. "How much?"

"The investigator we use on occasion charges a hundred an hour."

She nodded. "Go ahead. I'll keep in touch." She took out a checkbook. "Would a retainer for five thousand be sufficient?"

"Quite," the older man said. "I enjoy mysteries. How much information do you have?"

"Her name was Marguerite Thibadeau. She would have been seventeen at the time and the birth would have taken place sometime in February of 1970. We don't know who the father was."

"Anything else?"

"She was staying with an aunt." She took out a notepad with the name and address on it. "The aunt died in a robbery three years ago. I looked for a birth certificate for the daughter but couldn't find one."

"I'll see what we can do."

She left the office, feeling that at last she might be making headway

She looked at her watch. She would have a good supper tonight, then leave early in the morning.

She stopped in the office of the hotel and asked for the name of a good restaurant.

"If you're in Memphis, you need barbecue," the desk clerk said. "One of the best is a mile away." She gave detailed directions.

As she went to her room to wash up and put on her more comfortable driving clothes, she noticed a familiar car in the parking lot. A long, lanky figure lounged comfortably against it. A large dog sat obediently at his feet. It greeted her with a short excited bark.

As her gaze met Gage's, her breath caught in her lungs. Her heart skipped a beat, maybe three or four.

She had never been so glad to see anyone in her life.

Meredith's blue eyes widened in astonishment, and then a smile crossed her lips. Pleasure ran through him at her obvious pleasure at seeing him.

He had expected surprise. Anger. Defiance. He'd hoped for acceptance. He'd been braced for anything but the momentary delight in her expression.

"I would ask you how you found me, but you would probably say you're a detective."

"I probably would," he said as her smile awoke something bright and warm in him. "You keep running off on your own."

"And if you found me, someone else could?"

"Will you stop reading my mind?"

"Why?"

"It might get you in trouble."

"I think I'm already in trouble." Her voice was husky, and the underlying sensuality of her words made it clear she didn't mean just the recent violent events.

She looked exhausted, as well she should be. But there was an indomitable quality about her, and she was still forging ahead. Alone.

That scared the hell out of him.

"Find out anything?" he asked.

"I might have a lead. An older lawyer who apparently knows everyone who ever practiced law in Memphis. He's going through lists for names of shady lawyers who might have been involved in black market adoptions."

"It's going to be a rather long list."

"That was a cruel blow."

"Present company excluded."

He found himself relaxing after the long, anxious drive. He'd imagined any number of scenarios, none of them good. He'd particularly worried about the fact that she hadn't talked to him before leaving.

"You brought Beast."

"You're also observant."

She grinned. "He's hard to miss. Where are you going to stay tonight?"

"Here. I bribed the clerk. I take it they're not too particular."

"How did you find the motel? I didn't tell Sarah where I was staying." Her eyes narrowed. "That *is* where you got the information?"

"Don't be angry at her. I wheedled it out of her only by saying you could be in danger."

"But she didn't know about this motel."

"She gave me the information about your great-aunt. I

simply put myself in your shoes. I'm glad your mind works logically."

"You mean yours does?"

He gave her what he hoped was an indignant look.

"I think we're both in a heap of trouble." Her voice gentled. "How are you?"

"That's my question. *I* didn't just bury my father, lose my mother and get shot."

"I'm numb. What did the shooting board say?"

"They're still investigating. I'm the departmental bad boy. I also suspect that another player is stalling a ruling."

"Need a good lawyer?"

"I think your plate is full already. But there's no way they can go against four eyewitnesses. They just want to string it out awhile . . . tie my hands so I won't get involved in something they disapprove of." His expression mocked such thinking.

She held out her hand. "Thanks for coming."

"I would have been here sooner but Sarah said you wanted to be alone. She's been keeping me updated on your calls. Then I just found myself on the road."

"I'm glad," she replied simply.

Something intense flared inside. He intertwined his fingers with hers, feeling warmth creep through him, a kind of belonging he'd never known before.

He let her lead the way, Beast on his heels. He then took the key from her—the old kind of key, not a card key—and turned it in the lock. They stepped inside and immediately Meredith moved into his arms.

Moments later they were in bed and their lovemaking was frantic. Part of it, he told himself, was the survivor's need to feel. To know she was still alive. He didn't want to think about the other part.

He told himself not to take advantage.

But they were in the eye of a storm that wouldn't let them go. His need was explosive, and so, he sensed, was hers.

She had lost so much. Her family. Her sense of safety.

He had killed. That moment affected him far more than he'd ever expected it would. There had also been a split second when he thought he would die, and that the woman he cared about might also die.

He would never forget the surprise on Fuller's face. He suspected it would haunt him for a long time.

He needed her as much as she needed him, and that need fueled the attraction that had always linked them.

He didn't prolong the foreplay. She was ready and so was he. Need drove them. Need for human intimacy. Need for each other. Need to live. To feel. To love.

His lips met hers as he lowered his body on hers. Hot desire raged through him as he entered her. Her arms wrapped around him, bringing him closer to her, and her body reacted to his every stroke. She caught his tempo and together they moved in a primitive dance that became a frantic, whirling race toward a peak he'd never reached before.

He felt her body shudder in climax, and he caught himself just before he did the same and quickly withdrew, spilling his seed on the sheet.

Then he lay back and held her, as her body trembled. "I'm sorry. I should have brought something. I was damned worried about you. Why in the hell didn't you tell me?"

"I'm not used to having people worry about me."

"I can remedy that." He showered her face with kisses, then moved to her neck. "You taste good," he murmured.

"So do you."

"You feel great."

"Hmmmmmmm. Likewise."

He touched her hair. It was soft and silky and smelled like roses. "Don't ever do that again," he said.

"What?"

"Run off without telling me."

She looked at him with eyes glazed by passion and lips slightly swollen from his kisses. "I felt like I had to. . . . I was a danger to you. If it hadn't been for me, you wouldn't have had to shoot Fuller."

"He was a powder keg, Meredith, and nothing anyone did was going to defuse him."

She shivered in his embrace, and he ran his hands up and down her arms.

"What about supper?"

She sat up. "Excellent idea. I haven't had anything since breakfast."

"Me, either. Any ideas?"

"The clerk here told me about a barbecue place. She said you can't eat anything while visiting Memphis until you eat barbecue."

"She's right."

"You've been here before?"

"I like the blues. They have some of the best in Memphis."

"You come up here for that?"

That reminded him how little they knew about each other.

He took a shower, and she joined him. She leaned against the wall as he soaped her, then she soaped him and they let the water rinse them off. They stayed there until the water cooled, then turned icy.

They took turns toweling each other as steam lingered in the small room.

He felt the stubble on his jaw. "I need to shave."

"No, you don't. I like the outlaw look."

The steam in the small room cloaked them. He caressed her face. "And I like the way the shower made your cheeks glow."

They moved closer together.

"Barbecue," he reminded her, his lips all too close to hers.

She nodded. "Yes," she said. The heat between them remained. The desire. The need.

Hell, the raw hunger. He willed himself to step back.

They needed to talk. And she hadn't eaten all day. Perhaps food would bring them back to their senses.

"I'll get dressed."

"That's a hell of a good idea." The air sizzled between them.

Then she seemed to break loose of the spell that had held both of them prisoner. She left the room with a look every bit as frustrated as his must be.

There was still tonight.

He would stop at the drugstore on their way back.

The thought enabled him to grab a towel, dry his hair with it and dress.

In less time than he thought possible for a woman to get ready, they were in his car. He told Beast to stay, and the dog looked disappointed but sat back on his haunches.

Ten minutes later, they were in a packed room that smelled like heaven.

He ordered ribs. She ordered a barbecue pork plate. They traded food, their hands touching. So did their gazes. They feasted on each other as much as they feasted on the food.

He kept telling himself it was the situation. They had nothing in common. Nothing at all. But the air between them remained dense, heated, explosive. He sat next to her in the booth, rather than across. He wanted to be near her, to touch her.

"What do you plan to do now?" he asked.

"Find the man in that photo."

"You don't know he's the father. And even if he is, he may not know what happened."

"No, but he knew my mother." Her face was wistful. "Something happened between the time the photo was taken and the mother I knew. There was no laughter later."

He wanted to say he had a lead on the young man. But he didn't.

A vague familiarity he couldn't mention yet. He'd tried

to find the files of Dom's conviction years ago. He wanted to see a photo. Oddly enough, the files were missing. He hadn't had time to contact the prison for one.

But wouldn't Dom have shown a greater reaction to Marguerite Rawson's death if they'd had a child together? Gage couldn't help but believe he was reaching.

Still, he planned to talk to Dom once he returned. But first he had to ensure Meredith's safety. He intended to be with Meredith every moment. His suspension had been a godsend. Otherwise, he would have been tempted to tender his resignation. One, he thought, that would be accepted with pleasure.

He didn't mention any of that, though. Instead he ordered dessert.

She looked at him with a small smile. "Why aren't you twice as big as you are?"

"My coach always wanted to know that, too. He wanted big."

"Coach?"

"I played football in high school and college."

She looked puzzled, as if she were searching her mind for a previous mention of it. Hadn't that been in his file? But then why should it be? Hell, he'd never finished.

"What did you play?"

"Quarterback. Injured my knee in my junior year. Shot my ambitions to hell."

"Ambitions?"

"I was going to be the next Joe Namath," he said wryly.

"I was going to be the next Clarence Darrow," she said with a wan smile.

He liked the way she said that. For the first time in years, the sting of failure faded. "Reality has a way of diverting ambitions, doesn't it?" he said. "Where did you go to school?"

"George Washington. My father wanted a son to follow in his footsteps."

His hand reached out and closed over hers. "You're a damned good lawyer."

"Even if I'm on 'the dark side?' "

"I'm sorry for that remark. I saw what you did for Nan. And I've heard about your work at the shelter. You just always . . ." He searched for the words.

"Irritated you?"

"I wish it were that simple. Irritated. Challenged. Bruised my ego. Even worse, attracted me."

She chuckled.

He looked at her suspiciously.

"Those are exactly the same words I would use as to my reaction to you."

"The same?"

"Well, I might throw in that I thought you were arrogant and obnoxious."

"That's cruel."

"I was wrong."

"No, you weren't. A lot of people say that about me."

"They don't know you."

"And you do."

"I'm getting there. Slowly." Her smile was like a gift.

His dessert came. A huge piece of Key lime pie.

He took a forkful and offered it to her.

She opened her mouth and ate it. "Hmmm, that's good."

They shared the rest of it, their gazes seldom leaving the other.

It was gone much too quickly. He ordered a barbeque sandwich for Beast, shrugging at her amusement. "I forgot his dog food."

"That should make him happy."

"That will make him ecstatic. You give it to him, and he'll be your friend for life."

They smiled stupidly at each other again. Gage wondered what in the hell was happening to him. He was acting like an adolescent in love for the first time.

Just then the waitress brought the sandwich and bill. Meredith started to protest as he took it, and he silenced her with a look. "You can pay for breakfast."

"Promise?"

"Promise."

It was an abrupt reminder that they were partners, two people working together to solve a mystery. Well, dammit, wasn't that what he wanted?

Meredith wondered how she had ever thought him cold and arrogant.

He'd said very little about her parents. Sympathy probably would have induced a fountain of tears. Instead he had transported her for a few hours to a safe place. A warm and comforting place.

He stopped briefly at a drugstore. She bought some shampoo while he made his purchases, then they returned to the motel. He drove around it several times, his eyes watchful.

"You don't think . . .?"

"I don't want to take chances."

Then he parked and they went inside. He unlocked the door and made it clear he wanted to enter first even though Beast would have probably scared the stuffing out of anyone who dared go inside.

Beast *was* ecstatic at their return and even more so about the barbecue sandwich. Surprisingly, instead of gulping it in two or three bites, he was very much the gentleman, taking it piece by piece and savoring it, then licking his chops in appreciation.

Then he returned to his place at the full-length window.

Gage took her hand and she looked up at him. Magic enveloped them. He brushed her cheek with his hand, then gently traced patterns along the back of her neck, the very lightness of the touch making it incredibly erotic. Her every nerve ending tingled with expectancy, and she was filled with an aching hunger as his lips moved from her mouth to the hollow of her throat with scorching thoroughness.

"You're beautiful," he whispered, and she felt beautiful.

Her fingers went to the back of his neck, catching locks of his hair, and she felt him tense, just as she had. The air in the room was charged now, dense with voltaic energy.

This time he was taking time to seduce her. His mouth returned to hers, played against it, loving, teasing. Every part of her body ached and quivered and strained toward him as she met him kiss for kiss.

When his lips parted from hers, he touched her face as if reluctant to lose contact.

She leaned against him, needing the warmth to fill the cold emptiness and fear of the last few days, the loneliness and grief. He was a loner. She knew that. There were no promises. But she would grab these moments and know that for tonight she was wanted.

His eyes searched hers. Then he kissed her again, but this time there was no gentleness, as if he were trying to banish something. Or prove something.

There was desperation, urgency, demand . . . a primitive need so strong it set ablaze every feeling part of her. She'd never thought herself a sensual person but now she knew how wrong she'd been. Her heart, her body, her senses were swamped by the pure animal vitality of him, the magnetism of his eyes, the magic of his touch.

She didn't care if there was a tomorrow for them. She needed him tonight. She needed to fill all the empty places in her heart.

There was tonight, and it was a gift she'd never expected.

She led him to the bed. She undressed him while he undressed her, both taking their time, fingers lingering and lips meeting. Then he lowered her to the bed.

He opened the packet he'd purchased, then moved next to her, stroking her skin, then leaning down to kiss her breasts. Jolts of electricity ran through her.

This time he entered her with tantalizing deliberation. Every sane thought dissolved as he proceeded with maddening slowness, each movement arousing sensations that made her clasp him with her legs, pulling him deeper and deeper inside. Heat flooded her as they moved together. Pleasure rolled through her like rumbles of thunder, each wave more powerful than the one before as momentum mounted, and she was lost in one great storm of flashing lightning and bursts of splendor.

twenty-four

Holly sat on the porch with Doug Menelo. The sky was a very dark blue and it appeared that a million stars were blinking down at them.

She'd never seen so many stars in New Orleans. City lights and smog diffused them.

But here there was no smog and few lights. The stars reigned in all their glory. A few lacy clouds paid court.

Fanciful thoughts. But she was full of fancy these days. Hope had replaced fear.

Harry was inside, sleeping. Doug had stopped over to fix a leak in the kitchen water pipes. She was beginning to rely more and more on him, even as a voice inside told her how dangerous it was.

The night they went to the movie, they'd returned to a rain shower and a leak in the roof. He'd fixed it the next day, along with some sagging steps.

It had been a natural progression of a relationship she'd not been able to end. She liked his company too much. She liked the way he made her feel, as if she were someone of importance. He was funny and kind and decent to the core. He was also straightforward.

She longed to discard the glasses she didn't need, to add a touch more of makeup, to forget the dye that made her hair so unmemorable. She wanted to look nice for him, not because she wanted to impress his friends, but because he made her feel more than she was.

She couldn't do that. Still, he liked the plain person she'd tried so hard to make herself into.

"Thanks for fixing the leak," she said.

"Thanks for the beef stew. It was terrific."

Pleasure flooded her. She had never cooked much until she'd left New Orleans. There had always been someone else to do it. She found a new joy in finding recipes and experimenting.

This recipe had been in a local fund-raising recipe book, and she'd added just a touch of red wine to it. It had been, she'd told herself, the least she could do when he was repairing things.

They'd had the rest of the wine with the meal although she had only sipped at one glass. She couldn't afford to get giddy.

She knew she shouldn't invite his attentions. She kept reminding herself that he was a lawman and she was an outlaw. But every time she vowed she wouldn't see him again, something happened that drew them together. And she didn't want to deprive Harry of his Saturday horseback rides.

That was the excuse she kept giving herself.

But she was getting in deeper and deeper. She had watched him as he'd fixed the leak. He stretched out on the floor, the taut muscled arms visible with his sleeves rolled up.

She couldn't imagine Randolph fixing anything. Except an election.

And every time Doug looked at her with those dark eyes, her heart skipped in response. . . .

"A quarter for your thoughts," he said.

"They're probably not worth more than that penny."

"Let me be the judge of that."

"It's just . . . everything is so lovely out here. Quiet. I've never seen so many stars before."

"You fit this land."

She glanced at him. "Why?"

"It's always taken courage to move and resettle, particularly alone. And a resilience." He looked embarrassed as he faltered for a moment. "There's a lot of strength in you."

Strength? She'd always been the weakest person she knew. She had allowed herself to be molded by her mother, then used by her father and her husband. She'd been reading a lot about abuse. She realized now that she had been emotionally abused for years. And she had allowed it to happen.

"I wish you were right."

He was silent for a moment. "If you ever need to talk . . . I'm a good listener."

Her gaze met his. Her heart caught. He was saying something else altogether. He knew something was wrong. He was offering his help. How she wanted to grab it!

"I'll remember that," she forced herself to reply lightly.

He sighed and his hand reached over and clasped hers. "I'm good at fixing things." It was obvious that he didn't mean pipes or roofs.

But he couldn't "fix" her problem, not without getting involved. Her husband and father wouldn't hesitate to destroy him. Or even kill him if he got in their way, as she had. And then what would happen to Jenny?

A shiver ran through her. He pulled her to him and put his arm around her. Then he leaned over and his lips brushed against hers. She'd never had a kiss like it. Gentle. Tender. Persuasive.

She couldn't.

She had killed a man, no matter the reason. She was married to a murderer. A very powerful one.

She pulled away. "I'm sorry. . . ."

"Liz?"

"It's too soon. It's much too soon," she babbled. She wanted him so badly. She wanted his touch, his embrace. She wanted to love and be loved.

He was watching her closely. Then he stood. "I'm sorry,

too. I took too much for granted." His voice wasn't angry. Just sad.

"I . . . I . . ." She shook her head, turned and ran inside. She didn't want him to see the tears, the anguish of wanting what he was so openly offering.

"Liz?" He stood in the doorway.

She swallowed past the enormous lump in her throat. "Please go," she said.

He was a large shadow in the doorway. He gave her a quirky smile that was part puzzlement, part hurt. Well, she had led him on. Even cooked a meal for him. What did she expect him to think?

Despite her plea, he stood there, compassion written on his face. It was obvious that he knew something was wrong, terribly wrong.

"I . . . loved my husband. I can't . . ."

But she feared her eyes were saying something else. She had taken off the glasses as she'd made supper, and she wondered whether she was looking at him with the same longing that was in his eyes.

"Has someone hurt you?" he asked softly.

"No. I just feel wicked. Unfaithful."

"Harry never talks about him."

He was persistent. He was also moving toward her. His hand went to her cheek and he wiped something away.

She didn't realize she'd been crying.

She struggled for her composure. She felt the palm of his hand against her cheek. For a few seconds, she leaned into it, treasured one of the few tender touches she'd known.

Then he took it away. "I'll always be there for you, Liz," he said. "No matter what."

But he wouldn't be. Not if he knew the truth.

"Thank you."

"Thank you for supper. I get tired of my own cooking." She heard a forced lightness in his voice.

"You worked for your supper."

"So I did."

He regarded her with somber concern mixed with frustration. Then he picked up the box of tools he'd brought.

"Are we still on for riding Saturday?"

No. She should pack tonight and leave in the morning before daybreak.

She nodded.

"Good night then."

"Good night."

The door closed quietly behind him but she still heard the sound of his boots against the wood of the small porch.

She wanted to run out after him. She wanted to tell him everything.

Instead she looked out the window as he pulled away. The stars were almost gone, shrouded by clouds that had grown from mere wisps to heavy, purple billows.

She looked down. Her hands were clenched in front of her as the sound of his car faded away.

Don't go.

New Orleans

Gage followed Meredith back to the city. They had stopped at a drive-through restaurant in Jackson, then at a rest stop to eat and let Beast out.

It was a gloomy day. The rain that had fallen on and off throughout the drive seemed to foreshadow the next day, when the funeral would be held.

She had placed a call to Mrs. Edwards and had asked her to contact caterers for the gathering after the service. It would be at her parents' home again. It would be the second one in a week.

She wished there had been a way they could have driven back together, but they both needed their vehicles. The break for lunch helped, even the fact that Beast slobbered all over her.

They sat next to each other on a picnic bench like any other couple. But despite last night—and the passion that had raged between them—they were not a couple.

He had been gentle and tender and passionate and fierce. He had made her body sing in ways she'd never thought possible.

And it had felt so very good when she'd gone to sleep in his arms and woke in them.

They hadn't spoken of love or commitment. The spectre of her parents' marriage haunted her, keeping her from uttering them.

She never loved me. She kept hearing those words over and over again as she drove.

Then why had her parents married?

If she knew that, then she might have more clues as to what had happened.

She suspected Gage had ghosts of his own. She looked in the rearview mirror. Gage was still right behind her. Beast's head visible on the left side. She smiled. When she had met him years ago, she never would have suspected Gage Gaynor of being such a complex man. She kept finding new layers to him.

She wondered if she would ever really know him. If she would ever have the chance.

They had decided she would stay with him tonight. She didn't want to be alone, and he didn't want her to be alone. She couldn't bear answering the phone and taking condolence calls and questions from curious reporters.

They arrived at his home at five P.M.

She parked on the street and met him at his car. He took her hand and together they went into his house, Beast at his heels.

He showed her the guest room. "Want a few minutes alone?"

"I need to make a few phone calls."

"Be my guest."

She really needed to make more than a few. She'd deserted poor Mrs. Edwards, who had to cope with getting the house ready and answering the phone. It had probably rung off the hook. She'd left Sarah to deal with irate clients.

She had never before abrogated her responsibilities. She had escaped, pure and simple. She wondered whether searching for information had been an excuse.

She used her cell phone and called Sarah first. "Any problems?"

"Nothing I can't handle. Reporters are all over the place, but the judge in the Keyes case postponed. He asked me to convey his sympathies."

"Judge West?"

"Yep, he has a heart after all."

"Thanks."

"I'll be at the funeral tomorrow."

"You don't have to—"

"I want to. And so does Becky. By the way, my kids are falling in love with that dog."

"No problem with the apartment?"

"No. He squeaked in under the thirty-pound pet limit."

"Can you keep him for a few more days?"

"The kids will be ecstatic. In fact, if you aren't going to keep him . . ."

"I'm sure Nicky would be happier with your children. I'm gone so much." Yet it was another loss for her. She had been getting used to Nicky's presence.

She hung up and felt a tear wandering down her face. She sat down on the bed. The tears started coming. Not because of the dog. Or perhaps because of the dog. For some reason, it was easier to cry over a small loss than a huge one.

The tears came in torrents. She hated that, but she couldn't stop. Her father. Her mother. Her home. And now the damn dog.

"Meredith?"

She turned away from the phone. And from the door where he stood. She tried to stop the flood of tears.

"Has something happened?" His voice was warm with concern.

"Something else, you mean?" She hated the self-pity in those words.

He entered the room and pulled her into his arms. "It's about time for a cry. You can't bottle it up forever."

"It's . . . the dog," she mumbled. "It's so darn stupid."

"Did something happen to Nicky? I thought he was staying with Sarah."

"Sarah . . . wants to keep him," she babbled.

She waited for him to make some smart comment. Here she was crying over a dog she'd kept all of a few days.

He didn't. He folded her in his arms and just held her.

"It's time, love," he said. "Let it go."

She yielded to the compulsive sobs that shook her even as she absorbed the comfort of his embrace. The tears came and came.

Finally, they slowed. Seconds later he was wiping the tears from her face with such gentleness that she started to cry again.

"I never cry," she choked out. "Not like that."

"Then you're due," he said.

"Thank you."

"Any time," he said with a lightness belied by the caring in his eyes.

Love. He had called her "love."

A meaningless endearment. Nothing more.

She straightened, brushed away the remaining wetness from her face. "I'm sorry. I'm not usually—"

"Hell, I would worry like hell about you if that hadn't come," he said with a smile that was as intimate as a kiss.

She knew her lips were probably trembling, and she was sure of it when he leaned over and kissed her with such tenderness that she feared she would explode in tears yet again.

Instead she put her arms around him and the kiss deepened. He tore his mouth away and rained kisses up and down her face, licking the tears she knew still dotted her face.

She felt silly and stupid for the outburst and yet she felt better as well. Only now did she realize how she'd bottled so many emotions deep inside. She supposed she had gone through every known major one in the past two weeks. Grief, fear, terror, confusion, regret, loss.

She swallowed hard. "I think I can use a cup of coffee."

"Laced with brandy, I think." He pulled her close to his side and they walked together to the kitchen. She ached to taste his kisses again, but she also feared it. She wanted him far too much.

He was addictive. Too addictive.

She waited as he poured whole beans into a coffeemaker and a strong aroma filled the kitchen. An occasional tremor ran through her body, remnants of the crying jag. The emotions were still there, rumbling under the surface like a volcano with repeated eruptions.

She willed them to behave.

In minutes, he had steaming cups of coffee in front of them.

Then he sat down and studied her face. She knew it must be red and blotched and swollen.

His lips turned up in a quizzical smile. "Why must you be so pretty?"

"But I'm not."

He stared at her with astonishment. "Then you've never looked in a mirror."

"My mother . . ."

Something like understanding crossed his face. "I hope you don't compare yourself to her."

She didn't answer.

"A mannequin might be lovely," he said. "But it's the heart that conveys beauty. I don't know about your mother, but I know I like and . . . admire yours." He'd hesitated as if seeking a word.

Of all the things he might have said to her, that was the most startling. A warm glow suffused through her. It was the finest compliment she'd ever received, made so by her conviction that he'd never said anything like it to anyone else. He was always direct. Matter-of-fact. Poetry was not usually a part of his character.

She sipped the coffee. She needed a jolt of reality, of

common sense. She needed to fall back to the ground after that unexpected statement.

She asked, "What now?"

"Ready to join the fray again?" A challenge was in his eyes.

To get her mind off the past few moments? It was remarkable how sensitive he could be. She remembered when she had thought him the most insensitive man she'd ever met.

"Yes."

"Good."

"You don't think Rick Fuller was behind anything else that happened?"

"Believe me, Rick isn't that smart. I wouldn't rule out that someone used him, though."

"I keep going back to why."

"Everything leads back to your mother's request," he said. "And the stakes have to be pretty damn high if they don't hesitate to attack a former assistant district attorney and someone of your father's stature."

"Then someone in the city knows where my sister is?"

He nodded. "It's a possibility."

The coffee was helping considerably. So did sitting across from Gage.

"What now?" she asked.

"We need to find the man in the photo."

"How?"

"I made a call while you were making yours. I asked someone at the department to research taverns within a fifty-mile radius in 1969 for one called Paule's." He paused. "I think I have an idea as to who the boy might be."

"Who? Someone here?"

"I can't say until I know for sure."

She understood that. Too many people had been jeopardized already. The image of Mrs. Starnes remained in her mind. "When will you know?"

"I just called. I'm going over there now."

"Someone you know?"

"Yes."

She wanted to persist. She had learned enough about him, though, to know that it would do little good. He might cut some corners, but she would never doubt his integrity again.

"Can I go with you?"

"I think it's better if I go alone. He might talk to me more freely. I doubt that he would if you were there. If it is the young man in the photo and he knows anything, I'll arrange a meeting."

She wanted to protest. But there was something in his eyes that told her it would do no good.

"I should go home anyway."

His gaze held hers. "Will you stay here? With Beast? I don't think any one knows I'm back, or even that we are working together. This is the safest place for you."

She considered it. She liked the way he asked. He didn't demand or order as her father had often done. It was a request, made for her protection. "Yes," she said simply.

His mouth curved with approval. "I'll bring back some food."

"That sounds good," she said.

"Pizza?"

She nodded.

"Don't answer the phone while I'm gone. Or the door. You have a gun with you?"

"Yes."

He reached out and took her hand. "Keep it with you."

"How long will you be?"

"No longer than two hours. Any more than that and I'll call you on your cell phone."

She nodded.

"You have my cell number?"

She'd memorized it days ago. "Yes."

He stood. So did she.

"You really are beautiful," he said.

She'd probably never looked so wretched as she did after the recent outburst, yet she saw sincerity in his eyes.

"You be careful, too," she said. It was an order rather than request. "If they know we've been together—"

"I'll be on guard."

"Too many people have been dying around me," she said. "I couldn't stand another."

"I have no intention of letting anything happen to me."

He touched her check, then she stood on tiptoes and brushed her lips against his.

"Promise," she demanded.

"Oh, yes," he drawled. His voice was husky.

And then he left.

twenty-five

Gage met Dom at the shelter, a large rambling building that included a small gym where Gage and Dom played basketball with some of the young residents.

The building had been donated years ago when Father Michael Murphy ran the shelter. Father Murphy had a silver tongue and had not only talked someone out of the building but had garnered substantial backing for his cause. Dom, who had worked with him since he'd been released from prison, had been Father Murphy's designated successor.

Though not as diplomatic as Father Murphy, Dom's commitment and dedication had kept the money coming. He received city, state and federal grants, and had managed to keep the stream of money flowing from sources long cultivated by Father Murphy. Still, he never had quite enough. The number of runaways kept increasing.

Gage knew Father Murphy had saved the bitter young man who had spent years in prison. He'd sponsored his parole, given him a job and paid his college tuition. And Dom had found his calling. His experience in prison had helped hundreds of kids in trouble. They loved Father Murphy but they related to Dom.

Dom was in his office, a frown on his face as he looked at bills. The frown disappeared when he saw Gage.

"Thank God. An excuse to delay this. I hate paperwork. And bills even more."

"How are the finances going?"

"As always, I can use more money. Some of the kids really need better clothes. It's hard enough for them to go to school with the other kids knowing where they live. It's harder when they don't have decent clothes to wear."

"I'll send a check."

"You send enough, but I'll accept anyway. Now, why did you sound so urgent?"

Gage closed the door. "I asked you a few questions the other day."

Dom waited.

"About Mrs. Rawson? Whether you knew her."

"I'm not senile yet, Gage. What is the point here?"

"Did your father have a tavern near Donaldsonville?"

Dom merely gazed at him. Watching. Waiting.

"Did you know Mrs. Rawson when she was Marguerite Thibadeau?"

"Why the interrogation?"

"People have been dying, Dom. I think they are dying because of something that happened thirty-three years ago."

Dom didn't move. His face didn't change. Gage knew that stare. He had seen it on his brother's face. In prison you learned to school your expression. But you couldn't always control your eyes.

Gage saw something there.

He played his trump card. "Did you know Marguerite Thibadeau Rawson had a child in February 1970? A daughter?"

He saw the implications of what he'd said register in Dom's eyes. A muscle flexed in his throat. "No," he said softly after a long pause. "I thought she had gone to Europe."

"What happened back then, Dom?"

Dom stared into the distance. Gage knew he had never married. He'd always laughed it off. An ugly ex-con who had fifty wayward sons had no business getting married.

Since Gage had also avoided matrimony like the plague for his own reasons, he'd understood.

Dom's hands played with a pen.

Gage waited.

"*My* daughter?" he finally asked.

"If the timing is right, it's a damn good possibility."

"Where is she?" Only the throbbing muscle in his throat revealed any emotion.

"We don't know. Mrs. Rawson told her daughter, Meredith, about it just before she lapsed into a coma. She asked Meredith to find her and split a trust. Meredith has been trying to find her, but there aren't any records."

"The bastards." Dom spit out the two words.

Gage waited. He'd wondered if the father knew. If he hadn't, then he would probably be of little help.

Dom rose from the chair and started pacing. Barely restrained fury radiated in the room.

"Who?" Gage finally said. "Who are the bastards?"

"Her father. Oliver Prescott."

"Prescott?"

Dom sat down abruptly. His face was like a piece of stone, his brown eyes glittering like agates. It was obvious he was trying to control himself.

"Dom, we need help. There's been an attempt on Meredith's life. Her apartment was trashed, a friend of her mother's was killed after agreeing to talk to Meredith. Now her father's been killed. I'm afraid they will try again to kill her." He stopped. "It all started when she started to ask questions about her half sister."

Dom picked up a paper weight, juggling it as if he wanted to throw it against the wall.

Normally, Dom was the most controlled man Gage knew.

Gage waited, even though he hated every minute away from Meredith. He believed she was safe at his house, but this whole sequence of events had been explosive.

Silence was a technique he knew worked while a demand for answers rarely did.

"Who was the friend?" Dom finally asked.

"A woman named Lulu Starnes. Starnes was her married name."

"That's why I didn't catch it," he said slowly. "A different name."

"Do you remember her?"

"She was Maggie's best friend. Her shadow. She would have done anything for her." He put his head in his hands. "I shoved her out of my memory, just as I tried to erase Maggie. It never worked."

"Why?"

"Maggie didn't believe me when I said I didn't steal the car, that the drugs they found weren't mine."

"When did that happen?"

"We were talking about getting married. Her father hated the ground I walked on. I was part Cajun, the son of a tavern owner. I was nothing in his eyes. Less than nothing. He tried to stop her from seeing me.

"I was eighteen, just graduating from high school. She was seventeen. I met her when she and some friends came slumming to my father's tavern. We had good Cajun food. Good Cajun music. One of her friends had heard about it. The moment I saw her I was a goner. She was beautiful. Golden hair. Wide blue eyes. She started dancing with an old Cajun, her eyes sparkling like a lake dusted by sunbeams.

"I asked her for a dance, thinking she would refuse. She didn't, and I thought we'd both fallen in love at that moment." He was obviously seeing her again as he talked. Gage could envision her through Dom's eyes.

"We started dating. Secretly. It made everything more exciting. At least for her. I was the community bad boy. I'd gotten into my share of fights. Borrowed a car on a dare. Stupid kid stuff, but I had a reputation."

Gage wished now that he had brought Meredith along. But then would Dom had opened up as he was now doing? It was almost as if Gage wasn't there at all.

Dom squeezed his eyes shut, as if he were in agonizing pain. "Only a few people knew about us. She knew her father would disapprove. Lulu was one who knew. About the only time we had together was Saturday. She would say she was going to someone's home and drive down to meet me. Sometimes Lulu would come along."

He shook his head. "It's hard to think of both of them dead. I liked Lulu because she liked me. And she often provided excuses for Maggie's absences."

Dom stood again, started pacing the room like a convict paced a small cell. Habit, Gage thought. Dom was obviously recalling something very painful. He was thinking, too.

"Then I met Oliver Prescott. He saw us at a jazz place in the French Quarter," Dom continued. "I shouldn't have taken her there. It was risky, but a friend of mine had a gig, and Maggie wanted to hear him. He came over to Maggie and asked to be introduced.

"One day when Maggie was on a field trip, he called me and asked if I would like to try his sports car. I'd admired it before. Like a fool, I jumped at the chance. I met him at his house and he handed me the keys. I'll never know why I was so stupid, but I was a kid with a kid's love for cars. And where I came from, we didn't see many imported sports cars."

He didn't have to continue. Gage knew what was coming.

But Dom did. "I was arrested an hour later. The car had been reported stolen. There were drugs underneath the seat.

"My family didn't have much money but they used every penny they could borrow to get me a lawyer. It was my word against Prescott's. And because I'd taken a joyride a year earlier, I was considered a repeat offender. My father lost the tavern, and I was sentenced to ten years."

Dom raised an eyebrow. "Even then that was a hefty sentence."

"I suspect someone talked to someone."

"Marguerite's father?"

He shrugged. "Never could prove it. Money ran out and so did my attorney."

"And Marguerite?"

"I received a letter from her, telling me she never wanted to see or hear from me again. After that I didn't care much about anything. I was attacked and fought back. Earned a few more years. Then I met Father Murphy."

"You must have run into Marguerite after your release."

"No. I think we both did everything we could to avoid it. She never said anything about a child. I didn't suspect. . . ."

He closed his eyes. His fingers were balled in a tight fist.

"Dom?"

Dom opened his eyes and looked at him.

"Prescott? Do you know what happened to him?" Gage asked.

"I was still in prison," Dom said. "It happened just before my release. But I sure as hell wasn't sorry to hear of his death."

That was convenient. He saw from Dom's face he thought so, too.

Another dead end. Dom obviously had no idea where Marguerite's daughter was.

"I want to find her," Dom said. "I want to help you."

"It could be impossible. There are no records in Memphis, not even a birth certificate. It's as if she never existed."

"It's not impossible," Dom said slowly. "If it was, someone wouldn't be so hell-bent to keep her hidden. There has to be reasons for the secrecy. So we start with the people around Marguerite and find out why they would go to such lengths to protect a secret."

"The deaths may not have anything to do with her."

"But you don't believe that or you wouldn't be here."

"No," Gage admitted. "I'm beginning to feel I'm in a maze that has no exit."

"How did you find out about me?"

"Mrs. Starnes had a photo of you and Marguerite Thibadeau in front of your father's tavern. You've changed, of course, but I seemed to recognize the way you hold your head. Still, I wasn't sure until I traced down the tavern and discovered it was owned by a Cross."

Dom looked at him curiously. "I thought you had been suspended."

"I've taken a personal interest."

"Why?"

"Meredith Rawson. She's opened something very nasty and she can't seem to close the door."

"Does she want to close it?"

"No. She's determined to find her half sister. She promised her mother. She wants to split her trust fund with her."

"I think I would like her," Dom said with a whisper of a smile.

"You would. You both think you are Don Quixote," he added wryly. "She wants to meet you, too."

"Does she know . . .?"

"I didn't tell her about you. She knows I had someone in mind. I wanted to be sure first." He hesitated, then asked carefully, "There couldn't have been anyone else?"

"No," Dom said flatly. "Not if the baby was born in February."

Gage believed him. "For what it's worth, I think the Rawson marriage was not a happy one."

"I'm sorry about that," Dom said, real regret in his voice. "I occasionally saw photos of Maggie. All the vitality was gone. The smile was different."

So he hadn't been as indifferent as he first indicated.

Gage wondered whether that was why he'd never married. Whether he had been as disillusioned as Gage had been.

"Will you come home with me? I think she would like to talk to you." Gage paused. "She lost both parents in a week. Now she's discovering that their lives were nothing but lies. I think she needs to hear that her mother was once happy."

"I'm not sure she was," Dom said. "I had thought so, but—"

A knock at the door interrupted them.

Dom opened the door, and one of his assistants came in. "Jayson's gone again."

Dom sighed heavily. "I can't keep him locked up here. Did any of the other boys say why?"

"He's probably after drugs."

"Did he take anything from here?"

"One of the other boys says he took money from him."

"Then he doesn't come back. Elliott, you've met Detective Gaynor, haven't you?"

"I've watched him play basketball."

Gage chuckled. "You saw me beat Dom?"

"I'm afraid I did."

"He owes me a dinner."

Elliott looked from one to the other. Despite the warm banter, tension was thick in the room.

Dom said, "I'll be gone for a few hours. Can you handle things?"

"I think so." Elliot left.

"I should warn you," Gage said. "Getting involved could be dangerous."

"It's not only Maggie's daughter," Dom said. "I want to know exactly what happened years ago. It could clear my name. Dammit. Eighteen years in prison."

"Eighteen? You said you were sentenced to ten."

"Some guys came after me. I knifed one to protect myself. Eight more years."

Gage sat up in his chair. "Why did they come after you?"

Dom looked at him for a moment, then realization crossed his face. "You think the attack was planned."

"Someone might have thought you would hunt Prescott down and discover who was behind him. There was no reason for him to frame you on his own."

"That's one reason no one believed me," Dom said. "And the fact that Maggie had disappeared."

"She didn't testify for you?"

He shrugged. "She wasn't there. I don't suppose it would have helped anyway. She didn't know about Prescott's offer but . . ."

But he'd obviously felt betrayed. Pain was in every word he uttered.

Gage had known Dom for a long time. He was passionate in his crusade to help kids but otherwise had always been a good companion who loved a glass of beer and good conversation. Now Gage realized how self-controlled Dom was, how little he revealed to anyone.

"And she never contacted you again?"

"No," Dom said, then paused. "She didn't say anything to her daughter about me?"

"According to Meredith, she just said a few words before lapsing into a coma. Apparently those few words took all her strength. She only said there was a daughter and she'd been born in Memphis in February 1970."

Dom gave a bitter chuckle. "Silent to the end."

"There had to be reasons, Dom."

"Yeah, she didn't want the kid of a convict."

"I don't think that was it." Gage stood. "Let's go."

Meredith paced restlessly. She looked through his bookcases. She'd discovered long ago that books revealed a great deal about a person.

But their eclectic nature told her little. There were mysteries, suspense, biographies, history, literary classics. He had stacks of *Sports Illustrated*. His CD collection was just as varied: jazz, blues, classical. A few oldies. No hard rock.

Beast stayed right with her, as if he knew he was to keep her safe. Or perhaps he, too, wanted companionship. Perhaps he even sensed her restlessness. And sadness.

Tomorrow, she would bury the mother she never really knew. And she couldn't even go home to get ready. Not without being in fear for her life.

She finally grabbed a book and sat down. For about two seconds. Then she was up again, staring out the window.

It was growing dark when she saw Gage's car drive up, another behind him. Gage got out and went over to the other car. The driver got out and she stared at him.

Recognized him. Dominic Cross. He was legendary in New Orleans.

The hard-driving director of a shelter for runaways and a passionate advocate for young people at risk. She had even met him several times, and she'd been intrigued by his craggy face. He must be in his mid-fifties, and his hair was short. If he was the intense-looking thin boy in the photo, he had gained weight. He had a powerful body now, and his face looked as if he'd been a fighter. Like Gage, his nose was crooked, and she doubted whether he'd broken it on a football field. Like everyone else, she knew he had once been in prison. It was a large part of every story in the shelter.

Her heart beat erratically. Could he have been the father of her half sister? It seemed impossible.

She went to the door and opened it before they reached it.

Gage gave her a victory signal from just behind Dominic.

So Dominic Cross had been her mother's lover all those years ago. She couldn't imagine a more unlikely one. And then she remembered the photo again. The laughter in her mother's face, the happy smile on her lips. The possessive way the young man had his arm around her. There had been an intimacy conveyed in that pose.

She stuck out her hand. "Meredith Rawson. I've met you before at the courthouse."

He took her hand and held it a moment. "Gage told me about your search."

Gage showed them to the living room. He stood, watching. "I think a drink is in order here."

"A beer," Dom said.

Meredith nodded.

Gage disappeared into the kitchen.

"I didn't know about the baby," Dom said. "I was arrested—bail was set very high—and I heard her father had sent her to a relative in Europe. I never knew about a child."

She heard the pain in his voice. "I think few people did."

"What did she tell you?"

"Very little. She knew she was dying. I think she wanted to give me something. Perhaps even you."

"She kept me from my daughter all these years," he said roughly. His hands trembled slightly.

"I don't know why. I don't even know how," Meredith said. "I wish I did. I wish I could tell you more." She realized that her own sense of loss in not knowing her sister must be magnified a hundred times in him. He had lost a daughter.

"What exactly did she say?"

Meredith tried to remember. "First she said 'You have a sister.' Then that she had been seventeen. Pregnant. Her parents were furious. I think she used the word 'mortified.' That 'Daddy' thought it would ruin his career. She asked me to find her. She said she was leaving her trust fund to me. And to her."

She remembered the shock she'd felt, the words that had beggared understanding. They were still vivid in her mind. "I asked her, 'How?' and she said, 'Memphis. I was sent to Memphis.' Then she asked me to promise again to find her. I did and asked whether my father knew. She didn't answer. She simply said . . ."

"What?" Dominic demanded. "What did she say?"

"She apologized and said she was sorry for not being a good mother. She said she 'didn't have anything left after . . .' Then she lapsed into a coma. She never regained consciousness."

A muscle worked in his face. "That's everything?"

"Yes."

"Nothing about me? About the father?" It was more a plea than a question.

"I'm sorry," she said gently. "I wish I could help more."

He seemed to collapse within. She ached for him. Heartbreak was in every gesture. Heartbreak and anger.

Gage returned with three beers, distributed them and took one of the chairs. He looked from her to Dominic and back again.

"I can go away."

Meredith shook her head, then looked at Dom.

"Stay," he said. "You're a part of this."

Gage visibly relaxed.

Dominic turned his gaze back to her. "Tell me everything that's happened. Gage told me some but I would like you to fill it out."

She'd wanted to ask him about her mother. Not only wanted to. Needed to. Yet he had the greater right. He'd lost a daughter as well as the girl he'd obviously loved.

"Did you go and see her?" she asked suddenly.

He nodded.

"The nurse told me she'd seen someone in the room when she went out to the desk for a moment."

"I'd read she was in the hospital when your father was killed." His face hardened. She saw the effort it took to control his fury. "I wanted to see her."

"There was only a shell left," she said.

He nodded.

"Lulu Starnes had a photo of her. Gage probably told you about it. I never saw her smile like that. She and my father . . . well I never saw an affectionate gesture between them. It was almost as if a wall had been constructed between them."

"I'm sorry to hear that," he said after a long moment. "I really am. I loved her. I didn't want to see her unhappy."

Meredith reached out and touched him. "I am so sorry."

"What did you do then?"

"I confronted my father about what my mother said. He knew she'd had a daughter, but he wouldn't tell me anything else. I think he knew it all. He just kept telling me to leave it alone, that I didn't know what I was doing by opening the past.

"Right after that someone tried to run me down in the hospital garage. My house was trashed. I thought it had something to do with one of my cases—I specialize in domestic cases. But then I started to go through my mother's yearbook, looking for her old friends. I hoped someone would know who the father might be, and that he might know something."

"Gage told me about Lulu," he said. "I remember her. She was shy and quiet but I liked her."

"I decided then the attacks had something to do with my mother and my search for my sister. Particularly when there was a dead end everywhere I turned. No birth certificate. No record of any kind. Then my father's death.

"When my mother mentioned Memphis, I immediately thought she must have stayed with my great-aunt, but that was also a dead end. She died in a robbery years ago. It seems every trail ended in violence."

She looked at him. "I'm reluctant now to bring anyone into it."

"It's my daughter," he said. "I want to find out as much as you do."

"Tell me what happened with you and my mother."

She listened intently as he told his story. His face rarely changed expression but his voice shifted from a gentle tone into a more angry one as he went from falling in love to being arrested.

"I know my mother didn't love my father," she said. "They even had separate rooms. I could never understand why they stayed married.

"My father told me a few days ago that she had never loved him. His voice was sad. Regretful. It was one of the first times I ever heard him say anything about the marriage. They just treated each other like strangers who didn't particularly like each other."

"That must have been hard for you."

"I thought it was normal when I was a child, that everyone lived that way. Many of my friends had divorced parents and some of the divorces were pretty ugly. I supposed I counted myself lucky that at least they didn't fight."

"Have you had time to go through your father's papers?"

"Which specific ton of them? He's an attorney." Then she caught herself. *Was.* Was an attorney. When was everything going to sink in? She knew from other people that there was a numbness, a disbelief at first. She still felt it.

She looked away. And into Gage's eyes. She saw understanding there. The empathy that had developed between them continued to fluster her. She'd always been suspicious of love. She certainly wasn't a believer in marriage.

But the heat of sexual attraction had forged something more than that. She enjoyed looking at him. She enjoyed just being with him. She loved watching him make coffee and the way he took her hand. She liked the feeling that puddled in the stomach when *he* looked at *her*. She had no doubt that he saw something no one else had. To him, she *was* beautiful, and that made her beautiful.

She was suddenly aware of the lengthening silence.

"Where do we go from here?" she asked.

Dom stood and paced the room.

Gage continued to sit. "Perhaps we've been going about it from the wrong direction."

Dom stopped. She stilled.

"We start here and now instead of in the past," he continued. "Who had something to lose? Something so important that they would risk killing someone of your father's prominence? And he wasn't the only one. I think Prescott's death is connected in some way."

He looked at Dom. "I want to know everything that happened thirty-three years ago. And I want Meredith to hear it. Then I want Meredith to tell you everything she knows from the time of Prescott's murder. Maybe we can find a common denominator."

Dom broke in. "You think whoever killed Prescott also killed Charles Rawson?"

"And Lulu Starnes. Perhaps even Meredith's great-aunt. Loose ends. That's if we're right in thinking that Marguerite Thibadeau stayed there during her pregnancy."

"But why?" Meredith asked. "What secret could be so important?"

"It was Prescott who framed Dom. Your mother's father was probably involved and possibly your father. Perhaps Prescott became a danger. The investigative reports said he was known as a heavy drinker. Perhaps he tried blackmail or said something he shouldn't have."

"But why would an adoption become so deadly?"

"There's no records. That means it was probably a black-market baby. Or an informal adoption. One friend to another. For some reason that friend may not want the world to know that his, or her, daughter isn't really a biological child."

"But why would someone kill for that?"

"That's what we need to find out."

Meredith was already beginning to think along new lines. Which one of her grandfather's friends had a daughter who was born in February 1970?

"It's a long shot," Gage said.

Dom looked at Meredith, then at Gage. "But it appears to be the only shot we have."

twenty-six

Gage accompanied Meredith to her mother's service and sat next to her. His presence was a lifeline.

He took her hand in his and held it tight. She didn't dare look at him. The sympathy in his eyes would reduce her to tears.

She didn't want to shed any today.

The church was filled even more so than for her father's funeral. The mayor was sitting behind her, along with a number of other local politicians. Justice Samuel Matthews, who had sent flowers to her mother in the hospital, was present, as were Judges Haywood and Johnston, who sat together with their wives. She mentally filed the names of each of them. She would go over them later with Gage and Dom.

There would be the guest book, as well, but not everyone might sign it.

She knew that Dominic Cross was somewhere in the crowd. She wondered whether his presence would interest anyone. They had discussed the possibility of him sitting with them, but it was best to keep the bad guys guessing.

They had also discussed the probability that if someone believed that she and Gage knew Dom's connection to her mother, all three of them would become targets.

A cold target. She had heard that expression somewhere. That's exactly the way she felt at the moment.

She knew that the only way she could reduce the danger was to give up her search. Both Gage and Dom had suggested that possibility.

But she didn't intend to do that.

Someone had killed her father. Someone had killed a friend of her mother's. Her great-aunt might well have been murdered. There was no way she could continue to live under that shadow. Nor would she give up her search for her sister or the truth about what had destroyed her mother's happiness.

She still had avenues to explore. Her father's records, for one. He kept meticulous notes on everything. She wanted to go through each of his files at the office. There was still the attorney in Memphis. And now they had one more piece of the puzzle: Dom's arrest. It placed Prescott's murder right in the middle of that puzzle.

Meredith was conscious of all the eyes on her. Sympathetic eyes. Curious eyes. Malevolent eyes?

The minister referred to her mother's many charitable endeavors, calling her the heart of the city. Meredith had chosen the music, distressed that she didn't even know what her mother's favorite hymns might be. She had selected her own.

She felt numb as the last prayer was said and the pallbearers escorted the coffin out. There would be a brief graveside service, then the reception at her parents' home. The second in a week.

Caterers were already there, along with Sarah and Becky, who had volunteered again to stay during the service and supervise. Gage had also sent his detective friend Mack to ensure their safety. The private detective had been mortified at losing her when she'd gone to Memphis. He had been told to stay with her whether she wanted his protection or not.

He wanted to make amends.

And then?

There were a million things to do. Both her father's and

mother's wills would have to be probated. She would have to make decisions about their estates, particularly the house.

More importantly, there was a killer—or killers—to be found.

There was, of course, the matter of survival as well.

She accepted condolences from those who wouldn't attend the graveside service, then rode with Gage in the limousine to the cemetery. She wondered whether she could get through the next few hours. Her heart cried, even if her eyes didn't. She still couldn't quite comprehend everything that had happened and the impact it would have on her life.

Gage said little, but his hand had been at the small of her back as they left the church. It was protective, proprietary and evident. They had discussed the wisdom of his appearing as an escort, but he had ended the discussion abruptly by saying he was going to be there . . . by her side.

Thank God. She felt wrapped in his warmth. It helped fill the emptiness that continued to haunt her. In the limousine, he'd recaptured her hand, entwining his fingers with hers.

"Do you think he was there?" she asked. She didn't have to say who. The killer. Or killers.

"I would bet my last dollar on it."

"The cream of New Orleans society," she said bitterly.

"Not all of them, love. Just one."

"Or two. Or three," she amended. "How many lives have they destroyed? And for what reason? Everything comes back to that."

He put an arm around her and pulled her close to him. They rode in silence the rest of the way.

They would discuss murder later. Now was the time to mourn.

Gage watched as the last person left the Rawson home.

Meredith had thanked Sarah and Becky for their help and sent Mrs. Edwards home. Then Meredith, looking exhausted, collapsed on a sofa.

She looked vulnerable, but he knew that wasn't true. She had a core of pure steel. His admiration had grown steadily in the past two weeks.

She gave him a wan smile. "I survived."

"With flying colors. I don't know if I could have done it."

She gave him a long look. "I have no doubts you could."

He liked that vote of confidence. He'd experienced any number of emotions today. One of them, he realize with dismay, that he was falling in love.

Dammit. He didn't want those feelings. She was emotionally vulnerable now.

No amount of practicality or reason could have kept him from her side today.

As for increasing the danger to Meredith, he didn't think it could become any more intense than it already was. Someone was determined to stop at any cost inquiries into events of three years ago. Each succeeding death only added to the desperate need to protect one particular secret.

He was very aware that whoever was behind the deaths would probably come after him now. He welcomed that. He was prepared.

He also realized they had more discreet ways of destroying him than murder. Most likely they would try to plant drugs on him or his property. Both his troubled history at the department and a brother who was serving time for drug distribution would assist any such effort.

He didn't intend for that to happen. Nor did he intend to discuss it with Meredith. He wouldn't give her an excuse to escape his protection again.

As smart as she was, she'd probably already considered the possibility.

"Want a drink?" he asked her now.

"I would love one," she replied, "but I don't think I should. I need to keep all my wits about me."

He sat down next to her. "Do you remember everyone you saw today at the funeral? I know some of them but not all."

"I think so."

He had taken the guest book after the service. He handed it to her. "See if there is anyone you remember who didn't sign the book."

She worked mechanically, jotted down a few more names, then gave it back to him.

"I think we can delete the mayor," he said. "He was too young at the time." He went through them all, crossing them off or putting a check next to their names as possibles. The possibles were people who were in their mid-fifties or older. Another requirement was someone with political power. Someone had exerted influence to have him taken off the Prescott case.

Newcomers—anyone who hadn't lived in New Orleans for the past thirty years—were crossed off the list.

When they finished, he had sixteen names of possible suspects, all of whom were considered among the city's elite.

He handed the list to Meredith. She studied it silently. "And now we see whether any of them has a daughter born in February 1970."

"Yep."

"They are all prominent enough to be subjects of newspaper stories. We can eliminate them one by one."

"Bingo," he said.

"We might be on the wrong track."

"But it's the fastest train we have now. You could go through your father's files, but that might take weeks, even months."

She stood, looking uncertain.

Overload, he realized. "Let's go to my house," he said, trying to interpret her uncertainty. "Dom can meet us there."

"And we have Beast," she said.

"Did Sarah say anything about Nicky?"

"She would like to keep him if no one claims him." She gave him a wry smile. "I thought about keeping him, but Sarah has children. She's home more than I am. Especially now. It's best for the dog." Her voice was wistful.

"There are always dogs needing a home," he said. "In the

meantime you can share Beast. He'll be more than happy to oblige."

Her smile was heartbreaking. He felt like Lancelot. Ivanhoe. All the heroes he'd admired as a boy. He'd never felt like that before.

He leaned over and touched his lips to hers. Gentle. Achingly tender. His heart caught, skipped a beat. His hand touched her cheek. It was cold.

He released her lips. "Let's get out of here," he said.

He locked the door as they left the house. She stopped suddenly as she saw a car parked across the street, then relaxed as she seemed to recognize it.

"Mack Thomas," he said. "He's been watching the house and my car. He's very chagrined that you lost him."

"He shouldn't be. I've been helping battered wives escape husbands for several years now. I know all the tricks."

"So should he," Gage said critically. Still, he gave a small wave as they walked to his car. "Do you want to take yours?"

She nodded.

"I'll follow you."

"And Mack will follow you?" she asked with a slight smile. "We'll look conspicuously like a parade."

"He will go ahead and check out the house," he said. "You can meander a bit."

"No one would go inside with Beast there."

"Beast, unfortunately, is a marshmallow. Anyway, it's just a precaution."

"I think I should go home. Alone. I don't want anyone else hurt because of me. I have a gun. I'll be careful."

"Isn't going to happen, love." The word slipped out, just as it had earlier. "I'm not going to leave your side."

She looked at him. "Even if I asked you?"

"No."

Her face clouded with fear, but this time he knew it was for him, not herself.

"The sooner we find whoever is behind this, the sooner

you can get your life back," he said. "It won't be soon if we're at cross purposes, or if I have to spend valuable time trying to find you. It won't lessen their need to get me out of the picture. I already know too much."

"And Dom?"

"I think he's put himself into the picture. He wants to find his daughter, and like you, he's hell-bent on doing it."

They reached her car and he opened the door for her. She slid in, gave him a rueful smile and nodded her head.

He hoped to hell she meant it.

Mack met them at the house, a grim look on his face.

Meredith and Gage had arrived within seconds of each other.

The moment Gage saw his face, he knew what had happened. "Drugs?"

"Cocaine in the bottom drawer of your dresser in the bedroom. Enough to charge you with distribution. I flushed it down the toilet but I think you should conduct a more thorough search."

"Beast?"

"Wobbly. Whoever planted it probably drugged him."

He went into the kitchen, aware that Meredith was right behind him. Beast was collapsed on the floor, tongue hanging out, eyes not as bright as usual. Gage dropped next to him, scratched behind his ears. "Bad day, huh, guy?"

Beast looked at him pitiably, as if he knew he failed miserably.

"I knew what I was getting," he told the dog. "That's okay."

The tail swished once.

Fury and relief flooded him. Beast was breathing fine. He would have to sleep it off. In the meantime, he wanted to check the rest of the house with Mack. He suspected the DEA or officers from the NOPD would be knocking shortly.

"What can I do?" Meredith asked.

"You take the kitchen. Look under the sink, the fridge, in

the coffee can—any place you can conceive of being a hiding place. Mack checked the most obvious hiding place, my bedroom. But they might have left a second stash."

He took his office. He went through every office drawer, peered behind books in the bookcases. Having been on the drug squad not so many years ago, he knew where to look.

"Gage!"

Meredith's voice. He hurried into the kitchen. She held a plastic bag filled with white powder.

"Where was it?"

"A can of coffee."

"They're not very imaginative," he said. He took the package to the bathroom and flushed the contents down, then the bag.

Meredith followed and he saw the worried look on her face. "Gage?"

Hell, she was an attorney, and what he was doing was destroying evidence. He suddenly realized he had placed her in an untenable position.

He tried to explain. "Meredith, if they find this, I'll be in jail in a New York minute. There's still people who would like to see me crucified. At the very least, I would be tied up administratively for days."

He could call and report it, of course, but his superiors might well have already heard from an anonymous caller. They would claim he called only because someone tipped him off.

She stared at him, and he saw her weigh the alternatives as well. Then she nodded.

They were still hunting when there was a loud knocking at the door.

He hoped to hell they had found it all.

He opened the door. Four officers—two NOPD and two DEA agents—stood there.

He knew the NOPD sergeant. "Joe, what in the hell are you doing here?"

The sergeant gave him an embarrassed but determined look. "We had a tip that you had drugs here."

"Convenient," he replied.

Meredith stood next to him. "Do you have a warrant?"

Joe looked at him inquisitively.

"My attorney," Gage said.

Joe Tipton blinked, then handed the warrant to Meredith. She looked it over. As she suspected, the tip came from an unidentified source.

She stepped back. "Go ahead," she said. "But don't tear up the place." She turned to Gage. "Want to make me one of your great cups of coffee?"

He looked down at her. She had on her attorney's face. Blank. Yet something danced in her eyes.

"Great idea," he said. He opened the door to the kitchen wide. They all entered. Mack was sitting in a chair, a magazine in his hand.

The sergeant stopped. "Mack?"

Mack stood. "Joe. What are you doing here?"

Tipton looked embarrassed. "We had a tip we might find drugs here."

Mack's brows furrowed together. "Here? Strange. Everyone knows how much Gage hates drugs. He spent years trying to save his brother. They gone nuts over there?"

Tipton's face reddened. "We have to look."

Mack lumbered up out of the chair. "You can look here if you want."

Gage watched Meredith's lips twitch. If nothing else, this had served to break into her grief. "What about that coffee? Mack, you want some?"

"I'd rather have a beer."

"Done," Gage said.

A DEA agent stayed with them. He stood and watched as Gage poured water into a percolator and took the can of coffee from the cabinet. The DEA agent stopped him. Looked inside. Sifted the contents. Then returned it.

Gage noted the agents were more careful than they usually were. Apparently they had been given rather specific information as to where to find the drugs.

When the coffee was ready, he poured a cup for himself

and Meredith, then opened the fridge and took out a beer. He offered it to the agent. "Want to check it before I give it to Mack?"

The agent looked embarrassed. "No. I think we got a faulty tip."

"I have a lot of enemies," Gage said.

"Don't we all?" the agent replied, looking as if he would rather be any other place than in a fellow cop's kitchen.

Mack gulped down his beer. Meredith sipped her coffee. If Gage hadn't been so angry, he would have enjoyed watching her play the game. He also realized that now this hadn't worked, more drastic means might be employed.

After another thirty minutes, Tipton returned with one of the other officers. "Sorry about this, Gage. I told them they were crazy but . . ."

"Do you know who received the tip?"

"Someone from Public Integrity. They passed it on to the drug unit."

The second DEA agent came in. "Nothing," he said with a disgusted grunt.

"Anyone in the department will tell you I hate drugs," Gage said. "I've never used them, and I despise anyone who sells them." He couldn't hide the quiet fury in his voice, nor did he want to.

Tipton shuffled on his feet. "We had to check it."

"And now that you have, you can leave," Meredith said quietly. "I buried my mother today, and Gage and Mack were kind enough to look after me. An anonymous tip may be sufficient grounds for some judges, but I find it very questionable. The department, and the judge who signed the warrant, will hear from me tomorrow."

"I'm sorry," Tipton said again.

They left quickly.

She slumped down in a seat. Emotionally and physically exhausted.

Mack went to the door. "I'll be outside in my car," he said.

They checked on Beast. He was still sleepy but his eyes

were brighter. He managed to get up and go outside, though he had a lolling gait like a drunken sailor.

She felt better, though, watching him. Whatever he'd been given wasn't deadly. Perhaps that would have been a real giveaway that drugs were planted.

When he came in, Gage kissed her lightly good night. "You go ahead to bed. I want to do some work tonight."

"I'll wait."

"No, you won't. You look exhausted. I'll be in later."

He was being a gentleman. Too bad she really didn't want a gentleman at the moment.

But she was too tired to argue.

Obediently, she went to bed, hoping he would soon join her, and resenting the fact that she did.

twenty-seven

Marty called as Holly was finishing up the last details of a laughing frog sculpture. "Can you have lunch with me?"

"If Harry can come. I haven't found a regular sitter yet."

"I know of one. I can vouch for her."

"Perhaps she won't be available?" Holly said hopefully. Since the episode at the library, she didn't want Harry out of her sight.

"Why don't I check?" Marty was at her relentless best. Holly was learning that quality well.

"Who is she?"

"A widow, like you. She's had four children of her own and six grandchildren. She loves children and is the soul of responsibility." Marty hesitated, then added, "She could use the money."

Holly sighed. Trying to outmaneuver Marty was a hopeless task. Now she would not only be refusing lunch with the person responsible for her livelihood but she would also be depriving a poor widow of food money.

"All right," she finally said.

"She'll be over there at one. Is that okay?"

"Perfectly." *Perfectly not.* But she knew she couldn't hide here in the little cottage forever. She had avoided Doug since going riding on Saturday, refusing several invitations for dinner. She'd pled a sore throat, then work.

The woman arrived at ten minutes to one. Holly remembered seeing her before at the library. Lanky with a weathered face that told Holly she loved the out-of-doors, Teresa Stevens was dressed in blue jeans and a plaid short-sleeved shirt.

She had a smile that instantly put Holly at ease, and she carried some children's books with her. Her face lit when she saw Harry and she stooped to introduce herself.

Holly liked her immediately and obviously so did Harry. There was an ease, a kind of peace, that radiated from her. So did competence. Holly liked the fact that she had brought the books.

"He's had a peanut butter and jelly sandwich," Holly said. "He can have a cookie. I should be back in an hour or so." She glanced at the books in the woman's hands. "He loves reading."

"I wish more children did," Mrs. Stevens said.

"Well, a book will make him very happy. In fact, it doesn't take much to make him happy."

"We'll get along just fine."

Holly knew they would and she felt better as she left.

Marty was waiting for her. "I thought we would go to the Copper Queen for lunch," she said. "My treat."

"I can't—"

"Yes, you can. I have a proposition for you."

Holly wasn't sure she wanted a proposition. But she surrendered to a tide stronger than herself and walked the block to the famous old hotel. She had taken Harry inside. It was a legend. John Wayne was said to have made the hotel a second home on his trips to his ranch across the Mexico border.

But she hadn't eaten there. It was one of those luxuries she hadn't felt she could afford yet.

She would have enjoyed it if she weren't so worried about Marty's "proposition."

Her friend didn't waste any time once they were seated. "The tourist trade will come to a standstill this fall,"

Marty said. "I've developed a website for some of the crafts in the store to even out my business. I've put several of yours on it and they've sold. I would like an assurance of a steady supply. Disappointed buyers can kill a web business."

"How many will you need?"

"I'm not sure. But I would like to depend on at least twenty a week to start."

"To *start*?"

Marty shrugged. "Don't let me scare you. Perhaps they won't continue to sell as well as I think they will. If they don't, I'll purchase what you've done and keep them in stock at my store, perhaps offer them to other craft stores in the Southwest."

A waiter came for their order.

Holly was grateful. She needed these few moments to think. Twenty sculptures a week was an enormous number. She thought she could do it, but it would mean eliminating walks into the desert, her trips to the library, reading time with her son.

On the other hand, it could mean financial security, something she needed desperately. Her money was going out faster than it was coming in. She was extremely careful, but she was fast beginning to understand the phrase "quiet desperation."

After several moments' consideration, she ordered a salad and shrimp. Marty got a salad and cheeseburger.

When the waiter left the table, Marty quickly returned to the subject. "Do you think you can do it?"

"How much?" Holly asked first. She was quickly discovering that money should always be a top priority.

"I thought I would price them at sixty dollars each, plus shipping. I'll pay you forty."

Holly did the math. Twenty times forty was eight hundred dollars a week. With that, she could quickly build a cushion to finance going somewhere else if necessary. But twenty a week? She was doing fewer than seven a week now.

"Do you think you can do it?" Marty persisted.

"Yes," she said. She *would* do it. It might be the only way she could really protect herself and her son. Perhaps she could buy her own computer. And computer games for Harry.

"You don't intend to leave Bisbee any time soon?" Marty said.

"No," she said.

"Good. I'll have a photographer take some photos, and we're ready to go." She hesitated, then added, "Is there any biographical information that might help? College art degrees? Shows?"

Breath caught in Holly's throat. Of course they would need some copy. She shook her head. "It's just always been a small hobby I did for fun," she said. "No shows. No big sales. In fact no sales at all."

That was a lie but a small one. Her sales in the past had been to one small craft shop in New Orleans.

"Then it's done," Marty said with a smile. "Maybe we'll earn enough money to fix up the house. I've always had to reserve what little profit there is in the summer to tide us through the winter. This could be our salvation."

The waiter returned with their salads.

"I want to celebrate," Marty said. "A glass of wine?"

Holly nodded. She thought a little celebration was in order as well.

Marty ordered the wine, then regarded her cautiously. "Tell me to shut up if you want to, but how are you and Doug getting along?"

"He's very nice," Holly said, hoping her voice didn't give her away.

"Just nice?"

"I've recently been widowed. I'm not ready to get involved again."

Marty's gaze seemed to go straight to Holly's heart. "He's a really good person."

"I know."

"He's in love with you."

"Did he tell you that?"

"No, but it's obvious when he talks about you."

"He can't be," Holly said with dismay.

Marty paid no attention. "I've seen you with him. You're as much in love with him as he is with you." She paused. "I hope you forgive a meddling old woman but I like both of you."

"I can't love him," Holly said.

"You're in trouble, aren't you?" Marty asked outright.

Holly didn't answer. The lettuce stuck in her throat.

"I was too, once," Marty said. "I asked for help."

Again silence.

"You can trust me. *And* Doug. That's all I have to say."

If only it were that simple. Whatever Marty's trouble was, it couldn't hold a candle to hers. Marty didn't stand to lose a child to a monster.

She tried to eat the rest of the meal, but her stomach was roiling. Had she been that obvious? Did Doug suspect something as well? What if he started checking?

The urge to run was strong again.

But then she looked across the table at the woman who had befriended her. The librarian, Louise, had become a friend as well. She was making a life, and now she'd been handed the pot at the end of the rainbow. Financial independence by doing something she loved.

Harry needed stability. He now had an extended family. She had a home and friends of her own.

Marty seemed to read her mind. "No one is going to force you into anything, Liz. I just wanted you to know we're here if you need us."

She would stay. This was her home. Hers and Harry's.

She would start on the sculptures tonight.

The glasses of wine came and with them their meal.

Marty held her glass up in a toast. "To Special Things and Garden Folk."

Holly raised her glass. "Garden Folk?"

Marty looked embarrassed. "We have to call your creations something. It was the best I could do at the moment. It's open to debate," she added hurriedly.

"Garden Folk." Holly tested it again. "I like it."

They clinked their glasses together.

A bargain.

NEW ORLEANS

Judge Matthews suggested a golf game to his son-in-law.

He'd had his house swept for listening devices. It turned up nothing. Still, he was becoming increasingly paranoid. Everything was going wrong.

Charles Rawson had been the weak link. He should have eliminated him years ago, but Rawson had been a prodigious fund-raiser for favored candidates.

Matthews had carefully constructed a huge power base with both personal and financial support. As a judge, he was careful about open support, but Charles had been his conduit, and meetings were conducted on golf courses or at private dinners. Little was accomplished in Louisiana without the approval of Judge Matthews.

He had been discussed for the U.S. Appeals Court but he had no interest in that. Federal judges were subjected to far greater scrutiny than state judges, even those on the highest state court.

He watched as Randolph approached the green. His son-in-law was not a particularly good golfer. He didn't have the patience for it. That was his problem in everything. He was thirty-eight and thought he should be president. It had been the arrogance and impatience that had turned his wife against him.

And that was a problem that simply couldn't be allowed to continue.

Matthews was prepared to take more drastic measures and concede that perhaps Randolph had been correct in suggesting that he employ more people to find Holly.

He had to admit he had underestimated his daughter.

He'd been sure she would surface by now. The fact that she had not meant she had resources or friends unknown to him.

She was not his blood child. He'd bought and paid for her years ago. She had been pliable for the most part. It had been unfortunate that she had heard a certain conversation.

The more he thought about it, the more he realized that she might have been planning an escape for some time. When his detectives had not found any of the usual leads— credit card usage, Social Security number offered, phone calls to friends—they started going backward, peering into every part of Holly's life.

The sculpting tools had led them to inquire at area craft stores. They finally found one who identified Holly as the seller of a few sculptures.

Samuel had no idea how many she'd sold or how long she'd been doing it. She would eventually run out of money, though, and that probably meant going back to selling sculptures.

He was convinced they would find her. But her absence was hurting Randolph's campaign. They needed a plausible explanation, one that would garner him sympathy.

That was the reason for golf today.

After realizing that Holly had overheard a conversation, he didn't intend to ever allow another conversation to be overheard.

Randolph sank his ball for a double bogey on the tenth green.

They got back into the cart, their conversation turning to Holly. How to find her. How to eliminate the problem without harm to Randolph's career.

"Our people are checking craft shops in the Southeast. She likes the ocean and it looks as if she headed in that direction. If they find nothing, then they'll move across the country," Samuel said.

"Isn't that a little like looking for a needle in a haystack?" Randolph asked.

"It's been explained to me that the sculptures that we found in her work area and at the craft shop are rather unique. If she's selling them, we'll find them." He paused, then continued, "If you'd paid more attention to your wife, you would have known about this. It would have saved us one hell of a lot of trouble." He was getting increasingly disenchanted with his son-in-law, but he had far too much invested in him to jettison him now. Randolph also knew too much.

"And when we do find her?"

"An auto accident on her way home to you," Samuel said.

"And Michael?"

"He'll have to be a casualty, too. He knows too much."

"I don't—"

"Do you want to go to prison for the rest of your life?" Samuel said. "That's if the death penalty isn't in play."

They reached the tee of the next hole. The discussion ended for several minutes as Randolph hit the ball into the woods. "You're going to have to hit a hell of a lot better than that if you want to impress anyone," Samuel said.

His shot went right to the green. Rolled a little toward the flag and came to rest two feet from the hole.

Once back in the cart, the conversation resumed.

"What about the Rawson woman and the cop? I take it your little plan to plant drugs didn't work."

Samuel didn't at all like the note of satisfaction in Randolph's voice. "He must have found them before the raid," Samuel said. He'd reamed out his employee for not being more imaginative in hiding the drugs. "We can't try that again. It has to be something else. I'm thinking."

"Don't we have someone with the police department? Couldn't Gaynor be killed in the line of duty?"

"He's on suspension."

"Get him off it. And off the Starnes case."

"I'll do what I can," Samuel said. "There's another problem."

"God dammit, there's always another problem."

"Dominic Cross was at the funeral."

"Do you think . . .?"

"I now have someone watching both Meredith Rawson's home and Gaynor's home. If they link up with Cross, we'll have to take care of all three."

"How?"

"I'm not sure. I just know I want this ended. Right now there's nothing to lead back to us. Nothing but your wife. Her DNA would connect her to the Rawson woman and unravel everything."

"The bitch," Randolph said viciously.

"We have to make sure they don't find each other. Holly might tell them about the night she left."

"No one would believe her over me."

"Either way, it would destroy your career."

Randolph slammed his hand against the front of the cart. "How long do you think it will take to trace those sculptures?"

"We have ten people working on it. They say two or three days. If that is what she's doing."

"That stupid little hobby," Randolph said. "I should have ended it."

"Then we might never have found her."

They reached Randolph's ball. He hit it into the rough.

Samuel shook his head as he tapped his ball in for a birdie.

twenty-eight

Meredith had woken up next to Gage. She had an emotional hangover from the day before, and he'd just held her last night.

To her surprise Gage brought her coffee in bed, along with a surprisingly good omelet.

He suggested that they meet with Dom at Gage's fishing shack on one of the bayous later in the morning.

"I didn't know you had a cabin."

"It's not a cabin. It's a shack."

"Okay, I didn't know you had a shack," she admitted, wondering whether he was just trying to divert her from a very bad yesterday.

"There's lots you don't know about me," he said with a hint of defiance.

"I'll grant you that," she said.

"I just think we shouldn't be seen with Dom," he said.

"No arguments here. I want to see your shack."

He called Dom on his cell phone and gave him directions.

Meredith watched as he put his canoe from the backyard on top of his vehicle. Two people getting away from problems.

Two hours later, they arrived, but not until Gage was sure they weren't followed.

The shack was exactly that. Minimal furnishings. A double bed, one big easy chair that was slightly torn. An unsteady table, some mismatched chairs. A small refrigerator and stove that ran on a generator. Meredith smiled. "You're right. It is a shack."

"It's a good place to use when I'm canoeing," he said. "But I do have a telephone line and modem. I sometimes come here to work and think."

Dom arrived an hour later and viewed the interior with furrowed eyebrows. "Didn't know you were a swamp rat."

Gage waved one hand toward the table and its mismatched chairs.

Meredith watched as he led the meeting. He ran through the list of those men who had attended the funeral, and crossed some off immediately if they didn't have children of the right age.

Dom recognized many of those who had attended the funeral and suggested knocking two more of them off the list. One of them, he knew, had two sons, no daughters. Another had lost his only child in an accident three years earlier. She'd been twenty-two.

Using the modem and his laptop, Gage then accessed the newspaper files on-line, searching one name after another, learning what they could about each one. Through news stories, they were able to eliminate seven more names of men who had been featured in various articles with their families.

They were down to seven names.

They zeroed in on those with a more detailed search. Another two were eliminated. That left five.

Two were prominent attorneys, one was an executive with an insurance company and a major contributor to charities in the city, one was Judge Samuel Matthews, and the last was the owner of one of New Orleans's premier restaurants.

Meredith almost asked Gage to cross out Judge Matthews. He was a state supreme court justice and one of the finest legal minds in Louisiana. Meredith had respected him for years. He had been reelected by a huge margin each time he stood for another term.

She also saw surprise on both Gage's and Dom's faces at his inclusion on their thinning list.

"It couldn't be," she said.

"He definitely would have a lot to lose," Gage said.

"So would the others, if murder was involved," she countered.

"True."

Dom studied the name for a long time. "His daughter is married to Randolph Ames, who is running for Congress. I attended a fund-raiser the other night for him. I hate the darn things, but some of my sponsors thought I should go since grants would go through his office."

"Was Matthews's daughter there?"

"No. I thought it was a little strange at the time. It was one of those affairs at which the candidate wants to show off his family values." Irony laced his last words. "Ames did say that she regretted not being there but that she was across the country, caring for an ill friend."

Meredith watched as Gage searched on Randolph Ames. A campaign website appeared as an option. A click.

She stared at the congressional candidate. He was a handsome man, but she already knew that. He, too, was an attorney and they had crossed paths more than once at Bar Association functions. She had never faced him in a courtroom, though. He did have a good reputation.

She also knew she'd probably met his wife at some function or another, but she couldn't remember any particulars.

"Try to find a photo of the wife," she said.

Gage clicked on one of the options on the website, and a photo of Ames, his wife, Holly, and a boy of about four appeared. A slight smile was on the mother's face as she looked down at her son, love glowing in her face.

Her stomach knotted and a suffocating sensation tightened her throat. Holly Ames's hair was the color of honey, deeper than that of Meredith's mother, but the clear blue eyes and delicate bone structure were similar.

Gage saw it, too. She saw the recognition in his eyes. The woman in this photo bore a strong similarity to the young Maggie in the photo, far more than Meredith did to her mother. Without looking for a connection, though, Meredith might not have caught it. Many people have look-alikes. Blue eyes were common enough, and so was blond hair. And the appearance of bone structure was often affected by hairstyle. Her mother had short hair; the woman in the photo had long hair.

She looked at Dom, who was staring intently at the screen. A muscle throbbed in his throat.

"Dom?"

He raised his face. Stared at her for a moment. "It could be her," he finally said in a choked voice.

The others agreed.

"Keep looking," Meredith said.

He scrolled down until he found an announcement of the state senator's candidacy for a congressional seat. The wife was not pictured. The story mentioned she was out of town to care for a sick relative.

"Something's wrong," Meredith said. "I've been around politics all my life, and I know how important a family is, especially in a congressional race. She should be at his side, particularly during the announcement."

He scrolled down the news articles about Ames again, and they read them all, including photo captions. No Mrs. Ames.

"That's very odd," Meredith said. "There's even a photo of him at the symphony ball. She should be there."

"Maybe there's a perfectly good reason," Gage said, trying to be the devil's advocate.

"Let's find her," Meredith said.

"We could be wrong," Gage reminded them all. "It's conjecture. There's no proof other than facial similarity and coincidences."

"I'll try to contact her," Dom said. "I could use the shelter as a pretext. Invite her to be on my board."

Gage shook his head. "You shouldn't be involved now. No one knows that you're working with us. I would like to keep it that way. And think of the shelter. Those kids need you."

They all stared at one another.

Meredith began, "Then I—"

"No," Gage said. "I'm not sure whether the attack on you was meant to be fatal or not. But I'm not taking any chances, not until we know more. Exactly what do we know about Randolph Ames?"

"He's given money to the shelter and has been active in a number of causes," Dom said. "But he's never been out to see it. I've always felt he's a little too slick and programmed."

Gage agreed. He'd seen Ames once when he was doing a photo op at the police department. Since Gage held all politicians in disdain, he'd pretty much ignored the entire event. Now he wanted to know more. A great deal more.

Someone wanted to stop Meredith from finding out the identity of her half sister. An ambitious husband or a prominent father would have excellent motives.

But Ames would have been a young child when Meredith's half sister was born. Why would he become involved in something that had turned so violent?

"I think I know who can help," Gage said reluctantly.

The other two looked at him.

"I know a reporter. I've given him some tips in the past. He's never revealed me as the source. I could suggest he seek an interview with Senator and Mrs. Ames."

Dom looked skeptical. It was obvious he wanted to take more direct action. "You sure you can trust him?"

"I'm not sure of anything, but I think he's the best route without tipping our hand."

"Will we be putting him in danger as well?" Meredith asked.

"An innocent query from a reporter? I don't think so,"

Gage said. "But he's persistent enough to get to her. If he doesn't, he'll damn well get suspicious and won't stop at anything to find her. He has one hell of an antenna if I point him in the right direction."

His gaze followed Meredith's to Dom. He obviously wanted to go after Holly Ames himself. Every time her name was mentioned, his dark eyes roiled with anger. His anger wasn't any deeper than Gage's. Dom had just discovered he had a daughter. Something precious had been taken from him decades ago. Now Gage risked losing someone who had become very important to him.

He knew Meredith wasn't going to stop looking, and he respected her for it. But she wouldn't be safe until they found her sister and uncovered the mystery around her.

"Can you tell us who the reporter is?" Meredith asked.

He hesitated, then shrugged. They were in this together. "Sanders DeWitt."

Meredith raised an eyebrow.

He knew why. DeWitt was the best investigative reporter in the city, particularly on police and city corruption. It was a measure of his faith in her and Dom that he mentioned it.

"Might we be putting Holly Ames in danger?" she asked.

"She's probably already in danger, if she's who we suspect she is." Gage watched as his words registered.

"Call DeWitt," she said in a low, choked voice.

He took out his cell phone and punched in some numbers. "Sanders?"

"Yep."

"Gage."

"Got something for me?" No Hello or How are you? DeWitt never wasted time.

"I might have. Need you to do something for me. It could be a big story for you, as well."

"What is it?"

"Do you know anything about the wife of State Senator Randolph Ames?"

"The future congressman?"

"That sure?"

"Sure as hell looks that way from here. He has the money and backing. What about him?"

"Seen anything of his wife?"

"No, but I haven't looked."

"Do me a favor and call. Tell him you want to do an interview. A family type of thing."

"I'm not a political reporter."

"You're anything you want to be on the paper."

A pause. "What am I looking for?"

"Her whereabouts. A friend of mine wants to reach her without anyone knowing about it."

"Including the husband?"

"Right."

"You think there's a story here?"

"I'll be honest. It could be nothing or it could be the biggest story of your career."

"Coming from you, I'll take it. I'll see what I can manage. My editor might be a little startled at my sudden interest, but hell, he's used to my quirks."

"Thanks. I owe you."

"You want to tell me who this friend is?"

"Not now."

"Stranger and stranger. Good thing I trust you and those instincts of yours. Call you back shortly." He hung up.

"He's going to make the calls," Gage told the others.

"What do we do now?" Meredith asked.

"Wait and see where his fishing expedition leads. He may find out that she really is with a sick relative. If she is, we can fly to wherever she is and get a sample of her DNA."

"And if she refuses?"

"We find a way."

She nodded.

"Dom?"

Dom didn't look happy. But after a moment he nodded. "The bastards," he muttered.

Meredith reached out and took his hand. "We'll find her," she said.

The call came an hour later.

"What in the blazes is going on?" DeWitt said. "I've never heard so much tap dancing in my life."

"Did you get a location?"

"Hell, no. Damndest thing I've ever heard. Most politicians would jump through hoops for this kind of interview. Ames is 'out of town.' I asked to talk to his wife. She wasn't 'available.' I asked where she was. I was told, 'Taking care of a relative.' I asked where. 'She can't take questions now.' What city is she in? 'Sorry, she wants privacy.'

"All this from an aide, as if he were programmed. I insisted on talking to the candidate himself. He couldn't be reached. Important session in Baton Rouge. I checked with our capitol guy. Nothing's going on. As far as he knew, Ames was politicking in New Orleans. Started checking back in our clips. No one has seen hide nor hair of Mrs. Ames in nearly seven weeks."

"You didn't leave it there, did you?"

"Hell, no. Called back and said there were rumors that Mrs. Ames has left our candidate, and could his spokesman verify or deny. He denied of course. I said the only way I won't begin speculating is if I hear from the lady herself. Otherwise, I'll really start probing."

"What did he say?"

"He sounded nervous as hell. Said he would get back to me, but I was all wrong. Mrs. Ames was committed to her husband and the campaign, but she had a family obligation. Hell, I checked on her family. There's damn little of it. Her mother is dead. She has two aunts, and neither of them has heard from Holly Ames in months. Her father is Supreme Court Justice Matthews. Couldn't reach him, either.

"Gotta tell you, Gage, I'm beginning to sniff a story here. Who is the person who wants to talk to her? I fulfilled my part of the bargain. It's time for you to fill in some blanks here."

Gage looked at Meredith and raised an eyebrow. They had talked about this. Meredith had told him to use his own judgment.

"Meredith Rawson."

"My God. The Meredith Rawson who lost her father in the hit and run? Who has been attacked, witnessed a murder and been shot at by a rogue cop?"

"An accurate assessment. Yes."

"Do the cops have any clues in the hit-and-run?"

"No. They are dismissing it as accidental rather than an intentional murder."

"You aren't?"

"No."

DeWitt cursed on the other end of the line. "Will you stop saying yes and no? This whole thing is beginning to smell like rotten fish."

"Try a little harder to find her," Gage said. "Without involving Ms. Rawson. Then we'll talk."

"I'll try the justice again."

"You might try to find out a little more about Holly Ames. Hobbies, community involvement—you know, things like that."

A silence. "You think something bad has happened to her?"

"I don't think anything. I just want to locate her without being involved." Gage paused, then added, "But as you said—it's beginning to smell. Someone else involved in the situation is also dead. Merely because of questions asked. Be careful."

An even longer silence. "You think Ames is involved? And maybe Judge Matthews? I need to talk to you."

"I'm not at home."

"And you're not going to tell me where you are?"

"No."

"I can call the department."

"You would never get anything from me again."

"Dammit, Gage."

"Find her," Gage said, and hung up.

Meredith made them all toasted cheese sandwiches. She included two for Beast since they hadn't brought his dog food.

He gulped his as the three humans sat at the table and ate. She liked Dom. It had taken a few hours. There had been awkwardness, even resentment. All this began with an affair that took place thirty-three years ago. If it hadn't . . .

But then there never would have been a sister. Her mother would have never known love, even as cruel as this one had been.

She was beginning to learn the value of love. The glory of it. The joy. She knew it every time she looked at Gage. She wondered whether he felt the same delicious shivers up and down his spine when he looked at her as she did when her glance wandered his way.

What would happen when the danger was over? When the partnership ended? When the adrenaline ebbed?

She didn't want to think about that. She wanted to know more about the man who had incited dangerous feelings in her mother and who had fathered her half sister.

"How did you meet Mother?" she asked.

"She and her friends came to my father's tavern. They'd heard we had a great Cajun band, and basically they were slumming. Except for your mother. She loved the music. She didn't laugh at the grandfather dancing with his six-year-old granddaughter." He caught the look on her face. "Yes, children came to eat and dance. You have to understand. Cajuns are big on family. It's the most meaningful thing to them.

"Your mother fell in love with my family, with the music. The others got bored and decided to go. I had danced with her. I didn't want to let her go. I offered to take her and her friend, Lulu, home.

"Maggie and I fell in love that night. I thought she was the most beautiful girl I'd ever seen. You've heard of laughing eyes. I had, too, but I had never seen them until that night. She glowed with life and vitality."

His regret and sadness seeped through her. She remembered her mother's unhappiness. Two young lives destroyed. Why?

"And it was Prescott who framed you?"

"Yes."

"And then someone killed him. So he obviously didn't act on his own."

"He could have been killed for some other reason," Gage interjected. "From everything I could discover, he had enemies. He was a gambler, for one thing."

"I could buy that if there weren't so many other deaths that are related in some way."

But they were getting away from the subject she most wanted to hear about. Her mother. "How long were you and my mother together?"

"Four months. Long enough to know we wanted to be married. My parents objected as much as I knew hers would. She wasn't Cajun. She wouldn't understand our ways. They wanted me to take over the tavern, but I'd never wanted that. I wanted to go to college and become someone important. Well, I became someone important, but not in the way I thought."

"Ah, but you have," she said gently. "You've helped so many kids."

"Except my own," he said. "Except my own."

After lunch, Gage asked her if she wanted to explore the bayou with him in the canoe. "I'll take the cell phone. There's not much we can do until DeWitt calls back."

"And Dom?"

"I already asked him. He wants to make some phone calls. I think he needs some time to absorb everything."

She understood. It had taken her days to absorb everything. She couldn't even imagine what it would be like to discover you'd had a daughter thirty-three years earlier. "Beast?"

"Beast will stay here. I don't think anyone knows about

this place, but he sure as hell will let everyone know if there's lurkers around.''

She liked the idea of being alone with him. She needed to relax. She liked Dom but there was no question that there was an unease between them. She was the daughter of his love and probably his enemy.

She watched as Gage dragged the canoe to the dock and nervously eyed it as he settled it in the water. She had never been in one, and she knew how fragile and easily unbalanced one could be. She was not good at balance. Neither was she good at grace.

He must have caught her apprehension because he grinned. "Believe it or not, Beast has gone canoeing with me. If he can do it . . ." He left the sentence unfinished.

Falling into a bayou full of alligators and snakes was not her idea of fun. But if Beast could do it, she certainly could. And the prospect of being with Gage in his territory was irresistible.

He got in first, then held out his hand to her. The strength in that hand helped as she stepped in. His other hand caught her and guided her down onto a seat. For a moment, she feared she would tip the boat, and then she caught the balance.

He sat down and handed her a paddle. "Just watch me," he said with a lopsided grin that made her want to do anything.

Beast looked dismayed from his spot on the dock.

"Not this time," Gage told him. "Take care of Dom. Guard."

The dog turned and trotted back to the shack.

Gage put his paddle in the water and made what looked like effortless strokes. She watched him for several minutes.

"You do the exact same thing on the other side. Try to match my rhythm."

Easier said than done. She leaned over and the canoe started to tip. She leaned in the opposite direction. She watched as he balanced the canoe. "Don't lean," he said. "Use your arms until you find the balance."

She tried again.

This time the canoe moved faster. She found her rhythm and started to look around. Moss hung from trees rising from the water. Water flowers floated on the surface.

She had never heard this kind of peace. There was the buzzing of insects, the call of a bird, the sound of the paddles, but there was a human silence. A breeze softened the heavy moisture-laden heat. The aroma of flowers and vegetation filled the air.

The world and its dangers seemed a million miles away. She was flooded with a sense of peace as the canoe sliced though the waters. An alligator sunned itself on a bank. A bird sang its song. She understood now the lure of the swamp and the bayous, the sensuous feeling of timelessness.

He turned and looked at her, his slow smile mesmerizing her. He knew that she was succumbing to the magic. "When the world gets too violent," he said softly, "I come here. Nothing changes here. I imagine it was like this five hundred years ago. I always get balance."

It wasn't a word she would have expected him to use. He'd always seemed more like an action person. Always in movement. Always restless. Here there was a peace about him.

Layers and layers. How intriguing to explore them. He was, she decided, the most complex man she had ever met. She wanted to lean over and push back a lock of sandy hair that fell over his forehead. There was a sheen of sweat on his forehead and he had unbuttoned his shirt so the breeze could reach his body. In addition to being the most complex man, he was also the sexiest. And at the moment, he oozed sexuality.

She almost dropped the darn paddle.

Whether or not he sensed her feelings, he guided the canoe toward a piece of land that jutted outward. He hopped out and pulled the boat up, then held out his hand to her. She took it, her hand fitting in his so naturally. He pulled her to him, against him, and he kissed her.

They had kissed before. They had made love before. But

this was on an entirely different level. She felt the kiss through to her bones. It was tender and savage, passionate yet comforting, soothing. It was both demanding and giving.

She leaned against him, absorbing the love and care inherent in every caress.

She wished they weren't standing in the middle of a swamp.

His cell phone rang.

She silently cursed the intrusion of modern technology in a place where time seemed to stand still.

She heard his side of the conversation.

"Yeah?"

"You have to be kidding." Not a question.

"You sure about this?" A question.

Then, "Public record now, right?"

A pause. "No one will know where it came from. Thanks, buddy." He snapped the phone closed.

She waited for an explanation.

"I told you about our floater. A man who was found in a bayou. We struck gold. A sample of DNA was taken. It matched up with a man named Carrick. So happened he was charged with rape while in the service. The victim refused to testify but he was given a discharge and his DNA went on file."

"The name meant something to you," she said.

"He worked occasionally for Randolph Ames."

He punched in some numbers on the cell phone.

"Sanders, it's Gaynor again. Any luck?"

She could hear the reporter sputtering over the line. It was clear he was very angry at being stonewalled.

"Well, I might have something else for you."

She noticed he let that tantalizing morsel sit a moment before continuing. "Ask the Ames people if they know a man named Carrick. Accused rapist some years ago. Now a body in the morgue. A floater with no hands and no head."

He listened for a moment, then said with some relish, "Look in your own morgue for photos of State Senator Randolph Ames. You'll discover Carrick in some background photos. Apparently worked as a chauffeur and bodyguard."

Meredith heard an exclamation from the receiver, then Gage said, "I don't know if he knew or not. I'm sure you can find out. But you didn't get it from me." He snapped the phone closed.

He turned back to her. His eyes were worried. "I don't like the idea that Holly Ames is missing," he said.

She felt a similar panic. She'd heard enough to send chills down her back.

He took her hand. "Let's get back. I really want to talk to Ames. By the time DeWitt finishes with him, he's going to be in a panic."

They paddled back without stopping along the way to gaze at birds as they had on their way out.

As they drew closer, she saw Dom pacing the small, rickety dock, Beast beside him.

Gage stepped out of the canoe as Dom tied it to the dock. Then Gage reached out and helped her from the boat.

He turned to Dom. "What is it?"

"They're closing down my shelter."

twenty-nine

Holly worked on her latest creation, Belle the Butterfly. She had steadily increased her production, enjoying every single moment.

She couldn't remember when she had been so happy. Nor when Harry had been.

She was finally beginning to feel safe. If Randolph hadn't found her by now, he'd probably cut his losses and made up some plausible story.

Now that she was concentrating on Garden Folk, she no longer went to the library every day. Instead she had invested in an inexpensive used computer. She still checked the New Orleans papers occasionally, but certainly not with the compulsion she had her first weeks in Bisbee.

The increased amount of work had not diminished her joy in creating. She now had the pig, the butterfly, the frog, the ladybug, a whimsical turtle, and a snail. Each one changed, according to her mood and the piece of metal she used.

It was the best of all possible worlds. She could watch Harry, and now he had the computer as well as the television, books and Caesar to keep him happily occupied. They went for a long walk every day, and that was their special time together.

Doug had gotten into the habit of dropping by two or three times a week, always with food. He knew how much Harry loved tacos, and he could whip them up in no time while she put away her tools. Sometimes Jenny came and sometimes not, depending on her schedule.

Doug and Holly would sit outside and have a glass of wine or beer and watch the sun set.

He would leave then, realizing that she had to get back to work. He was the most undemanding, most patient man she had ever met. He just seemed to enjoy their company.

It was frightening how much she looked forward to his knock on the door and how much she liked looking at his face. It was such a pleasant face. The sun had bronzed it. Intriguing laugh lines drew attention to kind and intelligent eyes and a mouth that smiled easily. The features were craggy rather than handsome, obviously carved by character rather than displaying the smooth good looks of someone to whom everything came easily.

She had never heard him say an unkind word about anyone. She couldn't remember Randolph ever saying a kind one.

Every day, she got nearer and nearer to telling Doug her story. Each time, she caught herself before the words spilled out.

She knew she would. That one day she would trust him enough to tell him. And that day she would be putting her life, and Harry's, in his hands.

The phone rang, and she picked it up.

"We've received three orders for your Garden Folk," Marty said happily. "Also received a call from a gallery in Florida asking about them. They want to purchase ten but they also want to know something about the artist for marketing purposes. Apparently it's an intimate type of place that likes to personalize everything."

"What is there to say?" Holly asked cautiously.

"Maybe something about how you became inspired to create them."

"I'm not a writer."

"Why don't I write up something and let you look at it?"

"Okay," Holly said without enthusiasm. "But I don't want anything about Harry or myself."

"I'll be sure to concentrate on the creativity part," Marty said. "Can you and Harry come to supper tomorrow? I'm having another little gathering to celebrate. About the size of the one we had, when you first came. Bring Doug."

She hung up before Holly could reply.

Holly slowly replaced the phone in the cradle. She knew that Bisbee now considered the sheriff and her a couple. Several comments had been made at the store where she shopped and at the library. *Are you and Doug going to the concert in the park? Are you and Doug going to the opening of the new restaurant?*

She saw the love in his eyes. She felt it in the way he touched her. In his infinite patience. She wondered if her eyes reflected her growing feelings for him.

Perhaps it was time to tell him. But then what, as a lawman, would he have to do?

Would it be fair to him? She would never know until she told him. And they couldn't continue as they were. He wanted more. He needed more. He deserved more.

Perhaps tonight . . .

NEW ORLEANS

Everything was unraveling. The damn reporter wouldn't give up. He had even turned up at campaign headquarters and barged into Randolph's private office. The last question had been like a dagger aimed directly at his heart. "Do you know a man named Carrick?"

Randolph wanted to say no. But that was one of the few things he couldn't hide. He knew Carrick had been in some photos with him. Damn the man for his incompetence.

Carrick had assured Randolph he could do the job without outside help. After all, Mrs. Ames could be no kind of threat. She hated guns. She hated violence. She was a timid mouse.

So what in the hell had happened in his house?

He certainly hadn't expected what he'd found. A dead man in his wife's bedroom. Both his wife and son gone.

He'd immediately called his father-in-law, who calmed him down and told him what to do. Carrick would have to disappear. As would Holly . . . once she was found. Immediately.

But Holly had proved more elusive than anyone had thought.

And now Carrick had been identified.

Randolph hoped he didn't look as rattled as he felt. De-Witt had just barged into his office with a breezy, "Thought you were in Baton Rouge, Senator."

Since that was what Randolph had told the staff to tell the reporter, he felt cornered. "The meeting was over earlier than I thought."

"And what meeting was that, Senator?"

The best defense is a good offense. That's one thing he'd learned well from his father-in-law. "I didn't know you had moved over to the political beat."

"I haven't," DeWitt said. "But you interest me, Senator."

He couldn't help but be startled by the pronouncement. "Why?"

"Your wife, for instance. No one has seen her for a while."

"I thought my office had explained," Randolph said stiffly. "She's looking after a sick friend."

"But why is she incommunicado? Rather strange, isn't it? I mean, she *is* the wife of a man who wants to be a congressman. I assume she knows there are obligations."

"I'm the candidate, not my wife," Randolph said. "Her private life is her own."

"The voting public likes to know the family situation of its candidates. Now, if she's left you for some reason, I think they have the right to know that."

"She hasn't left me."

"Rumors say otherwise."

Randolph recognized the trap. "It hasn't been a problem." Of course he'd heard rumors and had been asked about Holly's absence by members of the press, who'd had the sense to back off when he and his father-in-law stared them down while delivering the story. But he knew that all too soon they would not be appeased and he would have to come up with Holly, her death, or a more convincing story about her absence. Visiting a sick friend. He'd not done too well coming up with that old saw.

"One phone call could clear this up," DeWitt said.

Randolph pondered the problem. He'd always had good press. He'd always courted reporters, taking them to dinner, to lunch, dropping news tips in their ears. He couldn't afford for them to turn against him now, and DeWitt was an important news figure in the city.

He could, of course, call the editor and ask why DeWitt was now covering a simple congressional campaign, but that might raise someone's antenna. Better to get a woman to call and pretend to be his wife.

"I'll try to arrange a call," he said.

"What about right now?"

"Her friend is dying. She is distraught. I'm not going to call and have her interrogated without some warning." He leaned forward in his seat. "I'll tell you something off the record. Holly is shy and sensitive. She doesn't like the political life. I'm sorry to say she doesn't care for reporters and has always avoided them. The only way I could convince her to accept my candidacy was to promise she would not have to be a public figure herself, that she could continue to raise our young son with privacy. I don't intend to break that promise," he finished righteously.

"When can I speak to her then?"

"I'll call you."

DeWitt gave him a look that said he wasn't buying any of it. "If I don't hear from you by tomorrow, I'll start asking some questions in my Sunday column," he said. "Now what about Carrick?"

"Can't say I know much about him. A friend asked me to hire him. He was my driver, nothing else. Then he disappeared."

"When?"

"I really can't recall the exact day."

"Perhaps your payroll records will."

"I'll ask my treasurer to check."

"Now?"

"He's not here now."

The reporter stared at him. Randolph met his gaze directly. He was good at that. It was an acquired art.

"Now I have a radio interview scheduled," he said, rising from his chair and holding out his hand.

DeWitt ignored it. "Did you know Carrick had a general discharge from the army?"

"No, can't say I did." He wasn't about to admit he did indeed know. "As I said, a friend asked me to hire him, said he was down on his luck. He was a good driver."

"Don't you do background checks on your staff?"

"He really wasn't on the staff. He was just there on an as-needed basis."

"You really should be more careful, Senator. He was accused of rape. I'm surprised you would want someone like that around your wife."

The damn reporter wouldn't quit.

"I'll take your advice," he said. "And now I really must go."

"Can I take you anywhere? Since you don't have a driver?"

Randolph knew he was being baited. He wanted to hit the damned reporter, or watch him being hit. He wanted to wipe away the smug, knowing smile. "No need. One of my staff will take me. I'll get back to you tomorrow about my wife."

He ushered DeWitt out the door. He knew that the reporter wasn't satisfied, that he would be back on the phone in the morning. Sanders DeWitt was renowned for his persistence.

He sat back in the chair. There was no radio show. Just as there was no wife.

He had to find a substitute. Fast.

He called Judge Matthews. He would know what to do. He always did.

Gage received a call from DeWitt.

"No more games," the reporter said. "I want to know what the hell is going on."

"What happened?"

"I'll tell you when I see you."

It was obvious DeWitt was not going to say anything more.

"Meet me in two hours at Calley's near Gibson," Gage said.

"Right," DeWitt said.

Gage hung up and looked at his two companions. "Want to meet with him?"

"I think the more he knows, the more he can help," Meredith said. "I no longer have anyone to protect." She looked at Dom. "But you do."

"They made their move," Dom said. "The only way I can fight back now is to bring the whole thing out into daylight and fight the code violations in court."

They all had decided that the sudden discovery of code violations was probably the result of Dom's appearance at Marguerite Rawson's funeral. A warning, perhaps. Or perhaps it had been intended to distract him.

Or destroy him.

In the past two hours, Dom had called in markers. His attorney was one of the city's top litigators and he was trying to find out more about the inspectors who tried to close down the shelter. He'd already gotten a ten-day suspension on the order to close.

The heavy-handed tactic could work to their advantage. They could use it to distract the senator and give him more than one position to defend. If he were tied to closing a shelter for kids, it could backlash in a big way.

* * *

DeWitt walked into Calley's at the appointed time, his gaze moving around the table with extreme interest if not surprise. He sat down. "What an intriguing group of bedfellows," he observed.

Gage wasn't interested in chatting. He had the most unpleasant feeling that something very bad might happen soon. "How was your conversation with the senator?"

"Uninformative except to discover he's an A-class liar. He promised his shy, reporter-averse wife that he would not inflict people like me on her. He said he would try to arrange a phone call tomorrow."

"It won't be her," Gage said.

"I need some questions to ask her so I'll know whether it's her." Then he sat back and searched every face. "Who wants to tell me what this is all about?"

Gage looked at Meredith. "It started with Meredith. You know that she was attacked in a parking garage and nearly killed."

Then each told their part of the story as DeWitt recorded it. When they had finished, he sat back and stared at them.

"You think Ames is behind this."

"And possibly Judge Matthews."

DeWitt raised an eyebrow.

"It's all about something that happened thirty-three years ago," Gage said. "Ames would have been about five years old."

"But why would Matthews want to keep an adoption secret to the extent of having people killed?"

"I don't know," Gage said. "We've considered every possibility we can think of. Maybe pride. Maybe something to do with an inheritance. Nothing else makes sense."

DeWitt's eyes were bright with interest. In fact, they fairly gleamed with the primitive instinct of the hunter. "If it's an inheritance matter, there should be a will somewhere. I'll research it. Wills should be in probate court."

"For the moment, I'm worried about Holly Ames," Meredith said. "What if . . ."

She couldn't finish the sentence.

"If she were dead, they would have found some better explanation by now," DeWitt said. "An accident of some kind. The longer she's missing, the more difficult the explanation."

Gage nodded. "I would just like to know if she disappeared of her own free will or was taken . . . somewhere." He didn't add the "alive or dead" that was implied nonetheless. Meredith didn't need to hear her fears repeated. He'd seen how her face had paled when she'd tried to say it. "If she left on her own, you can bet Ames is looking for her, too."

"What do you know about her?" DeWitt said.

"Damned little. Some stuff in campaign literature. A few mentions of her in news stories. Nothing more than her attending Tulane University and being a stay-at-home mom."

DeWitt looked lost in thought, then abruptly shook his head. "Often when a politician begins to run for office, he seeks publicity in a small community paper. Features showing him to be an ordinary Joe. I'll check the neighborhood papers in his senatorial district. Perhaps there was a feature."

"How long will it take?"

"Five minutes," he said. He grinned at their surprise. "I make a point of being friends with the local rags. It's surprising what they know."

He retrieved his cell phone from his belt, flipped it open and started dialing. On the second call, he found a writer who had interviewed Mrs. Ames.

Gage could hear only one side of the conversation—the clipped questions, then effusive thanks.

DeWitt looked pleased with himself when he finished.

"Carol Ellis, an associate editor, did a feature two years go. She really liked Mrs. Ames. Said she was very retiring but had a sweet smile and tried her best to answer questions."

"Any clues as to where she might go?"

"No, but she said Holly Ames had an odd hobby. She was a metal sculptor. She even showed Carol some kind of garden critter—a dancing pig. She kept insisting it was just a 'silly' hobby, but Carol sensed it meant a lot to her when

Carol praised one of her pieces." He paused—for effect, Gage knew. All reporters had a flare for the dramatic. It went with the job.

"And . . ." Gage prompted.

"Carol suggested a gift shop might be interested in selling them. Mrs. Ames didn't seem interested but she took the shop's card."

"What of Ames?"

"He wasn't there."

"Did you get the name of the gift shop?"

"Yep. Mary's Crafts and Gifts. On Magazine Street."

"Let's go." Meredith said. "Perhaps they might know something about Holly."

DeWitt shook his head. "I'm going to probate court, see if I can't find the wills of Judge Matthews's father and mother. It's a long shot, but I'm with you. I can't figure out anything other than money that would cause Matthews to risk everything. Then I plan to go through all our files on him and the good senator. Maybe I can pick up some oddity."

Dom stood. "I have to go to the shelter and make sure the kids understand what's happening. Then I'm with you."

"Tonight," Gage said. "Let's meet at, say, nine."

DeWitt nodded. "Where?"

"At a shack I own not far from here. Can you drive down here again?"

"Give me the directions."

Gage wrote them down. "Honk your horn when you arrive. We might be a little cautious."

DeWitt raised one eyebrow, nodded, then left without saying anything else.

Gage and Meredith reached Mary's Crafts and Gifts just before closing time.

They both browsed, then approached the middle-aged woman at the desk. "Are you Mary?" Meredith asked.

"Yes," the woman said. "Mary Sartain. Can I help you?"

"I saw a metal sculpture that someone bought here. It was a dancing pig for a garden. I was hoping you might have another."

"That must be Holly's work," Mary said. "I don't have any in stock now. Couldn't keep them in. She made only a few a month."

Meredith didn't have to feign disappointment. "Do you know where else I can look?"

The woman looked as she was trying to make up her mind about something, then shrugged. "I haven't seen her recently. Perhaps two months or so. But I did see something on a website that looked familiar. Perhaps if you give me your name, I can order one for you."

"Would you mind sharing the website with me?" Meredith said. "Of course I would pay you for your trouble."

"It's not that. It's . . ."

"What?" Meredith said.

"It's probably not her work at all. I got the impression her husband didn't like her selling her work. Someone else was in here. . . ."

"Who?"

"I don't know. But he was looking for her, too."

"Do you know where she is?" Gage had entered the conversation. He started to pull out his wallet. Stopped.

Meredith knew he had been about to show his badge. But he didn't have one now. Because of her.

The woman shook her head. "No."

"Did you tell him about the website?"

"I didn't like the way he looked," she said. "I did not."

Meredith decided to tell the truth. It was the only way they were going to get information. "I'm her sister. I'm looking for her. I have reason to believe she might be in grave danger."

"But surely her husband . . ."

In for a penny, in for a pound. She didn't have time to be nice. "He might be part of the problem."

The woman looked at both of them. Meredith took a card from her purse. "I'm Meredith Rawson. This is Detective

Gage Gaynor with the police department. We really need your help."

"You do have her eyes," Mary said. Yet she still hesitated.

Meredith liked the fact she was trying to protect Holly. There must be something about her sister that people liked, that they wanted to protect.

Finally the woman seemed to make up her mind. She turned on the computer on her desk. "I regularly check out new craft sites," she said. "I'm always looking for something new, unique. Holly's art was that. Whimsical and fun. I can't be sure this is hers, but it has a certain style that I would almost swear is her work."

She turned the screen so Meredith could see it. Special Things. The address was in Bisbee, Arizona. She stared at a display of items called Garden Folk.

"Is there anything about the artist?" Meredith asked.

"No, I already checked. No information available."

She and Gage looked at each other.

"Thank you," she said, and preceded Gage out of the shop. She felt jumpy all of a sudden, restless and expectant. After all that had happened, she might finally have a solid lead. The look Gage had given her said he felt it, too.

"We can fly out later tonight," she said.

"Not from New Orleans," he countered.

"Surely you don't think . . ."

"I don't know what to think," Gage said. "If Judge Matthews is involved, he has tentacles in every parish in Louisiana and every part of government. He's a kingmaker in this state."

"Then where?"

"We'll drive to Birmingham and catch a flight from there."

"What about Beast?"

"Maybe DeWitt will keep him."

Meredith looked dubious.

"He does have charm," he defended the dog.

"Perhaps on further acquaintance," she said with a small grin.

"If necessary I'll board him. But if they would kill a woman for no better reason than she was a friend years ago, they wouldn't hesitate to kill a dog."

"Why didn't they do it before?"

"Maybe they didn't want to make me mad," he said.

"Didn't work," she said, keeping her voice light even though urgency was eating her alive. What if Holly was in danger? What if they might lead someone to her?

Dom was at the shack when they arrived. Beast was lying at his feet. The dog rose lazily, went over to them and sniffed.

Dom stood, a beer in his hand. "I have people looking into the background of the building inspectors. In the meantime, we have ten days. We've always met every building code."

"What about the kids?"

"They'll be okay for a few days. They're not exactly sure what's happening but they trust me. I told them it would be okay." He studied their expressions. "You've found something?"

"We think she might be in Bisbee, Arizona."

"Where in the hell is that?"

"Just north of the Mexican border. East and south of Tucson," Meredith said. She had called Sarah's cell phone on the way to the cabin and asked her to look up the town and find the best way to get there from Birmingham.

"And?"

"There's a flight from Birmingham to Phoenix. We can catch a flight from Phoenix to Tucson."

"Make it three tickets," Dom said.

"The shelter?"

"Paul Simonsom is handling the legal matter. My two assistants can handle the shelter itself until I return. They've been bugging me to take a vacation. And it's probably better that I'm not there. I might just try to hurt someone."

They waited. Nine o'clock. Nine-thirty. Meredith started

to worry. They needed to head out if they were going to catch the morning flight.

Then Beast barked as a car honked from down the road. Two minutes later a car drove up to the cabin, and DeWitt got out. Beast ran out as if he was going to bite off his leg. Just before he reached DeWitt, he stopped, sat and panted eagerly.

"You still have this monster?" DeWitt asked. "This is a hell of a place to find."

"That's the idea," Gage said.

DeWitt went inside, saw the minimal furnishings and chose a straight chair.

"Found a will. Wasn't easy but it is public record."

"And . . . ?"

"Judge Matthews stood to inherit only half his father's estate unless he had issue. Not adoption. A blood child. How archaic is that?" He shrugged as if to ignore his own question. "A child was born to his wife in Memphis, February 15. A girl. It happened four months after his father's death."

Silence filled the cabin. "Blood tests done?" Gage asked.

"Yes, the executor demanded it. But they could be faked. So could the birth certificate."

"We didn't look for one under Matthews," Meredith said.

DeWitt looked at them. "We still don't have any proof of murder. Fraud perhaps, but that will work only if we find the woman and get new blood tests."

"We might know where she is," Meredith said.

"Where?"

Gage shook his head. "The fewer people who know—"

"Hell with that, Gaynor. What if something happened to you or Meredith? No one would ever know what happened."

Meredith felt a new chill creep down her back. She nodded in agreement. Someone else should know . . . just in case. DeWitt would profit the most by handling the information with care and keeping it to himself until the time was right to release it. "Bisbee, Arizona."

"I know it. An artist colony."

"We're going to drive to Birmingham and get a flight to Phoenix in the morning."

The reporter looked torn. "Wish I could go, but I just received a call from Ames. I can talk to his wife at ten tomorrow morning. I think I should do so. I'm also looking into the closing of the shelter. My usual source in that department wouldn't talk."

"I have a favor," Gage said.

DeWitt's expression was cautious.

"Look after Beast for me. I don't want to leave him at home."

"You've got to be kidding. My wife would kill me."

"She'll love him," Gage said. "He brings in the morning paper."

"She likes cats. Small ones."

"Beast is very tolerant."

"Gaynor, you're out of your mind."

"Just for two days. If it doesn't work, you can drop him at a kennel. He'll not be happy but it's better than dead."

DeWitt looked at him as if he were mad. "Right. Lay on the guilt," he muttered.

"It's for the good of the story," Gage cajoled. "You can put his steak on the expense account."

"Steak?" DeWitt's voice was strangled.

"Well, hamburger will do in a pinch."

Meredith saw the wicked gleam in Gage's eyes.

"Damn you, Gaynor."

"You won't be saying that when you win the Pulitzer for your exclusive story. Besides, he's a good guard dog."

"Yeah. Maybe I won't have a home to guard." But he took the dog's leash. Beast followed happily enough.

An hour later Gage, Meredith and Dom were on the road to Birmingham.

thirty

New Orleans

"We might have found her," Samuel Matthews told his son-in-law as they met for breakfast. They sat in the corner of an out-of-the-way restaurant and talked in low voices. There was no one nearby.

"Where is she?"

"Arizona. A little town near the Mexican border called Bisbee."

"How . . .?"

"The craft business. Our guys found a sculpture on the Internet. It's almost identical to the one she left at your house. Of course, there are hundreds, probably thousands, of people doing this type of thing, but there is a very close resemblance. My people are flying down in a private plane to check it out. There's a nearby airport."

"They know what to do?"

"Yes."

"I want my son."

"Impossible. He's smart. You know that."

"We can keep him away from anyone for a while. I can hire someone to look after him."

"The decision has already been made," Matthews snapped, cutting off the conversation. This damned business had already taken too long. Court was in recess, but he had a dozen cases to review, several opinions to draft.

Dammit. He stood to lose everything because of a moment's carelessness. Randolph had assured him that the house was empty when they'd had the unfortunate phone conversation, that Holly was taking Mikey to the preschool they had so carefully selected. He hadn't known the boy had a stomach upset, that she was waiting for a call from the doctor and had picked up the phone when he'd called.

He hadn't known until he heard a click on the phone that someone had overheard him talking about campaign money from gambling interests—from, in fact, gambling interests that reached deep into organized crime. Any hint of involvement would destroy his career.

It was damnable bad luck for him and stupidity on Randolph's part.

He'd never felt much for Holly. Although she was a beautiful woman, he'd always considered her weak and not very intelligent. But she'd fulfilled her role quite nicely until now, and in turn he had assured her a powerful husband and prosperous life.

How could he not have seen the rebellion that lurked inside? She'd always been such a compliant little thing.

Now he could end it once and for all, and settle back into his life. The friendships of some of the most important people in Louisiana, even Washington. He was powerful. Respected. He had worked every day of his life to get to where he was, and no little fool was going to end it.

He shrugged. "Anyway, it's too late. They have their orders. We need to start thinking about some press releases for you."

"I have that call, remember?" Randolph said. "DeWitt will be at my office this morning, expecting to talk to my wife."

"I have you covered. One of my people has found a woman in California. He's filled her in completely. She knows all about Holly. Maybe that will get DeWitt off your back."

"I don't know. He's damned persistent."

"Well, in a couple of days, he will have a grief-stricken husband and father to interview." He handed Randolph a number. "Tell him it's a cell phone. Memorize it, because you should know it by heart."

"Have you found that damned cop and the Rawson woman?"

"No, and Cross has disappeared as well. That's why we have to get rid of all of them. They can't find her or Mikey. They can't get her DNA, or the whole damn mess will unravel."

Randolph closed his eyes. Then opened them. "What if they find her first?"

Matthews detected a thin note of hope in Randolph's voice. He decided to placate the man. A little.

"I've thought about that. I've told a friend of mine on a confidential basis that your wife has stolen your child, that she is mentally unbalanced. He issued a custody order. Perhaps we won't need it. But we have it if we do. Holly will do or say anything to keep Michael. We can bargain with her. Then we can take our time in solving the problem." He looked at Randolph. "I never leave anything to chance. You should know that by now."

He didn't like the look on his son-in-law's face as he nodded. Perhaps he'd overestimated Randolph Ames's ambitions. He hadn't expected this sudden sentimentality.

He would keep a closer eye on him, especially in the next few days.

No, he never left anything to chance.

BISBEE

Holly answered the phone after listening to it ring for several moments. She was in the midst of one of her pieces. But the insistence alarmed her.

By now most of her friends knew that if she didn't answer, it was because she couldn't.

She picked up the phone.

Marty's voice was as insistent as the ring had been. "Liz, I have to see you immediately."

Holly didn't like the tone. It was almost frantic. Marty didn't get frantic.

"Where?"

"Somewhere Harry can't hear us."

"My porch. Or your shop."

"I'm on the way."

"Do you have someone to watch the shop?"

"I'm closing it." She hung up.

Holly suddenly felt cold. Whatever made Marty decide to come over had to be urgent. This was her busiest season, and Marty very seldom locked the door against potential customers. She might be an ex-flower child who still liked her hair long and clothes flowing, but she also wanted to survive. She had become what she had once most hated: a capitalist.

Marty was on her doorstep in less than five minutes.

Liz gave Harry a glass of milk and some cookies, then found a movie she'd rented and he hadn't seen yet.

Then she went outside and sat on the steps with Marty. "What is it?"

"All of a sudden, I started getting a lot of queries about your work," Marty said. "At first I thought it was the novelty, but I just received a call from someone in New Orleans."

Fear froze Holly. She prayed her face didn't reflect the pure terror she felt.

Apparently not. Marty continued as if the world hadn't just ended.

"She was worried. She was afraid she might have made a mistake. She said two people—a man and a woman—came in looking for one of your metal sculptures. They started out by saying that they had seen one and wanted one for themselves. When she said she would try to find one for them, they said something else altogether. One said she was your sister and feared you were in danger. The other said he was a detective. The woman did look a little like you—same eyes, she said. They appeared so worried. . . ."

"And Mary—" Holly caught herself.

"Mary Sartain." Marty confirmed the name. "She'd seen your sculptures when hunting through craft websites. She showed it to these two people."

"I don't have a sister," Holly said hopelessly. It didn't matter what she said. Her house of cards had finally tumbled. She hadn't thought it would happen. Not after all this time. What a fool she had been.

"I can stall them," Marty said, "but all they have to do is ask anyone here a few questions about a woman who sculpts with metal. A woman and her son."

"Thank you for telling me," Holly said. She had to start packing. She had to leave immediately. "When did she talk to them?"

"Yesterday. Then she worried about it all night. She called me this morning."

"Thank you. I have to go. . . ." Her voice trailed off. She felt cold, so cold. And numb. She didn't want to lose what she'd gained here—a home, friends, a sense of belonging as she'd never had in New Orleans.

"What's wrong, Liz? Tell me. I'm not going to judge you. I was involved in some nasty things years ago. I have no right to judge anyone. It's obvious you and Harry need help."

"I can't get you involved."

"I am involved. I'm your friend. So are Doug and Russ. Let me call Doug."

"He's a lawman."

"He's also in love with you."

"I can't do that to him. I can't make him choose between duty and me."

"I can't imagine anything you could have done that would make him have to choose."

"Imagine the worst possible thing." She couldn't keep it in any longer. "It's in the envelope I gave you."

"An abusive husband?" Marty probed.

"If he was only that."

"Then what?"

There was no resistence left. She had just regained her life. She loved this life. She knew Harry was happy for the first time. She knew she was.

"My husband tried to murder me. I woke up to noises in the house. Someone with a gun, and the key to our house, and the numbers to our alarm system."

Marty didn't say anything, just waited.

"I used my husband's gun. I shot him. Harry was in the house and—"

"Dear God," Marty said. "And I thought you were a timid soul."

"I was. I am."

"The hell you are. You picked up and ran and made a life for yourself. But did you ever think about going to the police?"

"My husband is a state senator. He's running for Congress. He's very powerful." She hesitated, then added, "So is my father."

Marty's face screwed up in a frown. "Your father?"

"He's . . . he's . . ." How do you tell someone your own father probably tried to have you killed? A father who was also one of the most respected jurists in the state of Louisiana.

Marty stood. "You can tell me later. Right now we're getting you the hell out of here. Get Harry. I know a place you can stay about fifteen miles from here. No one knows about it. I always thought I might need a place to hide. There's plenty of canned food. A well. Worse comes to worst, I'll take you across the border. They will never find you then."

"I don't have papers for Harry."

"A few of my friends have questionable backgrounds as well. In an hour, I can get a forged copy of a letter of permission from your husband to take him across the border. Now come on and get off your ass. Ten minutes and we'll be on our way. I'll take care of this sister of yours."

"They might come after you."

"An old activist like me? Let them try. Now about the sister—do you have any idea who it could be?"

"No. It's just me. I always wondered why there wasn't another child. My mother once said it was my father's fault, that she wanted a dozen little girls like me."

She heard herself and trembled. It was long ago. Her mother had wanted a doll, and that was what she'd made Holly into. Holly shook her head and rose. "I'll be ready in a few moments."

"You can follow me. I want you to have a car."

Holly didn't waste any more time. She'd wasted enough.

She gathered up their clothes; there weren't many. Then her tools. Harry looked at her with wide-eyed surprise as she packed what books they had. Marty helped carry them out to her car.

"I don't want to go. I want Sher'f Doug," Harry said, his mouth drooping.

"Just for a while," she said, knowing it would probably be forever. She felt sick to her stomach. Worse. "I thought we would go out and explore the desert."

"Is Caesar going with us?"

"Of course he is."

His face was dubious. She remembered the last time she had rushed him out of his home. She closed her eyes for a moment. It wasn't fair. It wasn't.

Within ten minutes, they were ready.

Holly didn't want to leave the little house she'd decorated and come to love and think of as a safe haven.

She bit back tears, took Harry's hand and called Caesar, who knew something was wrong. He hung back, his tail tucked between his legs. He didn't want to leave, either.

Then she tugged Harry outside and put him in the car seat. She picked up Caesar and plopped him inside. Marty had already started her little Bug.

As they pulled away, Holly didn't look back. She hadn't looked back at her house in New Orleans, either. But that had been because of fear. She'd hated the house.

It was totally different when she was leaving a place, and people she loved.

The funky little store was closed.

Disappointment coursed through Meredith. She'd felt during these past few hours that she was reaching the end of her search. Anticipation had built inside her. She would finally meet her sister.

Gage and Dom had napped on the plane. It had been late reaching Phoenix and they had just barely made the connection to Tucson, where they rented a car. She'd had no sleep. Questions kept running through her mind during the drive to Birmingham, the two flights and the drive from Tucson to Bisbee.

Only adrenaline kept her going.

But it was three o'clock Arizona time and they'd expected to find the shop open. Finding it closed was a huge downer.

They went to the businesses next door, one an art gallery, the other a small grill advertising tacos. The owners of both expressed surprise that the shop was closed.

"She'll be back soon," one said.

Meredith took out a photo of Holly that they'd printed from a newspaper article. "Do you recognize this person? She's my sister. Holly. We had an argument years ago, but now I realize how important family is, and I'm trying to find her." She couldn't explain the true story, or they would be here all day.

Both owners—one a man and the other a woman—glanced at the photo, then shrugged. "Can't recall that I have," said one.

"Doesn't look familiar," said the other. "Never heard the name."

"She's a sculptor," Meredith tried again. "In metal. I think she does work for Special Things."

"Wouldn't know anything about that," said the man who owned the taco business.

"Still doesn't look familiar," said the woman in the art gallery.

The three left the store and stood on the street.

"I would have sworn they recognized the photo," Dom said.

"Then she has friends."

"Protective ones."

"Maybe Mary Sartain called and warned them," Meredith said. "Just in case something was wrong."

"And the whole town is in on it?" Gage frowned.

"It couldn't be," Meredith said. "There wasn't enough time."

"Let's start at real estate companies," Gage said.

Holly followed Marty. Fifteen miles out of town, Marty turned down a dirt road that very nearly didn't exist. They bumped over ruts and across a dry stream bed and came to a stop at a cabin abutting a bare hill. One lone cottonwood struggled for existence in front.

Holly got out of the car, unstrapped Harry from the car seat and met Marty.

Marty unlocked the heavy door and opened it.

It was hot. Stuffy. But the furniture looked comfortable and Marty turned on lights, so it had electricity.

"A generator," Marty explained as she handed Holly her cell phone. "Keep this with you."

Holly's heart felt tight. Constricted. She had just gotten over fear. And now it had come tumbling back into her life, taking it over again. She didn't want to hide for the rest of her life. She didn't want it for Harry. She didn't want it for herself.

But the fear. God, it was overwhelming.

"I'm going to tell Doug about this place," Marty said.

"No."

"You don't have a choice any longer," Marty said. "I know him. He has been my friend for years."

"But his duty—"

"There's something more important to him than that," Marty said. "Integrity that supercedes what others might call duty. He knows about me. He knows that I participated in something unlawful long ago. He's never told anyone." Her mouth slanted at Holly's start of surprise. "Trust me," Marty said. "Trust him."

Holly hadn't trusted anyone in a very long time. But Doug had protected Marty's secret.

She knew she had nothing to lose.

She nodded.

Doug heard about the queries about a woman and a boy immediately. Mr. Santos from the taco shop called first. Then Mrs. Carson from the art gallery.

"Thought you should know," Mr. Santos said.

"Maybe I should have told them," Mrs. Carson worried.

"You did right," he reassured both of them.

He left his office and drove to Holly's house. Her car was gone. Still, he knocked. No one answered.

He sat in front of the house for several minutes, then decided to try Marty. She might know something. He might also get a glimpse of the three people asking questions about someone who sounded very much like Liz.

He found them in a bar across from Special Things. It was quite obvious that they weren't tourists. They were staring across at Marty's store.

He wandered in and ordered a Coke. He sat at the bar and studied the trio.

A pretty young woman. A man in his early fifties who looked like an ex-boxer and a man who looked like a cop. He could always spot them. Their eyes never stilled. Just as this one's didn't still.

He finished his Coke and sauntered over. "How do you like our little town?"

The woman looked disconcerted, then smiled. "I like it," she said.

He stiffened. Her eyes looked just like Holly's. So did the smile.

Nothing else did. She was slim, but more roundly built than Holly. Taller. Her face didn't have the fine bones that Holly's did, and the nose was larger, yet the accents were similar. So was the musical quality of their voices.

"Good," he said. "I'm the county sheriff. Anything I can help you with?"

He saw them stiffen this time. He didn't wear a badge on his shirt, nor did he carry his gun in an obvious place.

The man he had pegged as a cop stood. He held out his hand. "I'm Gage Gaynor. Detective. New Orleans."

"Doug Menelo. You here on official business?"

"No. Vacation. My girl is trying to find her sister. Meredith's mother just died and left them both a rather large estate."

"What's her name?"

"Holly," the woman said. "Holly Ames." She pulled out a photo. It was Liz.

He shook his head. "'Fraid I can't help you. Don't know anyone named Holly."

The woman persisted. "She might be using another name. She has a son. She might be in a great deal of danger. We have to warn her."

"Now that sounds mighty interesting. Care to tell me more about it?"

"That would take time. We need to find her."

"I have all the time in the world," Doug said as he settled down in a seat overlooking the window. The others had to turn away from it to talk to him.

"We're looking for the person who runs the shop across the street," Gaynor said.

Doug saw Marty then. She'd parked in the city lot and was walking toward her store. He didn't want her talking to anyone until he had.

"Marty sometimes goes to the bank about this time of day," he said. "It's two blocks down."

"She'll be back, won't she?"

"Doubtful. She's a free spirit. Often takes off early."

He watched as Marty turned the CLOSED sign to OPEN. He hoped the town's newest visitors didn't notice.

He got up. "You said your name was Gaynor?" he said. "What division?" He intended to call the NOPD as soon as he could.

"Homicide."

Doug didn't like the sound of that at all. "Well, good luck to you. If you want to find Marty, you might try the bank first, then her house. You go straight up this road. Just keep climbing until you reach the last road, then turn right. Ask anyone."

He rose and went to the bar, paid for his soda.

Then he sauntered out, went down the road and came up to the back of Marty's store. He pounded on it.

Finally, Marty answered.

"You're going to have company soon. A New Orleans detective and some woman who claims she's Liz's sister."

She didn't look surprised.

"Where is she, Marty?"

"At a cabin fifteen miles from here." She went in and jotted directions for him on a notepad by the telephone. "It's an old miner's cabin I fixed up."

"I think I know it," he said. "What's this all about?"

"She'll tell you. She's ready now, I think." Marty hesitated, then added, "She needs you."

"Keep those folks busy."

"I can do that."

He returned to the sheriff's office, called the New Orleans police department and verified they had a Gage Gaynor in homicide.

"Where did you say you were?" a voice on the line asked.

He hung up. He wanted to talk to Holly first.

Doug decided not to use his official vehicle. Instead he jumped in the Jeep. Heart speeding he started west.

•   •   •

A pounding shook the door. Marty left the storeroom and went out to check. She expected the three people Doug had described. Instead two men in sports coats stood there. They couldn't have looked more out of place if they wore devil suits in Disneyland.

She had just locked the door again and now she shook her head no.

The pounding grew more insistent.

She turned away, lowered the shades.

Then she heard a click in the door. She started for the phone. She didn't make it.

She'd always known she needed better locks.

That was her last thought before losing consciousness.

thirty-one

Gage found the owner on the floor in the back of the shop. Her head was cut and she was moaning.

Dom administered first aid while Meredith called the police department and an ambulance.

They had tried Marty's home only to find no one there, then returned to the store. The CLOSED sign was still up but the door was half open.

They went inside, and Gage found the woman on the floor. Blood seeped from a cut on her head. He thought the desk in the shop had been searched—or perhaps the woman simply was messy.

He stooped beside her.

"Gage?"

"Over here," he answered, moving aside as Dom and Meredith joined him.

"Someone hit her very hard," Gage said. "She's alive but just barely. Her pulse is thready and I don't like the sound of her heart."

"Could someone have followed us?" Meredith asked.

Gage shook his head. "I don't know how. We had a rental car. There couldn't have been any kind of tracking device. And I watched. No one tailed us."

"Maybe they tracked her through the website as well," Dom said.

"But now someone may know where she is, and we don't," Meredith said.

Gage stood. "That sheriff . . . He might be able to help."

The police arrived, screeching up to the door and parking in the middle of the street.

Two officers entered. One knelt next to the woman. "Marty?"

"A head wound," Gage said.

"Who are you?"

"We found her," Gage said. "The door was open and we came inside. She was on the floor along with the telephone. She must have been trying to reach it."

"I asked your name."

"Gaynor. I'm a tourist. But I'm also a homicide detective with the New Orleans Police Department."

"Have any identification?"

"Driver's license. No badge. I shot a man several days ago and I'm on suspension until the shooting board meets."

"He shot to save my life," Meredith added. She didn't want them to think Gage was a trigger-happy renegade.

"And who are you?"

"I'm an attorney from New Orleans."

"Christ," one of the officers said in a low tone.

Then the ambulance arrived and two paramedics rushed in, checking the woman's pulse, then heartbeat. They prepared to load her on a stretcher.

The woman moaned again, and Meredith moved closer to her.

A police officer joined her. "Marty?" he asked. "What happened?"

"Doug," the woman managed to say. "Contact Doug. Tell him to hurry to—"

She lapsed into unconsciousness.

"Must mean Sheriff Menelo," one of the officers said. "I know they're friends." He took a radio off his belt and asked his dispatcher if he could locate Sheriff Menelo and tell him to meet them at the hospital, that Marty had been badly injured.

"I suspect my chief is going to want to talk to you three as well," the officer added.

"We'll go to the hospital," Meredith said, catching the gazes of Gage and Dom. They nodded.

This woman, Marty, was their only lead at the moment. They had struck out everywhere else.

Meredith worried that time was growing short. If the sculptor *was* Holly Ames, then had Marty given whomever was here her address?

If her half sister was hiding under another name, why? What did she fear?

The same violence that had followed Meredith?

She knotted the fingers of one hand in a ball. She would have bet that the sheriff earlier had recognized the woman in the photo. Meredith just hadn't understood why he tried to hide it. Unless he knew something that made him protective. If so, he was an ally.

They needed an ally in this town.

They would be taking a risk, but she had the feeling time was short.

Doug had a radio in his car and he heard the call. Marty had been attacked and had called for him.

She needs you.

Those words echoed in his head. But Marty had asked for him. She was in poor condition, according to the dispatcher. Perhaps she had something more she had to tell him.

Torn, he finally stopped, turned around and headed back to Bisbee. Liz should be safe enough where she was. As sheriff, he had covered all of Cochise County at one time or another. He'd patrolled for illegals and smugglers as well as caches of stolen Indian artifacts. Otherwise he wouldn't have known of the cabin's existence.

He put the flashing light on top of the Jeep and pressed

his foot down on the gas pedal. Ten minutes back. Then he would return.

Who would have hurt Marty? Every one in Bisbee respected her. Some might argue with her defense of down-and-outers or her opposition to many of the newcomers who wanted to change Bisbee. But crime—particularly violent crime—was not a major problem in the city.

He knew it had something to do with the three tourists and Liz.

He wanted to talk to them again. He should have pressed the point when he'd seen them. But he'd realized from the first day he'd met Liz that she was running from something. He had not wanted to excoriate the wounds. Now he wished he had.

He reached the hospital three minutes later.

He parked in front of the emergency room and ran through the doors. He stopped only briefly at the desk. "Marty?"

He didn't have to elaborate. Everyone knew Marty.

"They took her up to one of the operating rooms."

"Her condition?"

"Critical. There's been bleeding in the brain."

His heart sank. She couldn't help him now. Still, he decided to go up to the waiting room to see whether he could find out anything more. He walked in and saw the same three people he had seen in the bar.

He went to the desk, heard the same information as he had below. "How long before they will know anything?" he asked.

"I don't know," the nurse said.

Then he went over to the two men and woman. "What do you know about this?"

"I found her," the tall detective said. "After going to her house as you suggested, we returned to the store. The sign still said CLOSED, but the door was unlocked. We went in and found her."

"You didn't see anyone there?"

"No, but it looked like someone had searched the place."

Doug remembered her jotting down directions to where Liz was hiding. Sometimes imprints remained on the next page of the pad.

"Do you want to tell me why you are really here?"

Dom stepped forward this time. "As we told you, we're looking for Meredith Rawson's sister, Holly. She's my daughter. I didn't know about it until a few days ago. It's a long story, but there's been several murders surrounding Ms. Rawson's search for her sister. If you know a woman with a small boy and who sculpts in metal, she could well be Holly Ames. And if she is, there are some people who would do anything to keep us from finding her."

"A husband?"

"Yes, a state senator. And her father is a justice on the state supreme court. Both men are powerful in Lousiana."

"And your role in this?" Doug stared straight at Gaynor.

"I'm here for Meredith."

Doug quickly made up his mind. He felt he was a good judge of people, and he instinctively trusted these three.

"Let's go," he said to Gage.

"I'm going, too," Dom said.

"So am I," the woman added.

He didn't have time to argue with them. He turned to Gage. "You have a gun with you?"

"No."

"I have an extra one in the car."

He started toward his car at a jog. He had a sick feeling in his gut. They reached his Jeep. The older man got in the front without asking. The other two piled in the back. Doug screeched off, putting the siren back on top of the Jeep.

Holly waited for Marty to either call or return. Her friend had promised to do so if she heard anything from the mysterious sister.

She also knew Marty would call Doug. She continued to keep her ears turned to the phone and her eyes on the nearly invisible road that led to the cabin.

Harry was quiet. More quiet than she had seen him since they had reached Bisbee. Even Caesar moved around with his tail between his legs.

She had explored the area behind the cabin, the mountain it backed up to. Marty had said it was full of hiding places. It had once hidden Apaches for months.

Holly fixed some pork and beans for herself and Harry, then looked back outside. It was late afternoon, and the sun was falling, casting shadows over the desert landscape.

Holly shivered with loneliness.

She looked outside again. She saw a trail of dust rising up from the distance.

Doug?

Her heart flip-flopped at the thought. She dreaded telling him the truth but it would also bring relief.

She should have told him earlier. She knew that. She'd allowed fear to overcome her instincts.

She looked back outside. The vehicle was closer. Not a Jeep. Not Marty's old Bug.

That fear she'd been trying to mask flared into full terror.

She grabbed the dog's leash and clicked it on. She couldn't leave the animal here and break Harry's heart once more. "Come on, Harry," she said. "Let's play a game of hide-and-seek."

"I don't want to," he whined.

That was so unlike him that she stopped for a moment. But urgency propelled her ahead. "Don't you want to come with Caesar?"

He stared at her for a moment, then slid off the sofa. "I suppose so. But I would rather go riding with Sher'f Doug."

She would, too, but instead she hurried him out the back, trying her best not to frighten him. She held his hand with her left hand and guided the dog with the other, moving as quickly as she could. They scrambled up to a ridge. She gave the leash to Harry and pointed out a direction. "You go ahead," she said. "Then I'll find you."

He gave her a dubious look but pulled the leash and

stumbled forward. She looked at the ground they'd just passed over. Footprints.

She took a branch from a shrub and backtracked, brushing away their signs. Then she caught up with Harry, who had stopped and was waiting for her.

She wished she had the cell phone with her. But in her frantic escape, she'd left it inside.

"Doug," she whispered. "I need you."

They went across the ridge, then started climbing again. She heard some shouts in the distance.

Her car was still parked in front. Perhaps she should have taken it and made a run from Bisbee.

Too late now. Panic had driven her. It drove her now.

She wished with all her heart she had a weapon. Why hadn't she taken a kitchen knife? Anything.

She did know she wouldn't surrender without a fight.

"Faster," she urged Harry. "Faster."

Meredith told as much of her story as she could, then Gage took over, and finally Dom.

The sheriff said little yet she realized he was fully absorbing everything even as he drove.

"Why?" he asked. "Why is she running?"

"I don't know," Meredith said. "Something terrible must have happened. We do know that an employee of Senator Ames was killed about the same time she disappeared."

"You never met her?"

"Yes," she said, "though we went to different schools. I met her at some fund-raiser or another."

"No recognition?"

"No. We don't look that much alike. I see more resemblance between her and my mother than she has with me. Since I never knew I had a sister, I never thought about it."

The sheriff was grim. His fingers were nearly white where they clasped the steering wheel.

"Should you call for help?" Meredith asked.

"Not until I know what in the hell is going on," he said.

"I did ask for a patrol car to patrol an area just north of here. They can be here within four minutes."

He loved Liz Baker. That much was obvious. He was going to do his damnedest to protect her. She glanced at Gage, and he nodded. He had caught it as well.

It was odd how well they communicated. They didn't need words.

They left the main road and turned onto something that barely resembled a trail. They bounced over rough terrain and Gage's hand tightened around hers.

Despite the dust that rose and smothered them in gray fog, she saw a small building. Then two cars.

One man was at the front door of the cabin. He held a rifle in his hands.

The sheriff uttered a curse, then took the radio in one hand and called for help. He turned on the siren, obviously to intimidate.

The man in the doorway stood his ground and leveled the rifle. He pointed it at the oncoming car.

The windshield shattered, and glass flew throughout the car. Meredith felt a sharp sting.

The sheriff turned the car suddenly as the shooter aimed again. Menelo zigzagged, and Meredith heard the report of the rifle again. But this time it didn't seem to hit the car.

"There's an extra pistol in the glove compartment," Sheriff Menelo said. "There's also a rifle in the trunk."

"I can shoot," Meredith said.

"So can I," Dom said.

Menelo slammed the car to a stop and jumped out, taking his pistol from his holster as he did so. Meredith spilled from the other side of the car and took cover behind it. Dom rolled on the ground with the pistol he had taken from the glove compartment, and Gage grabbed the keys Menelo threw to him and opened the trunk, taking out the rifle.

Meredith could have believed it was all choreographed ahead of time.

The window in the cabin broke and a rifle poked out.

Meredith glanced over at the sheriff. His face was like stone.

"Liz and her son might be inside," he said. He hollered out, "Liz?"

No answer.

Then, to the gunman, "There's no way out. More cars are coming. Come out with your hands up."

Silence. Then the rifle moved, obviously searching for a target. But the shooter didn't seem to aim at them.

"Go," Menelo said.

They ran for cover. Gage followed Meredith to a shallow gulch and shielded her body with his. Dom and the sheriff followed.

Dirt rose as bullets peppered the ground in front of them, but the gulch protected them.

Menelo glanced at Gage. "Can you get to the back? It looks like there's only one shooting."

Gage nodded. "Stay here," he told Meredith. "Don't move. You don't have a weapon."

She nodded. Reluctantly.

He leaned over and kissed her. "I love you, Ms. Rawson."

Then he was gone, sprinting toward the cabin, zigzagging as he did so. Menelo kept the shooter occupied by shooting slightly above the window. It was obvious he didn't want a stray bullet to go inside.

Meredith prayed as Gage reached the side of the cabin and disappeared behind it.

She heard a siren. The backup car was on its way. Most likely more calls had gone out.

But where was Liz Baker? Was Liz Baker really Holly Ames?

Was she already dead?

And Gage? He was taking so many chances. She wondered whether her breath would stop coming every time he was on duty.

Shots. Different sounds. Then Gage appeared at the front door. "Call an ambulance."

She ran toward him. So did Menelo.

"Liz?" he asked.

"There's only one here," Gage replied. "And he's wounded."

Holly heard the hunter behind her. He was making no attempt to mask his movements.

Harry was exhausted. The dog was panting. She didn't know if she could run another step. They couldn't go any farther.

She heard a siren in the distance. Then shots. She stopped. Listened. But then she heard a rustling of brush beneath her and understood the pursuit had not ended. She urged Harry onward again.

Doug was here. She'd known he would come. And now he would probably come after her. He would be a prime target for the man chasing her.

She stopped, looking around. They were high. Near the edge of a cliff.

Harry had caught her urgency. He'd suddenly understood danger. So apparently had the dog. He didn't bark. He just went where led.

She saw a cottonwood not far from where they were. It had been struck by lightning and was charred.

She stopped and kneeled. "Harry," she said. "You must do something for me. No matter how hard it is."

His eyes grew big.

"Do you see those bushes over there? Near the tree?"

He nodded.

"Take Caesar. Hide behind them, and if you see a man, toss a rock toward that ledge. Can you do that?"

His lip trembled. "I don't want to leave you."

"You won't be far away. You can always see me."

She heard a rock fall. It wasn't far from them. "Please, Harry."

"I can," he said.

"Don't let him see you. I just want him to hear the rock land. Right over in that spot." She pointed out a spot.

" 'Kay," he said.

She hugged him. "I love you," she said.

"I love you, too."

"Now go. And find a good rock."

He dragged the dog away, and she watched as he hid himself. She went close to the ledge and sat as if she couldn't go any farther.

In seconds, a tall, well-built man appeared. His gaze moved around, catching her. She watched as he glanced down at a photo, then back at her.

"You're going to pay for making me go to all this trouble," he said as he approached her. "Where's the kid?"

"I didn't bring him."

"You lie. I saw the coloring book. Two plates on a table." He drew closer. "I won't hurt him."

"You heard the siren. The police are here."

"Hick cops," he said arrogantly. "They're probably dead by now. Now where's the kid?"

A thud behind him. Harry's rock. The man quickly turned toward the sound and she ran toward him and pushed. He stumbled, took a step, then started to swing around, grabbing for her. A flash of color flew past her, a low growl filling the air. The hunter put up his hands to protect himself, dropped the gun and stepped back into nothing.

Holly grabbed the dog's leash and pulled him back as her hunter went over the cliff, his scream following him all the way down.

thirty-two

Meredith heard the scream. A man's scream.

Doug turned to one of the two newly arrived officers. "Take care of the man inside the cabin. You," he said to another, "come with me."

He started toward the back of the house and up a trail behind it, moving faster than Meredith thought possible. Gage was next to him. Dom behind.

She followed.

Gage turned. "Stay here."

"Not on your life," she said. "It's my sister."

He shook his head and took off.

The trail was difficult, rarely used and barely visible in the gathering dusk. Yet they could still see what must be recent footprints. They were clear and pronounced. Someone in a hurry.

"Liz?" the sheriff called out as they continued to climb. Meredith glanced to the side and saw a body sprawled out on the ground far below, limbs at an unnatural angle.

"Sheriff," she shouted.

He stopped, turned and said something to the deputy beside him, who peeled off and headed toward the figure. The sheriff continued to climb, his gun ready in his hand. Gage still carried the rifle, cradling it in his right arm. Of all of them, he seemed to move the most easily, his rangy body taking the climb gracefully and surely.

Meredith's heart pounded faster with each step. What had happened up above? That could have been her half sister and nephew lying broken on the ground, the family she'd never met, never known. She prayed that they were all right.

She heard a voice. A woman's voice. Low. Scared. "Doug. Here. I'm here."

Breath rushed back into her throat. She stepped up her pace and reached the summit of a ridge in time to see a lovely young woman throw herself into Menelo's arms. He held her tight for a moment, then finally released her.

"Anyone else around?"

She shook her head.

Menelo holstered his pistol, leaned down, picked up a small boy and held him as if he were a precious object.

Meredith stood back and watched.

Gage put an arm loosely around her shoulders. Dom was staring transfixed at the man, woman and boy, who were totally oblivious to anyone else.

The woman finally turned and looked at them, bewilderment in wide blue eyes. Cornflower eyes. A lighter blue than Meredith's. Her hair was short, dark, unlike the blond tresses Meredith had seen in photos. Her face was streaked with dirt, possibly tears, but even that couldn't disguise her beauty.

Meredith walked toward her. "I'm Meredith Rawson," she said slowly. "I think . . . I believe I'm your half sister." She couldn't wait to say it, not when she had come so close to losing all the family she had left. Not after the secret had been stifled for so many years. How close had they come to it being too late for the truth?

Too close.

"That couldn't be," the woman said. "I don't have any—"

"Thirty-three years ago my mother was seventeen. She had a child out of wedlock, a girl, in Memphis, Tennessee. The child was taken from her. She tried to find her, but couldn't. There were no records. At the same time your mother was in Memphis, Tennessee, but we don't think she had a child. We think you were given to her."

Bewilderment crossed the woman's face. Liz Baker's face. Holly Matthew's face. "But why?"

"We don't know exactly. We have some good guesses. But a DNA test would confirm your parentage."

Meredith held her breath as she watched the words take hold. Holly looked up at Menelo, who was still holding her son. She took one of the boy's hands and held it tight. A frown creased her brow as she obviously tried to absorb what was being said. Meredith knew how hard it must be for her.

"You mean my father . . . isn't really my father?"

"It's possible."

"Then who . . . ?"

Dom, who had been silent until now, stepped forward. His face was a mask of control but his brown eyes were roiling with emotion. "I think I am," he said. "I didn't know about you until a few days ago. I—" His voice broke.

Meredith wanted to hug Holly. She wanted to hug the boy. She knew Dom must be fighting every fiber of his being not to do so.

The officer who had been dispatched to check the body below arrived. "Dead," he reported to Menelo.

"What happened?" Doug ask Holly softly.

"I was . . . waiting for you. So much I needed to tell you. I saw the car approach. I knew it wasn't you, so I took Harry and Caesar . . ."

For the first time, Meredith noted the nondescript Benji-type dog that huddled close to Holly, its leash trailing on the ground. "He saved our lives," Holly said. "He went after . . ." A tear started rolling down her face as she knelt and hugged the dog.

The aftermath of fear, Meredith thought. She was becoming all too familiar with it. "There's another man down in the cabin. He's been injured. Perhaps he can tell us who sent them and why."

"It was my husband," Holly whispered, looking up at Sheriff Menelo, her heart in her eyes. "He sent them. He sent someone to kill me in New Orleans. I overheard a conversation I shouldn't have."

Menelo's eyes closed for just a fraction of a second, and Meredith saw the pain he felt for Holly. "I thought it might be something like that," he said softly, putting his free arm around her.

"I killed the man he sent," Holly said. "I knew no one would believe me. My husband is . . ." She was trembling. Her entire body trembled. Her eyes were glazed with tears.

Meredith couldn't stop herself from reaching for her free hand. Holding it tightly. "They'll believe you now," Meredith said.

"Why?"

"It's a very long story," Meredith said. "Maybe we should go down."

But Holly wasn't ready yet. She looked at Dom, obviously trying to see something of herself there. She bit her lip. "My father—Judge Matthews—is part of it. He's untouchable. He and my husband—"

"No one is untouchable," Dom said roughly. "With your DNA, we can prove he defrauded his father's estate. We have a witness alive below. There's been other murders, and if we can tie him to them, he'll have to talk to avoid the death penalty."

Holly looked at him again. "You're Dom Cross, aren't you? I've read about you. You work with children."

He nodded. Meredith could tell how much he wanted to go over to her. Meredith dropped Holly's hand and moved away, making room for Dom. Or maybe they both needed more time.

But Holly held out her hand to him.

Tears gathered behind Meredith's eyes.

Holly Ames looked fragile but there was a gentleness and kindness in her that glowed. Obviously, there was also strength. That she had escaped a murder attempt, made a new life with friends who apparently would do anything for her, then survived this last attempt on her life proved that.

Pride surged through Meredith. And admiration. Her heart swelled with a sweet poignancy.

In the last few weeks, she'd lost her family. Now, as Gage took her hand and squeezed it, she knew she had discovered a new family.

Gage watched the reunion in the soft twilight. A lump formed in his throat. He thought of how Meredith had fought for this moment, had never ceased looking despite all the roadblocks thrown in her way.

Her sister had the same grit.

He thought of Clint. Of his middle brother, Terry, who had died in a gang fight. Of his mother who simply didn't have the emotional or financial ability to cope with raising three boys.

He had tried to help them, but he wondered whether he had ever done enough. He realized now he'd kept an emotional distance from Clint, terrified that he would lose him as he had lost Terry.

No more. He would make sure Clint had everything he needed to succeed. Particularly love. And support.

He could do that now. He had closed down years ago and hadn't realized it. Whether it was due to Debbie's betrayal, Terry's death or his mother's, he didn't know. He just knew it had happened.

Meredith awakened his heart with her own passion and guts.

He leaned over and kissed her. "I love you," he whispered.

Her face transformed in front of him. He'd always liked her face. Integrity radiated from it. Honesty. But now she looked truly beautiful. God, he loved her.

"We had better get down before it gets any darker," Menelo warned.

They started down the path, this time Gage leading the way, his hand clasped with Meredith's. Menelo carried the boy. Dom steadied his daughter. Gage could only imagine what Dom was going through.

How would he feel at suddenly discovering he was a father?

Emotion surged through him. It was so strong, he almost stumbled. He tried to identify it. *Tenderness*. That was it. And love so powerful, it could overcome anything.

They finally reached the cabin. An ambulance had taken away the wounded shooter. The sheriff called his office and ordered that there be an around-the-clock guard on the gunman.

Menelo then talked softly to Meredith's sister. Gage heard the name, "Marty." Holly's face crumpled at the news, and Menelo called the hospital. "Marty's in recovery," he said. "She's going to be okay."

Gage watched the interaction between the sheriff and Holly. They couldn't keep their eyes off each other. And the moment Menelo sat down, the boy crawled up in his lap. It was obvious that Holly and her son had a protector. A strong, competent one.

Starting with Meredith, they told the story to Holly. Dom finished with the events of thirty-three years earlier: his arrest, his imprisonment.

Holly's eyes filled several times. "I'm so sorry," she told Dom.

His hand trembled slightly in his lap. "Believe me, everything was worth it to find you. And my grandson."

"We still need the DNA," Menelo warned. "We can get the blood work done at the hospital tonight and drive it to a lab in Tucson first thing in the morning. Until we get the results and get the prisoner talking, we have damned little proof."

"What about tonight?" Meredith asked. "Could there be anyone else out there?"

"I want Liz to stay with me," Doug said. "With added protection." He paused. "If that's what she wants to do."

Holly nodded. "Thank you. Harry will love that."

"I wish I had more room, but I don't," he added regretfully. "But the Copper Queen is a great hotel and I'll assign a couple of troopers there. We can have breakfast at my place, then drive to Tucson."

Meredith broke in. "I think Holly—or should we call you Liz?—needs some time to absorb this. I know I did."

"It's Holly. I always felt a little uncomfortable with Liz."

"Holly." Doug tried it on his tongue. "I like it, too. And Harry?"

"His given name is Michael. I always called him Mikey, but he really has become Harry to me."

Harry had been drowsing with the sheriff's arms but perked up when he heard his name. "Like Harry Potter," he said.

"And you are a little wonder, just like him," Holly said. "You were so brave and smart." She looked up, pride all over her face. "He threw a stone and distracted that man . . . and then Caesar knocked him down."

"I'm impressed," Meredith said, smiling.

"I want to be just like Sher'f Doug," Harry said, and closed his eyes again.

Hours later, Gage and Meredith shared a glass of wine in their room at the Copper Queen, a legendary hotel which, they were told, had been a frequent haunt of John Wayne.

Dom had retired to a room next door. He had calls to make, he'd said, but Meredith felt he really just needed time alone.

So did they.

But first Meredith wanted to call Sarah and tell her all was well and ask if anything needed her attention.

Sarah answered on the first ring. "Thank God, you called. I've been worried."

"It's been a busy day. We found my sister."

"Are you sure?"

"As sure as I can be without the DNA test. Any problems?"

"Other than having a boss who has been a target of some madman, nothing."

"I think it will soon come to an end," Meredith said.

"Oh, someone from your father's law firm called. Associates have been going through his files to divide the cases and decide if any required follow-up work. They found an envelope made out to you."

"Where is it now?"

"It's in the office safe."

"Good. I should be home tomorrow. I'll check it then." She hung up.

Gage had taken off his shirt. He looked terrific, but then he always did. He gave her a quizzical look.

"Sarah says my father's law firm called about an envelope an associate found in one of his files. It was addressed to me. I can't imagine why he would put something there instead of giving it to me."

"I'll call about flights tomorrow afternoon," he said.

She hesitated. She'd told Sarah she would be back, she needed to go back, but she really didn't want to leave her sister. Not now. "We won't know about the blood tests then."

"Menelo will let us know."

"I like him."

"I do, too," Gage said. "I noticed he threw away the rule book a couple of times."

He reached out to her and pulled her against him. Both of them had a few cuts from flying windshield glass but nothing serious, and now all she wanted was to lie in his arms. They both had been exhausted, too exhausted to do more than order a hamburger from room service, take a shower and lie on the bed.

His lips touched hers and all the exhaustion fled. There was something in his eyes that hadn't been there before. A commitment. A comfort along with passion. As if he'd settled something deep inside himself.

She touched his cheek, feeling the roughness of a new beard. Then she buried her fingers in his hair, savoring the closeness, drinking in the essence of him.

"I love you, Meredith Rawson," he said, his lips brushing the words against her skin. He'd said it earlier, but then adrenaline had been running in all of them.

The earth moved and the heavens thundered, all within her soul.

She moved her hand, her fingers tracing the crinkles around his eyes, the almost invisible dimple until he smiled.

"I love you," she said. "More than I thought it possible to love someone."

"I have a lot of baggage," he said. "My brother should get out of prison next week. He will have to stay with me awhile."

"Need a good lawyer to help?"

"I was depending on that," he said with the slow rare grin that had always captivated her.

"What other baggage?"

"The Beast."

"I adore Beast."

"He will try to push you out of bed."

"I can hold my own."

"You can, indeed," he said.

"There was something else," she said.

"Nothing important. Not now."

"What was it?"

He shrugged. "The differences between us, between our backgrounds."

She sat up. "I didn't know you were a snob."

He smiled at that. "I was engaged in college," he said. "A girl from a very good family. I was a football jock. A hero. Then I injured my knee and was told I couldn't play football again. She was gone the next day."

"Did you love her?"

"I thought I did. She was everything a poor kid from the slums ever wanted. Beauty. Class." He played with her hair.

"Doesn't sound like much class to me."

He shrugged. "I had my shallow moments. But it hurt, and for a long time it was hard to trust again. Then my job got in the way. It's difficult being a cop's wife and it's hell on a marriage." His gaze never left hers.

He was asking a question.

"It's difficult being *anyone's* wife or husband," she said.

"But I never thought love meant asking someone to change what they are. And you, my love, are a cop down to your toes."

"Is that a yes?"

"Was that the question?"

"I think so."

"Once more with feeling," she said.

He hesitated. "I just want you to know what you're getting into. Clint. The job. I can try to get another one."

"Yes, I know what I'm getting into. No, you are not to get another job, and no, I am not going to let you go out the door again," she said. "So yes, I will marry you despite that decidedly unromantic proposal."

He grimaced. "I'm not good at romance, either."

But he was. He was always there when she needed him. He accepted her without question. He made her smile. He filled what had always been an empty place. He warmed all the cold places.

He offered all the romance she needed.

She nibbled at his lips. His mouth claimed hers.

And then they became very, very romantic.

"I'm so sorry I had to lie to you."

Holly's gaze met Doug's.

She had gone to the hospital with him, checked on Marty who was asleep but doing fine, and waited while he talked to the injured man. He would live, Doug had reported back to her. And he was already talking. He named someone she didn't know, but now they had a trail to follow.

Then they had gone to Doug's home. She'd been there before when he had cooked steaks. His sister and niece lived right across the road.

Harry was tucked into a second bed in Jenny's room.

Doug made her some hot chocolate.

He brushed a short curl off her forehead. "You had good reason. You must have been terrified."

"More than that," she said.

"You'll probably have to go back to New Orleans and make a statement about the night you left. Your statement should be on the record. But not until we know we can protect you. If the DNA proves what Gaynor and Meredith believe, Judge Matthews's credibility will be destroyed."

"I know." She shuddered. She didn't want to ever see Randolph again, or her father. The man she'd always thought was her father, but who had never acted as such. Now she understood why.

"When this is all sorted out, do you want to return to New Orleans?" he asked cautiously.

"No. This is my home."

He touched her face with such gentleness she wanted to cry.

She lifted her face in invitation.

He accepted. His lips touched hers with infinite tenderness, like a whisper. He deepened the kiss until she was swirling with the magic of it. His hands massaged the back of her neck, and she was filled with delicious sensations and a warmth that crept into every fiber of her being.

He released her lips and picked her up, taking her into his bedroom.

He undressed her, gave her one of his shirts to wear, then guided her down on the bed.

He took off his shoes. But then he lay next to her. Holding her. Caressing her. Teaching her to trust.

Teaching her the meaning of love.

Samuel Matthews heard from the investigator who had sent the two men to Bisbee.

"One's dead. The other is talking. I'm getting the hell out of the country while I can. You might do the same."

Samuel lowered the phone. He had thought he'd put enough distance between himself and the people he'd paid to take care of problems. He had no doubt now that everything was falling apart.

DeWitt was looking into the adoption and his father's

will. Holly was alive and the DNA would prove she wasn't his child. When one thread was broken, the others would unravel quickly enough.

He blamed Randolph. If his son-in-law hadn't hired an incompetent to rid himself of Holly, perhaps none of this would have happened. But now it was quite likely Samuel's role in Cross's conviction would become known, as well as his connections with dubious campaign funds and the death of Prescott so many years ago.

He knew one thing. He would not go to prison.

He went through his desk, shredding some documents and burning them in the fireplace. He did leave two documents that would destroy Randolph Ames.

He drank some of his expensive brandy, smoked a cigar and looked around at the photos on the walls. Samuel with the president. Samuel with three governors. Samuel with a U.S. Supreme Court justice. The latter had been his goal once. Perhaps he had never stopped hoping.

He had another glass, went into the bathroom and straightened his tie.

Then he went downstairs and picked up his keys.

No note. No obvious suicide. No warning to Randolph.

He got into his car and backed out.

He knew just the place to run his car off the road.

A tragic accident.

It would be a grand funeral.

Gage and Meredith heard the news when they landed in New Orleans. There was no reason now to fly to Birmingham. Holly was found and was being protected. Dom had decided to stay in Bisbee for a few more days. He wanted to get to know his daughter and grandson.

The television from a bar boomed out the news: *Supreme Court Judge Samuel Matthews Dead In Accident.*

They exchanged glances, then Gage took out his cell phone and dialed DeWitt. He should have done so last night, but they both had been exhausted.

"Sanders," he said. "What have you heard?"

He listened for a moment, then asked, "Could it have been a suicide?"

Gage nodded as DeWitt obviously asked a question. "Yeah, we found out a lot. We found Matthews's daughter. Two men had been sent to kill her. One's dead. The other was wounded. He's talking." Another pause. Then, "Can you wait before printing anything? I don't want Randolph to get away as well. Okay. Will you pick us up at Meredith's office? She has to retrieve something there."

He listened for a moment, then grinned. "Yeah, bring Beast."

He folded the phone shut.

"Let's get a taxi and go by your office to get the envelope your father left you. DeWitt will meet us in the parking lot. He's chomping at the bit."

An hour later, DeWitt was waiting for them in the parking lot of her building. Beast was taking up the whole backseat.

"I'll get in the front," Meredith said as the dog made moaning sounds at seeing them. She watched the dog slobber all over Gage as he tried to squeeze inside. Then she took a look inside the envelope and stiffened.

The date was the same as her father's death.

She quickly ran through the three-page document. It was a confession as well as a letter. She read it silently, feeling the guilt within the letter. Her father had been devoured alive by it.

She silently handed it to Gage and ignored DeWitt's quizzical looks. He would have to read it for himself.

They arrived at Gage's house and went inside. He made coffee while DeWitt read the letter. Her father had meant for it to be read. That much was obvious.

"My God," DeWitt said, and put it down on the table.

It was all there. Matthews's desperation for a child when he was sterile, Marguerite's parents desperate to hide a pregnancy that her father thought might destroy his career. To keep the secret they had to destroy a young man—not only destroy him but to do it in such a way that Marguerite would never speak to or of him again.

There was so much more. Young Prescott was a gambler. He'd been paid to frame Dom, then got greedy and tried to blackmail both families. Charles Rawson had been an ambitious young man in the law firm ruled by Marguerite's father. Charles had lusted after Marguerite and was seen as a perfect match for her. He'd sold his soul to make that happen and had helped frame Dom, then murder Prescott.

The final wound was the deepest. Marguerite had been forced into the marriage. If she didn't do what was asked, Dom would never leave prison alive. His life for hers. Rawson had always loved her, always wanted her, and she hated him for what he had done. She agreed to a marriage without love. She wouldn't sleep with him.

Until he raped her. Meredith was the result.

He never touched her afterward. They both had punished each other until the last day of their lives.

Gage reached over and touched her. "I'm sorry," he said.

"I know now," she said. "It's always better to know."

But a tear dropped on a page.

"They gave me you," he said. "And I am grateful to them for that."

She smiled through the tears.

And then they prepared a case to bring Randolph Ames to justice.

Together. Just as she knew they would always be together.

BISBEE
SIX MONTHS LATER

"It's over, darling," Doug said after getting off the telephone. "They found him guilty."

Holly looked outside at Harry playing with Caesar in Doug's yard. She had been staying with him since arriving back from New Orleans. They had left New Orleans immediately after she was released from testifying. She hadn't wanted Harry there when the verdict came in.

And she'd wanted to go home. Doug *was* her home.

She'd testified for one long day. Randolph's attorney had tried to destroy her. She had known that going in, but she had withstood the barrage. And was stronger for it.

Randolph had refused to grant her a divorce but Meredith was working on it.

As for Meredith . . . they had become very good friends in the past six months. The DNA had confirmed that they were sisters, and Meredith had directed half her mother's trust fund to her. It was a considerable amount.

Holly hadn't wanted to take it. She was finally convinced to do so only after being told it was her mother's dying wish. But she planned to give much of it to charity—a large chunk to Dom's shelter and another for a shelter in Bisbee. The rest would go for Harry's education.

She relaxed against Doug, wondering how life could have gone from so bad to so good within a year. Harry was five now. He'd had nightmares for a while after the incident at the cabin but they had faded.

Doug took her hand and led her outside to watch the sun set.

They sat on a porch step. Then Doug unexpectedly dropped to his knees and she looked at him in surprise.

He fumbled in his pocket, then took out a box and gave it to her.

Hands shaking, she opened it and looked at the ring. It was a sapphire. A blue that matched her eyes.

"Will you marry me?" he asked. "I didn't want to ask until this was over, but, well, dammit, I can't wait any longer."

Her heart ached with love for him. "The divorce—"

"Meredith said she can expedite it. She and Gage are getting married in June. Would you . . . I mean, every woman wants her own wedding, I suppose, but I thought . . . maybe you two, ah . . ."

He was babbling. Doug never babbled.

He knew how happy she was at finding Meredith, at having a sister. He was asking her if she wanted the moon as well as the sun.

"Yes," she said simply.

He kissed her for a very long moment, then they looked up at the sunset, hands entwined.

"It's so beautiful here," Holly said.

"It pales in comparison to you. When I first saw you—"

"In my glasses and brown hair?"

"I thought you were the most beautiful woman I'd ever seen."

"I was plain."

"You've always had a glow about you."

Her fingers tightened around his. "It's our glow," she said.

And she knew it would be there forever.

epilogue

The double wedding took place in Bisbee, in the church that Doug and now Holly attended.

There had been an easy agreement in the location.

Holly had only bad memories of New Orleans, and Doug had friends throughout Cochise County.

Neither Meredith nor Gage cared where they married. They just wanted it done.

But the four of them did want to do it together. Hatred and destruction had brought them together. Now love bound them together—a new family forged by respect and trust and caring. They wanted to celebrate that together.

And Meredith and Gage had become enthralled by the funky town with a big heart, though not enough to move there. Gage liked being a cop in a big city. He liked the action. He liked the energy. Meredith wanted to continue her work in domestic abuse.

Their jobs remained in New Orleans but they were fast considering Bisbee their second home.

Half the town seemed to be at the wedding. The four had debated over which bride should come first, then decided Meredith as the younger would.

Both men stood at the altar with their best men. Clint

stood next to Gage. Harry, bursting with pride, was a pint-size best man for Doug.

Jenny led the procession as flower girl, and Marty was Holly's maid of honor.

Gage watched as Meredith walked down the aisle, followed by Sarah, her one attendant.

She hadn't wanted white. She hadn't wanted a veil.

She was beautiful. She always had been to him, but never so much as at this moment. Her eyes were luminous. A sky blue princess-style dress floated around her body as she walked toward him.

He couldn't bear to think how close he had come to losing her.

When she reached him, her hand folded into his, and she turned to watch her sister, who started down the aisle on Dom's arm.

Holly was struck-blind gorgeous. Gage watched with amusement as the groom next to him blinked several times. Gage had come to like Holly very much, particularly her wonder at everything and her total lack of awareness of her own beauty.

Yet it had always been the prickly attorney who made his heart race and his blood turn warm. Warm, hell. Hot. Steaming.

His hand tightened around hers and they exchanged secret smiles. As always, they seemed to know what the other was thinking.

He'd moved into her house, renting his own to Clint. The rent was darn little in the beginning, but now Clint had stayed in his job in computer troubleshooting for six months, had even been promoted already, and spent his spare time at Dom's shelter, helping kids.

He was going to make it.

The minister spoke the words. Gage knew them. He had been to weddings. But the words had never really meant anything to him.

Now they did.

"In sickness and in health . . .

"For richer or poorer . . .

"'Til death do you part."

And then came the best part. "You may kiss the bride."

His. She was now his. And he was hers. That was the best part. They were friends, lovers, partners.

His lips took hers possessively. For a long moment. Maybe two.

A few twitters came from the congregation.

He glanced at the couple next to them. They had not quite finished their kiss.

Well, he had always been competitive.

He returned to the kiss, still wondering how this miracle had occurred, how one person could be so supremely happy and content. It had all started with violence and deception followed by more of the same. He knew there would be future obstacles. There always were. But for the first time in his life, he believed in happy endings.

The twitters became louder and he reluctantly drew away, just as Doug did. They glanced at each other and grinned. Doug lifted Harry up in his arms, and Jenny and Marty hugged Holly, then Meredith.

It was done.

There was a celebration waiting. A huge one.

A celebration of love and life and family.

He offered his hand to Meredith.

An ending. A beginning.

He was ready.

In 1988, **Patricia Potter** won the Maggie Award and a Reviewer's Choice Award from *Romantic Times* for her first novel. She has been named Storyteller of the Year by *Romantic Times* and has received the magazine's Career Achievement Award for Western Historical Romance along with numerous Reviewer's Choice nominations and awards.

She has won three Maggie awards, is a three-time RITA finalist, and has been on the *USA Today* and Walden's bestseller lists. Her books have been alternate choices for the Doubleday Book Club.

Prior to writing fiction, she was a newspaper reporter with the *Atlanta Journal-Constitution* and president of a public relations firm in Atlanta. She has served as president of Georgia Romance Writers and as a board member of River City Romance Writers, and is currently president of Romance Writers of America.